THE
MURDER
OF
EDDIE
WATCHMAN

RICHARD N. RYAN

Library of Congress Control Number: 2015903751

ISBN: 978-0-9908624-0-6

Dedication

To my parents, John P. and Doris L. Ryan,
who gave me the means, and to my wife,
Cindy, who always believed

"I am a man and therefore have all devils in my heart."

Father Brown, Fr. The Hammer of God

APRIL, 2005

The guy comes from out of nowhere, which I guess is appropriate, seeing how that's what we are in the big middle of. One second I'm standing there in the calm spring evening watching the plane descend, the next he's right up behind me in the dark, telling me to stand still. Somehow I know from his voice—call it training—that he's speaking from behind a gun, so I do what he says. I'm irritated. How had he been able to come up on me? What he says next—on the ground, face down—doesn't help matters any.

Has to be a cop, I'm thinking, probably Navajo, and some of them no doubt know how to move through brush. But if he's Navajo, I'm in luck. They rarely patrol with backup, so this guy is likely alone.

I start down—but onto my back and with my arm over my face. I can see he can't tell the difference in the dark, and when he bends over to frisk me I do what I have to do. I kick his gun away with one foot, and when he looks up to see where it's gone, I crush his jaw with the other. He falls on his face at my feet. I scratch around for a rock, and cave in the back of his skull, which starts me feeling better. Sneak up on me.

The rest of the evening goes as planned, except now we have a body and a Navajo police cruiser to get rid of, but I'm on it. The pilot and I quickly transfer the goods to the cruiser, along with the body. He follows in my truck as I drive my dead friend down to the water's edge where the boat is, get out and roll him over the drop off into the deep water. Carey and I load the boat, he takes off, and I return the pilot to his craft, watch him lift off, then head for home—all in under an hour. Damn, we are good.

Wouldn't you know, I thought, it would be Pete and Paul who spotted the roof of the vehicle sticking out of the water? This lake draws characters like a magnet. I always figured it had something to do with all that water in the middle of all that dry. It just pushes people off center. But these two'd been here so long and collected so many crazy stories that I'd heard they hadn't paid for a drink up at the Windy Mesa for years. So I knew getting the straight skinny out of them wasn't going to be easy, especially as rattled as they were.

And I'd forgotten that they finish each other's sentences, which made me crazy.

"We was just trolling close to shore…" said Paul.

"And he looked up and seen it," added Pete. "So we had to move in…"

"For a closer look," finished Paul.

What do they do, rehearse these things? I wondered.

"Then we seen it was a cruiser," said Paul.

"A Navajo cruiser," corrected Pete.

I felt my stomach roll over and my pulse quicken.

"That's what I meant," said Paul.

"Well, that's not what you said," Pete replied.

They stopped and looked at each other. They'd been friends for so long I realized that they actually had begun to look like each other, just like people and their pets.

"You sure about this?" I asked, hoping, but I knew.

They nodded, together.

Paul took a sip of the coffee I had brought after I had seen how shook up they were. "That's not all we saw," he said.

"There was a body," Pete jumped in.

I felt my skin flush with anxiety.

Paul nodded. "In the cab," he said.

"In the passenger's seat," Pete added.

"It looked pretty rough," Paul said. They looked at each other again, and both shook their heads.

"What do you mean?" I asked.

"Like it had been there for a while," said Pete.

"Anything else?" I asked. Now I had to know.

"The sun in the windshield. We saw something shiny," said Paul.

"We think it was a badge," said Pete.

"On his shirt," added Paul.

"A police badge?" I asked.

They nodded again, together.

Of course, as head ranger, I had dispatched a boat immediately to secure the scene once Pete and Paul had calmed down enough to give me a location. I'd also called the bureau office in Flagstaff to get them started. Now Luke and I were headed out there to take a look ourselves. I offered a silent prayer, not that it wouldn't be Eddie—after all, how many Navajo police officers and their cruisers were missing?—but for help in dealing with what was coming. Luke was quiet. I knew he was steeling himself for the same thing.

The late October sun had dropped so that we passed through alternating shadow and sun as we headed up the channel, the air chill or warm depending, but the sky between the steep walls of the canyon maintaining a steadfast Prussian blue. The lake was down so low there were places we felt like we were at the bottom of a well.

Luke was at the wheel. Men and driving, I thought, although to be fair to Luke he wasn't bad that way. It was all about competence with him. Gender, appearance, color—none of that mattered if you could do the job. And frankly, I had to admit that he could handle a boat better than I. Especially when we were in a hurry and there were so many warning buoys for barely submerged rocks and lake bottom.

There wasn't much we could do at the scene until the federal forensics guys showed up, which probably wouldn't be until morning. We gave the overnight gear and provisions we had brought to Silas. He'd surrounded the cruiser with buoys and attached police tape to them, then done the same with stanchions on shore, for which I was secretly grateful. I couldn't approach the cruiser and what was inside it without possibly contaminating the crime scene.

Silas also had called in the car number on the cruiser's roof. I gazed around at the water and rock. What a desolate place to meet your maker, I thought with a chill.

Luke and I moored the boat, and then got out to look around. There wasn't much shore, just the shelf on which the cruiser sat. After a few minutes, Luke started up the steep rock face directly behind the cruiser.

"You be careful," I said. As usual, he was wearing his Tony Lamas, not the best climbing shoes. I was pretty sure he slept in them.

In about five minutes he disappeared over the top, but reappeared a minute later.

"It's what I thought," he said. "There's a road up here."

Just then, the call came through on the radio. The cruiser number came back. It was Eddie's.

SARAH

I fell into bed that night more tired than I could ever remember being, but sleep did *not* come. I kept seeing Eddie's cruiser, dirty white and filled with lake water like an aquarium. Only nothing alive was in there.

After a while I got up and, opening my top dresser drawer, retrieved a small deer hide medicine pouch. I returned to bed and spread its contents on the coverlet. A small packet of corn pollen, a piece of turquoise and one of onyx, a tiny earring of stamped silver, a twist of lamb's wool. And as I held each object, I remembered.

Eddie seemed always to have been around, in school, riding his bike in summer with the other boys, in and out of my parents' trading post—just one face among others.

But when I finished school at NAU and moved back in with my parents, suddenly he seemed *there*. My dad had backed the truck up to the wool shed to unload my stuff and the next thing I knew Eddie was asking me which boxes went where as he carried them in.

Truth be told, I was a little embarrassed to be back. There I was, one of the few kids, white or Navajo, to go on to college from our small community, retreating back to where I'd begun. I felt like I was hiding out, probably because I was. Many friends I'd graduated high school with had moved on. Most were working, some were married. All of them seemed to possess a sense of purpose that I sorely lacked.

College had been so scheduled it was like having a job; classes to attend, papers to write, books to read, exams to study for. And of course, there had always been plenty of social activity going on to fill in the gaps.

Then I graduated, and at a single stroke, all of that was cut off. I felt lost, so I scurried back to the only world I knew. And there was Eddie.

Of course, we had bumped into each other during my years away, but my focus then had been school work and new friends and college guys. I simply had overlooked him; he'd always been a piece of the scenery back home.

But helping unload he suddenly seemed to have separated himself from the background. All at once, he was standing there, a fully formed man, with a kind smile, strong looking hands and bits of lint stuck to his shirt and ball cap from helping bundle the wool my father bought every spring.

He began sticking around the trading post after work. Often my mother would invite him to stay for supper. After we'd eaten, he'd help me wash dishes, and we'd sit out on the porch in the lengthening spring twilights and talk. He'd smoke a couple of cigarettes and soon I asked him for one. I'd never smoked before, and I never have since, but I lied and told him I'd picked it up at school. I didn't feel very adult, because I remembered thinking it made me appear more sophisticated.

Eddie helped ease me back into the community, catching me up on what my old high school friends were doing, inviting me to softball games and dances. He himself had taken some community college classes, but confessed that school wasn't for him. The two of us were on different planes intellectually, but emotionally we were both searching for ourselves, each hoping the other could somehow mirror the person emerging. In that sense I supposed that what we were doing was essentially selfish, but it hadn't struck me that way at the time.

The two of us talked, I told myself, but mostly—I was now ashamed to say—I talked and Eddie listened. He was good at that. It was part of what had made him such a good cop.

One Saturday morning he asked if I'd like to go riding that afternoon after the post closed. There was a place he wanted to show me. We rode out toward the mesa, winding our way up through the juniper and piñon trees to a shake abandoned years before. We unsaddled the horses and lay the saddle blankets on the ground inside. The roof, once cedar boughs freshly cut every summer and draped over sapling joists, was now gone, the cedar posts still erect in the ground, providing us with the only sense of shelter we needed, the whole shaded in late afternoon by a huge old cedar tree. Our lovemaking was open to the crystal blue sky, our union permeated by the smell of horses.

We began riding out more and more frequently, often after supper in the long warm summer evenings. As was typical of young people, we believed we possessed a great secret, of which no one else alive was even remotely aware. That we believed so was evidence of how dimly aware we were of our own situation. Of course, although my parents didn't know where the two of us were disappearing to almost every evening, they did realize what was happening.

Riding out to the old shake became like our lovemaking. We would begin by trotting side by side, but as we got closer, and once in sight of it, we spurred the horses on faster and faster. We would arrive panting, our horses blowing and stamping as we hobbled them and turned them loose to graze as we turned to each other.

As a lover, Eddie had been sweet and gentle, yet undeniable as the tide is undeniable, rising slowly yet irresistibly until our wavering individualities were erased and we lost them and joined together. Both equally inexperienced, we made up for in ardor what we lacked in skill.

At dusk, we walked the horses back, Eddie turning off on the road to his parents' house, I continuing on to the trading post. Our skin was still warm with the other's skin, each of us still tasting and smelling the other, the sounds of our cries and our sighs still echoing in our ears.

Looking back, I thought it was that loss of identity, that momentary ceasing to know ourselves, that drew us so. Even more blissful than satisfying the physical urge was shirking our shared obsession with what the future held. Making love, there was no future, time itself stopped, and in that oblivion we could take a rest from the hectoring question our future had become.

A sense of timelessness seemed to have encapsulated that entire summer. I carried it now in the medicine pouch Eddie gave me one evening at the shake. Opening it, I can relive the slanting rays of the sun on Eddie's face as he unbuttoned my blouse, the cushion of cedar duff under our blanket, my hands tracing the smooth arc of his back as he lowered his mouth to mine.

Maybe the lovemaking changed, maybe time passed was all, but as summer became fall and fall winter, we abandoned our visits to the shake. Once that happened, it was like awakening from a dream. Our visits became more about talking again, and as we talked we awoke to the world around us. It was almost as though we had passed through some sort of portal together, and once through we could never go back.

There had been a brief but awkward period in which we truly thought we were meant for each other, but the more we talked the more we realized we were looking for different things. I was still restless, but I knew the only way to satisfy that was to move on. I had contacted a couple of grad schools, and had talked several times with my father about practicing law. Eddie had said that being so close to me had started him thinking about children and a wife.

I entered law school the following fall and soon after that Eddie went away to the Navajo police academy in Toyei. Our paths, once set, intersected thereafter only in friendship.

One by one, I collected the objects, returned them to their pouch, and replaced the pouch in the drawer. In bed, I turned over on my stomach to go to sleep, the image of Eddie's sodden cruiser again before me. Oh Eddie, I sighed. Shi' kis. 'My friend.' What happened to you?

First the endless drive up. I just couldn't get used to the distances out here, everything so far away. *What? Are the miles longer out West?* I wondered.

"How far you gotta go to check out a murder around here?" I asked Frank. "Back in the projects in D.C. we never went further than around the block."

Frank looked at me and chuckled.

"That a taste of what you call black humor?"

"That's good, Frank. A double entendre."

We get to park headquarters, and all six of us are crammed into an overheated one-windowed room barely big enough for the table we were sitting around. Go figure.

Frank. Before we go in, "Let's leave a small footprint here."

This for me. Huh.

Head Ranger Sarah Tanner, a tall woman at the head of the table, was running the meeting. Seemed to know what she was doing. She should. All of them go through the academy just like me and Frank.

Tanner started with herself and went around the table. "This is my partner, Officer Luke Russell of the park service. And most of us know Frank Doyle, special agent out of Flagstaff. He and his partner are here because the deceased was a Native American found within the park boundaries.

"Our local coroner and one of our Page docs, Jordan Hunt. He helps us with any inside-the-park fatalities and finished the autopsy on the deceased this morning. He'll be giving us some preliminary results a little later."

This guy looked to be in his mid-40s—a very fit mid-40s. I didn't normally go for older men, but thought I might make an exception here. I looked at him long enough to give him a chance to look back, but all I saw was him and Sarah glance at each other with what I sensed was something more than professional interest.

Sarah looked down at her paper on the table.

"These last two are newcomers. Frank's partner is Special Agent Luanda Wilmington. Flagstaff is her first assignment out of the academy. Welcome."

I smiled.

"And Tommy Two Clouds, newly with the Navajo Division of Public Safety."

The Indian guy sitting beside me stood up. He was so tall it looked like his hair was brushing the ceiling. Taking the initiative, I extended my hand and said, "Yah-ah-teh."

It flustered him.

Now what? I wondered.

He shook my hand, but instead of getting Yah-ah-teh back I got Hau kola.

"I'm Lakota, actually," he said.

Oops.

But he was smiling.

A clerk appeared at the door.

Sarah asked, "Coffee anyone?"

No one wanted. Just as I was about to suggest we get on with it, Sarah began, reading from a file.

"Deceased was a 39-year-old Navajo police officer, Eddie Watchman," she said. "Stationed in Kayenta. With the force 13 years. Left behind a wife and three kids."

She paused. I noticed everyone at the table was looking down at it.

"Last known whereabouts?" I asked. Keep it moving.

"The night of April 29 Eddie answered a domestic dispute call north of Inscription House," Sarah said, pointing to a spot on the wall map behind her. "About here.

"Radio transcriptions as well as residents there confirm he arrived at 9:15, spent about an hour getting everybody settled down, then left. Called in to say he was going to check something out. Didn't say what. That was it."

"*Nobody* up there knows anything?" Frank asked.

Sarah shook her head.

"Navajo police talked to everyone the day after the disappearance, but no one came forward."

Frank glanced over at Tommy.

"We'll check it out tomorrow."

Tommy nodded.

Sarah turned to Luke, the Marlboro Man if I ever saw one.

"Dive team found nothing around the vehicle, which looks like it sank to where we found it," he said. "Probably was pushed in from a road up above when the lake was higher."

"How much higher?" I asked.

"Right on 60 feet."

I was amazed. "Sixty feet! What happened? The dam spring a leak?"

"It's an unusually big drop," he said, "but we've had big fluctuations before. Spring and summer of '73 was a wet El Niño cycle. The lake actually rose 55 feet in three months due to a combination of runoff from an unusually heavy snow pack and spring rains. On the other hand, remember that this lake is both a hydroelectric and irrigation system, so it's not unusual to lose a lot of water over the summer, especially with the drought we've been in lately."

He checked his report. "Eddie's gun was missing. And he was sitting in the front passenger's seat, not the driver's seat, which was moved back for a much taller person."

"Forensics estimates it was positioned for a driver at least six feet tall," Frank added.

"How tall was Watchman?" I asked.

Jordan checked the autopsy. "Five-foot-nine."

"So someone else may have driven it," Frank said, "possibly the murderer."

"Beyond that, there's one other thing," Luke said, looking around at us. "I'd like it to stay in this room.

"Lab reports a trace amount of high-grade marijuana found loose inside the vehicle."

I looked at Jordan.

"Autopsy show any in the officer?"

Everyone, but especially Frank, looked at me as though I'd tracked dog shit into the room.

"Blood chemistry was negative," said Jordan. "Negative for anything illicit. No alcohol even," he added, looking at me.

I smiled as warmly as I could.

He returned to his report.

"Condition of the body, given the water temp and the closed windows, fits with the time of disappearance, about six months. His jaw was broken in three places, but cause of death was blunt trauma to the back of the head."

Frank. "Weapon?"

"From the shape of the wound, something rounded. Possibly a rock."

Officer Two Clouds cleared his throat.

"You mean somebody in the back seat with a rock?"

Jordan shook his head.

"Our guess is Eddie was attacked and killed outside the vehicle, then loaded into the passenger's seat before being pushed into the lake. We found what we think is a small amount of blood on the fabric of the passenger's seat. We'll know more when we get fabric analysis back from forensics."

"Water sixty feet down would have been pretty cold, wouldn't it?" I asked. "Would have slowed bleeding considerably. Maybe he was killed in the cruiser."

Jordan looked at me with what might have been a little respect.

"There was too much blood loss and too little on the seat."

Nice try, I told myself.

"So we're left with why someone would go to that much trouble to hide the body and the cruiser," Frank said.

"Hopefully we'll answer that question when we find where he was killed," Sarah replied.

"You mean 'if,'" Frank said. "There's a lot of open ground out there. What say we take a look at the cruiser this afternoon?"

"It's as good a place to start as any," said Sarah.

Out in the hallway afterwards, Tommy was standing there, grinning down at me.

"Sorry," I said. "Just trying to be neighborly."

"No problem, it's just how many Navajos you see with my height?"

"I haven't seen all that many Navajos in the first place. So how did you end up down here from up in, is it South Dakota?"

"I was raised around here. Navajo couple, close friends of my parents, adopted me when my folks were killed."

"How did they die?"

"Car wreck. I was too young to remember."

He turned to Jordan, who put a hand on his shoulder.

"So who's your family?" the doctor asked.

"The Tsinnajinnies, out by Kaibeto."

"Your dad work for the railroad?" Luke asked.

"That's my uncle Lemuel. My dad works at the mine."

"What's his name?"

"Leonard. My mom's Daisy," said Tommy.

"Well, we're glad to have you with us. We'll get to the bottom of this," said Jordan. "I just had a question for Luanda."

Tommy wandered off, looking for someone else to impress with his height.

"That was a pertinent observation in there about the bleed out rate. You're interested in forensic work?" Jordan asked.

"I think I want to specialize in it," I said. "I've applied to get back to the academy...Another thing...You know any alcohol would be long gone after six months."

"I know, but I just wanted to let you know we checked," he said.

"What about blood pooling?"

Jordan nodded.

"Another thing told us he died outside the cruiser. He was upright in the seat, but there wasn't much blood in the buttocks or the back of the thighs."

"You said his jaw was broken?"

"Smashed is more like it. Looked like..."

"So, is this your first visit to Lake Powell?"

I turned and there was Sarah.

"I've been here six months and I'm ashamed to say I haven't even been to the Grand Canyon yet."

"Looks like you're about to see more of the Grand Canyon State anyway. You staying in Page?"

"Holiday Inn."

"Why don't we have a drink at your place this evening after we've been up the lake?" she suggested.

"Not me," said Jordan, heading for the door. "I have to get back to the office. Heavy afternoon ahead. Keep me posted."

"Will do," Sarah said.

"Sounds good to me," I said, "as long as I don't have to drive."

TIC DOULOUREUX

Carey threw the paper into my lap, stood there waiting for me to pick it up.

"Hey, asshole. I'm watching *Survivor* here. Fuckin' amateurs, can't get outta their own way to save their sorry asses."

"You better read it," he said. "They found him. Shit! I knew they would."

I knew he was talking about the cop. The lake had dropped so fast, it didn't take a rocket scientist to figure somebody'd discover the cruiser sooner or later.

Next commercial, I scanned the story, which occupied the whole front page of the *Chronicle*. Nothing I didn't already know—except— "Holy shit!" I said. "Jordan Hunt!" I laughed.

"Who the hell is he? And what's so funny?"

"The city coroner, evidently…and an old acquaintance."

Yes indeed, I thought. *Old Jordan and I go way back.* So after everything, we both end up back here, back where it all began…

I feel that high-altitude sun, so direct, burning the back of my neck, making me sweat as I pedal up the mesa to Jordan's house, my little brother Stevie hollering at me from behind to wait up.

Being at Jordan's house is always better than being at home, even on days like this, when he steps quietly out the door, closing it noiselessly behind him, to tell us we have to find something to do away from the house. Sometimes Jordan's dad plays touch football with us out in the yard—that's the best—but not today. Today the house has a stricken feeling, like everyone in it is holding their breath. Today his dad is "unwell." That's the word he uses. Only years later did I understand what it meant.

We go to the garage, gather up poles and a tackle box. The lake seems far enough away, and it's the perfect place to unveil the little surprise I borrowed from my dad. We fly down the hill, over the bridge, and out to the marina at Wahweap, where there's a battered aluminum rowboat tied up, purchased by Mr. Hunt for the enjoyment and amusement of us boys. A quick stop to buy bait, and we're rowing into the middle of the bay, the light glorious. There's not a shadow in the world, except perhaps for the one I have tucked inside my shirt.

We all throw lines over after I help Stevie bait up, and damn if it isn't Stevie just a minute later who hooks the big walleye. I take his pole from him and haul it into the boat, where it flips around, gnashing its mouthful of needle sharp teeth. The next second Stevie bursts into tears. He's scared to death of the thing and swiftly climbs around behind me, almost falling out of the boat.

Jordan and I bust out laughing, we're laughing like hell. He brings an oar up to club the thing, but by now the blue steel shadow is out of my shirt. Jordan's face changes. His laugh goes high pitched, like he's strangling.

Even Stevie shuts up when he sees it.

I watch a guy on TV leap from a 30-foot cliff into the water.

I'm still laughing as I point it down and pull the trigger.

We're all momentarily deafened by the explosion, but there's nothing to hear anyway until the bottom of the boat begins to fill with water and I shout the baddest word I know.

"Fuck!"

We tear our shirts off and try to stuff the hole, but it quickly becomes clear that we're sinking. Jordan grabs the oars and tries to row, but the boat is settling under us. We have to swim for it.

On the screen, the guy is swimming out to a rock—'bout a hundred yards. Powder puff.

We're a thousand yards from shore, way beyond the limit Jordan's dad set when he gave us the boat, but what choice do we have? We jump in and start swimming. Jordan and I are side by side, but Stevie quickly falls behind.

The guy is floundering, struggling. Is he gonna make it?

I go back for Stevie, get him across the chest with one arm, stroke with the other. But he just goes limp on me. Dead weight.

"Kick! Kick!" *I scream. He does, but weakly.*

I can see the shoreline is closer. A bad feeling tells me not close enough.

A second guy jumps from the cliff, starts swimming for the first.

I catch up with Jordan, who's slowing down, coughing and gasping.

"Too far," *he says, his voice the same as it was back on the boat. He stops, tries to tread water, but he starts to sink.*

The second swimmer reaches the first.

I let go of Stevie and grab Jordan. We're only twenty yards from shore. I stretch my legs down. Where the hell's the bottom?

A few more strokes and I can touch.

I push Jordan toward shore and turn for Stevie.

But the water's smooth.

Stevie's gone.

Gone.

I watch the two swimmers crawl up on the rock together. "Fuckin' amateurs!"

I jumped up and threw the paper back at Carey, who looked at me like, 'It's only a frickin' TV show.'

SARAH

The tourists had pretty much thinned out by that time of the year, so it wasn't hard to spot Luanda in the lounge. Besides, any young woman as pretty and as black as Luanda would stand out anywhere, never mind in a town as white as Page. She was at a window table looking down at the dam.

"Man, that's a lot of concrete," she said. "How long it take to pour all that?"

"Nine years. 1956 to 1965. Four million nine hundred and one thousand cubic yards."

She whistled softly. "My father worked construction. He always loved the big jobs."

I told her Jordan's dad had been chief engineer on the project.

"Local boy, is he?" she asked.

"Jordan? Born and raised right here in Page."

"I'll bet you could even show me where," she said

"What makes you think so?"

She shrugged one shoulder, so I knew she was fishing. "The meeting this morning," she ventured.

"Is it that obvious?" I asked.

"Only to someone who's looking around herself," she said, and we both laughed.

"We're just getting started, so I guess he's fair game, although I think you'll find he's otherwise engaged, and not to me."

"Oh?"

"His practice, his dad, the hospital. He has priorities."

"His dad's still around?"

"Lives with Jordan. Moved in after Jordan's wife moved out a couple years ago."

"Not a priority?"

"He hasn't said much about her."

The waitress came over and we ordered.

"So where's Frank?" I asked.

"On the phone to Window Rock, putting a file together on Officer Watchman."

I apologized for the reception she'd gotten at the meeting that morning. "It's just that Eddie was a big part of a small family up here," I explained. "We all take it personal. I grew up with Eddie's wife."

"On the reservation?" she asked.

"My dad's a fourth-generation trader, owns a trading post over by Crystal, near the Arizona-New Mexico state line. Ella's taken the kids back there to her family for now."

Luanda looked out at the lake. "He wasn't much older than me."

We had visited the site of the cruiser that afternoon. The day before, the dive team had done their thing, then forensics floated the cruiser out, with Eddie still inside, on a salvage barge. The cruiser was now in a boat hangar at Wahweap, and Eddie was in the hospital morgue.

"Luke's having a hard time," I said. "He and Eddie used to hunt together."

Luanda turned back to me. "That Luke, he doesn't show much. How can you tell?"

"It's all part of the cowboy ethic. His family's ranched this country since his great grandfather painted it."

"What do you mean?" she asked.

"Luke's a great grandson of Charles M. Russell, the painter."

"No kidding!"

"Yeah, he's even got a couple of originals hanging in his trailer, and a bronze in the living room—calls them his retirement plan."

"Hope he has honest neighbors."

"Nobody comes around the ranch he doesn't know about, trust me…Oh, and speaking of coming around, I got a call this morning from the AP stringer in Flagstaff asking about Eddie," I said. "They covered his disappearance last spring. I told him what we know, except for the marijuana. I gave the same stuff to George at *The Chronicle* here in Page when he called."

"Hopefully we'll find the perpetrator and be done with it," said Luanda. "Frank, Tommy, and I are driving out tomorrow to talk to the people who saw Eddie last."

"The domestic disturbance call?" I asked. "Check with Frank, but I'm pretty sure the Navajo police interviewed them after Eddie disappeared."

"They find anything?"

"Not much, but now we know what happened to Eddie, it's good you're going back. Only watch your step. Those domestic problems have a tendency to reignite."

"We'll pack a fire extinguisher," she said, and raised her glass.

My father was in the kitchen when I finally got home that evening—cooking dinner, thank God. The office had been wall-to-wall all afternoon, then rounds at the hospital. I draped my lower extremities over a stool at the counter, on which I rested my upper extremities.

"Cocktail hour's already started. I'm one up on you," Grady said, raising his glass of tea. "Care for one?"

"Sure, only leave out the six sugars and the crushed mint," I said.

Grady shook his head as he poured me a glass. "God didn't make this stuff to be drunk straight," he said. "Not like bourbon."

Of course, we both knew he hadn't touched a drop of that since he'd put my brother Merced in the hospital thirty years earlier.

"Drink yourself into a diabetic coma with this stuff," I said.

"We all gotta go somehow. You going out to run today? You got time before dinner."

I responded by laying my head on my arms.

"Guess not, then. I'll go ahead and get things ready. Anything new on Eddie?"

I told him about the meeting that morning with Frank, Luanda, and Tommy.

"Of course, you're the expert, but if you ask me, I'd look for somebody local, I mean out on the res. Ten to one he was killed by one of his own people."

I raised my head and smiled at my father. "As a matter of fact, Dad, we've got three people going out tomorrow to check out the guy who saw him last," I said.

Grady answered by looking smug.

"But for what it's worth, I think you're wrong," I said.

He cocked an eyebrow at me. "Oh?"

"The kind of murder you're talking about is usually a crime of passion. You know, a domestic squabble, a falling out among friends, usually involving alcohol."

"So what makes this one different?"

"Well, for one, Eddie suffered two potentially fatal injuries. His mandible was driven nearly up into his brain, and his skull was crushed from behind. Now, the latter is consistent with the type of crime you're talking about, but the former most certainly is not.

"Second, whoever killed Eddie went to a great deal of trouble to load him back into his cruiser, seatbelt him in, drive him to the lake, and dump him in. It's unlikely that someone in a drunken rage would do that."

"It would sure help to know where he was killed," said Grady.

"Which is why we've got people going out tomorrow to his last known location."

"Okay, let's eat!"

We sat down, and Grady said, "I told you I'm heading over to New Mexico Tuesday, didn't I?"

"Another demonstration, right?"

"Another power plant. Can you believe it? I'm telling you, Jordan, these power plants, they're the new dams. Same strategy as fifty years ago: build them in some out of the way corner where nobody lives or where the people who do live there are disenfranchised already—you know, Indians, poor ranchers. Promise 'em all kinds of high-end jobs, for which none of 'em will qualify, so the company of course will bring in its own people, leaving the grunt jobs to the locals. You've got local communities falling all over themselves to offer the power company tax breaks and building incentives.

"Only these coal-fired plants are worse than the dams. At least the dams only screwed up the rivers they backed up. These plants—even with all the new high-tech scrubbers and combustion technology and all that—are huge polluters! They promise the locals tax revenues, which the local government pockets and the people pay for with higher rates of lung cancer, emphysema, leukemia, you name it. It's a devil's bargain, I'm telling you. You're trading human lives for energy that's gonna be shipped to Phoenix or Albuquerque or some other God-forsaken sinkhole."

I held up my hands. "Dad, you don't have to convince me. I'm a doctor, remember? In a place where we've got our own power plant. I see this stuff all the time."

He paused long enough to blink. "And the coal they burn, most of it's strip mined, so there's more land torn up. Tell you they put it all back the way it was. Restoration they call it. Like you could put an egg back together after you've cracked it open and eaten what's inside.

"People have to start thinking renewable. Wind. Solar. Geothermal. It's the only way we're going to save the planet. Huh, the planet, hell. Save our own selfish asses. The planet will survive."

"So, don't forget that conference is next weekend," I said, trying for a change of topic.

"The one in Phoenix? Just a couple of days, right?"

"It's the one on methamphetamine toxicology."

"So are you taking your lady friend, then?" he asked.

"Sarah? No, she's on duty that weekend. Besides, I don't think we're quite there yet."

"And where would that be?" he asked. His eyes twinkled.

"C'mon Dad, lay off."

"Jordan, you've been back almost five years. How many chances do you think are gonna come along in a small town?"

"Dad, it's not the lottery, okay? Maybe you and Mom found each other early, but I'm still looking around."

Grady's eyes changed. Mentioning my mother had been a mistake.

"You're right there, son. Found her early, lost her early."

"I'm sorry, Dad. I didn't mean to—"

He raised his hand. "It's okay, son. It's like this house, keeping it the way she had it, like a museum. It's not right, I know, but I can't let go."

I came around to his side of the table and put my arm around his shoulders.

"Nobody's asking you to, Dad. The house is fine just like it is."

Grady was quiet for a moment, then he raised his head. "It's like rafting down the river, son, and you latch onto a boulder just before you hit the rapids. You don't let go until you're sure what's ahead of you."

He looked around the room. "This place is my boulder."

I had never said it to him, but I'd tried to show him in the years since I'd come back that it was okay to let go. He didn't have to hang on so tightly. But he'd shown no signs of letting loose. Funny, I thought. Here I am trying to latch on while he's trying to let go.

SARAH

There was a voice mail waiting for me when I got back to the office after drinks with Luanda. A Mrs. Belkow, Space 14, needed to see me immediately, very important. Isn't it always? On the other hand, most people don't realize that an area the size of a national park at any given moment holds the population of a small city. Problem is, that population changes daily, making it pretty difficult to keep track of the bad guys, so I figured 'best to check it out,' and drove over to the campground.

Space 14 was a 35-foot Wanderer fifth wheel with a wooden plaque that said: "The Belkows – Norm and Judy" affixed to the gooseneck. Parked beside it was a late-model one-ton Dodge Ram pickup with a Cummins diesel.

Mrs. Belkow must have been standing just inside, because no sooner had I knocked than the door opened, she poked her head outside, looked left and right, then motioned me in, jerking the door shut behind her. She snapped the lock.

Judy Belkow was a small woman from whose compact frame time had melted any extraneous fat and whose hair was a dark, unnatural red. Mr. Belkow, although absent from the room, announced his presence in the trailer with a wreath of fresh cigar smoke hanging just below the ceiling. I introduced myself.

"Norm said I shouldn't call you, Officer Tanner, but I felt you should know," she said.

Somewhere in the depths of the trailer, Mr. Belkow cleared his throat.

"What should I know, Mrs. Belkow?"

"Well, late this afternoon Norm and I were out for our regular walk before dinner. You know, just through the campground."

I nodded. Mrs. Belkow obviously had this well rehearsed, so I just let her roll.

"Well, two spaces down, Number 16, a man named Harris pulled in last Tuesday. Let's see, was it Tuesday? Yes, Tuesday, because I got my hair done in town. The space was empty when we left, but he was there when we got back.

"Well, today he called us over, said he had something to show us if we could keep a secret. I looked at Norm, and he seemed all right, so we let him show us. It was a pot, you know, one of those Anasazi pots. The rim was broken in a couple of places, but he had the pieces. Showed us how they fit together, like a puzzle, didn't he Norm?"

A grunt issued from another room.

"Anyway, he was really excited, said it was his greatest find ever, in twenty years he'd never found anything like this. Said it would fetch a lot of money, more than enough to cover his whole trip. Said a friend of his had found one like his but not nearly as nice and had sold it for almost five thousand dollars!

"Well, we stayed a few more minutes, then I told Norm we had to get back to our walk if I was going to have dinner fixed on time. Harris reminded us it was a secret, but I was careful not to agree to keep quiet because I knew I was going to call you, Officer."

I asked if Harris had mentioned where he found the pot.

"I don't think so, did he, Norm?"

Another throat clearing.

"Nope."

I had her give a brief description of Harris, then thanked her and told her she'd done the right thing. I listened, but there was no sound from the back of the trailer. I told Mrs. Belkow I'd check it out.

Back out at the truck I got Luke on the radio. He drove up a few minutes later and we walked over to see Harris. The campground, about half full this time of year, was mostly retirees in trailers. Pretty quiet.

Space 16 was a camper in the back of an old Chevy half ton, Utah plates, expired, pulling a trailer carrying an 18-foot Bayliner. A slovenly man in his thirties answered my knock.

"Mr. Harris?" I asked. He nodded.

"I'm Officer Sarah Tanner, park police. This is Officer Russell. Are you alone?"

Another nod.

"Mind answering some questions?"

"Guess not. What's going on?"

He stepped down out of the trailer, closed the door behind him.

"Mr. Harris, I have information that you're in illegal possession of an Anasazi artifact found within the boundaries of the recreation area."

Maybe he'd been drinking. I didn't smell anything, but he just stared at me.

"An Anasazi pot, Mr. Harris," I prompted.

"No!" he blurted out. "Who told you that?"

I said that wasn't important, asked him again if he'd found a pot.

"I don't know anything about pots. I just came down to fish for a few days."

"Up the lake somewhere, off in a side canyon?" I prodded. "I know you guys network. Someone clued you in?"

"Like I said, just fishing."

"Let's not play games, Mr. Harris. I have an eyewitness who saw you with the pot."

I was taking a chance that he might realize it was Mrs. Belkow, but I was sure he'd shown the thing to anyone else who was interested.

"Don't I get to confront my accuser?" he asked in a voice one decibel short of a whine.

"This is only an investigation, Mr. Harris, not a court of law," I said. "Now, we can take you into custody, get a warrant, search your truck, your trailer, your boat, find what it is we're pretty sure you have, and then place you under arrest.

"Or you can cooperate now, simplify the process, which, in my experience, the judge views favorably. But we're not going to wait long, Mr. Harris, so you need to make up your mind."

There's always a moment during an encounter like this when the suspect has to go one way or the other. Guilty or innocent doesn't matter. They have to decide to cooperate or just keep shucking and jiving.

I guessed Mr. Harris chose the latter, because he mumbled something about something in the cab of his truck, headed that way, then bolted for the sagebrush.

"Damn!" I said, and the chase was on.

Fortunately, Luke keeps himself in ferocious shape, not working out so much as working around the ranch evenings and weekends. He had Harris down and cuffed before I came puffing up. I helped bring him to his feet.

"Well, Mr. Harris," I said between breaths, "looks like you chose the long road. Now Officer Russell here is going to transport you to the city jail in town, where you'll stay until your hearing, probably tomorrow. Any questions?"

Once we had the warrant, it didn't take long to find. Wrapped in an old army blanket, tucked behind the front seat in the cab, was a corrugated pot about six inches in diameter—probably Early Basketmaker. Judy Belkow was right: two small shards fit perfectly into the lip. It was in such good condition; hard to believe it was probably close to a thousand years old. Harris had been right about one thing: it was quite a find.

JORDAN

I sat up late reading that night, but my thoughts kept returning to my father and this house. Most days he had a sense of humor about it, living in what he called his 'time capsule' or his 'time machine.' But tonight my mother's memory must've been close somehow and had reached out and touched him. I understood. Some things were never very far from my thoughts.

The whole town has turned out, of course. I mean, this is Ladybird, the president's wife! Right here in Page! Everything is closed: businesses, stores, even school. Everyone has gathered on the top of the dam, where a stage and bleachers and row upon row of folding chairs have been set up under a blue sky perfect for the dedication ceremony.

Tic and I are seated facing town, and we watch as the motorcade bearing Mrs. Johnson, a line of black Lincolns and Cadillacs, crests the mesa and begins winding its way down to us. So many black cars, it could be a funeral procession only there's no hearse.

I look to my right at the steel-arch bridge spanning the river gorge. Our teacher told us that newspapers and radio and TV stations from as far away as Phoenix and Salt Lake City were there, and I can see there are several cameras aimed our way. The black cars start out on the bridge past the cameras, which swivel to mark their passing.

On my left, Grady has taken his seat on the bleachers behind the stage, along with some other employees of Merritt-Chapman & Scott Corporation, which built the dam. The mayor is up there too, along with a lot of people I don't know.

Grady is peering at something to his right, and when I turn, I see the door to the elevator leading to the top of the dam open and about a dozen crew-cut Secret Service agents, all the size of football players and all wearing black suits, come boiling out. All heads turn their way. A thrill of anticipation courses through the crowd—she's coming! But, I'm wondering how all those guys fit into that elevator.

The agents form a corridor between the elevator and the stage to let Ladybird pass.

"These boys know what they're doing," someone in the crowd says.

And then here she comes. Everyone's cheering and clapping, but we can't really see anything until she mounts the stage and takes her seat. She looks like the type of grandmother anybody would want to have: smiling, nicely dressed, well-poised. Like a lady. I guess that's where she got the name.

We all stand while the band plays "The Star Spangled Banner." The mayor remains standing to give a short welcoming speech, but I'm not paying attention 'cuz I'm too busy visualizing the next step of the program. Eventually he sits down and we get our cue.

A large space has been left open directly in front of the stage. A lot of kids from Page School are going to re-enact the building of the dam for the First Lady. Mr. Keys, our principal, thought this would both entertain and inform Mrs. Johnson, who hadn't been here for much of the actual construction.

He's taken direct control of the production from the start, and now he signals us to begin assembling our props into what he calls a tableau vivant. Off to one side, a shed-sized replica of the White House goes up (Mrs. Johnson's current home, Mr. Keys had taken pains to point out to us), and he takes a seat inside. He's going to play President Dwight D. Eisenhower, who began official construction of the dam back in 1956 when he pressed a button in the White House and set off the first explosion to begin preparing Glen Canyon for its new occupant. I think it's a good part for Mr. Keys because he looks a lot like the picture of President Eisenhower in our history book, balding with a friendly face— grandpa to Ladybird's grandma.

Some of the older boys move into place the chicken wire and papier mâché canyon walls they built in shop class, and then Tic and I go to work. We're in charge of the explosives, a single cherry bomb actually, that Grady helped us rig with a hot wire connected to a 9-volt dry cell and a button in front of Mr. Keys in the White House. The firecracker is packaged inside a brownbag lunch sack stuffed with a mixture of flour and cayenne pepper to simulate the dust from the explosion. The sack is glued in the bottom of a bucket turned on its side at the base of the west wall. At Mr. Keys' touch, the canyon will be filled with dust.

I am especially proud of the dust mixture, my own creation. Realism, realism, realism, Mr. Keys kept stressing to us, so I was especially careful of the color I chose from my mother's spice rack to match the sandstone walls of the canyon. Cinnamon was too brown, paprika too red, but cayenne was just right. Tic and I are ready, holding the bucket steady, waiting for Mr. Keys to begin speaking his part.

Earlier in the week, he had received a copy of the speech Ladybird was to give and had shown it to all of the students in the play. In it, she honored the eighteen men who'd perished in the dam's construction, pointing out that their sacrifice had not been in vain, enumerating the benefits that would flow from the dam for the greater good of all.

Mr. Keys said he was glad she hadn't drawn an analogy between the dam and Vietnam, where her husband Lyndon had the United States so deeply mired. He thought everybody in the audience would be glad she hadn't. I didn't know much about what was going on in Vietnam, so I had to assume Mr. Keys was right.

Suddenly the crowd quieted, and although we can't see him from behind our paper-thin canyon wall, we know Mr. Keys has stood up to speak. Sure enough, he's right on time. We tighten our grip on the bucket, waiting for our cue, and here it comes. Mr. Keys speaks the words "the first step toward making the desert bloom," and presses the button.

Our contraption works perfectly. The bucket even magnifies the flat bang of the cherry bomb into a resounding boom, the "canyon" instantly fills with red dust, and the crowd breaks into applause.

Unfortunately, although all the little kids have been warned that there is to be an explosion, Mr. Keys has failed to alert the Secret Service. In an instant, pandemonium erupts on the stage. Chairs are sent flying, people are knocked down. Men are shouting, women scream. The agents form a reverse huddle around the First Lady, every man facing out, ready to lay down his life for her. Somebody later said one of them had tackled her to the stage, but we doubted that, although this is only three years after the assassination of President Kennedy, so maybe he did.

Anyway, it gets worse. A breeze funnels the cloud of pepper up onto the stage, where it acts like tear gas, and there's an extended convulsion of sneezing and coughing until the cloud finally dissipates, after which Mr. Keys stands up and arbitrarily announces that the remainder of the play is being cancelled, but Ladybird graciously requests that it continue, and Mr. Keys just as graciously accedes.

Our part finished, Tic and I return to our seats. I glance up at my father, who's also regained his seat, and he's glaring at me as though the whole incident is my fault. If he believes it is, it must be, I think, and guilt consumes me.

The play continues, and my occasional glance at Grady tells me he's still upset, although a couple of times I see him shading his eyes and looking up the mesa toward town. Then I remember. My mother is supposed to have driven back into town from her teaching job in Kaibeto to attend the dedication ceremony, and she hasn't arrived yet.

The next time I check the stage, I catch one of my father's assistants leaning in to whisper something. Even from a distance I can see all the color drain from Grady's face. He disappears from the stage one moment, and the next he's leaning over me, Merced and Niles in tow.

"We have to go. There's been an accident," is all he says.

I'm confused. "You mean an accident here at the dam?" I ask, but my father is stone-faced.

I ask again as we climb into the car.

"No," he says. "A car accident. Your mother."

Now we're all too afraid to ask any questions, and we sit silently as we cross the bridge. I look out his side of the car. The ceremony is still in progress, all the cameras and onlookers facing that way. None of the cameras turn toward us as we pass. The dedication must be more important than what's happening in our car.

There's an ambulance in front of the hospital when we arrive. Dad makes us wait in the foyer while he goes in to talk to the doctor. Everyone around us is talking in whispers. Nobody looks at us, even though everybody seems to know who we are and why we're there.

My father is gone for what seems like hours, and when he finally emerges from the hospital's corridors his eyes are terribly changed. It's only when he gets closer to us that I realize he's crying, something I've never seen him do before. It's something I will see him do many times in the days and weeks to come.

I never saw my mother again. The casket was closed at the funeral, and for several years after that I had a recurring dream in which I understood that there had been a mistake, that my mother hadn't been buried in the Page cemetery. Then she'd pull up outside our house and come smiling through the door, a stack of books clutched in one arm and a bag of groceries in the other, asking us boys to go out and fetch the rest of the bags from her car. In the dream, I go outside, but her car is a smoldering wreck in the driveway, and when I go back inside to tell her this, she's gone.

LUKE RUSSELL

Next day, Sarah and I had Harris show us where he found the pot, a small side canyon a couple hours up the lake. It was a beautiful fall day. The cloudless blue sky reached down to the many shades of sandstone red on the horizon. The water, smooth as glass, reflected the blue of the sky. Along the way, I filled Sarah in on some of the history of Glen Canyon before the dam was built.

"The Sierra Club called it 'The Canyon Nobody Knew,'" I said. "Of course, this was after they'd used up all their political capital blocking a dam in the Bureau of Reclamation's site of first choice, Echo Canyon, at the confluence of the Green and the Yampa up in Dinosaur National Monument. Somebody once joked that Glen Canyon was the canyon only the *Sierra Club* didn't know.

"The place actually has a long and colorful history. As evidenced by our friend Harris here"—he gave me a blank look—"prehistoric people like the Basketmakers and the Anasazi once lived in the canyon, but they were long gone by the time the Spanish first explored this area in the 16th century. In 1776, the two Spanish priests, Dominguez and Escalante, were searching for a convenient route linking the Spanish settlements in New Mexico with those in California, but they turned back somewhere near Cedar City and crossed the Colorado at the mouth of Padre Creek, which became known as the Crossing of the Fathers. Now underwater, of course."

I continued as we made our way up the lake.

"Over the next century, the Spanish and then the Mexicans, under the guise of converting the Indians to Christianity, raided this area for Navajo slaves and livestock. But very few of them settled here. The country was just too rugged and dry. By 1848, the Americans owned it all, and they sent several surveys out—Wheeler, Hayden, and Powell among them—but only Powell actually came through here, and even he limited his explorations to the river and a few major side canyons. Once the Mormons settled Salt Lake, they began filtering into this triangle formed by the Colorado, the San Juan, and the Clay Hills to the east, along with Indian traders, cattle ranchers, scientists, and adventurers.

"Gold prospectors big and small tried to make a go of it in Glen Canyon. Cass Hite set up shop at the mouth of Ticaboo Creek in the 1880s, and brokered claims up and down the river for years after that. Glen Canyon was 'nature's sluice box,' they said, figuring that gold from all the side canyons had worked its way into the river over the millennia. The Hoskaninni Mining Company anchored a big dredge near the creek, but the gold, by the time it had washed in from all the side canyons, had been ground too fine to recover. 'Flour gold' they called it. Eventually it was only the little guys who were able to sustain themselves on what they could pan. Cass Hite lived for years on what he sluiced out of what he called his Bank of Ticaboo. When he died in 1914, his friends buried him in front of his cabin. The Park Service attached a buoy to mark the spot, but the chain broke in a storm. Hite Marina is named after him.

"All those old timers testified to the canyon's legendary beauty, its floor sprinkled with cottonwood trees, its sandstone walls, hundreds of feet high in places, streaked with desert varnish, home to dozens of waterfalls after a passing thunderstorm. My grandfather came through here in the 1880s after he left Missouri, although he never painted any part of the canyon so far as we know. He gave away so many of his early pieces that it's hard to know everything he painted.

"Before they closed off the dam in 1963, the government surveyed most of the historic and prehistoric sites in the canyon. Still, a lot of unexplored territory was eventually covered with water, which means we'll never know what's down there."

I laughed.

"Of course, this drought is bringing a lot of it back to the surface. Eddie's cruiser wasn't the only thing exposed. As you can imagine, we've found all kinds of boating trash—props, anchors, rope, outboard motors—even a boat and a couple of ski-dos. Not to mention an airplane. And anything that can be dropped overboard—sunglasses, eyeglasses, bottles, propane tanks, all kinds of tools, guns, binoculars, coins, silverware, watches, jewelry. All kinds of fishing gear—rods, reels, lures, fishing line, tackle boxes. Water skis, snorkel gear, scuba tanks. It's like uncovering a lost world.

"It's really amazing. We're seeing parts of Glen Canyon--waterfalls, canyons, caves—under water for forty years; old mining equipment from the days of the uranium boom back in the '50s; Anasazi ruins, but of course they're now in shambles because the water dissolved the mud and plaster used to hold the walls together. The water's also ruined any artifacts left behind—pots, feather weavings, wooden tools, baskets—unless they were made of stone…'course, everything's going to come back to the surface someday," I said.

"What do you mean?" Sarah asked.

I shrugged. "One thing the dam builders either didn't reckon on, or ignored—this whole canyon country was created by erosion. The emerald green Colorado River you see below the dam isn't natural, it's a product of the dam. Where do you think the name Colorado came from?" I asked, then answered my own question. "Those early Spanish conquistadors. It means reddish-brown, the color of the water.

"Look at the San Juan today. It carries so much silt at certain times of the year that it creates sand waves which ride upstream on the sand carried by the water. So where do you think all that sand and silt and rock're gonna end up?"

I looked around. "Right here. Eventually it'll pile up high enough that the river will overflow the dam, and that'll be the end of Lake Powell."

We beached on a sand bar at the mouth of a small side canyon right next to the marks left by Harris' boat the day before. Sarah checked the name on the topo map—Muley Twist Canyon.

The lake had originally risen about a half mile up the canyon, killing off the trees and underbrush, now making hiking easy. The couple of miles after that were a different story, and by the time we'd reached the ruin—a small granary at the top of a talus slope on the canyon wall—we'd all worked up a good sweat. I looked at Harris, surprised that a guy as doughy and out of shape as he seemed to be could have made it this far. I guessed even a little greed went a long way.

We scrambled up the slope, stood catching our breath at the top while Sarah checked the coordinates on her GPS and marked them on the map.

"How in hell you even know this was up here?" I asked Harris. "You didn't just wander into it."

"Just got lucky, I guess," he said ironically.

"Hell you did," I said. "Somebody tipped you off. You want to tell us who?"

He just stared down the slope.

"Judge'll view it kindly," I prompted. "Maybe balance out last night's attempted escape."

Harris took a seat on a flat rock nearby. "Guy in Page said he knew a site, never been dug," he said. "Drew me a map for a hunnert bucks."

"You're a trusting soul," I said.

"Guy said he'd fence anything I found. Get me good money."

"Name?"

"He didn't say and I didn't ask."

"All right. Description."

Harris sat for a moment. "Guy was about…" he started, then hesitated. "Uh, maybe I better not."

"Why not?"

He glared at me. "I just changed my mind, all right?"

"So why the change of heart?"

"None of your fuckin' business."

"Let's watch our language. We got a lady present."

"Did the guy threaten you?" Sarah asked.

Harris turned, started down the slope. "I'm going back to the boat," he said.

Sarah started to follow him, but I held her back.

"Let's finish up here."

"But Harris—" she began.

"Give him time to think about it," I said.

I looked around.

"Besides, where's he gonna go?"

Hiking back to the boat, I asked, "You thinking what I'm thinking?"

"About Harris?"

I nodded.

"As a suspect in Eddie's murder?"

"Why not?" I asked. "He's out diggin' a ruin, Eddie catches him red-handed, Harris gets the drop on him somehow and kills him, dumps his body in the lake away from the ruin. End of story."

"So he murdered Eddie over an old pot?"

"Or some other artifact."

Sarah pointed her thumb over her shoulder, indicating the site we'd just left.

"That's worth killing for?"

"Let's ask Harris," I said.

TOMMY TWO CLOUDS

Out beyond the last power pole and the end of the water line we found the small family compound: a newer looking trailer, two hogans and a scattering of outbuildings falling down. Half a dozen vehicles stripped for parts settled in the sand. An empty sheep pen waited on the perimeter.

We pulled up at the older hogan, the type hardly seen anymore, built years ago of cedar logs with a mounded dirt roof. Smoke came from the stovepipe.

I blew the horn and immediately three dogs charged the cruiser, barking like hell with their front feet up on the doors.

"Native home security system," I told Frank.

He nodded. "Seems to be working."

After a few minutes, I blew the horn again.

"I knew we should have called ahead," I said.

Frank chuckled. I'm not sure Luanda got it.

Finally the door cracked open, and an old man wrapped in a coat—one leg of his jeans hung up on the top of his boot—headed for us. He called to the dogs; they began jumping around him like puppies.

I rolled my window down and explained in Navajo why we were there. He nodded once, saying yes, yes, stared down at the ground, then out at the horizon.

"Is there something wrong?" Luanda asked from the back seat. "Can't we come in?"

I motioned to her to wait, and in a minute the old man turned for the hogan and waved us in.

"Just be careful of the dogs," I said as we got out. Sure enough one of them, looked like a German Shepherd only with the legs of one o' them wiener dogs, made a run at Luanda. She turned on it, threw up her arms and shouted. The dog backed off.

"Impressive," said Frank. "Bureau training?"

Luanda shook her head. "Growing up in a bad neighborhood."

Inside, the hogan was as warm and tidy as I somehow knew it would be. We settled on some rickety wooden chairs, and the old man offered us coffee, speaking in Navajo all the while. As near as I could make out, he was talking about how dry it had been. No water, no water, he kept saying. Even the spring down in the canyon nearby was almost dry. He went on to complain about his arthritis, that he could barely walk. He was lucky to have a grandson to take the sheep out every day.

Frank seemed to be settling in, but I could see Luanda was getting impatient.

At one point the old man looked directly at me and spoke. I laughed, and explained that I'm actually Lakota.

"What's he saying?" asked Luanda.

"That I'm really tall for a Navajo."

"Does he know anything about Officer Watchman?" she asked.

"I don't know. I haven't asked yet."

The old man asked who Luanda and Frank were. I told him FBI. He smiled and nodded. "Washington," he said. He asked what we were doing away out there.

I explained about Watchman being found, that he was last seen here, and that we wanted to know about what had happened that night.

He turned in his chair and looked out the one window at the trailer across the yard. "It's my son and his wife," he said. "They don't get along. I don't know why. They both drink. They were fighting and my grandson got a hold of the..." Here he paused, put his hand to his ear and said, "Yah, yah, yah."

"A cell phone," I said.

He nodded. "He called the police. 911. The officer came much later. By that time, the fight was over. I had the kids with me."

"The officer put my son in the cruiser. It was a warm night, so he drove him a few miles down the road so he could sober up walking back home."

I explained this in English to Luanda and Frank, who looked at me in surprise. "No arrest?" asked Frank.

I told them it was not unusual in such cases for an officer to do this rather than transport the man all the way to Kayenta. Too much time and trouble and paperwork, otherwise.

"We need to talk to his son," said Frank, opening his notebook. "What's his name?"

"Kenneth Klain," I told him. "But we already know all this. We interviewed him when Watchman first went missing, but he wasn't much help. He'd been too drunk that night to remember much, said he was blacking out by the time Watchman arrived."

"But now we have a body, and a probable cause of death," said Frank. "How do we know he didn't kill Watchman?"

I shrugged. "It just hadn't seemed very probable at the time," I said, "especially if Klain had been as drunk as he'd said he'd been."

But I knew Frank was right. Back then Eddie had only been missing. Now he was dead.

"Did the officer say anything else before he left?" I asked the old man.

He thought for a moment, and then shook his head. "He was on the radio, but I couldn't hear what he said. Then he left."

Like the traditional Navajo he was, the old man pointed with his lips in the direction Watchman had gone—west.

"He didn't go back the way he came?" I asked, and knew at once I should have rephrased that.

"Yes," he said, meaning I was right, he hadn't gone back the way he came.

Frank had caught the lip pointing and a hint of the conversation.

"He's saying Watchman headed west when he left, not east?" he asked.

I nodded. The cruiser with Watchman inside had been found in the lake, due west but many miles from here. Somewhere between this compound and the lake he had met his end.

"Let's go talk to Kenneth Klain," said Frank.

The old man walked us out to my cruiser, running interference between us and the dogs. We were safely in the vehicle when he looked up at the sky and lip pointed again, this time at a small plane passing overhead.

"More and more," he said in Navajo. "Even at night. This place is getting crowded. Next we'll have power and running water."

He chuckled. "Then I can buy a TV, big screen, and turn it up real loud when my son and his wife are fighting. My grandchildren can join me."

Even from all the way across the lumberyard where he worked in Tuba City, it was plain to see that Kenneth Klain was the polar opposite of his father. Where the old man was sinewy and hardened by years of outdoor labor, the son was flabby from too much fried food washed down with too many beers. The late fall sun shone on the greasy highlights of his face as he walked, squinting at us, across the yard to the office.

I could see he remembered me when he saw me. I introduced him to Frank and Luanda.

He looked worried. "FBI?" he asked. To me, in Navajo: "What's going on?"

I told him we'd found Eddie's body, and that we had some questions for him.

"He's dead? The officer?" he asked, scared now.

"Mr. Klain, tell us what you remember about Officer Watchman taking you away that night," said Frank.

Kenneth was quiet for a minute, staring at the floor.

"Well, I was pretty drunk, so I only remember some pieces," he said. "I remember the officer was okay, he didn't hit me or anything."

"You two didn't fight?" asked Frank. "You didn't hit him?"

Kenneth shook his head.

"What about the cruiser? See any boxes or bags in the back?" Luanda asked.

Kenneth shook his head slowly. "I can't remember," he said.

"When Watchman let you out of the cruiser, did you see anything?" Frank asked.

I could see that Kenneth was really trying to reach back, but there wasn't much there to begin with. He cleared his throat.

"I guess it musta been when I was walking back. I just remember lying on the ground, looking up at the stars, and one of them was moving," he said, looking up and tracing his finger above his head.

Frank and Luanda looked at each other. "You mean like a shooting star?" Frank asked.

"No, slowly," Kenneth said.

"You sure it was a star, not a plane or a satellite?" Frank asked.

Kenneth shrugged. "I thought it was a star," he said quietly.

"Was it blinking?" Luanda asked.

Kenneth looked at her with the lost eyes of a true drunk.

"I can't remember," he said.

We left Kenneth in the office while we stepped outside.

"I still say he could have killed Watchman, even if he doesn't remember it," said Frank. "Keep in mind this guy beat up his wife. He has a propensity for violence."

"But then you're saying he stole the marijuana, loaded Eddie back into the cruiser, drove it all the way to the lake, and walked back home…dead drunk," I said.

"We only have his word as to how drunk he was," said Frank.

"And the marijuana would have been a big temptation," added Luanda.

"If it was even there at that point," I answered. "And how do we know what quantity? Enough to kill for? Forensics found only a trace in the cruiser.

"And here's something else. We know Eddie was killed by a blow to the back of the head, but what about his busted jaw?"

"Klain could have done that," answered Frank.

"But why?" I asked. "Why kill Eddie *and* break his jaw?"

"Klain could have broken his jaw first in a fight, then killed him," said Luanda.

"And what happened to the pot?" I asked.

"Who the hell knows?" said Frank. "Maybe he smoked it all up himself. All I'm saying is that this guy was the last one to see Watchman alive, and now Watchman's been found—murdered."

"But it's all circumstantial. We still have no hard evidence that Klain killed Eddie."

"He's right," said Luanda. "We still have nothing to hold him on."

Frank looked at the two of us, threw up his hands in disgust, and said, "Fine. But Tommy, you tell Klain we're going to be keeping an eye on him. Tell him he's our number one guy right now."

"I will."

"Now I'm going back to Flagstaff. Wilmington…you coming?"

LUKE

Back at park headquarters, we settled Harris in an interview room. Sarah came in with the tape recorder while I made coffee.

Sarah seated herself across the table from Harris, who sat there nonchalantly sipping his coffee. I leaned against the wall behind him.

She turned on the recorder, identified herself, me, and Harris, gave the date and time of day.

"Mr. Harris, we've got some questions about your whereabouts on and around April 29th of this year," she began.

"Last April?"

She nodded.

He sat silently for a minute, looking at the wall behind her.

"I don't remember exactly, but I was probably out at the compound," he said.

"Compound?"

"Out by Poverty Mountain."

"On the Arizona Strip?" I asked.

Harris nodded. "The old Calder place."

"You're not with that group of survivalists out there, are you?" I asked, leaning forward.

Harris turned his head in my direction. "It ain't against the law," he said in the same tone he'd used in the campground the night of his arrest—somewhere between defiance and fear that he'd say too much.

"Besides, we ain't survivalists, we're militia," he said proudly.

I snorted a laugh. "For all the difference there is. Just a bunch of wannabe soldiers playing army out in the boonies."

"Things are gonna change," Harris said quietly. "You just wait."

"Well, while we're waiting, let's get back to April 29th," said Sarah.

"So what's that all about? I told you where I was."

"We believe a Navajo police officer was killed that night."

"You mean that one was on the news? The one was at the bottom of the lake? I didn't have nothin' to do with that...no ma'am."

Harris was shaking his head vigorously. "Nothin' to do with that," he repeated.

I came forward, leaned on my hands on the table beside Harris, looked down at him.

"Harris, we've already got you for looting, but we could turn up the heat on high and throw in a murder charge you can't prove where you were."

Harris looked up at me, now a sheen of sweat on his face.

"You check with the others at the compound," he said. "They'll tell you."

"I'll bet they will."

Sarah watched Harris' face light up with another idea.

"And why would I kill a cop?"

"That's easy," I said. "He caught you digging a ruin, or in possession of artifacts, just like we did. Trust me...you didn't make it that hard. Only Officer Watchman caught you out somewhere alone, not in a campground like we did, and you got the jump on him."

The sweat was beading on Harris' face.

"Or let's try this on for size," Luke continued. "I've been told you and your militia buddies traffic in drugs, stolen goods, whatever comes along, as a means of supporting your silly little war games. Now let's suppose you were mixed up in that and Officer Watchman caught on."

Harris stared into his coffee cup.

"You want me to go on?"

"Mr. Harris, let's go back to the map," said Sarah.

"What about it?"

"Why not make it easier on yourself and identify the man who drew it for you?"

For a moment, the look on Harris' face told us he was going to do just that, but then, just as it had out at the ruin, something stopped him.

"He'd kill me if I told you."

"Did he tell you that?"

"He didn't have to. I just knew it."

Sarah glanced at Luke.

"Where were you two going to meet if you found anything?" Luke asked.

"He said don't worry, he'd find me."

Harris sat up straight. "Look," he said, "bottom line is I go to jail for pot hunting, even for murder, at least I'm still alive."

"I'll say this, whoever sold him the map put the fear of God in him," I said out in the hallway.

"Do we have enough to hold him?" Sarah asked.

"On looting and possession of artifacts—yes. But even on that he'll only be fined because he showed us where the site was."

"Not enough for Eddie, though."

I shrugged.

"There's nothing places him anywhere near where we found Eddie and we still don't know where he was killed."

"Could Harris have been out near Inscription House the night Eddie disappeared?"

"Who knows? Nobody claims to have seen him out there. Besides, it's unlikely Eddie would have caught somebody pot hunting at night."

"So, we let him go," she said sadly.

"We'll hold him long enough to send somebody out to Poverty Mountain to verify his story, but if that checks out, which it will, he's out of here."

TIC

It was a contest, see, a race between us and the rising water, who could get to the ruins and the pots inside them first. It was a game, and for once my daddy and I were on the same team.

You see, they closed off the dam in 1963, on a Friday the 13th in September as a matter of fact. I looked it up. Started backing up the Colorado River into Glen Canyon to form Lake Powell. Soon after that the old man started bringing me along on his pot hunting trips, trips like the ones he'd been taking for years up along the Colorado and the Green, the Paria and the Escalante. By the time I was born, he'd scoured that country from the Kiaparowits Plateau to Grand Gulch, from Waterpocket Fold to Recapture Pocket. Never kept a map, no directions, nothing the rangers might find, just had every ruin marked in his head. We're not talking about the big ones here, of course, the ones everyone visits like Mesa Verde and Navajo National Monument. Those are all protected and patrolled. I'm talking about the thousands of tiny outposts abandoned a thousand years ago when the 25-year drought forced those ancient people to move closer to reliable water sources like the Colorado and the Rio Grande.

We lived out on the Arizona Strip then. We only moved to Page once they started building the dam. Daddy hated that dam and the government in Washington, so far away, that built it. I think we moved to Page just so he could torment himself with watching it go up. He hated it not just because it was taking away a lucrative source of income. He just hated the destruction of that beautiful canyon and all that was in it. He hated the idea of all those "new people", as he called them, moving in. Never mind the tourists.

Along with building the dam, the Bureau of Reclamation had sent teams of archeologists all through those canyons to map and dig all the ruins before they were flooded. All the ruins they could find, that is. Between them and what my father called "the week-enders" and "the vacationers," they'd picked all the low-hanging fruit.

"But none of them has what I got," he'd say, clapping his arm around my shoulder, "the best climber in these parts since the ancient Anasazi theirselves."

That was my job. Most kids grow up climbing trees. I grew up climbing canyon walls, scavenging for the pots, tools, and other artifacts the Anasazi had left behind. Every summer from the time I was school age, we'd make several expeditions into the boonies, motoring up the rivers or driving overland to the remote canyons that held what we searched for.

"You find enough of these sites," he told me, "and after awhile you can spot where they're likely to be."

And not just caves and overhangs close to the ground. Those were obvious and many had already been dug. No, he was talking about the granaries and outposts tucked back into gaps and cracks away up on the canyon walls.

During the years we dug together, his eye was always sharper than mine. As carefully as I learned to scan a canyon wall, he was usually first to spot the bit of rock hand piled on rock or the bird droppings or some indication of an alcove high above us. Then we'd walk the base of the cliff, looking for the ancient hand and foot holds chipped by the Anasazi, or some vertical crevice they'd used to climb.

And then I'd start. If we couldn't find the old route, I'd make my own. Free climbing, with a couple of gunny sacks, a trenching tool and a length of rope knotted to my belt. No ropes, no pitons, no carabiners. Just me and the rock face.

"If them ancient ones could do it that way, so can you," my daddy would tell me, and up I'd go.

Once at the site, I'd look for anything on the surface that looked manmade, then carefully start shoveling aside the sand or bird shit or whatever else had accumulated over the centuries. Usually I found nothing, but when I found something it went into the sacks to be lowered slowly down to my father waiting patiently (or not) below to sort it out.

We were never squeamish about burial sites. We'd heard the Indians talk about ghost sickness and all that, but it was just bullshit to my dad, and so it was to me. The summer I turned nine, away up on Comb Ridge, we found a little niche just big enough for a mummy and the room needed to lay it in there. Tucked in around it must have been a dozen pots, most of them intact.

I swept away the sand, and up by the skull I found a necklace of turquoise, shell and coral that I knew was worth a fortune. My excitement growing, I tucked it into the sack, then reached for the last and largest pot, set into the deepest recess of the tiny cave. Turning it in my hands, I heard a rustle, looked up, and found myself facing the ass-end of a skunk, poised to spray.

I ducked back, but too late. He cut loose and hit me full-face. I yelled and jerked upright, slamming my head against the rock ceiling of the alcove. Blinded and half-crazed, I scrambled backwards and nearly out into thin air.

Far below, I heard my father shouting "What the hell's going on?"

My eyes, my nose, even my mouth was on fire. I didn't know where the hell the skunk went. Away was all I wanted. But climbing down was always harder than going up because I couldn't see where I was going. Now I was nearly blind. There was no way I could make it down. I shouted this to my father.

"Stay there," he hollered, and soon I heard him grunting and cursing his way up the cliff face to me.

Using my rope, he rigged a climbing harness on me and lowered me to the canyon floor, then climbed down himself.

"I didn't know you could climb," I said.

"I didn't either, not anymore," he said. "And I'm sure as hell never going to do it again."

It was then I heard how shaky his voice was. I laughed in spite of myself, and pretty soon he laughed. Of course, then, after I'd washed out my eyes in the creek, I had to climb back up and lower down all that I'd found, but that was good, the both of us laughing together out there by ourselves.

But all that changed after Stevie drowned. Then the whole thing turned into strictly a business proposition. We'd gear up and head out for a few days, but now it was just directions and orders. There was no more talk, no laughs. The old man had never been too good at those things, anyways. Now it was: "Get your ass up that rock, and if you fall, I'm leavin' you here." I believed him.

And back home, the treats and little extras were gone. Now it was a brief counting out of what he thought was my share of the sale of whatever we had found. He'd put it in my hand, and walk away.

Most of the main canyon was flooded by then, anyway. All that was left were some of the side canyons and the mesa tops. The sites there were fewer and smaller. "Pretty poor pickins," Daddy would say. And soon after that, we stopped going out altogether.

SARAH

"You know what I hate about funerals?" I asked.

"What's that?" said Jordan.

"The same thing I hate about weddings."

"Oh?"

We were crossing the res under a cloudless autumn sky, heading for Eddie's funeral in Crystal, caught between the somber purpose of our trip and the red rock beauty of the landscape in the golden October sun. We had just passed another field full of stunted corn plants that had died early in the summer for lack of a monsoon.

"Look at that," I said, "there aren't even any cattle or sheep to eat the dead corn. Ella told me everyone's sold off their livestock. No water. No grazing."

"So what, besides the obvious, do you hate about funerals?" Jordan asked.

"Oh. Well, I hate how they bring everyone together, and everyone's so close for a few hours or a few days, then it's over and everyone just goes back to their own lives, and their own worries, and everything. And all that closeness is lost…same with weddings."

"Maybe not lost. Don't the newlyweds carry it on in some way?"

"You're right. Then I guess in that regard a funeral is worse."

A few miles down the road, I gazed out the window.

"I wonder how many times this sand has been piled into dunes, to be pressed back into rock, only to break down into sand again," I said.

Jordan eyed me from the driver's seat.

"Contemplating eternity, are we?"

"I guess in preference to my navel."

"That's a matter of opinion," he said, and I punched him in the arm.

Dad had tried running the trading post for a round of seasons after Mom died, but his heart wasn't in it. She'd always been the spark that lit the place, he said, and without her, what was the point? She must have kindled him in the same way, for he didn't outlive her much beyond that year. Ernest found him passed away in bed one spring morning when he came to open the store.

I had Ernest mind the post after that, but he was playing a losing hand. With more roads paved and more people with cars and pickups, the locals could more easily reach the 7/11 in Tsaile and the new Bashas' in Fort Defiance with their lower prices and greater variety.

Also, Navajos for years had been moving away from the traditional economy of wool, mutton, piñon nuts, rugs and baskets, and jewelry, as well as the extension of credit by traders. Most people now had salaried jobs and borrowed their money from credit unions and banks, not traders.

"Place looks homey," said Jordan as we got out of the car and stretched.

I was still paying Ernest a little to keep the weeds chopped and the trees going, but for me the place carried a heart-wrenching air of abandonment.

"Yes," I said, "the place still *looks* the same. Just doesn't *feel* the same."

Stepping up on the porch, I ran my hand over the cut sandstone wall of the store, still standing as true as it had when my great-grandfather Tanner had erected it with the help of his "Navvies" back in 1883.

We went in through the front door of the store.

"For years, not much changed around here," I said. "My grandfather put in the first gas pumps back in the '20s, but this was still a bull pen when we moved in."

"A bull *what*?" said Jordan, looking around.

"A bull pen. They called it that because the trader stood in a big cage in the middle of the store, along with all the goods he had for sale, which were hung from the inside walls of the cage or stacked behind glass fronted display cases. Customers picked out what they wanted and he unhooked it from the wall or took it from the case and sold it to them over the counter."

"Sounds like the traders didn't trust their customers," Jordan said.

I nodded. "But remember that dad was a lawyer before he started trading. He thought it was wrong to presume the customers guilty until proven innocent. It went against his grain, so he soon remodeled the store into what you see now."

We walked through the empty store and out the back, where the feed barn, always dilapidated, had further succumbed to gravity.

Looking up, I chuckled. A battered basketball rim, now netless, hung crookedly from the splintered boards above the barn doors.

"How many hours did I spend shooting baskets out here?" I asked. "But it paid off, I guess. Helped put me through NAU."

"Basketball scholarship?" Jordan asked.

"Partial," I said, then laughed. "But more importantly, it made me popular in high school, despite—or because of—my being the tallest girl in our class."

The door to the house was unlocked. I had called ahead to have Ernest come by to sweep the place out and lay in some firewood. Jordan set our bags by the door. I put the sack of groceries we'd bought in Kayenta on the kitchen counter.

I stood in the center of the living room, looking slowly around, suffused with the feeling that I was back at the center of my universe. The bookcases, still filled, lined one wall. The old Steinway quarter grand stood in the corner. I walked over, raised the lid, and plinked out a few notes.

"Not too badly out of tune," said Jordan.

I walked from room to room, surveying the wide floor boards for water stains. "Roof still doesn't leak," I said.

"They knew how to build them back then," said Jordan.

"The house dates from the same year as the trading post. My grandfather wired it for electricity and Dad's the one who put in the indoor plumbing. Can you believe they were still using an outhouse and a pump on the back porch when we moved in?"

I opened a couple of windows front and back to air the place out, then dug a couple sets of musty sheets from the linen closest. Jordan helped me hang them to air on the clothes line by the back door.

"We'll take care of the rest of it when we get back," I said. "We'd better head for Ella's place."

*****

Adella and Marcus, Ella's two oldest, and a half dozen of what I guessed were cousins were chasing each other in front of the Watchman doublewide when we pulled up.

"Sarah!" the two shouted in unison, racing up to me, pinioning my legs between them.

"What's in the bag?" asked Adella.

"Yeah, the bag!" said Marcus.

"As if you didn't know," I said, reaching in. I pulled out a Frisbee for each of them, then a scale model big-wheel monster truck for Marcus and a soccer ball for Adella.

Ella stood in the front door holding the baby.

"Hi! C'mon in," she said.

Inside, I set the bag down, and took the baby from her. "Now, this one I haven't met," I said.

"This is Eddie."

"We just call him Junior," Adella chimed in.

"Well, hello Junior. Welcome!" I said. "I brought him a couple of sleepers. Hope they're the right size."

Jordan was standing behind me.

"Ella, this is Jordan Hunt. Jordan, Ella Watchman."

The trailer was crowded with relatives in for the next day's service, but everyone cleared the living room so we could talk. The aroma of mutton baking in the oven drifted from the kitchen. We sat drinking coffee, talking about the kids and helping Junior, who was just starting to walk, launch himself from one of us to another.

"He must be going on a year now, isn't he?" I asked.

"Couple more days," Ella said. "He was born six months to the day before Eddie went missing."

I noticed but didn't comment on her marking other events from that date.

The kitchen door swung open, and Ella's mother came in.

"Well, Sarah! I didn't see you come in. I'm sorry, but this place has been crazy for a couple of days, everyone getting ready for …"

"Tomorrow."

She hugged me. "Thank you for coming," she said. "You look well."

"So do you."

"Too busy around here to get sick."

She turned to Jordan, extended her hand. "I'm Marie Salt, Ella's mom."

"Jordan Hunt. A friend of Sarah and Eddie's."

"Thank you for being here." She turned to Ella. "Ella, give me the baby. It's time for his bottle." She picked Junior up and headed for the kitchen. On the way she collared Adella and Marcus. "You two know better than to be kicking that ball inside the house," she said. "Get outside with the rest of the kids."

"So how do they seem to be doing with Eddie gone?" I asked Ella.

"Well, Marcus just started Kindergarten, so I don't think he really understands what's happened. And Adella knows he's gone, but I get the feeling she doesn't understands everything that means." She laughed. "Does that make sense?" she asked.

"And what about you?" I asked.

She looked out the window for a minute at the kids playing in the front yard, organizing her thoughts. "You know, he was missing so long, I think I knew he was gone a long time before you found him. I knew Eddie wouldn't stay away without letting me know somehow where he was."

She turned back to us. "Back in June, Tommy Two Clouds hired a hand trembler, and we all drove out to where Eddie was last seen, but all the trembler could tell us was we were still too far from Eddie to pick up his trail."

"Like I told you on the phone, once Eddie was found in the lake, the Park Service got involved in the investigation," I said. "You okay talking about it?"

She nodded.

"Did you talk to Eddie the night he disappeared?" I asked.

"Not after he went on shift. It was like he fell off the face of the earth, that's how Tommy put it. And I guess since he was in the lake all this time, he did…in a way."

"Did Eddie ever mention a man named Kenneth Klain?" Jordan asked.

"Isn't Klain the name of the family Eddie had gone to see about the domestic disturbance?"

I nodded.

"Tommy told me that name," she said. "But Eddie never mentioned it, not that I remember…But you know what?" she said, getting up and going down the hallway into another room. She returned in a minute with a file folder. "Once they found Eddie last week, I began cleaning out his things. I found this in his desk. He kept a little office in a corner of the family room."

She handed it to me.

"It looks work-related," she said. "Maybe it will help. But that's all I've found."

"Thanks, baby," I said.

We heard a chainsaw sputter to life in the back yard. Ella looked out the window.

"That's just dad, bucking a load of logs he and Tommy felled last weekend," she said. "He and mom have been such a big help since Eddie went missing."

"Sounds like Tommy's been helping too," I said.

"He's been great. Honestly, I don't know what I'd have done without him. The family all likes him, except my dad is always teasing him about being too tall for a Navajo. He's over at the cemetery now, seeing to—"

I watched her eyes fill with tears.

"Come here," I said, putting my arms around her.

After a minute, she said, "He just helps out where he can: groceries, treats for the kids, chores around the house, helping my folks."

Jordan went to the window.

"Looks like your dad could use some help," he said. "I'll be out back."

"So I guess Jordan is a good friend," Ella said after he left.

"What makes you think so?"

Ella looked around, spread her hands to indicate the trailer and everything surrounding it. "I don't think you'd bring a casual acquaintance into all this, would you?"

The burr of the chainsaw waxed and waned outside, blending with the sound of kids playing out front.

I laughed and shook my head. "Ella Watchman, you've had my number since our first day back at NAU."

Now we both laughed.

"I guess you could say Jordan and I have an eye on each other," I said.

"Well, you *have* brought him back to the old stomping grounds. That tells me something."

I got up and went to a bookcase on the far wall, picked up the picture of Eddie in his dress uniform from the top shelf.

"That's Eddie when he graduated from the academy," said Ella, coming to stand beside me.

Now it was my turn to mist up, Ella's turn to hold me.

"It's okay, Sarah. Eddie told me a long time ago about you and him…Just promise me one thing," she added.

"What's that?" I asked, my voice breaking.

"You'll find whoever killed him."

I embraced her and we laid our heads on one another's shoulders.

"I promise, baby. We will."

The sun was down by the time we got back to the trading post. The air held a chill. There had been no point in having the power turned on for one night, so Jordan filled and lit a couple of kerosene lamps while I brushed marinade on the steaks we'd brought in the cooler. He fixed a fire in the wood stove. Opening the bottle of pinot noir we'd brought, he poured us each a glass.

He picked up the folder Ella had given us, sat at the kitchen table leafing through it.

"Looks like Eddie's notes from some of the cases he was working on," he said. "Man, these Navajo cops see it all—burglary, DWI, assault. You'd almost think he was working in Phoenix, not out here."

"The problem is they're spread so thin. Each officer probably covers an area the size of a city."

"Hmm. Rooney. Sounds familiar," he said.

I turned off the faucet in the sink. "I'm sorry. I didn't hear you."

"Eddie's got notes here from an interview he did with a guy named Rooney in Page. I think he's a former patient."

"Along with everyone else in town."

"Are you saying they're all *former* patients?" he asked with a smile.

"You know what I mean."

He took a piece of paper from the file. "Looks like he was questioning him about a possible Phoenix-Page drug connection."

We both stopped and looked at each other.

"Are you thinking about the traces they found in Eddie's cruiser?" I asked.

He nodded. "I think we need to track Mr. Rooney down come Monday morning. Pay him a visit."

"Let's make it a date. I'll go with."

"Dinner by lamplight," I said. "So romantic. Now if I could just play the piano and eat at the same time, we'd be all set."

"Well, maybe you could play while I eat," he suggested.

"Forget it, mister. I'm one who enjoys eating her own cooking.

"Which is quite good, by the way."

"Mmmm…lamplight," I said. "We used to lose power so often when I was a kid we always kept plenty of these lanterns around. I loved how soft the light was, and how the shadows moved as you carried one through the room.

"I mean, I was Laura Ingalls Wilder in the *Little House on the Prairie*. A little older, and I was Willa Cather's *Antonia*.

"My mom taught me to read before I started school. I used to sit in that window seat right over there, breathing my dad's pipe smoke, hearing the fire crackling in the stove, warmed by the late-afternoon sun coming through the window. It was a safe, secure, complete little world, and I'm fortunate to carry it with me to this day."

Jordan put more wood on the fire after dinner. I opened the piano and began absent-mindedly picking out a melody while he settled in on the worn leather sofa.

"Mom was afraid I'd grow up a heathen," I said. "So, she got a priest from Flagstaff to come out once a month and hold a service here in the living room. "

I accompanied my narrative with the opening bars from Ravel's "Bolero."

"We'd move the furniture around, and some of our neighbors would come in."

"You play well," said Jordan. "Who taught you?"

"My mother. I'm good, but she was amazing. Studied at Julliard. When she met my dad, she was the pianist for the Houston Opera Chorus.

"Eventually, she let me play when we sang during the service." I started into a medley of "Nearer My God to Thee," "Gather by the River," and "The Old Rugged Cross."

"You seem to have a broad repertoire."

"You mean for someone who grew up in a trading post?" I shrugged. "My parents were extraordinary people," I said. "My mom came from a well-established oil family in Houston. She was tall, slender, with long, delicate hands. I get my dark hair and eyes from her. She could move so gracefully. My dad used to joke that she didn't walk, she floated.

"He'd been a partner at a big Houston law firm for a dozen years before they met, but Mom's folks were still disappointed when they got engaged. Dad's family was Mormon, so maybe to help smooth things over, he joined the Episcopal Church. They settled into a big house in Houston, but three years later, when my mother was pregnant with me, Grandpa Tanner died and left this place to Dad."

Switching to "Sweet Betsy from Pike," I said, "So they packed their things, including this piano and Dad's law library, along with ten Black

Angus cows and a big German Shepherd named Rex, and moved to the res."

"No tall Shanghai rooster?"

I laughed, and puckered out my lips at the bookcases behind the piano. "As you can see, his law books are still on the shelves. By the time I left for college, I'd read most of my dad's library, even a few of the law texts, which I guess is what eventually led me to law school."

"And yet you still point to things with your lips like a Navajo."

"Oh, we were isolated. No doubt about it. We had no TV, not even a newspaper. I started school ignorant of *Sesame Street*, Charlie Brown, and the Pledge of Allegiance, none of which sat well with my first grade teacher. I remember spending the entire one-hour bus ride home that first day rehearsing my speech about why I should never go back to that school."

I played the opening bars from the *Looney Tunes* cartoons.

Now Jordan laughed.

"Mom listened to me plead my case, then we sat down for an hour and played piano duets. Next day I went back to school. It was the first time I realized I could work out hard feelings through music, something I've done many times since."

Next was Aaron Copland's "Appalachian Spring."

"But mostly this was a great place to grow up. There were always horses to ride, steers to chase, canyons to explore, petroglyphs to find. As you can imagine, most of my friends were Navajo. Eddie was one of the closest."

Eventually, I ran out of things to play from memory…and it was getting late.

"C'mon, you can help me clean up the kitchen," I said, putting the lid down on the keys.

"Let me gather the sheets off the line first, okay?"

"Fine."

A slug of cold outside air followed him back into the kitchen. It sent a chill through me.

"You've got two sets of sheets here," he pointed out.

Unsure if he was trying to tell me something, I decided not to dance around it.

"Yes, I thought you could bunk down on the sofa," I said.

If he was anticipating an alternative arrangement, he kept it to himself.

"I'll wash, you dry," I said.

"Sounds good."

I pulled some blankets from Mom's old cedar chest and we made the beds, then curled up together in front of the stove. Jordan wrapped one of his blankets around my shoulders and pulled me close.

"Thanks," I said.

"My pleasure."

He tightened his arm around to me and I lifted my face to him. We kissed, taking our time, until I pulled back.

"You okay with our sleeping arrangements?" I asked.

"You're the lady of the house."

I smiled at him. "You are such a gentleman. It's one of the things I really like about you."

"And what are some of the other things?"

I laughed. "Sorry, but I want our first time to be special, and I'd feel a little funny having it be here. Does that seem odd?"

"This place holds a lot of memories for you. Maybe we shouldn't add to them tonight."

"Thank you for understanding, but it's not just that. It's tomorrow, too."

"I know."

*****

In the dream, Eddie and I are riding out to the old shake, the dazzling full sun of summer on our backs. An exhilarating sense that all things are possible pervades me. Side by side, we're going nowhere and everywhere. Anything could happen. Eager for our rendezvous, we gradually surge ahead, faster and faster. Now we're galloping. The wind is in my hair. Beside me, I hear Eddie whoop as he spurs his horse on. The thrum of our horses' hooves on the ground fills the air. I turn to smile at him, to share with a look this longing for him. But now it's no longer Eddie on his horse but in his cruiser, which is full of lake water. I can see it sloshing around in there and him at the wheel as he slowly begins pulling away from me. I shout to him, but he won't turn to look at me. I'm riding as hard as I can to keep up, but he's leaving me behind. He disappears over a rise and I'm left on the road, longing to go with him but somehow knowing that's not possible. I sit my horse, watching as the plume of dust from his truck dissolves slowly into the sky, the scent of horses strong in the still air.

LUKE

Rooney's trailer was an older one, on a street in what Jordan tells me is Page's original trailer park, built by the Bureau of Reclamation back in the 50s to house those working on the dam. On the way in, he points out one of the original trailers.

"Ours was just like that. I mean, they were all the same. Government issue," he said. "We lived here before Grady had the house built."

Rooney's place is not what I was expecting—junked cars and trash. Two old birches shaded the trailer and the meticulously kept lawn in front of it. Late blooming mums lined the herringbone brick walkway to the front door. Looked more like the home of a retired librarian than a drug dealer.

A late-model Impala sat at the curb. As we approached the trailer, I noticed that the front door and the windows were new, the originals replaced.

Our knock brought a black man to the door, medium height but of a very slight, almost feminine, build. High cheekbones underscored long-lashed, almond shaped eyes. A delicate hand rested on the handle of the screen door.

"Yes?" he asked. Not hostile, nor sullen, which is what I was expecting. Just wary, which I had discovered years ago came with the uniform.

"Julian Rooney?" I asked.

He nodded.

"I'm Officer Russell with the National Park police. This is Officer Tanner, and Dr. Hunt. May we come in?"

"What for?" he asked. Again, not hostile, just deeply cautious.

"We have some questions about an interview you did last spring with a Navajo police officer, Eddie Watchman."

"You mean the one they pulled out of the lake last week?"

I nodded. "The same."

He hesitated. For a second, I thought he was going to tell us to go to hell, but he unlatched the door.

The trailer was as clean and orderly inside as it was out. Looked to be expensively decorated, too. Rooney seated himself on a loveseat by the window, lit a cigarette, while we arranged ourselves around the living room.

"Mr. Rooney, what did you and Officer Watchman talk about?" I asked.

"You must know the answer to that or you wouldn't be here," he answered impassively.

"We have reason to believe he suspected you of dealing drugs in this area through a connection in Phoenix," I said.

He was quiet for a moment; just stared at me.

"You know, that's exactly what Watchman said to me," he said. "And I'll tell you exactly what I told him."

"What's that?"

"That is pure, if you'll pardon my French"—with a nod to Sarah—"bullshit.

"What's more, as you've probably noticed, I'm a black man, a black man out here among all the Mormons and Navajos. I'm already conspicuous. Why would I want to raise my profile even higher?... On top of that, I'm a man, of—how shall we say—a certain sexual persuasion, one that's none too popular around here? So I have lots of reasons to keep my head down."

I have to admit the man was talking sense.

"And besides, even if I was dealing, do you think I'm going to just come right out and tell you? Uh-uh, sorry. You're going to have to do all those police things. You know, gather evidence, interview my acquaintances..." He looked directly at Jordan. "Maybe even stake me out."

He raised his eyebrows, which I now noticed were plucked, and tilted his head at Jordan.

"Isn't that how you say it in police parlance, Doctor?" he asked.

Jordan didn't look the least unsettled.

"Mr. Rooney, six months before we found him last week, Officer Watchman disappeared somewhere out between Inscription House and the lake. We think he was murdered out there, then dumped in the lake. Can you account for your whereabouts on the night of April 29?"

Rooney tapped his cigarette on an ash tray.

"I'd have to check my calendar, of course, but I can assure you I was nowhere near Inscription House that night or any other night. I've never even been there during the day."

"Why don't you do that?" I asked.

He turned to me, batted his eyes.

"Do what, Officer?"

"Check your calendar."

"Oh."

Rooney went into a back room, returned with a date book.

"Let's see. April 29. Here it is. I was working that night, actually."

"Where?"

"Wahweap. I was tending bar."

"Who's your supervisor down there?"

The name he gave me was the woman in charge of food and beverage services at the lodge. Wouldn't be hard to check out.

Jordan cleared his throat.

"Julian," he said. "I checked the hospital files before we came over here. You showed up at the ER last winter."

"I remember," said Rooney. "I kind of overdid the holidays, and my hepatitis C got the better of me."

"That's right. I saw you, remember?"

"How could I forget any contact with you, Doctor?"

Jordan ignored the compliment, if that's what it was.

"You remember how you contracted that?" Jordan asked.

"You asked me the same question last winter, Doctor, and I'll tell you again. The casual gay relationship is built around the exchange of bodily fluids. So, you figure it out."

"No exchange of contaminated needles during intravenous drug use?" Jordan asked.

Rooney set his cigarette in the ashtray and pushed up both sleeves.

"See for yourselves," he said. "Clean as a whistle."

"So just what do you do for a living besides tend bar, Mr. Rooney?" I asked.

"In the summer—wait tables, mow lawns, minor landscaping," he said. "In the winter—interior painting, some decorating."

"Much call for that around here?" I asked.

"Enough," he said. "And when there isn't, I live off the favors of friends."

I knew I didn't want to go there. "You do this here?" I asked, indicating the living room.

He nodded.

"Other than Wahweap, where do you tend bar?" Sarah asked.

"Oh, all over. You know how busy summer is here. This summer I worked mostly down at Wahweap. I'm still filling in on weekends."

"Just out of curiosity," said Jordan. "How did you end up in Page?"

Rooney rolled his eyes. "How many times have I asked myself that same question?"

Back in the car, I said, "The yard, the house, the neighborhood. The whole low profile thing. I think he's trying too hard."

Jordan nodded. "Got to be covering up something," he said. "It's about more than just being black…and gay."

"I agree, guys," Sarah said. "It's all too pat. But with the traces in Eddie's cruiser and Rooney's name in his notes, there's got to be some drug connection here."

"No sign of anything in his house," Jordan said.

"He's too smart for that," I said. "He'd be dealing out of another location, like a rented storage space, a friend's house. But not here. Neighbors would object to so much coming and going."

"Page police have anything?" Sarah asked.

"Nada," I said. "But we can ask them to keep an eye on him."

"You mean stake him out?" asked Sarah. "Isn't that how you say it, Doctor?" She batted her eyes at him.

"Give me a break," he said.

*****

Back at the office, I had a message to call George at the *Chronicle*. Figured I might as well get it over with.

His voice was bright, which immediately irritated me.

"I heard you and Sarah Tanner and Jordan Hunt paid Julius Rooney a call this afternoon," he said.

"You're on the ball today, George."

"Page is a small town. This have anything to do with the Watchman case?"

"What makes you think so?"

"Oh, just that Rooney is one of our less upstanding citizens."

"And?"

"Word around town is he's dealing drugs."

Did he know about the traces we found in Eddie's cruiser? "You think Eddie's death was drug-related?" I asked.

"Was it?"

"Not as far as we know, right now."

I thought about the mention of the Phoenix-Page drug connection in Eddie's notes, but decided it was too tenuous right now to bring up.

On the other end I could hear George, stymied, shifting gears.

"Last spring, we talked to Kenneth Klain after the Navajo police questioned him about Eddie's disappearance," he said. "We went back out there Friday, talked to Kenneth. He said the Feds came to see him. Anything happening there?"

"You'll have to ask them."

"C'mon Luke," he practically whined.

"Frank Doyle said they didn't have enough to hold him for Eddie's murder, if that's what you're asking."

"Hmm. You know, Rooney did some interior decorating for some friends of mine last winter. Do you think he's gay?"

"I'm not going to speculate on that, George. Besides, what would that have to do with Eddie?"

"Oh, you know, morals charge, that sort of thing. Maybe Eddie knew something we don't and was blackmailing Rooney, squeezing him."

I could feel my blood pressure ticking upward.

"Listen, George, why don't you call me back once you're really on to something? In the meantime, don't waste my time on speculation, okay?"

"Fine, Luke. I'll catch you later."

He hung up.

Damn fishing expedition—the little prick.

TIC

I knew him the second I saw him in his outer office, but he didn't recognize me until he saw my name on the new-patient chart, then his eyes got big and he smiled. Damn it if I hadn't imagined it just like that, his face and everything.

"Holy Hannah, Tic Douloureux! How the hell are you?"

"Well, I've been better or I wouldn't be here," I replied, reaching out my hand. Smart him off a little.

"What are you doing around here?" he asked, raising one hand palm up, shaking my hand with the other.

"Seeking some goddamn medical attention," I said, smiling just as big as I could, knowing I never felt better in my life.

He actually looked abashed—embarrassed that he'd dropped his professional veneer. I marveled. Still the Boy Scout.

"C'mon. Let's go back here," he said, leading the way to an exam room.

"I mean, are you just passing through...visiting...what?"

"What."

"You mean you're living back here? That's great!"

I nodded. "Bought me a boat...living on it down at Wahweap. Just got back."

We caught up for a while. We had both gone into the service right out of high school. I told him as much as he needed to know about my time in, where I'd served, sure that he would take me at my word and not check it out. Who would lie to Jordan Hunt?

"You were Army, right?" I asked.

"Rangers. Been out about five years." I looked around the room. "Uncle Sam put you through med school?"

"In return for signing away a large part of my life."

"I know how that goes."

We both chuckled.

"So, your dad still around?" I asked.

"Oh, yeah. Too ornery to die. Still in the same house, even."

"And what about you? You married?"

"No. You?"

"Never could find one'd have me. But I'm surprised about you. You were fighting 'em off with a stick in high school. Football hero. Basketball star."

He laughed. "Well, all that's a long time in the past, Tic."

Oh yes, the well-deserved Hunt reputation for modesty, I thought. Again I marveled. Only a man who was still above us, gazing down at all us mere mortals walking around on the ground, could profess such modesty.

"How your brothers doing?" I asked.

"Well, Merced's building a business empire down in Phoenix. I tell him it's all luck, but the truth is he works hard."

"You know what they say, 'The harder I work, the luckier I get.' And what about Niles?"

"Oh, he's still out there inventing things and trying to sell them. His latest gadget is a penstock and turbine getup that generates electricity using falling water by day, then uses part of the power generated during the day to pump water back to the uphill storage tank at night."

I nodded. "Ingenious."

"Says he got the idea from the dam here in Page."

"He always was kind of a science nerd."

"That hasn't changed. He's on this energy kick, rides a bike everywhere. I tell him he's keeping himself in such good shape he'll probably live an extra twenty years and use up all the extra energy he saved riding his bike."

"Good point."

"He tells me he'll probably be hit by a bus. What do I say to that?"

We both laughed.

"No, all he needs is a more or less constant infusion of cash from Merced and me. He'll either die a millionaire or dead broke…no in-between."

"Well, at least you've got it."

"Don't be fooled by what you see here. I'm in hock up to here. In fact, I'm doing post-mortems on a cash basis for the county."

"Hey, I saw that in the paper."

"Oh, about Eddie?"

"I thought I moved back here to get away from all that shit," I said.

"I don't think anyplace is safe anymore."

He was more right about that than he knew.

"So what's the problem?" he asked.

It took me a second to remember why I was there, but I don't think he noticed. Guess we were both slipping.

"Damn headache's been plaguing me for a week," I said.

He took my vitals.

"You say you just got back? It's probably altitude change, a little dehydration," he said. "Welcome back to the Colorado Plateau. Drink more water."

"I was thinking more like a beer."

"Sure," he said. There was an awkward pause. "Uh, just say when."

"I'll call you."

He seemed good with that. I knew he would.

As I walked out, we agreed we'd both come a long way from Page High, but I wondered as I walked to my truck, Had either of us moved a step past graduation day?

JORDAN

In my office flipping through the files of patients I'd seen that day I got to Tic's. His visit had stirred so many memories of our shared boyhood, but all of them were colored by the tragedy of Stevie's death. The ambivalence I felt about renewing our friendship made me ashamed. Tic had been like a brother to me back then, but I felt like he'd been toying with me today. I was pretty sure he hadn't been any sicker than I was, although he had seemed…fragile, I guess. As though the years since our childhood had hollowed him out somehow. Or maybe the whole thing was just his awkward way of getting back in touch, and I decided that if he could do that the least I could do was meet him for a beer some night after work.

I leaned back in my chair and let my thoughts spool back.

*****

Out on the playground, I overheard Tic telling anyone who asked that it was his little brother Stevie busted his lip the night before while they were wrestling.

"Yeah, I had him pinned, then he looks up at me, and Wham! The little shit head butts me!" Followed by a rueful laugh.

But I knew better. I knew the second he walked into class that morning. It wasn't the lip itself, it was the way he looked around the room, then ducked his head and kept it down.

I knew because I'd seen a split lip like that before, but it wasn't Tic's. It was Merced's, after my dad had come home in a bad mood one night from the Windy Mesa and Merced had unwisely back-talked him.

I even knew the trick of getting your brother in on the story to cover you, just like Stevie was telling his pals today how he laid one on his big brother. The whole thing just made me feel sad.

That night, Grady stayed later than usual at the Windy Mesa, and it was my turn to ride my bike down there and bring him home. He normally made it back by bedtime, his spiked breath filling my nostrils as he kissed us each goodnight, but occasionally, for whatever reason, it took him longer to drink his fill.

I leaned my bike around the side and stepped quietly in the door, hoping to get Grady's attention without attracting anyone else's. Looking around, I noticed Tic's dad sitting by himself at the bar. Over in the far corner sat Grady at a table with Pete and Paul. I couldn't hear them over the noise in the bar, but I could see they had him hooked with what was most likely one of their fabulous fishing yarns. I tried my standard trick of staring intently at my father until he looked my way, which actually worked more times than not.

But not tonight, so I slipped over to the table, where he wrapped a meaty arm around my waist, and introduced me, not for the first time, to Pete and Paul, who nodded their acquaintance. I knew this was where things could get dicey with my dad. He knew why I was there, but I didn't know how he'd respond. Would it be the cold, closeup stare and a shove back toward the door or a warm squeeze and a polite request to let him finish this one and he'd be out?

Luckily, it was the latter, and I headed back outside to wait. My eyes readjusted to the dark, and I noticed Tic sitting in the front seat of his dad's battered pickup in the parking lot. He rolled down the window.

"Saw your dad in there," I said.

He nodded. "Your dad here, too?"

"Yeah, he'll be out in a minute. How's your lip?"

"Okay." We both kind of looked around for a minute.

"My mom sends me when my dad gets like this," he said. "Sometimes I have to drive him home."

"You know how to drive?"

"I have to scoot the seat way up, but I can do it."

I was impressed. I was about to say so, when the bar door opened and Dad came out.

"Grady," I said. He started my way.

"You call your dad by his first name?"

"Yeah, I guess. See you tomorrow."

"Okay."

I went around and got my bike. Grady lifted it into the back of his truck, and drove us home.

*****

"You won't believe who came in today," I told Dad.

His look told me he wasn't in the mood for guessing games.

"Tic Douloureux," I said.

That put a smile on his face. "From high school?" he asked. "What the hell's he doing back here?"

"Didn't say."

"Well, how's he doing?"

"Okay, I guess. We're going to get together for a beer sometime soon and catch up."

"Old Tic. He still look the same?"

"Pretty much. Seemed distracted by something, though."

"Tic? Mr. Focus? Mr. 'I'm Gonna Reach My Goal and Nobody's Stopping Me'?"

"Brought back a lot of memories seeing him."

The mood in the room was suddenly somber. Dad reached over, put his hand on my shoulder.

"I'm sure it did," he said. "Buying that boat for you boys was a mistake. Always regretted it."

"Boat wasn't the problem," I said, thinking of Tic and that damn gun.

For a minute we were separated by our thoughts, then I chuckled.

"That little Stevie could surprise you. I remember the Douloureuxs had that big Rottweiler staked on a chain in front of the trailer, and one morning Stevie says, 'Hey, you guys, watch this.' He walks toward the dog, fishing for something in his pocket. Tic tells him to stay outside the chain.

"That dog, he must have weighed twice what Stevie did, he charges to the end of his chain, barking like hell. Stevie just holds up the piece of bacon from his pocket, and that dog sits like his butt's been stapled to the ground. We can't believe it.

"He reaches out with the bacon, and Tic yells Stevie! but by then Stevie has placed the bacon on the dog's nose. He's as still as a statue.

"For a whole minute, Stevie and the dog stand there, stock still, staring at each other. Then Stevie steps back, says 'Hup!' and that dog flips the bacon into the air and swallows it in one motion. We all started cheering and clapping. How that little guy taught that dog to do that, even he couldn't tell us."

Dad laughed, but said, "I never did like you boys hanging around down there at Tic's."

"Oh, it was all right. It was just a big junkyard. Old cars up on blocks, construction trash, anything his dad and his uncles could scavenge. He even had an old single-engine plane down there once. God knows where he got it."

"You can bet he didn't buy it," said Dad, and we both laughed.

TIC

People say a dog's mouth is cleaner than a human's. But I said it wasn't true, thinking of all the times I'd seen Chopper licking his dick and his balls. That's why I'd been so careful about cleaning the bite, even though the iodine made my eyes tear up it stung so bad. I didn't want rabies or something.

My dad had been right. We all knew to the inch where Chopper's chain ended, and we all made sure we stayed outside that circle. If I'd been dumb enough to get too close, he said, then I deserved what I got. What he didn't know was I'd been taunting Chopper again, jabbing him with a stick until his mouth frothed. It was just that on the last lunge, he'd gone for my hand instead of the stick.

I'd vowed to wait until the wound healed, that I'd use the time to think of a way to take care of that old devil dog. Now I was ready. My parents were at work, my brother at school. I'd stayed home sick.

The trickiest part I'd already done. The rest had been easy. Feeding Chopper was my job anyway, so grinding up one of my mother's sleeping pills and sprinkling it over his food was no problem. The hardest part was sneaking out last night with a hacksaw and cutting through one of the links in his chain while he slept. One of the links close to where the chain attached to the stake driven into the ground. I needed a long length of chain still attached to Chopper's collar to make the plan work.

Arranging everything in the weed-filled lot down behind our trailer my dad called the "equipment yard" had taken a few days, but he rarely went down there when he was working, so he hadn't noticed.

Now I was standing on the rickety porch Dad had hung from the side of our trailer. Chopper stood a few feet below me at the end of his chain. I was getting him started the way I always did, locked in a staring contest. He always won. Other dogs always started barking right away and I'd win, but not Chopper, because he wasn't some ordinary dog. He had the devil in him. Well, today I was going to let that devil out.

Still staring, I moved slowly off the porch to the end of the trailer, where I'd stockpiled a heap of stones. Screaming like a banshee, I began pitching them at him, sometimes hitting him, sometimes missing, but quickly driving him into a rage.

"Devil dog!" I screamed. "Devil dog! "

He lunged at me, barking furiously, snapping at the air as if it were my hand, craving another taste of my flesh.

"C'mon! You want me? C'mon!" I taunted him.

He lunged again.

"That's it, you son of a bitch!" I shouted. "Jump! Jump!"

And then it happened. With a Ching! sound, his chain snapped, and the chase was on.

Around the end of the trailer and down among the junk cars, rusting farm equipment and piles of scrap lumber we swooped. I'd counted on Chopper's chain slowing him down, but he came at me faster than I'd thought. I was ready for him, though. One by one as we sprinted through the yard I tore off pieces of an old shirt I'd pinned to my jacket and threw them down. Behind me I heard him pause long enough to make sure these weren't parts of me, then resume the chase.

It didn't last long. I flew past a pair of defunct tractors, then down a corridor I'd formed using whatever wood scraps and spare machinery parts I could find, at the end of which was a ramp I'd improvised with sheets of old plywood. Now came the moment of truth. Would Chopper follow me?

I raced up the ramp and launched myself over the deadly trap I had prepared for him, first over the many-toothed cutting bar, then the rusty tines of a winnower I'd carefully positioned beyond it. Rolling as I hit the ground, I turned just in time to see Chopper, his chain trailing behind, leap from the ramp. His eyes, blazing, burned into me. He drew back his lips in a vicious snarl.

I'll never forget how his expression changed, from murderous to dumbfounded, as his chain caught between the teeth of the cutting bar, jerking him to a halt in mid air above the sharpened tines of the winnower – then driving him down onto them.

Another foot and he would have cleared it. I suddenly went weak as I realized I had no idea what I would have done if he had. I shivered. But now he lay impaled on a half dozen rusty tines, frothy bubbles of blood dripping from his mouth.

He didn't struggle for long. I got up close to his face as his eyes glazed over.

"So who's the devil dog now?" I whispered.

One long, last, low growl was his only reply.

I walked away, but I realized he had come out on top once again. He was free of the torments of this world, but I was still here. In a way, I envied him.

A FREE MARKET ECONOMY

The two young guys who enter the Wahweap lounge mid afternoon threaten to upset the equilibrium that's settled over its only two occupants. Rooney is tending bar, and Carey has been there pretty much since the place opened at noon, calloused hands wrapped around an Miller Genuine Draft, thick fingers clamped on a chain of unfiltered

Camels. Periodically, Rooney sets another cold one in front of him, empties his ashtray, and the two of them go back to watching the Lions lose yet another Thanksgiving Day football game.

The few employees and guests remaining at this time of year only serve to make the place feel emptier.

Buzz cuts under ball caps, clean shaven, the young men look as though they're barely out of high school, maybe what Carey might have looked like forty years ago. A couple of buds taking a break from what's probably their first job out of high school, they're excited to be going out fishing for a few days. No doubt there's a flashy new pickup towing a streamlined something out in the parking lot. They're in debt up to their eyeballs, but what do they care? They have a lifetime to pay it all off.

Carey gives them a quiet stare from under his battered, sweat-stained cowboy straw, and they both settle down on stools, order beer.

"See your IDs?" Rooney asks.

They pull out their wallets.

"You guys here for the Parade of Lights?"

"Never heard of it."

"All the locals deck out their boats with Christmas lights, trees, you name it, parade down to the dam and back. Compete for prizes, although this year with the low water I heard they're just going to circle around out in front of the marina here."

"Well, we're going out fishing for a couple hours, but we're staying here tonight."

"Find yourselves a couple strings of lights, join the parade."

They both nod, and turn to look out the picture windows while they drink their beer and discuss their trip. Outside, the sun dodges a cloud and shines weakly down, muting the colors of the panorama through the plate glass windows. At the marina below, parade contestants are putting the finishing touches on their boats.

One last swallow, and the two turn back to the bar, motion Rooney over.

"Dude, you know where we can score an o-z of ganja?" one of them asks quietly.

Rooney glances over at Carey, whose eyes are fixed on the TV but whose ears, Rooney is pretty sure, are tuned in their direction.

He leans over the bar. "I can probably fix you up," he says softly. "I get a break in about an hour."

Sure enough, no sooner have they arranged quantity and price than Carey turns to them, points at them with a nicotine-yellow index finger.

"You boys looking to score, I can fix you up right now," he says in a voice scarred by half a million cigarettes. "Know you're anxious to get out on the water. Them fish are waitin'."

They look at Rooney as if to inquire what, if any, the protocol is here, but Carey steers them through.

"Better price than the Queen of Spades here, too," he says.

Climbing down from his stool, Carey adjusts his rodeo buckle under his overhanging beer paunch.

"C'mon out to the parkin' lot," he says, brushing the last of his beer out of his handlebar mustache and off his unshaven chin. "We'll take a drive. Sample some product. Do a little business."

Glancing apologetically at Rooney, they leave their seats and follow Carey.

He and Rooney exchange looks.

"Hey, keep the beer cold and my seat warm," Carey says. "Don't worry. I won't be long."

He returns in about 30 minutes, hoists himself back up on his stool.

"Another satisfied customer," he says, splaying out a handful of cash.

"Why don't you mind your own business?" Rooney asks.

"Hey, it's all business, Queenie. Just building up a loyal customer base. You know, word of mouth."

"Go peddle your wares someplace else. And stop calling me that."

Carey leans forward on his stool.

"What, you got a lock on this place? Your manager know that? Maybe we should go discuss it with her."

"If you don't mind explaining to her where you just went with those two."

"Just driving around, introducing a couple of out-of-towners to famous Lake Powell."

"What are you, the Welcome Wagon?"

Carey adjusts his hat, pushes back the hair that straggles from beneath it.

"Hey, Bub, you might not have noticed, but we're livin' in what you call your free market economy here," he says. "Competition's what it's all about."

"There's ways of eliminating the competition."

"Oho! Now we're gettin' down to business. Well, I'll tell you what, Sweetheart, I'll show you mine, you show me yours. We'll see who's bigger. Whaddya say?"

Carey looks around, lowers his voice.

"I feel it's only fair to warn you, though, I got a lotta back up. In other words, mine's bound to be bigger."

Carey's cell phone rings. It's Tic, wondering how the sale went.

"No problemo," says Carey. "Yup, took it right out from under him. In fact, I'm sitting right across from him. Sure, hold on a second."

He hands the phone to Rooney.

"Wants to talk to you."

"Who is this?"

"We're on a no-name basis here, Rooney."

"You seem to know mine."

"And a whole lot more. I know where you live, what kind of car you drive. I even know you're queer as a three-dollar bill."

"Fuck you."

"Sorry, but I'm not so inclined. But I've been checking you out for business reasons."

"What the hell are you talking about?"

"You see, Rooney, Wahweap is my turf now. In fact, all the marinas, the entire lake, is now mine. And I have a business proposition for you."

"Stick it up your ass."

"Already told you I'm not interested. But here's my idea. Simply put, you go to work for me."

"No way in hell."

"Now let's not be too hasty," says Tic. "Here's how it works. You continue to deal from the bar, only I'll supply the product. Everything else stays the same."

"Except my cut, that right?"

"Well, we can iron out the details later."

"Suppose I just say no."

There is an ominous pause on Tic's end.

"Suppose yourself in concrete waders at the bottom of the lake."

Now Rooney pauses, thinking.

"Look, I got a good connection in Phoenix, lots of local customers," he says. *"How does 'partners' sound?"*

"Not interested. I've already got an iron-clad connection and a fool-proof delivery system. As for customers, well, you've already met one of my salesmen. What do you think?"

"I think you're full of shit."

"Rooney, this is a one-time offer. I need the help and I'm willing to be reasonable. Oh, and if you're thinking about going to those two rangers who were at your house a few weeks back, I wouldn't. There's some very interesting information they'd like to know about that Navajo cop found in the lake last month."

"I had nothing to do with that."

"But they don't know that, do they? They're looking for somebody to hang that on. It could be you. Now be an obedient boy and hand the phone back to my man. Think about what I said. Only don't think too long."

LUKE

I'm not even sure what I was doing there. A blind man could see that Jordan and Sarah had eyes only for each other. What the hell was I, their duena? I was thinking about offering to go sit at the bar, when this new friend of Jordan's—Tic—walks in.

Tic. The hell kinda name is that, anyway?

Be nice, boy, I told myself. Jordan invited you, and Jordan's a friend, although why he wanted this guy here on top of me being here I couldn't say. The place was feeling crowded.

Jordan made introductions. "Tic and I went through school here together way back when," he said. "He just moved back."

Yes, I shook hands like I was supposed to, sat back and followed the small talk, just watching.

Until I had to ask Tic, "So where'd you move back from? You still got family back here?"

"No, sorry to say, both my parents have passed," he answered. "What about you? You from around here?"

Before I could answer Sarah jumped in, being cute.

"Oh, Luke's the closest thing to a celebrity we've got in these parts. His great grandfather was Charles M. Russell, you know, the western painter. Luke's family owns a ranch up by Kanab."

"Thank you, Sarah, for telling everything you know," I said, wanting to thump her. She must have seen the look on my face, because she stopped talking, but it was too late. I could swear for an instant I saw antennae on Tic's head. "Your granddaddy leave you anything?" he asked.

I hate to lie, but I wasn't about to divulge anything to this guy. "Mostly memories," I said. I watched the antennae disappear. *Thanks again, Sarah,* I thought.

"Ranching's a hard way to make a living," he said. "Between that and rangering you must have your hands full."

"Keeps me off the streets and out of the pool halls," I said. "So what's your line of work?"

"Well, I guess you might say I'm between engagements right now."

"Tic just retired from the Navy," Jordan said.

Tic nodded. "Just shy of thirty years in."

"Any plans now?" I asked, deliberately pushing that. Maybe I was wrong but I had a feeling Tic was like a lot of guys I'd seen down at the lake over the years, smooth on top with a lot of ugly baggage below.

But Jordan interrupted. "Hey, you guys. What is this, twenty questions? C'mon, I'll buy the next round."

After we'd all had a couple more, Jordan went over to the juke box, came back grinning, pointing at Tic, and said, "See if this brings back memories." The next thing we heard were the opening chords of "Aqualung" by Jethro Tull, not my taste, but Jordan and Tic were singing along:

"Sitting on a park bench…Eyeing little girls with bad intent"

Then they both crack up. I looked at Sarah, but she was clueless, too.

"Feeling like a dead duck…Spitting out pieces of his broken luck"

Fortunately, that seemed to be all they remembered of the words. They stopped singing, at least, which was a kindness. Jordan turned to us.

"Sorry," he said, still laughing. "Tic's nickname," followed by more laughs.

"Aqualung?" asked Sarah.

"Yeah, you know, when we were kids, we spent all kinds of time down at the lake. Used to compete with each other, cliff diving, stuff like that. We'd throw a can of Coke out in the water–"

"*Coke*! You mean, *Bud*!" Tic interjected.

"Well, later I guess it *was* beer," said Jordan. "And we'd see who could find it on the bottom. Whoever found it drank it…and Tic–"

"Let me guess," said Sarah.

"How he stayed under so long…" said Jordan, shaking his head. "Anyway, when the song came out–"

I probably shouldn't have, but I couldn't resist.

"Holding your breath must have been a real asset in the Navy," I said.

Again, something shot through Tic, but then it was gone, and he smiled.

"How exactly did you mean that, friend?" he asked. I noticed his eyes weren't smiling.

Jordan said: "As a matter of fact, Luke, it *was* an asset. He doesn't like to talk about it, but Tic here was a bona fide Navy SEAL."

"No kidding," I said. "You earned your Budweiser?"

Now this *was* interesting. Navy SEALs don't just fall off trees.

"Things around here must seem pretty tame in comparison," I said.

"Most of it was training. Pretty routine," Tic said.

I knew I'd get no answer to any question about what action he'd seen, but Sarah didn't.

"So where did you serve?" she asked. "Iraq? Afghanistan?"

"I'm sorry, but I'm just not at liberty to say."

We all just kind of stared at each other for a moment, until Tic said, "Hey, anything new on that Navajo cop you found at the bottom of the lake, when was it, last month?"

"His name was Eddie Watchman," I said.

Tic nodded. "So, any leads on who did him? I read he was murdered."

"Blow to the head, as far as we can tell," Jordan said.

"From what I read, sounds like he was killed, put in the cruiser, and dumped in the lake, that right?"

"Looks that way."

"Any idea where he died?"

The fact was, other than Kenneth Klain, we had no suspects, and no idea where Eddie had been killed, but I'd be damned if I was going to tell this guy that.

I said, "Well, the investigation's ongoing, so we're just not at liberty to say."

Tic laughed. "Turnabout's fair play. Hope you track him down. You need any help, I've got time on my hands."

Don't hold your breath, I said to myself. Which reminded me of something.

"So Tic, why didn't you go the full thirty years?" I asked.

"What's that?" he asked, turning back to me.

"You said you were in the Navy just shy of thirty years. Why didn't you run out the time?"

He stared at me. I could see the wheels turning. Good.

Finally, he said, "You know, Luke, every man reaches a point in his life at which he's simply trying to avoid being overcome by the weight of his personal history. I guess I just reached that point sooner than most."

Now you tell me what the hell that meant.

Christmas Day, I came over early to help Jordan and his dad fix dinner. Merced and Niles were flying in from Phoenix later that morning and we wanted things ready before we picked them up at the airport. The sun had just come up in a cold, clear sky. Still no sign of snow. I wondered if winter was going to be as dry as summer had been. Jordan and I were sitting over coffee in the kitchen, which looked like something straight out of the '60s. I asked him if it ever bothered him.

"The decorating? Y'know, for the most part, I don't see it," he answered. "Besides, there's the whole thing with Dad, and leaving it like Mom left it."

"But that was forty years ago," I said.

"I know it seems weird, but what's the harm in it?"

I told him it was creepy, like stepping back in time.

He looked around the room. "I guess that's the point."

"Only in a house full of men," I sighed.

"I've made some changes since I've been back," he said. "Air conditioning, a new furnace."

"But the wallpaper, the curtains," I pointed out. "How old is that Emerson radio on the counter? Even the linoleum tile on the floor… which is worn out, by the way."

He looked down. "Maybe we can find something to match it. The refrigerator crapped out a few years back, but we were lucky to find another in the same color."

"But avocado green and harvest gold?" I asked.

"You have to admit it fits the color scheme. And the radio still works, by the way."

Grady walked in then, said, "Anybody like breakfast?"

Jordan and I headed to the airport just before noon. I'd met his brothers last summer, when they came up for a long weekend and we'd all camped out down at the lake. We'd had a riotous good time. Even Niles had joined in. He was quite accomplished on the guitar, and one evening we'd all sung far into the night, our voices echoing like a pack of coyotes from the walls of our little side canyon.

"So, you're the oldest, then Merced, then Niles, right?" I asked.

He nodded.

"And what does Merced do down in Phoenix?"

"Right now he's organizing a group of investors behind a software startup."

"Did you say he was an attorney?"

"He's got a law degree, but he's not practicing per se."

"And what about Niles?"

Jordan shook his head and smiled. "Niles. Who can say what Niles is up to? He's got so many irons in the fire even he can't keep track of them."

As Niles and Merced crossed the tarmac from the plane, I said Merced looked tired I thought. Jordan said that was usual, but okay. "You'll see, he'll still be chipper as the day is long," he said.

Niles was looking all around him, as if he'd never been in Page before.

"What do you suppose he's looking for?" I asked.

"I asked him once. He said, 'Anything.'"

I laughed. "What a bunch."

Jordan and Merced sat up front on the way back to the house. I was in the back seat with Niles, who was peering out the window at whatever we happened to be passing. Merced looked at me from the front seat, but spoke to his brother.

"Jordan, you sly dog. You didn't say you were bringing Sarah along!"

"Didn't I tell you?"

"No. I think you're coveting her, but you'd better be careful, or some younger man is going to swoop in and snatch her away."

"That's only if some older man doesn't smack him first."

I interrupted. "Are you two fighting over me?"

Jordan turned and smiled. "No, but that doesn't mean we won't before the day is over."

"Behave," I said.

"He started it," Merced pointed out.

Back at the house, Grady had prepared a wassail in a huge crockery bowl, an heirloom his great grandparents had brought over from England.

"The recipe's a hand-me-down as well," Grady said. We stood around the bowl in the living room as he ladled out a steaming portion to each of us.

We were about to raise our cups in a toast, when I said to him, "None for you?"

In the corner of my eye I saw Jordan glance at Merced.

Grady saw it too. "All right," he said. "We're not going to tiptoe around this all day." He turned to me. "Sarah, I'm an alcoholic. I'll have been dry for exactly twenty-one years on Labor Day of next year, and that's all we need say about that."

"It's remarkable you can be so upfront about it," I said.

"Years of serious psychotherapy," he replied. "It's also helped that I've concocted a more forgiving beverage that has been my mainstay for all those many years. It's a blend of spiced tea, sugar, and mint. Key's the mint. It's gotta be fresh. This time of year, produce guy at the Safeway orders it in special for me. Summer, I grow a bed of it, three of four varieties, actually–"

"Grady," said Jordan.

"Sorry," Grady said. "Just let me say that if, at any time, I can mix one up for you, don't hesitate to ask."

Jordan said, "Of course, if you do drink one, you get no dessert, because you'll have had all the sugar your pancreas can tolerate in one day."

Grady raised his glass to us. "Okay, Mr. Party Pooper Doctor. Now, with that out of the way, can we all relax and enjoy?"

After dinner, all the guys stood up on Grady's cue and moved toward the kitchen to commence clean up. I asked if I could help.

"The rule here is if you cook, you don't clean up, and vice versa," Grady said. "Merced, why don't you stay and entertain Sarah while we take care of the kitchen?"

"With pleasure."

Jordan turned at the kitchen door. "I'd put you on your honor, buddy, except I know Sarah has better taste in men than that."

"Better taste? She's dating you, isn't she?"

"Exactly."

"Uh, guys. Hello. I'm still here," I said, waving from my seat.

"Sorry!" they said together.

"Let's go sit in the living room," Merced suggested. "It's more comfortable." He topped off my wine glass, which I carried into the living room, where we sat opposite each other in wing chairs by the fire. "So how are things down at the lake?" he asked.

"Oh, pretty quiet this time of year. Cold weather and water aren't a good mix."

"Although, I understand from Jordan that you had some excitement this fall."

"Pretty sad. We were all close to Eddie."

"Any recent developments?"

"Did Jordan tell you we have a suspect?"

Merced nodded. "Guy named Klain?"

"Kenneth Klain. We think he's the last one to have seen Eddie."

"He in custody?"

"No. The FBI interviewed him but didn't think they had enough to hold him."

"What do you think?" he asked.

"I think he's a long shot."

"Why is that?"

"I think Eddie was too smart and too experienced an officer to be taken down by a single drunk."

"So, whodunit?" he asked, chuckling at his little joke.

"There's a wild card in there somewhere," I said. "But I grew up with Navajos, and my gut tells me it isn't Klain."

"Jordan says you're from a trading family."

I nodded, took a sip of dinner wine. "Fourth generation. My folks own the trading post at Two Grey Hills. My grandparents owned the posts at Crystal and Sanostee…and leased the post at Carson."

"So, how'd you end up a Park Ranger?"

"Figured it would be a way to use my degree and live in a beautiful place."

"Jordan told me you went to law school."

"ASU. He said the same about you."

"I went to U of A, although I've never practiced. It's come in handy, though, in what I do."

"Sounds like you're currently into a little investment banking."

"That's one thing. What about you? I imagine knowing the law helps in your job, too."

"As you can imagine, we face a lot of jurisdictional issues," I said. "You plop a national recreation area down in the middle of existing federal, state and county jurisdictions, and you spend half your time deciding who responds to what. Keeps it interesting."

In a bit, Jordan called us back to the table for coffee and dessert.

"I tell you guys Tic Douloureux was back in town?" he asked as he parceled out pieces of pie.

"I thought he shook the dust of this little town from his heels for good," Merced said.

"Apparently not," Jordan said.

"You two were pretty close as kids."

"Yeah, but we had kinda drifted apart by high school. Things changed after his brother drowned. He changed."

"You gotten together much?"

"Just for a beer last week."

"Well, he got mixed up in that rape down at the lake your sophomore year, didn't he?" Merced asked. "Girl…what was her name? Eventually refused to press charges.

"And what about the guy got beat up so bad the following year, on the road out to Copper Mine. Tic's name came up in that, too."

"He joined the military out of high school, didn't he?" Grady asked.

"Navy," Jordan answered. "I lost track of him after that."

"Hopefully, the service straightened him out. That guy was headed in the wrong direction."

"So what's he doing back here?" Merced asked.

Jordan shrugged. "He didn't say. Retired. Sounds like he's living on a boat down at the lake."

"Gotta be a step up from Trailer Town."

"Where he used to live with his folks?" Jordan said. "They're both passed."

"You mean the family's lost that single-wide?" Merced asked. "Oh, the humanity."

Grady went to bed soon after that. The boys decided to stay up for a while and play cards. They asked me in as a fourth. Niles dealt as Merced mixed another round and handed around cigars. I was surprised to see Niles was still drinking. He hadn't said a word all day.

I asked him, "So what're we playing?"

"Euchre," he said.

"Never heard of it," I said. "You're going to have to teach me the rules."

As Niles was explaining, Merced asked, "Remember when we used to do this when we were kids? Playing acey deucey, betting pennies up in our room?"

"Until we discovered girls, that is," said Jordan.

They all laughed.

"All except for Niles," said Merced. "He learned to play euchre from a girl, didn't you, Niles?"

Niles nodded, a shy grin on his face. "Best of both worlds, right? Girl named Arvella. From Indiana. Her dad came to work at the dam."

"I understand your dad was chief engineer on the dam."

"Only during construction," Niles said. He glanced at Jordan, as if seeking permission to continue. "Things got a little out of control around here after that."

Merced snorted derisively. "A little," he said.

"That was when your mom died," I said.

"And Dad went completely off the deep end," Niles said. "He wasn't often sober over the next ten years, not until–"

Here he paused again, looking at Jordan, who nodded, but Merced finished the sentence.

"Until he almost killed me."

Something told me not to ask. This was terra incognita for me, and I sensed that even the boys themselves rarely visited here.

Merced cleared his throat, drew on his cigar. "Part of it was my fault," he began. "I was showing off. It was the summer I turned thirteen, and we were down on the lake Labor Day weekend, water skiing. As usual, dad had been drinking. We had a little Boston Whaler back then, with a 75-horse Johnson on the back, and that thing ran like a scalded dog. Anyway, Dad was at the wheel, swinging me wide, and he cut his own wake, so I decided to go for some air and try a 360. Of course, I flubbed it and went down. Dad saw what had happened, so he cut back to pick me up. I was in the water holding my ski up so he'd see me, and Jordan and Niles were pointing at me and screaming at him, but damned if the drunk son of a bitch didn't run right over me.

"I didn't even try to duck. I just figured he'd see me. Anyway, I was lucky, I guess. He hit me so hard he shoved me far enough under that I missed the prop. It's a miracle he didn't break my neck. Of course, he knocked me out colder than a mackerel, and then what does he do? Instead of jumping in the water to look for me, he just flops down in the bottom of the boat and breaks into tears, moaning and crying my name. Thank God Jordan had his lifesaving training, or I'd have been history."

"You were in the hospital for almost a month as it was," Jordan said.

"Anyway, to the best of our knowledge, he's never touched another drop since," Merced added.

"And neither has Merced's head been the same since," Niles put in.

Merced offered him a mock salute. "And thanks for that," he said. Everyone laughed.

By the time cards were over, the guys had reached a consensus that I'd had too much to drink to drive home, especially considering that I was a law enforcement officer, and that I should stay the night on the sofa. The boys had always slept in a dormitory upstairs at one end of the house, so a bed wasn't available. I was inebriated enough that I didn't really care.

Jordan brought down a couple of blankets and one of his pajama tops, then busied himself in the kitchen. When I was ready, I called him back into the living room.

He ducked his head in the door. I love to see a grown man act shy, only I knew it wasn't an act with Jordan.

"Get in here, Mister," I said. He obeyed. I pulled him close.

"Thanks for the field surgical kit," he said.

"You're welcome. Figured it will come in handy down at the lake sometime. So tell me, a girl named Arvella taught Niles to play euchre. Girl ever teach you to play anything?" I asked.

"This," he said, his hand at the back of my neck, his mouth on mine.

Whoever she was, she'd taught him well. Or he'd had lots of practice. Or both.

The alcohol. The overheated room. His lips and tongue on mine. My head was in a lazy spin. I pulled him closer, feeling his arousal. He moved his hands up under my top, caressing my back, pressing my hips into his. I could feel the warmth of the fire on the backs of my legs as I leaned into him, slowly losing myself in the erotic heat building between us.

I drew back, still holding his arms as I lowered myself to sit on the edge of the sofa, pulling him down to kneel before me. He moved in close, and I twined my legs around his waist. Now we were part to part. Again we joined lips.

Fortunately he was still dressed, because just then the kitchen door banged open and Merced was standing there. I grabbed a blanket and Jordan got to his feet.

I think Merced was more embarrassed than we were.

"Damn!" he said. "I'm sorry, you two, I didn't realize–" he sputtered.

"What did you need, Merced?" Jordan asked.

"I just came down to see if Sarah needed anything before I turned out the lights," he stammered.

"Thought you might tuck her in, did you?" Jordan asked.

"No, looks like you're taking care of that."

"Well, don't leave the lights on. I'll find my way."

"I don't doubt it, brother," he said, and backed into the kitchen.

Jordan turned back to me, but the moment had passed for both of us. I lay back on the sofa.

"Well, go ahead, then," I said.

He tilted his head.

"Go ahead and tuck me in," I said, and pulled the blankets up under my chin.

TIC

Although the day after Christmas was bright, the sun held no warmth. A chill, steady breeze blew off the lake out of the northwest. I decided to drive up to Anne's place for some huevos. Halfway up the mesa, here came Jordan and another guy out for a run. Coupla Boy Scouts.

I rolled the window down, shook Jordan's hand, squinted into the low winter sun.

"Christ, is that you, Niles?"

"Welcome back to Page," he said between breaths.

"Same to you. Listen, I'm headed up for breakfast. Why don't you two meet me at Anne's?"

"Give us about 20 more minutes," said Jordan.

I used a napkin to wipe the condensation off the inside of the window, waved to Niles and Jordan as they walked up. Niles took a minute in the parking lot, hands on his knees, gathering his breath. Pussy.

"So you boys have a nice Christmas?" I asked. "Nice a you, Niles, to come up from Phoenix. I'm sure your daddy appreciated it."

"He does like having us all together," he said. "What about you?"

I shrugged. "I'm all alone in the world anymore. Which is probably better."

Neither of them knew what to say to that. They ordered coffee. I got a refill.

"So what happened to your eyeglasses, Niles?" I asked. "You were always the geek of the family. Mr. Science Fair. You win that every year in high school, did you?"

He glanced at Jordan.

"And junior high," he said.

I nodded. "See you lost the plastic pocket protector, too," I said. "Or maybe you don't need one with your sweats."

Another glance. I reached across the table and patted him lightly on the cheek.

"Just jazzing you, kid," I said with a smile. "Lighten up."

We ordered breakfast.

"So Niles, how *are* things in the inventing business," I asked as sincerely as I could.

He paused, finished what was in his mouth.

"Well, I've built a working prototype of what I call a gravity recycler," he said. "Don't want to waste any of that gravity," I said, but I smiled.

"That's kind of a misnomer. It's actually a device that stores a portion of the energy generated by falling water, then uses that combined with solar to pump the water back uphill, where it falls again and generates more energy."

"A perpetual motion machine."

"Well, not exactly. It just gives you more than one fall out of some of the water."

"Ingenious."

"Thanks, but so far I've only tested it on a small scale. I'm sure bigger would be better, but it's also more expensive, and I don't have it. Merced is working on that, but no luck so far."

I laughed. "The Three Musketeers. You know that's what we used to call you Hunts among ourselves? All for one and one for all. I can see that hasn't changed."

"Who's we?" Niles asked.

Ah, a bite.

"Oh, you know," I said. "I always had my little 'entourage.'"

"Jordan tells me you were a SEAL. What was your specialty?"

"Lead Climber."

Niles nodded. "You were always pretty good on the cliffs down at the lake."

"Oh, you have no idea."

"So what brought you back to Page? Not exactly the land of opportunity."

"Well, your brother here's doing all right. Medical practice, hospital shareholder. And I'm sure he's getting a little action down at the lake."

Niles was actually the one who blushed. Now he wanted to play. "You got anybody in the way of a significant other?"

I gave him a long stare. "Never gonna happen," I said quietly. "I lost my dick in Afghanistan. IED blew it clean off."

That really threw him for a loop. I held off as long as I could, then broke out laughing. The look of relief on his face was priceless.

"Well, on that merry note, I need the restroom," Jordan said.

Once Jordan was gone, I fixed Niles with another stare and leaned in so I could talk softly.

"The little joke was just my way of saying keep your fucking nose out of my business. You think you know me from when we were kids. Well, a lot of water's gone through the dam since then, you little asshole. Trust me, you don't want to fuck with me. I don't care if you are Jordan's brother."

He had no comeback for that.

Jordan returned, it was time for me to head.

"Niles," I said, shaking his hand. "Great to see you again, buddy. Good luck with the gravity thingamajig."

"Thanks," he said without expression.

"Now don't forget what I said."

He just stared at me.

"When you coming back?" I asked him.

"We usually plan a get-together at the lake each summer."

"Well, I'm sure I'll see you then."

JORDAN

Not until Tic was out the door did I realize how tense Niles had been as I watched him relax, letting out a long breath.

"What's up, little brother?"

Niles shifted in his seat. "Dad said last night he hoped the service had straightened Tic out. I don't think it did."

"Why'd you say that?"

"While you were taking a leak, he got right in my face, threatened me."

"What about?"

"How the hell do I know? Told me to stay out of his business. I was just making conversation, for Christ's sake. I wasn't prying."

"Well, you know Tic was always a little sensitive about family."

"Family, hell. He's always had a mean streak a mile wide."

"Tic?"

"When we were kids, for some reason, he never showed it to you. But we all saw it. And felt it."

"Well, you really did have a pocket protector," I said, trying to kid him.

"And you needed braces. So what?"

"Hey, settle down. You know Tic had a rough home life. Lost his little brother."

"Even you said last night that you and Tic grew apart in high school."

"But that had more to do with the friends we chose, or the ones who chose us."

"Exactly. His 'little entourage.' Gang is what it was."

"You're really upset. What got you started?"

"C'mon, Jordan," he said. "You heard the stories same as Merced and I did."

"You mean all that about killing his dog?"

"Among other things."

"Why would he want to kill his dog? Aside from the fact it was vicious."

"And who do you think taught the dog that?"

"Niles. Where's all this coming from?"

"I don't trust someone whose eyes don't smile when he does."

"Is that right? I didn't notice."

Niles shook his head and smiled as he rose from the booth. "My big brother...loyal to a fault."

"To family and friends, anyway," I acknowledged.

"So where does Tic fit in?" he asked.

SARAH

"A bad conduct discharge! Are you sure?" Jordan asked over the phone. "That's not good."

"Luke said he double-checked for just that reason."

"What put him on to Tic in the first place?"

"That night over at the Windy Mesa before Christmas. Luke said it seemed odd, a guy in for close to thirty years just hanging it up. I had to admit I agreed with him."

"That's it?"

"Luke said, and I quote: 'On top of that, I didn't like how he was all questions and no answers.' So he did some checking. You know Luke."

"A BCD. Tic. What happened?"

"We don't know. Luke's still checking. I just wanted to give you a heads up."

"Boy, that's bad. Almost thirty years, and now no pension, no health benefits, no nothing."

He sounded shaken. I wanted to take his hand.

"I know you two go back a long way, but remember that Luke didn't want you blindsided, that's all."

"Tell him thanks. I know he means well."

"He's on your side, Jordan."

"But that doesn't automatically put Tic on the other side."

"We'll have to find out more."

"So I wonder what old Tic's doing for do-re-mi."

I said, "Good question."

JORDAN

"I mean, no ropes, Jordan, no backup, no nothing. My first mission, and just the four of us free climbing the sheer rock face. Then we came under small arms fire."

He set his beer on the bar. He spoke so softly I had to lean in to hear him.

"It's dark, and cold as hell in these mountains. The Afghanis can't really see us, so we keep climbing toward the cave, just trying to get close enough to lob a couple of grenades inside.

"They know what we're trying to do. Those fuckers. What they lack in gear they more than make up for in guts and brains. Now I understand how they chased the Russians out back in the '80s.

"I'll be honest, I hated my job training climbers, but I'd have given my left nut to be back in Little Creek at that moment.

"But we keep climbing. All the while, I'm whispering status reports on my headset to my CO back at forward base, and he's urging us on." He gave a bitter laugh. "Fucking armchair quarterback...I stretch for my next handhold. A round shatters an outcrop by my head, lacerating my face with splinters of rock. I'm sliding, clutching at anything to stop myself. I jolt to a stop feet first on a four-inch ledge. I'm blinded by blood in one eye. Worse, I feel around on the face. I'm stuck here. There's no way forward or back."

His face changed. Christ, his voice changed. A chill ran up my spine.

"Dad, I'm stuck! I can't move! What do I do?"

"You pussy! Get your ass up to that cave!"

"There's no handhold. If I move, I'll fall!"

"Don't make me climb up there, you little fucker!"

His voice changed back.

"They're zeroing in on us. A round stitches the air by my shoulder. I close my eyes. Weld my chest, legs, nuts, everything to the rock.

" 'Team leader, what's your status?'

"My CO. He sounds so calm, I want to laugh, but terror grips me, grips me so tight I can't breathe, can't stop the tremble starting in my legs."

"I'm gonna fall! Help me!"
"Tic. Listen to me. Reach down and unhook the rope from your belt."
"I can't! If I move, I'll fall!"
"There's a small tree growing out of the rock about ten feet over your head. Look up, you'll see it."

"Slowly, carefully, I look up, just in time to see one of the bad guys pop up against the night sky with an RPG launcher on his shoulder. A huge explosion to my left. I watch equipment, pieces of Dylan and Rocker fly into the air.

"Without realizing it, I jump, fall until I crash into a small tree, hang on.

"You asshole! The tree was below me!"

He sat there at the bar for several minutes, collecting himself. Looked at me, said, "And that, my friend, was Afghanistan. Desertion under fire."

"Doesn't sound like it to me," I said.

"Doesn't matter. They said it was. A year in the brig, and the Big Chicken Dinner."

TIC

What I didn't tell Jordan: Of course, we make it back to camp, I didn't help myself. I honestly believe I'd have been OK if my CO had just thrown me in the brig and been done with it, or kicked my butt up around my shoulders and relieved me of command. Instead he made a big mistake. He tried to talk about it.

"First, I blame myself for what happened last night," he began.
"Sir?"
"I should never have okayed your promotion, put you in charge of those men."
"I was qualified, sir."
"On paper, yes. But we both know out here paper doesn't mean dick."
"But sir—all those years at Little Creek—I earned the right to be here."
"Son, let's be honest. The only thing changed your career in the Navy was 9/11. Hadn't been for that, you'd still be back there pushing recruits up that damned climbing wall."
He tapped my personnel file, which lay on his desk. "It's all in here, Douloureux. High school bad boy; lucky to graduate. Join the Navy— see the world. But you needed action, someone's ass to kick. Heard the SEALs needed climbers, and that was your ticket.
"Smart enough to out-think the psych profile, but you just kept getting your dick caught in the wringer. Why is that, Douloureux? I'd a' been your CO back then, I'd a' washed you out and been done.
"But it says here you could climb like no man before or since, so the Navy compromised on you. Tucked you away at Little Creek, figured you'd finish out your time there and no one would get hurt.
"Then came 9/11, and everything changed. Suddenly we were out in these mountains, and you became too valuable an asset to be lingering at the rear.
"But in all the excitement, the SEALs forgot something—a tiger can't change his stripes. Not what we do. It's too close to the bone. In fact, it is the bone. Your job here is more than just a job, it's what you are. It's your identity, your core. But with you Douloureux, I always sensed there was something else—something that didn't belong—something that sooner or later was going to get between you and your mission. What do you think that is, Douloureux?"

"I respectfully submit, sir, that the captain seems to have all the answers."

He shook his head. "I can't put my finger on it, but I know it's what caused you to freeze out there last night."

"I respectfully submit, sir, that you're wrong. I simply had no place to go."

"No, you froze, Douloureux. You panicked. And now two men are dead."

He's zeroing in on me just like the bad guys last night, I thought—zeroing in—and I'm going down.

Only I'm not going down alone.

First I lock his office door. He sees that, he reaches for the phone, but I'm too fast for him. I come for him right over his desk, send him into a file cabinet, hoping to break his back.

Down on the floor, he's blocking everything I've got. The office is tiny, so I stay in close, trying for his eyes, throat, and groin.

Of course, he's doing the same. The only difference is, I'm younger, stronger, and faster. I know it. He knows it. Even so, he holds out longer than I thought he would, living proof of how far good training can carry you.

Ultimately, I get his ear in my teeth. Do a Mike Tyson on him.

Only thing kept me from killing the son of a bitch was I knew I'd hang for it. Even so, the corporal kicked through that office door just in time.

TIC

I love old ranch houses, don't you? They're always sort of worn around the doorposts and thresholds, and the nail heads shine through in the wide plank floors. The smell of old wood smoke is never entirely gone. They possess such an air of permanence, of stability—Luke's especially, which was built of cut sandstone blocks with walls eighteen inches thick. Quiet as living in a cave. They're broken in like an old shoe. Of course, now *this* one had been broken into.

- 92 -

The paintings weren't hard to find, hung on either side of the living room fireplace, built of river cobbles. I stopped to admire them before taking a tour of the rest of the house. On the left was an Indian war party riding towards a sunset, one brave turned in his saddle for a last look at where they'd been. I shook my head. Somebody else fucked over by the feds. Even Russell had understood that.

On the right hung an oil of a trapper sitting his horse while it drank from a mountain stream. On the opposite bank, an Indian and his mount are doing the same. The bronze, a mare with her two colts, was bolted to the floor in front of the living room picture window, which looked out on the Kaiparowits Plateau to the west. Too bad, I thought. But even unbolted, the thing weighed probably a thousand pounds. Carey was stationed out on the highway to alert me to any company, but even the two of us couldn't have budged that thing.

Either Luke had somebody coming in to clean, or he was an old maid, because the place was neat as a pin. Well, I was going to take care of that.

A pair of antique kerosene lanterns were the first to go. They shattered nicely, as did the mahogany framed mirror I tore from the dining room wall. Seven years bad luck—hell, I already had a lifetime. What was seven more years?

"Pry into *my* life, you asshole!" I shouted. "How do *you* like it?" I asked, clearing an old kitchen clock off a side table and onto the floor. An entire corner cupboard full of cut glass and old plates bit the dust.

"Make me look bad in front of my only friend, fucker? I'll show you bad!" I screamed, toppling a grandfather clock onto its face. The chimes mixed satisfactorily with the sound of breaking glass.

By the time I was done, the place looked like an earthquake had hit it. Maybe I went a little nutso, but this guy needed to understand he better not fuck with me.

I bubble wrapped the two paintings and slipped them into the small duffle bag I'd brought. Standing in the living room amid the carnage, I looked wistfully once more at the bronze, then headed for the truck to pick up Carey.

"C'mon in. The bubbles are wonderful!" I raised my champagne flute and sank to my chin in the hot tub.

Jordan shook his finger at me. "Bubbles or no, remember alcohol and hot tubs don't always mix."

"Duly noted, Doc. Now take the rest of the day off and get in here."

He snapped me off a smart salute and climbed in.

After a cold afternoon of cross country skiing, the water's hot caress was wonderful. My tired limbs were disappearing into the heat.

"The in-suite Jacuzzi was a great idea, Jordan."

We had wanted to downhill ski, but the drought was still on and the slopes at Telluride were pretty skied off, so we'd spent a little extra on the room instead.

He laid his head back on the edge, eyes closed, immersed in the same bliss I was. When he cocked an eye open at me, I set my glass on the edge of the tub and motioned him over.

I'd been excited all day about picking up where we'd left off Christmas night when Merced had barged in.

"Help me out here, big boy," I said, and soon our suits were floating free on the bubbles. Underwater, I straddled his hips as I moved my mouth over his, our tongues flicking at one another. I reached down. My hand told me he was almost ready.

Sliding myself up and down, I gently began gliding both of us to full arousal. Each long, delicious stroke evoked a groan from me and a throb from him. My nipples, erect, maddened, brushed the hair on his chest. He took me in both hands and picked up the tempo of my slow glissando, leaving me free to focus on the deep kiss in which we were locked.

Ever the tease, he leveraged me high enough to slowly caress my sex with his, eliciting a gasp from me that made him chuckle. Taking himself in one hand, he focused the action on one spot, drawing another gasp. He then began inserting and withdrawing himself, but the water made penetration difficult.

"You're thinking what I'm thinking, aren't you?" I murmured in his ear.

"That's about the size of it."

I saw what he meant as he stepped from the water and grabbed a towel. He wasn't kidding.

Once in bed, I laid back, then reached delicately down and showed him what's coming. Grasping himself, he again caressed me as he had in the tub, and I murmured my approval. After the hot water, our foreplay and the sight of his arousal, I was so ready that he entered me easily in one long, glorious stroke.

Then it was no holds barred, and if that sounds like a wrestling match, it was. He pinned me to the bed with a deep thrust, which he held, throbbing deep inside me. Alive to all of it, I felt myself beginning to contract around him. I locked him to me with my arms and legs, and he rolled over onto his back. On top, I controlled the tempo, and raised myself gradually, then dipped teasingly down, then all the way down to sheathe him in my warm darkness. Eventually, I freed myself and moved over his chest to thrust my wetness against his open mouth. Then I was riding his face, pinning his head to the bed, muffling his excited cries as he gave me the good tongue lashing I deserved.

At last, I slid myself back down onto him, and he rolled me over in preparation for delivering the coup de grace. I gloried in every sensation: the soft crush of his pubic hair on mine, the gentle bounce of him against my upturned ass with every stroke, his chest crushing my breasts between us.

Later, after dinner, as we stood before the fire, he pressed himself against me, saw the surprise in my eyes.

"What my mother used to say must be true," I told him.

"What's that?"

"It's good to keep a hard man down."

His eyes widened. "Your mother said that?"

"Or some variation thereof."

We dropped our robes right there on the floor, made a pallet of them on the plush rug before the grate. I was on my back as he lowered himself into me. After our lovemaking earlier, all my tissue was raw, oversensitive. I was stimulated at the mere touch of his part to mine, and climaxed at his first penetration. Such must have been the case with him, for he quickly spent himself.

We were dozing in the comforting touch of skin on skin.

"Penny for your thoughts," he said.

I hesitated. Should I tell him? The words were out of my mouth before I could decide.

"I was thinking about Eddie."

He came up on his elbow and I turned my head to face him.

"Just now?" he asked.

I sat up and pulled my robe around my shoulders.

"If this is going to go on," I said, taking him by the hand—"and I hope it does—there's something you should know. A long time ago, at a point in my life when I had no idea what was coming next, Eddie and I were lovers."

"When was this?"

"After college. I wasn't ready to go to work, mostly because I had no idea what I wanted to do, so I retreated to the res. Went to work in my parents' store. Spent most of my free time cooped up in my room, reading and thinking about my future, being careful not to do much about it.

"Eddie and I had known each other for years. He was a couple grades behind me in school. He was always a good-looking kid, and while I was away in Tempe he'd grown into a handsome man. We'd see each other in the store. This sounds silly now, I know—"

Jordan cupped my cheek in his hand. "It's okay."

"Well, I was reading through most of Thomas Hardy. *The Return of the Native. Tess of the D'Urbervilles. Jude the Obscure.* I was drawn to his women, so conventional but so restless, so ambivalent. It was a way to see myself. So I guess I fashioned myself after them."

I giggled. "I even started smoking. Unlike a Hardy novel, thank God, I didn't destroy myself, or Eddie. It lasted less than a year."

"What happened?"

"Once the first blush was off, we started comparing notes on the big picture. He wanted kids and a wife to care for them, and I got some direction by figuring out where I didn't want to go. I feel like I did set things right, though."

"How's that?"

"I introduced him to Ella."

*****

"We both know who did this," Luke said, standing in the wreckage of his living room.

"I'm not jumping to any conclusions," I said,

"That's because it was you who tipped him off."

I made a T sign with my hands. "Whoa! Time out, cowboy! Lots of people know you have the paintings."

"Past tense, you mean."

"Okay, okay, but how many times have you loaned them out on exhibition for fundraisers, and such? They weren't your best kept secret."

Luke looked around the room. "I figured the paintings would be a target. I didn't count on all the collateral damage, but I guess it fits."

"How's that?"

"I did kind of rub his nose in it that night."

"What makes you so sure it was Tic?"

"The same thing that made me sure he wasn't showing all his cards that night—my gut."

"Well, you were right on that one," I conceded. "The court martial and the dishonorable discharge."

"Which, of course, were not his fault," Luke said.

"That's what he told Jordan, anyway."

I looked around. "So what does your gut tell you about installing a security system now, like I suggested years ago?"

"Kind of like closing the barn door after the horse is gone, isn't it?"

"So you're sticking with the yard dogs. After the great job they did this time."

"Hey, it's not their fault they're susceptible to a treat and a scratch behind the ears. He must have come in several times over the past few weeks while we were gone and befriended them."

"They probably led the guy around the house pointing out the good stuff."

"Well, whoever it was knew it had to be done on a Tuesday."

"Why's that?"

"Only day of the week I'm on duty and the two hands drive to Kanab for supplies."

"Which suggests surveillance."

"Something else Tic would specialize in, no? Also, anybody that careful would have a lookout posted with a radio. They were skilled. It wasn't a couple of crack heads."

"We can contact Page police. Have him picked up."

Luke shook his head. "No point in that. He'll have that base covered. No, I'm going to bide my time. You know what they say about paybacks."

He looked over at the picture window. "At least I've still got the bronze."

TIC

His house was just where I remembered it, outside of Bluff on a stretch of high ground overlooking the icy river. Same as when my old man and I used to sell him the pots we'd dug, only now it was completely surrounded by landscaping inside a high fake adobe wall with a wrought-iron gate, a big garage and a swimming pool out back. There was a brand new Mercedes pulled up beside the fountain outside the front door.

I called ahead—was the only way Carey and I got by the security system, told him I had something he'd want to see.

He'd remembered my father when I called. He should, seeing's how it was my dad helped make him the rich asshole he was today. All those years of my old man grubbing in the dirt, only to have to sell it to this guy for pennies on the dollar—this guy who then sold to museums and private collectors around the world and made millions.

Fat fucker, greasy and doughy, like a big ball of fry bread before it's patted flat and goes into the hot fat. Plump fingers with manicured nails.

Inside the house was like a museum. Navajo rugs behind glass on the walls, and spread over the hardwood floors; pots in display cases everywhere you looked.

I carried the box, set it down on the desk in his study. He hovered over it like a fat bluebottle fly about to land on a pile of shit—which he was, only he didn't know it. First, I pulled out the two Russells, propped them up on the sofa.

"My my, what do we have here?" he asked, pulling up a chair opposite the paintings. "Be a good lad and hand me the magnifying glass from my desk, would you?"

While he examined the Russells, I wandered over to a glass case in the corner, recessed ceiling spot highlighting it. Inside was a Kayenta water jug in black and red. Completely intact. Not a nick or scratch on it.

"How'd you come by this?" I asked.

He glanced my way, returned to the paintings. "That was dug from Keet Seel about a hundred years ago. Dates from the 13th century."

"Gotta be worth a fortune," I said.

"A small one, anyway." He turned to me, cleared his throat. "These paintings appear to be originals."

"Because they are."

"How in the world did you come across two authentic Russells in this God-forsaken corner of the world?" he asked, then answered his own question.

"Forget I asked you that," he said with a wave of his hand. "As you can imagine, it doesn't pay to inquire too closely in my business. Still, I must determine their provenance before I can be sure of their authenticity."

"Determine their—what did you say?"

"Their provenance, their origin, their source. Only then can I establish a price and locate a buyer. You understand."

I returned to the box, reached in and pulled out the .357 I'd placed beneath the paintings.

"Now, *you* understand," I said, pointing it at him. "This is *my* 'provenance.'"

"Now, just a minute," he said, getting to his feet.

"Have a seat."

Which he did. I told Carey to get over to the bar by the door leading out to the pool and fix us all drinks. Which he did.

Then we talked. I mean—I talked—and he listened while I went back over the years, recounting every single pot and scrap of jewelry and arrowhead and tool of bone and stone and wood that my father and I had spent days roasting in one side canyon or another to dig up and lug out to him.

"And that doesn't include everything my father brought you before I came along," I added. "Only to have you Jew us down to rock bottom time and again, my dad walking away with barely enough to cover the cost of gas and grub. Meantime, you're on the phone with half a dozen private collectors bidding up the price, selling it for ten times—a hundred times—what you paid."

He shrugged. "Tricks of the trade."

"You had us by the balls, and you knew it, so you just squeezed as hard as you could, didn't you? I mean, what were we gonna do, go t' the cops? Try to sell the stuff ourselves?"

"Exactly the point, my boy," he said. "You had no contacts, no buyers. I did."

I started to speak, but he raised his hand and said, "What we're arguing about here is a simple matter of supply and demand."

"Yeah, and where would you've been without our supply? Out there digging up that stuff yourself, you fat fuck?"

"By the same token, where would you have been without me creating the demand? Selling it at a roadside stand to tourists with no money, waiting for the next highway patrolman to stop by?"

Carey laughed at that. I frowned at him and he shut up.

"That's a good point," I said, "but here's another one. All that's in the past. Now we're gonna squeeze back."

He looked around the room. "You're going to rob me? I can assure you that all of this is fully insured, so go ahead."

"No, we've got no way to get rid of this stuff, so here's what we're gonna do."

I moved up closer to him on the sofa and lowered my voice. "First, you pay me for the paintings—today."

He started to object. "I don't have the cash—"

Waving the gun in his face shut him up.

"Then you're gonna start liquidating your accounts—see—savings, CDs, IRAs, treasury bills, stocks and bonds, the whole portfolio. One account at a time, then you hand the cash over to me."

Now he was sweating, but he wasn't ready to cave.

"And if I tell you to fuck off, like I always told your old man?" he asked.

That earned him a swat upside the head with the .357.

While he was bent over, groaning and pressing his torn ear against his head, I said, "Here's what. Me and Carey'll pull your pants down, bend you over that desk, and shove the barrel of this gun as far as we can up your ass, then ask you where your safe is. Hesitate and I pull the trigger and blow your brains all over this beautiful rug.

"Then we find the safe ourselves, clean out this museum you call a house, sell what we can, and call it even.

"Or we can do it the easy way, which, frankly, I prefer because I have no desire to see that fat pimply ass of yours. Or one of these rugs ruined."

Carey laughed.

I told him, "Like you said, what we're arguing about here is a simple matter of supply and demand. You've got the supply, we've got the demand."

I stood up, reached down and grabbed his shirt front, yanking him to his feet. I shoved him toward his desk.

"So let's get to work."

SPRING EQUINOX

The old man, stirring a pot of posole on the wood stove, didn't see his grandson peeking in the single window of the old hogan. He was still stirring when the door opened quietly behind him, and the barrel of a gun slowly came around the jamb.

"Bam! Bam bam! Bam!" shouted a voice.

The old man jumped, dropping the spoon into the posole, and cursed in Navajo. Fishing to retrieve it, he looked up to see the boy standing in the doorway holding a revolver out in front of him with two hands. A grin spread slowly over his grandson's face.

"Now I gotcha! Hands where I can see 'em!"

The grandfather didn't move, just stared at the boy.

"You heard me. Put 'em up!"

The boy's finger crept to the trigger.

The old man was putting his hand out for the gun, his mouth forming the word "No!" when the boy squeezed.

The sharp bang deafened them both. The slug blew by the old man's ear and buried itself in the cedar log ceiling. The revolver flew from the boy's hands. They stared wide-eyed at each other for a long moment, then the old man crumpled noiselessly to the floor.

"Grampa!" the boy cried. He ran to the old man, tried to lift him from the floor. Slowly, grandfather seemed to make sense of where he was. His bright eyes focused on the boy, who peered in turn into the face of his cheii.

Suddenly the old man broke into laughter. "You crazy kid!" he said in Navajo. "You almost blew my head off! Help me up, you little bastard."

The old man walked over and picked up the gun.

"Where did you find this?" he asked in Navajo.

"Out by the road that ends at the lake."

The old man sat at the table. He turned the pistol over carefully in his hands, noted the serial number stamped on the base of the butt. He looked up at his grandson.

In Navajo he said, "We'd better call the police."

FRANK DOYLE

"Thank God the kid missed when he pulled the trigger," I said, stepping out of Two Clouds' cruiser.

"Too bad he didn't hit one of the dogs," Luanda said under her breath.

"What was that?"

"Nothing, sir."

I looked around. "This may not be the *middle* of nowhere, but I bet you can see it from here."

Forensics had been there long enough to mark a basketball-court sized area into a grid of numbered squares, which they were now working one by one. Jordan, standing at about center court with Sarah, waved us over.

"Jordan, Sarah," I said, shaking hands.

"Frank. Luanda. Tommy."

"What've you got?" I asked.

He pointed at the ground. "Here's where the boy found the gun. You can still see a partial imprint in the sand."

"We got your call on the serial number," I said. "It's Eddie's."

"We guessed as much. The Smith and Wesson is standard issue for Navajo police."

He pointed at the ground. "The hoof prints are the boy's horse. The smaller tracks are the sheep he was herding."

"Damn, that's going to contaminate the scene."

"Don't worry. We think we found the rock that was used to kill Eddie. Your people already bagged it for the lab, but its location, shape, and condition are pretty conclusive."

"What was its condition?" Luanda asked.

"We found a few strands of hair and what we think is blood on the underside."

"Anything else?" I asked.

"Preliminary soil samples near the rock also show traces of blood. Depending on what we find in the way of quantity, we think it may be where Eddie bled out after he was killed."

"And before someone loaded him back into his cruiser and drove him to the lake," I added. "Just FYI, we took Kenneth Klain into custody in Tuba City as soon as his father called about junior finding the gun. This thing's turned into a real family affair."

"So you still think Klain is our man?" Sarah asked.

"Christ, his house is only a couple of miles down the road," I said. "We had to pass it on the way in here."

Sarah looked around. "You're right. His place is probably the closest residence."

"Well, you got somebody else in mind?"

She just shrugged.

"Hey, Frank, come take a look at this."

One of the forensics guys was squatting over something on the roadside.

"Looks to be wunna those 'lectric camping lanterns," he said. The thing had been run over a couple of times. The lens and bulb were gone, but he was right.

I called Tommy over. "You guys carry anything like this in your vehicles?"

He shook his head. "Not standard issue, but a lot of guys buy whatever they need to get the job done, so it coulda been Eddie's."

"Then again, it coulda bounced outta anybody's truck coming down the road," said the tech.

I told him to bag whatever was left of it and look at it back at the lab.

I asked Tommy, "So the lake is down this road? Where they found Watchman?"

"About three miles."

"Let's go talk to Kenneth Klain—again."

SARAH

Tommy ducked into the little room behind the one-way mirror.

"Sorry. Got another call," he said. "Anything?" He nodded toward the room on the other side of the glass, where Frank and Luanda were seated at a table with Kenneth Klain.

"Been about thirty minutes," I said. "Not much."

He had his notes from his first interview with Klain a year earlier. I handed him ours from our talk with Klain the previous fall in Tuba City.

"He hasn't deviated from what's in there, anyway," I said.

In the other room, Frank was laying out various scenarios for Kenneth.

"Now we know why you hid the body and the cruiser. It was too close to your house."

"I didn't kill him," Kenneth said, his chin tucked down.

"How do you know that? You said you don't remember."

Kenneth only shook his head.

"Funny that it was your own boy who found Eddie's gun. Guess the whole thing backfired on you," ventured Frank.

"Why would my own son lead the cops to me?"

Frank shrugged. "Maybe he didn't know what his daddy was up to."

"And what about the pot, Kenneth?" asked Luanda. "What did you do with it? Sell it? Smoke it? Give it away? Stash it somewhere out there? It's been a year. Gonna be stale by now—rodents and bugs into it."

"There wasn't any pot."

"And I suppose there wasn't any gun either, was there?" Frank asked. "Did you and Watchman wrestle over the gun?"

"Why would he have his gun out?" Kenneth asked.

"Maybe you were coming at him with a rock. Or maybe you just snuck up on him and bashed his head in! And once he was down, you broke his jaw for good measure!" Frank shouted.

Kenneth looked as if he were ready to burst into tears.

"Klain say anything else about a moving star?" Tommy asked.

"Luanda already brought that up. Nothing."

Jordan was shaking his head.

"The broken jaw doesn't make sense. I mean, his jaw wasn't broken, it was shattered. That would take a precisely timed, powerful blow. Kenneth lacks the skill, not to mention the strength. This guy is essentially a sponge with legs, not a kick boxer."

"So, we're looking for someone who is?" I asked.

"Could be," he said. "But the pot doesn't make any sense either. So let's say it was Eddie's. He wouldn't have answered a call with it stashed in the back, just driving around with it."

"And how could someone dead drunk have realized the value of the pot even if it was there, then be sober enough to kill Eddie, stash the pot, and drive Eddie's body to the lake and dump it in?" I pointed out. "Wouldn't he just have dumped the pot, too?"

"That's what I told Frank last fall when we questioned Kenneth," Tommy said. "Problem is we have no way of knowing how drunk Kenneth really was that night."

In the interview room, Kenneth had broken down and was sobbing. Frank looked disgusted. Luanda went to get the deputy.

LUANDA

Two days later, I called Sarah.

"Looks like Eddie was killed out where the boy found the gun," I said. "Lab says the DNA matches on the hair and the blood."

There was only silence on Sarah's end.

"You okay?"

Silence, then Sarah said in a small voice, "Sorry, but knowing the place makes it more real somehow."

I told her I understood.

"Also, the quantity of blood in the sand accounts for what Eddie was missing when we found him in the lake."

Nothing from Sarah.

"You still there?"

"So, that's where he died," she finally managed to squeeze out.

"I'm sorry, Sarah," she said. "I know he was a friend."

"It's okay. It's all just come back."

We each observed a few seconds of silence.

"We checked his gun, too," I continued quietly. "No prints except for the boy's. Just too much exposure to the elements."

"Fired only once," I added. "By the boy."

"So the gun was out of the holster," she said. "But Eddie never got a shot off at whoever killed him."

"Guess not."

"Well, if Kenneth was drunk, it seems unlikely he could have disarmed Eddie before he killed him."

"Unless he just somehow caught him off guard."

"Eddie was too good a cop for that."

"Anyway, we checked the lantern, too," I said. "Two outdoor stores here in Flagstaff sell it, but no dice on who bought it."

"It may not even have been bought in Flagstaff."

"You're right. And anybody could've lost it out there, not necessarily anyone connected to Eddie's death."

There was another pause, then Sarah said quietly, "Maybe it's just a place where people lose things."

LUKE

St. Patrick's Day was only a week past and already the spring winds had begun. Not only were they earlier this year, they came earlier in the day. Mornings are usually calm, but the wind greeted me as I stepped out of my cruiser and headed into a 9 o'clock meeting at the visitor's center at the dam. I guessed that by lunch we'd have dust in the air like fog.

This time of year, visitors were scarce this early in the morning. Usually, I took a minute and stood at the huge windows overlooking the dam. Seems like no matter how many times I see it and the huge chasm it spans, I'm always impressed by the sheer scale of it. But today I headed straight for the conference room. I just wanted to get this over with.

Perfunctory introductions all around. Seemed everyone felt like I did. I don't know why, but the wind always puts everyone's teeth on edge. It makes horses spooky, even cattle. Maybe it's all that air moving without being able to see anything actually move, except the trees and the sand. At any rate, everyone there seemed wound tight.

Part of the problem, of course, was the lack of any visible progress in the case. Eddie had been found in October and here it was March, and all we'd done is talk to people. At least it seemed that way, not only to the public but to our supervisor as well.

Which brings up another part of the problem. Ted Wooster, our regional superintendent, was a political appointee, one of those know-nothing gasbags who had raised enough money for the party to earn a highly-paid post directing people who really did know their jobs. He seemed to think that the mere fact of his appointment meant he knew what he was doing. He'd come down from Salt Lake at the behest of the Secretary of the Interior on a "fact-finding" mission.

I'd been in a couple of meetings with him previously and knew that before we were through today, he'd manage to second-guess at least one of the decisions made by every person present, and spew enough fatuous advice and opinions to irritate everyone except maybe for Tommy, who just seemed to be a perennially happy guy. All of this without having the foggiest idea of what he was talking about.

He didn't disappoint.

"Let's get started, shall we?" he asked, checking his watch. "Now, you all know why I'm here, but I want you to carry on as if I weren't."

Then what's the point of this meeting if you're not here?

"So let's get a snapshot of where we are," he was saying, "and I'll wait 'til later to voice my concerns and those of the secretary."

Frank began, speaking directly to Wooster.

"Assuming you've read my reports and Luke's, you know we believe we've found where Eddie Watchman was murdered."

"Yes, where his gun was found," Wooster said.

"Along with blood, hair, and other evidence."

"I understand a boy found it?"

"Kenneth Klain's son. Out herding sheep."

"But didn't you search the area yourselves after interviewing" — here he checked his papers — "Klain's father, was it?"

"Mr. Wooster, do you understand how big an area we're talking about?"

"Superintendent," he said.

I saw Frank bristle. So much for pretending Wooster wasn't here.

"Superintendent," he repeated through clenched teeth. "This is an area of many square miles."

"Hm. You got a lucky break, then. Tell me more about Klain."

"We believe he was the last to see Eddie alive, but we have some serious doubts that he was the murderer."

Again, Wooster leafed through his papers.

"He says he was too drunk to really remember what he did."

Frank nodded.

"But also too drunk, we believe, to have killed Eddie, driven him to the lake, belted him into the driver's seat, and stashed the pot we believe was in the back of the cruiser," he said.

"Where'd the pot come from?"

"Forensics found only trace amounts," Frank said. "We think there was a lot more and that it belonged to whoever killed Eddie."

"But you don't know," Wooster said. "Maybe Watchman was smoking it."

Sarah practically jumped out of her seat.

"Excuse me, sir, but that's just plain impossible," she said.

"And how do you know that?"

"Eddie was a personal friend," she said. "I know."

Wooster just shrugged, which started Sarah on a slow burn.

"So, what was Watchman doing out there in the first place?" he asked.

"That's the 64-dollar question," said Frank.

"I take it you have no 64-dollar answer."

Frank just stared at him.

Wooster looked at me.

"What kind of media coverage has this gotten?" he asked.

"Local newspaper and radio, AP out of Flagstaff with a couple of mentions there and in Phoenix," I said.

"We got a call yesterday from the *Lake Powell Chronicle* about the discovery of Eddie's gun," said Frank. "I told them where we'd found it west of Klain's place, what else we found, but that's about it, which of course immediately sent them out there, for all the good it did them."

"Are you sure you should have told them anything?" Wooster asked.

"They told us, actually. I have to give George credit. He's got pretty good connections with the Navajo community. They trust him. But I warned him to stay out of the area, on penalty of arrest. Don't want them tramping around on any evidence."

Wooster looked smug, as if to say Frank should have kept his mouth shut.

"You mean anything else you haven't found yet," said Wooster. "So you think he was murdered there, but then driven in his own vehicle to the lake and dumped in, cruiser and all."

Frank nodded.

"For some reason, the murderer didn't want Eddie's body found in that place," he said. "Oh, and another reason we doubt it was Klain is forensics says the driver's seat had been slid back by a man of taller height, but never returned to the position where Eddie would have had it."

"How tall was Watchman?"

"About 5'9'."

"So how tall do they figure this other guy was?" Wooster asked.

"A lot taller than Kenneth Klain, who's only 5'6'."

"So if it's not Klain, who is it?"

"We arrested a pot hunter last fall, right after we found Eddie," I said. "Thought maybe Eddie might have surprised him digging pots. But we had no way of tying him to the location where we found the cruiser."

"So, basically, you have nothing," said Wooster.

"We're looking at one other guy," I said. "Grew up around here, dishonorably discharged from the Navy. We think it's no coincidence that Eddie was murdered not long after this guy moved back here."

Wooster shuffled through his papers.

"None of this was in any of the reports," he pointed out.

"It's still too preliminary," I said. "But another reason we doubt Klain killed Eddie is because Eddie's jaw was crushed in a way that suggests a trained killer."

"Soon after Luke discovered the dishonorable discharge, his house was broken into and some property was stolen," Sarah added.

"And you think it was this guy," said Wooster. "What's his name?"

"Tic Douloureux," I said.

"So, have you questioned him?"

"Like I said, we don't have enough to bring him in," I said.

"So, how tall is he?" Wooster asked.

"We don't know exactly, but approximately the same height as whoever pushed that seat back."

I thought Wooster was going to pat himself on the back.

"You understand, law enforcement is not one of my specialties," he said.

No, those would be fund-raising and ass-kissing, I thought.

"So, I'll leave the investigation up to you."

Which left us right where we had started.

"So, what impact is all this having on park operations?" Wooster asked us.

"Even with the bureau involved, the investigation is taking up a lot of our time," Sarah replied. "And summer's right around the corner."

"Looks like your preliminary reservation numbers are down," said Wooster. "That should ease the load a little."

"Yes, sir, except that regardless of numbers there's a lot to do to get ready for summer—ordering supplies, interviewing and hiring auxiliary personnel, lots of administrative things.

"And once people start showing up, things really get crazy. Spot-checking boat registrations, patrolling the lake and the marinas, answering emergency calls, paperwork of course, educational presentations.

"And even slightly smaller crowds are still going to be enormous," I said.

"We've submitted a supplemental budget request," Sarah said.

"Don't get your hopes up," Wooster replied.

"How about shifting some of our routine responsibilities to other personnel in order to focus on the investigation?" I asked.

Wooster waved his hand.

"If you can," he said. "I don't care. Is it really taking up that much of your time?"

"I think I speak for all of us when I say we fear this isn't over," I said.

"Well, the secretary wants this resolved, if possible, before the summer season," he said. "Not only because of visitor numbers, but because of danger to the public."

"It's not like we don't want it solved, either," said Jordan. "All the local business people are concerned that no one's been arrested. They don't want this hanging over Page now that visitors have already begun arriving. Remember, lots of these people spend time out on the lake themselves. They're already concerned about the low water, limited access to many of the side canyons, more navigation obstacles."

Wooster didn't seem to give a shit about Page's problems, but suddenly his face lit up with another bright idea.

"Haven't you had to close one of the marinas because of low water?" he asked.

"We closed Hite last summer," I said.

"Well, there you are. With one less marina to oversee and that much less lake to patrol, you've got the extra people you need."

Problem solved.

Wooster and I walked out together. He strode to the windows, stood gazing at the dam, up the lake, and down the canyon.

"Quite a bathtub ring we've got going, eh?" he commented. "I understand snow levels are below average again this winter. "

"Not as bad as last winter, but still not good," I said.

"Everything's so big, it's hard to get an accurate picture of exactly how far down we are," Wooster said.

"Spring runoff has begun, so it's actually coming up," I said. "As of yesterday, we were 103 feet below maximum."

Wooster shook his head.

"A catastrophe in the making."

So what are we supposed to do about that? I wondered. *Go piss in it?*

He turned to me, looked me in the eye.

"Keep those reports coming, Luke."

"Yes, sir."

Unfortunately, the fact that your supervisor is clueless doesn't mean he can't bring pressure to bear. In that regard, the park service is like the military: shit always flows downhill.

SARAH

On the 29th of April, we were all at Eddie's grave in Crystal to commemorate the year since his death, or at least the last day on which he'd been seen alive.

I kneeled and plucked out the few weeds that had managed to sprout in the mound of dirt despite one of the driest winters on record. I was thinking about Eddie's funeral last fall when we'd all said goodbye to him. It'd been so hard to walk away from here and leave him behind in the cold ground. I had a feeling it wasn't going to be any easier today.

Ella had told me on the phone that she wasn't sure she could participate.

"Have you been out there this winter?" I'd asked.

"Yes, but only with Tommy. Does that sound strange?"

"No, baby."

"I feel like I'm dishonoring Eddie in some way."

"You're not."

Only when I told her that Tommy would be along this time had she agreed to come. Now she straightened two pots of plastic flowers standing by the headstone.

Luke stepped up and stuck something into the loose soil—an elk antler in which he had carved the shape of a uniformed Navajo police officer.

"This here's part of the last one we hunted together, friend."

We all stood quietly, honoring Eddie with our silence.

"And we'll hunt down whoever did this," Luke added. "I promise."

Tommy stepped forward, took off his hat. "I never met Officer Watchman. I've heard he was a fine policeman. I know we miss him on the force."

Ella wanted to talk, so she and I walked among the graves while the men stood and chatted.

"I wanted to ask what you thought about me and Tommy moving in together," she said.

"You feel like you're ready to try again?"

She nodded. "Tommy's been so helpful to me. Adella and Marcus treat him like their dad, and Junior's too young to know the difference."

"You're still pretty young yourself, with three kids to raise."

"I just don't know about Eddie. I mean, I still love him. I'll always love him."

"But he's gone, Ella. And Tommy's here."

"I don't know what Eddie would say about that."

"I think he'd be happy knowing his children have a father again, don't you?"

She blushed. "I guess, but what about Tommy?"

"Tommy's a good man. He's still really a boy in a lot of ways, but he's doing a man's job, and he's growing into it. Maybe he could grow into the right person for you."

She nodded. "We'd have to find a place of our own. We couldn't live with my parents."

I smiled. "Jordan and I have been talking about the same thing."

"How's it going?"

"I'd have to leave park housing. No loss there."

"Is Jordan ready?"

"I don't know. He's lived with his dad for so long. They sort of take care of each other."

"And that's the problem?"

"That's what he says, but I think it's just a smokescreen."

"For what?"

"Want some pop psychology? Do you know how his mother died?"

"No."

I briefly related the circumstances as he'd told them to me.

"What I think is it's given him a permanent attachment disorder—fear of commitment."

"He's never married before?"

I nodded. "Once. It didn't last long, which doesn't help."

"Maybe he's overcommitted: his dad, his job."

"Could be. Still, it's hard to accept that someone you love doesn't have time for you."

We walked a little further, Ella pointing out the graves of friends and family.

"Were those notes I gave you last fall any help?" she asked.

"Eddie had talked to a Julian Rooney, but he had nothing to tell us. We still think there were drugs involved," I said. "I called you when we found the gun last month and arrested Kenneth Klain, but he was so drunk the night Eddie disappeared, he hasn't been much help, either. And I told you we did a thorough forensic search of the area around Eddie's gun. We're pretty sure that's where he was killed. Why he ended up in the lake we still don't know."

"Any other suspects?"

I shrugged. "Luke's been checking out an old friend of Jordan's, guy discharged from the military, moved back to Page about the same time Eddie was killed."

"What do you think?"

"Luke thinks the same guy broke into his house at the ranch and trashed the place. I agree with that. Eddie's murder I think is a long shot."

"Sarah, I know Eddie would appreciate everything you guys are doing."

"I'm sorry it's not more. But like Luke said, we'll keep at it. I can promise you that."

LUKE

"Luke? Hate to bother you, but I think we got a problem down here you might be interested in."

It was Theda Caswell, the food services manager at Wahweap.

"What's up, Theda?"

"Well, co-worker in the lounge tells me last night that the bartender's dealing dope from behind the bar."

"You think he is?"

"Hell, I don't know. He's only part time, but he's been with us for several years."

"Who is it?" I asked.

"Julian Rooney."

A little light blinked on inside my skull. I tried to keep my voice neutral. "You gotten any other complaints?"

"Not that I remember. Rooney's done a good job for us. Register's never been short. Inventory's always checked out. Customers seem to like him."

"Let me get back to you, Theda."

Later, I realized we should have moved slower, asked more questions, but it seemed at the time that so many people wanted answers, and I thought this might lead to one.

What's more, Sarah agreed we needed to move, so we set things up immediately.

Arranging a sting at a place like Wahweap was easy. We'd nailed a cocktail waitress several years back for the same thing. Guests come and go all the time, most of them tourists on a swing through the Southwest, some of them looking for a little more fun than the law allows. Nobody knows who's who.

We brought in a new guy, Franklin, young ranger just hired and working out of Bullfrog Marina way up the lake. Hadn't been at Wahweap more than a couple of times.

The next night Rooney was working we wired Franklin up and sent him in.

After a couple of beers, he popped the question with us in the audience in the van outside. He and Rooney arranged terms, and a few minutes later Rooney was carrying something from his car in the parking lot back into the building.

When he discreetly passed it over the bar a minute later, Franklin told him he was under arrest.

Once booked and seated in the interview room, Rooney asked if he could smoke.

"This is by regulation a smoke-free environment, but for you, we planned ahead," I said, pulling an ashtray from my pocket and sliding it across the table to him.

Sarah had turned on the recorder, identified the three of us.

Rooney lit up, inhaled deeply, and exhaled slowly.

"Thank you, man. I appreciate you making an exception," he said, batting his eyes at me.

"No problem. But now we need to get down to some of that police work you advised us to do when were at your house last fall."

He took another drag, sat back in his chair.

"Except I don't think entrapping people is lawful, is it?"

"Nobody coerced you into making a deal with Franklin," Sarah said. "That was a clean bust and you know it."

"Okay, okay."

"So Rooney, you remember our little talk last fall at your place, is that right?"

He nodded. "That Phoenix-Page connection? That dead cop?"

"That investigation is still open."

"And I'm still on the hook, that it? Even after you found out I was working that night?"

"Doesn't mean you weren't mixed up in it, somehow," I said, "accessory after the fact—you get the idea."

"So, I'm not the only one on your list?"

"Now you've been busted, son, means you just moved to the top of the list."

"Somebody set me up, could only be one person, same one's been holding me on a string all along." He shook his head. "Shit, you're talking to me, I'm at the bottom of the food chain, you understand?"

"That's what we figured," I said, although I knew no such thing.

"I'm like one of those little crawdads you find in the lake, just food for the bigger fish."

"So who are the bigger fish, Rooney?" asked Sarah

He just stared at her. We could almost hear the wheels turning.

"Look, I know when I've been caught, all right? But if I tell you what I know, you got to guarantee me some protection."

Sarah and I glanced at each other. I nodded okay to Rooney.

"Well, I know who's the big fish on this end," he said.

I knew Sarah and I both had Tic's name on our tongues, and when Rooney spoke it, we looked at each other and tried not to smile.

"Now Rooney, I want you to tell me exactly how you know this," I said.

"Simple. He's my man."

"So the stuff you were selling to our guy tonight —"

"Came from him," Rooney finished. "He had me on a 70-30 split, the fucker…said he'd kill me if I didn't cooperate."

"But how do you know it was coming from Phoenix?"

"Where else?"

"Oh, Salt Lake, Denver, maybe even LA, come right up I-40 to Flagstaff," I said.

He shook his head. "No, this stuff is only grown in Mexico. It's that new hybrid shit, grows year round."

"You talking about the stuff they call Columbians?"

"Yeah, can't be killed with herbicides."

"How does it get here?"

"Semi full of bales through Tucson into Phoenix, then re-packaged into kilos and distributed in passenger cars."

"How do you know Tic wasn't just moving the stuff for someone else local?"

Rooney shrugged. "He told me he was the main man around here. Besides, I never heard about anyone else."

"This is all good, Rooney," said Sarah, "but right now it's just your word. We need more."

Rooney hung his head. "Shit. You sure about this witness protection stuff?"

"We're tied into the federal program, Rooney," I said.

"But I've heard about people being found and killed."

I nodded. "I won't say it hasn't happened, but it's exceedingly rare."

"I just want to remind you I'm putting my life on the line here."

"We know that, and we won't let you down."

He silently weighed his options. "Okay, I know how you can make sure."

Sarah and I held our breath.

"You know where Tic docks his boat here at Wahweap?"

"We can find it," Sarah said.

"Okay, well that's where he stashes it."

"On the boat?"

Rooney nodded.

"Where exactly on the boat?"

"There's a storage locker, down in the cabin, all the way forward," he said. "Stuff is in a gym bag under a couple of life vests."

"Describe the bag."

"Phoenix Suns. Purple and orange. Got their big insignia on it." He took a deep breath and let it out slowly. "Okay if I have another smoke?"

SARAH

The marijuana was right where Rooney told us it would be, a couple of keys stuffed in a Phoenix Suns gym bag under some life jackets in the forward hold.

Tic showed up while we were on board, which made arresting him easy. I was beginning to think we'd have it all wrapped up that night.

Tic didn't struggle. "Guess I should have seen this coming," was all he said.

We put Rooney in the holding cell before we brought Tic in, him on one side of the table, Luke and I on the other. Jordan was in the observation room behind the one-way glass.

He leaned back in his chair in the interview room. For what it's worth, I thought he looked pretty relaxed—considering.

"So, this must all be Rooney's doing," is the first thing he said.

"Rooney?" I asked.

"Yeah, Julian Rooney. Tended bar here in the lounge."

"We know who Rooney is, Douloureux," said Luke, leaning in a little closer. "You two know each other?"

"I live on my boat here at Wahweap. Do most of my drinking in the bar."

"What's Rooney got to do with this?" I asked.

"C'mon. I heard it all went down tonight, Rooney walking out in cuffs. Next thing you're searching my boat. Didn't take much to put two and two together, figure he must have stashed that trash on my boat."

"When would he have done that?" asked Luke. "We arrested him in the lounge and brought him directly here for questioning."

Tic tapped the side of his head. "That Rooney, he's cagey."

We waited for him to explain.

"You don't get it? He must have hidden the stuff on board a couple of weeks ago."

"But you're saying he put it there before he was busted? How'd he know he was going to be busted?" I asked.

"Selling pot in a bar, Officer Tanner? That's what I'm saying. Rooney knew it was bound to happen sooner or later."

"So he bought himself a little insurance, that it?"

"Exactly. Hiding the stuff on my boat is his get-out-of-jail-free card."

I glanced at Luke. He looked skeptical.

"Tell you what," Tic said. "I'll bet he knew exactly where it was on the boat, didn't he? Led you right to it."

"But, why set you up, some guy he only knows from the other side of the bar?" Luke asked. "You never bought any pot from him, did you?"

Tic managed to look offended. "Me? Wacky tobacky? Nah, never have."

"So, why would Rooney single you out?"

Tic leaned across the table toward us, lowered his voice.

"Here's what I think. Couple weeks ago, Rooney was working, I closed down the bar. I think I was the last one there. Anyway, I say good night, walk back to my boat, climb on board, turn around and who's standing there but Rooney.

"'What the hell do you want?' I ask him.

"He just stands there for a minute, mumbling something about how I just always seemed friendly at the bar.

"Now believe me, I was never more than polite. I just felt kinda sorry for him, you know? A blind man could see he was queer, and way out here in place like this, gotta be lonely for a guy like that—I mean—black *and* queer.

"Then he says something like, 'You're nice, but you're a dangerous man, too, aren't you?'

"I said, 'What the hell are you talking about?'

"He just keeps standing there on dock, looking at me, and it hits me. He's coming on to me!

"I jump back onto the dock, get right in his face and tell him to get the fuck away from me and stay away from me.

"He reaches out his hand toward me. I slap it away and shove him backwards and he falls.

"I told him he was a goddamned queer and if he ever so much as looked at me like that again I'd kick his ass so far up around his shoulders he'd look like the Hunchback of Notre Dame."

He took a deep breath, leaned back.

"Like I said, I knew he was queer, but believe me I never gave him any encouragement."

"So this is payback for rejecting him?" I asked.

"How the hell do I know? You asked me why he'd tap me. Maybe he figured he'd kill two birds with one stone. Set me up as payback and get himself off the hook for selling."

Luke got up, walked around behind Tic, leaned against the wall.

"Really, how hard would it be to stash something on my boat? You were just there. It's never locked. Just ask Jaime down there. He'll tell you. The cabin door's *always* unlocked.

"And here's something else. Couple nights before he comes on to me, I'm sitting there at the bar, things are slow, and he tells me he's a suspect in the murder of that Navajo cop you found dead in the lake. Right out! Just like that!"

I started to say something, but he held up his hand.

"Wait, there's more. He also told me you thought he was involved in buying drugs from a gang in Phoenix."

"Why would he tell you all that?"

Tic shrugged. "Make himself look important? I don't know. Maybe if he was sweet on me he was just trying to impress me. But now that's he's been busted, maybe it's true. The heat's on and he just wants to point the finger at somebody else."

He looked at both of us.

"All right, you think I'm making all this up. Then do this. Check the stuff Rooney was selling in the bar with the stuff you found on my boat. Dollars to doughnuts it's the same."

"Thanks for the tip," I said, "but we're already checking that out."

"Okay, that's a wash, I agree." Again, he leaned toward me across the table. "But there's one more thing you need to check out."

He turned his head, made sure from the corner of his eye that Luke was listening. "It just occurred to me, but after what Rooney told me about him being a murder suspect in a case involving drugs, I'm wondering if there wasn't pot found in that dead cop's cruiser."

I looked up at Luke, who had moved up behind Tic.

"Of course I have no way of knowing if there was, but if so, is there any chance that the stuff Rooney was selling—and that he planted on my boat—is the same as what was in the cruiser? Because if it is, that, in my mind, would be a pretty strong link between Rooney and the death of that cop."

Nobody said anything for at least a minute.

"Course, if it *is* the same, and Rooney's telling the truth about you being his man, that would link you to Eddie Watchman's death," I said.

He just winked at me and smiled. "Jordan's gonna miss the boat, he doesn't pick up on you, honey."

Jordan, who'd been standing behind the one-way glass, was out in the hallway shaking his head after that last remark. He smiled at me.

"I think he likes you, Sarah."

"Give me a break. He's just manipulating us for all he's worth. I mean, are we supposed to believe that story about Rooney coming on to him?"

"Rooney batted his eyes at me last fall at his house."

"Oh, please."

"Seriously, how do we know Rooney didn't? Not only that, it's interesting that he knew exactly where the pot was. He even named what object it was hidden under, described the duffle bag."

"But he could have seen all that while picking up pot from Tic."

"Or he really did stash it there to frame Tic just like Tic says," Jordan replied. "All I'm saying is that right now it's just Rooney's word against Tic's."

"Can I intervene here?" Luke asked. "And suggest we at least check the pot?"

It took a couple of days, but we had the FBI lab compare the pot from all three sources and it was just what Tic had said it would be—all the same stuff. Columbians, usually grown in Michoacan, in the mountains west of Mexico City.

"Which just means Rooney is telling the truth," said Luke. "Tic is distributing this stuff from his boat, Rooney was dealing for him, and the fact that it's the same stuff we found traces of in Eddie's cruiser actually implicates Tic, not Rooney, in Eddie's death."

"But Tic's story is also perfectly credible," I said. "Rooney set him up as payback and to get himself out of the spotlight. So it comes down to 'he said, she said.'"

"Oh Jordan, come on," Sarah said.

I held up three fingers. "Look. Who's been busted for dealing here? Rooney," I said, counting on one. "And whose name is in Eddie's notes? Rooney's." I counted on the second. "Third, you found the pot on Tic's boat, but you have no evidence it's actually his. It could've been planted."

"But there's still the question of how Tic knew about the pot in Eddie's cruiser," said Luke. "Only a handful of people knew that."

"But he didn't know. He was just surmising," I said. "It's not his fault he guessed right."

I watched them look at each other. I could see the doubt in their eyes.

"All right," said Sarah. "I'll tell the DA we'll go with possession only on Tic."

"At that quantity bail should be substantial," said Luke.

"Well, I'm going to argue that he be released on his own recognizance," I said.

They both looked at me as though I'd grown a second head.

"Sorry, but I think Rooney's lying. Just like we all agreed at his house last fall, the whole thing's too pat. On top of that, I think you two are fixating on Tic for no good reason."

"Few months ago, I had a million good reasons, smashed all over the floors out at the ranch," said Luke.

"And what's that based on, Luke?" I asked. "A bad feeling you got at the bar that night, and the fact that Tic was dishonorably discharged, then lied about it? He told me what happened over in Afghanistan."

"And you told us," said Luke. "My gut still tells me there more to this guy than meets the eye."

Ultimately, Luke and Sarah were right. The DA not only refused to release Tic, he put him under $50,000 bail. I agreed to post his bond, and requested that Tic be released in my custody. Luke was still skeptical, but Sarah was impressed.

"Jordan, you honestly believe he's innocent, don't you?" she asked.

I looked her right in the eye. "He was my friend a long time ago. He saved my life. I think he's being framed. What else could I do?"

LUKE

Rooney, of course, continued to protest his innocence, told us that Tic was setting *him* up and for the same reason, to deflect the focus of the investigation from himself. We questioned him again about the circumstances of Eddie's death, even though his alibi about working that night had checked out. When we pointed out that he was selling the same pot that we found on Tic's boat, he stuck by his story that he'd been working for Tic, who was distributing from his boat. We also pointed out that the pot was the same stuff linked to Eddie's death, and he went right back to his alibi, so we were going around in a circle.

Of course, Rooney denied he'd ever come on to Tic, that theirs was strictly a business relationship. In fact, he said he hated Tic for sending Carey to rob him of his sales at the bar, which made sense. And he'd only been on the boat to pick up more dope, which is how he knew where it was.

Finally, just out of curiosity, I asked him since he was dealing for Tic, why would Tic cashier him in the first place?

"I've been worrying about that same thing all along," he said.

TIC

Night after Jordan sprung me, I paid Rooney a visit in Page's city jail, where they'd transferred him from the holding cell at park headquarters. Quietly, I apologized for getting him fired and subsequently arrested, but told him he could take comfort in the fact that he was right. I had set him up to take the heat off myself. As compensation, I offered to pay his bail, which was surprisingly low. Rooney told me he'd only been charged with possession and sale. I asked him if there hadn't been any charges related to the murdered cop, and he said no, but that he figured those wouldn't be long in coming.

I could tell he was ambivalent about me springing him, that he was afraid I'd kill him for ratting me out. But I assured him he'd served his purpose and now that I was out there were no hard feelings. So rather than stay safely in his cell, he decided to run for it. Which I knew he would.

*****

"Keep digging," I say, pointing the gun at the smaller one, who's leaning on his shovel, looking over his shoulder across the lake at the setting sun. He turns back, gives me the same look he's been giving me since Carey and I jumped them last night down in Water Pocket Canyon south of Page: Fuck yourself.

"What about him?" he asks, noticing that Rooney has also stopped.

I get up, walk over to Rooney's hole, also near the water, the lake only a couple of feet away.

"Almost done. You got more left to do. Keep digging."

"This stuff is like wet concrete," says the one had the 'fuck you' look.

"See, now you're whining. And that's your whole problem in a nutshell, you and Rooney here. You're both lazy, and that's made you careless."

"Careless had nothing to do with you selling me out to the rangers," says Rooney.

"But you're the one walked right into that sting. Careless.

"Then Adolpho here coming up from Phoenix. Yeah, yeah, I knew you were cutting your own deals on the side, Rooney, but in this business, you got to play 'em closer to your vest.

"I mean, you worked for me, what, almost six months? You think that was gonna go on forever? You gotta plan ahead. Like that marijuana on my boat. I stashed that stuff in that locker, like, the day you went to work for me."

I go back and sit down, watch them dig. The sun has dropped behind the sandstone ridge on the far side of the water. Not much of a glow. No wind today, unusual this time of year, so the air's clear, and still warm.

"And you, Adolpho. What were you thinking, hombre? You weren't a hundred yards off the highway to make the drop. Carey and I coulda rounded you two up with our dicks in one hand. Now you're telling me you can't dig anymore."

"What are we digging for, anyway?" asks Rooney. "There's nothing buried here."

"Don't worry. There will be. Soon."

I watch their faces. Even two dumb fucks like these are getting the picture. Finally, I say "All right, drop the shovels. Into the holes. Sit down, facing the water."

"Sit down?" asks Adolpho, looking down at the wet sand. "What for?"

"Just follow directions."

Once they're seated, I get down on the ground and check. "Rooney, you're good," I say, motioning over Carey, who zip ties Rooney's wrists behind his back.

"Adolpho, you got a little more work to do."

He stands up, and I can tell there's going to be trouble.

"Why don't you just shoot me now? I ain't diggin' anymore."

"That's going to spoil some of the fun, but if that's the way you want it."

I put the hammer back on the .357 and touch the muzzle to his forehead.

He stares at me. *Coldblooded fucker,* I'm thinking.

But I'm glad I wait, because in a couple of seconds, he grabs his shovel and starts digging.

There's a chill gathering in the air, but there's still plenty of light.

"Okay, vato. Now start filling Rooney in."

He gives me the look again, but this time he does like I tell him, and in a few minutes Rooney's buried up to his chin.

"That's good. Now pack it down tight. That's right. Okay, your turn."

I'm surprised how readily he sits down in his hole. Still, I cover him, carefully, with the gun, while Carey zip ties him and begins shoveling him in.

As I pat the sand down under Adolpho's chin, I explain, "Now you boys both been in Phoenix this time of year, right? You know how hot it gets, how everyone cranks the AC. Well, that creates a huge demand for power, and where do you think that power comes from? Why, right here at our very own Glen Canyon dam. They open the penstocks, the water rushes down, spins the turbines, and generates electricity. In fact, there's so much water released it raises the river level downstream several feet. And, of course, it drops the lake level.

"But once the sun goes down, Phoenix starts cooling off, power demand drops, and the whole system reverses itself."

I get down in their faces. "You two following all this?"

They just stare at me.

"That's right. They close the penstocks, and the river drops—but the lake? You guessed it. Even with the drought, we're getting enough inflow this time of year to raise the lake overnight. It's like tides in the ocean, only these are manmade. So by tomorrow morning, this whole beach will be under several feet of water—and so will you."

I watch this register.

"You have to look at it this way, boys. You're in the unyielding grip of something bigger than yourselves, something inevitable. The sun has set, the desert's cooling, the air conditioners are shutting down. It can't be stopped. Look, it happens to all of us at one time or another. You can't buy your way out of it, bargain your way out. It's just your turn in the barrel. It's all about control, you understand? I have all the control. You have none. You're between a rock and a hard place. I'm the rock and there's the hard place," I say, pointing to the lake.

"Neither of which is gonna change. So you have to change." I touch my chest. "In here. Your only real choice is submission, utter and absolute."

Rooney looks up at me. "I dig the submission thing, man, but let me lay something out for you."

I say nothing.

"All right, let's say I go back to those two rangers and tell them I lied about you being my man," Rooney starts.

"Recant?"

"Absolutely. I was working strictly solo, and when they busted me I was afraid they'd find some way to connect me to that dead cop so I planted that stuff on your boat to set them on you."

I wait. "That's it?" I watch his eyes harden on me. "So they lock you back up in their safe little jail again? Away from bad old Tic?"

I shake my head. "You can't turn back the clock. Besides, I gave you your chance to run, posted your bail, and you blew it."

"Listen, man, I was planning to leave town. I just needed one more score to fund my departure."

The desperation in his voice sends a sexual charge through me. I feel immense.

"C'mon, man," he pleaded. "They'll send me up for dealing, and when I get out, I'll be history."

I give him a little smile. "You're already history, Rooney."

His face changes. Now he's angry.

"So what was with all the fucking games, you sick asshole?"

I shrug, still smiling. "Just more fun that way."

That shuts him up.

It's nearly dark. A few early stars have burned their way through the deepening blue of the sky. I squat down in front of them. The water has nearly reached their chins.

"Now you two don't know each other very well, but here's your chance to get acquainted."

I turn and look out over the lake. "You've only got probably five or six hours, so I wouldn't wait. Maybe you can discuss further what we've talked about here this evening—and Adolpho, don't worry about the load you hauled up from Phoenix for Rooney here. The proceeds from that sale will go toward a worthy cause."

Now he cranes his neck to look up at me. "Mis compadres are going to find you, man, and when they do they're going to make this look like a mercy killing." Then he spits in my face.

I want to club him, but more than that I want him conscious for what's coming. I stand up, wipe my face, and smile.

"Oh, and before we go, I wanted to recall for you a little prayer that kind of sums it all up. You probably heard it before. Goes something like this: God, grant me the serenity to accept the things I cannot change; the courage to change the things I can; and the wisdom to know the difference. You all have a nice night, understand?"

Miles away, the water rushes down the penstocks, pushes past the turbines and flees downstream, but one by one, the air conditioners in Phoenix begin clicking off, and one by one, the turbines shut down for the night. The penstocks close, and the water in the lake begins its inexorable rise.

SARAH

For some reason, Luke's startled response when I barged into his office early the next morning just made me more irritated.

"C'mon, cowboy," I said, tossing him the keys to the cruiser, "we need to get over to Rooney's muy pronto."

"What's going on?"

"I'll explain while you drive. C'mon!"

As we pulled out of the parking lot, I told him, "City jail called first thing this morning. Rooney made bail last night." I slammed my hand on the dash. "Damn! I *knew* we should have filed the additional charges right then and there, not waited to hear from Frank."

"How the hell'd he get out?" Luke asked.

"They said some old whiskey Joe showed up with the requisite amount, signed the papers, and he was gone."

"What name did he sign?"

"I don't know, Carey something."

"How'd a guy like that have money like that?"

"That's the point, Luke! It's not his money. It's Tic's!"

"But why would Tic bail him out?"

"I'm afraid I already know why, but let's get to Rooney's to make sure."

His place showed all the subtle and not-so-subtle signs of abandonment. No car in the drive, flowers beginning to wilt in the window boxes, an issue of the *Chronicle* tossed onto the front walk.

No one answered our knock. "Let's make sure," I said, trying the knob. It opened.

Inside, scattered evidence of a hasty departure: dresser drawers and closet doors left open, no toiletries in the bathroom, the evaporative cooler left running overnight from the day before.

In an unconscious gesture of frugality, I turned it off.

"I guess we didn't sell him on the witness protection program," I said.

"That might have been a long shot, anyway, if this whole dustup only turned into a drug beef and not murder. Rooney knew that."

"I sure hope he knows what he's doing now."

"Don't be too hard on yourself, Sarah. Guy like Rooney's lived by his wits all his life, he's going to do what he knows."

I made sure all the doors and windows were locked before we left.

Luke picked up the paper off the walk. "Yup, this bird's gone."

"But I have an unhappy feeling we're going to see him again, very soon."

HEADS

It's never the money, it's always the time, she thought, rolling over in the California king in the upper stateroom of the 75-foot houseboat they'd piloted up from Wahweap the day before. Ron was still asleep, so she slipped naked out of bed to the French doors opening onto the balcony and walked outside.

It had taken her months to finally break Ron away from his commercial brokerage in Long Beach, away from nurturing this client through this sale, that client through that purchase. He was making money hand over fist, but the man's life was not his own. They'd lost three different houseboat deposits before he'd finally seen enough daylight in his schedule to get away. Thousands of dollars, but there was plenty more where that came from. She'd learned to not sweat the money.

The sun had been up only a few minutes, but already it was beaming its warmth upon her face, her breasts, invading her pubes. Holding the rail, she leaned her head back, letting her long dark hair fall free down her arched back as she stretched. She felt the warmth revitalizing and re-energizing her, arousing her body from the long night's sleep, just as it did when she sunbathed nude by the pool at home.

Ron had been anxious at first about leaving. During the flight to Flagstaff and the drive to Powell he'd been itchy without a phone to his ear and a keyboard at hand, but he had handled the houseboat transaction with his usual aplomb, and before she knew it they were on their way, Ron at the wheel singing "Sailing, sailing, over the bounding main."

When they'd finally anchored at dusk yesterday, it was her turn, and she'd known exactly what to do. First a stiff drink, freshened while they floated in the onboard Jacuzzi, the stereo and the lights set low. The huge bed had afforded plenty of room for their antics after that. They had fallen asleep in one another's arms. After a night like that, everything seemed to be put back in its proper place.

She looked toward the beach at the end of the side canyon in which they were anchored and imagined lying in the warm sand, soaking up its heat until she was drenched with it, then into the cool, limpid water to drain the heat away. Then back to the beach, repeat cycle until cocktail hour.

Not wanting to awaken Ron, she climbed down the outside ladder to the lower deck, unhooked the gate in the railing, and slipped over the side into the water. She was only a few languid strokes from the beach, where she lay face down on the sand, which was exactly the temperature she had imagined it to be.

She dozed for a while on one side, then turned over to bake the other. Must tan it all and tan it evenly, she said to herself, and smiled, thinking, two more weeks of this. I can do it.

Her stomach gurgled, and she realized she was hungry. In their hunger for each other last night, they'd overlooked dinner, but the refrigerator onboard was stuffed with goodies. I'll wake Ron up with the smell of fresh coffee and bacon, she told herself. The thought made her stomach gurgle again.

Exhilarated, she jumped to her feet and sprinted into the water. But three steps in she tripped and fell flat in the shallows, tripped over something hard like a rock, yet not a rock: it moved. She rose to her knees and turned, waiting for the sand in the water to settle to see what it was.

Still in bed, Ron was twilighting, holding Sheila close, reliving their lovemaking of the night before, his mouth on hers swallowing her moans and cries as he thrust into her again and again, her long lovely legs locked at the small of his back. Dozing, he reached down and fondled himself, feeling it stiffen to full attention. God, she'd been wild.

Absently, he reached out to her side of the bed, awakening enough to realize she wasn't there and to understand he was hearing screams, but not like those of the night before. Sheila was somewhere outside, screaming in terror. He leapt from the bed and ran to the railing. Sheila, nude, was crying and backing away from something in the water on the beach.

"Sheila?"

She turned to him, pointed at something in the water.

"Heads," he thought he heard her cry.

"Cause of death, drowning," I said. "Both had water in their lungs."

We were in the morgue in the basement of the hospital.

"How long they been in there, Jordan?" Luke asked.

"Been dead about a week when our little sunbather found them."

I pulled back the sheet on Rooney.

Sarah sniffed. "Smell's not as bad as I expected."

"The water and the sand are both on the cool side this time of year, which would have slowed decomposition. Otherwise, no surprises here. Skin is jaundiced from the advanced hepatitis C with which I diagnosed him last year. Eyeballs and the rest of his face would have been, too, if we'd found him earlier."

Sarah shivered. "You guys have to keep it so cold down here?"

"Sorry. Hate to be crude, but it's the same principal as the meat locker over at the Safeway."

"I know, I know."

She turned over one of Rooney's hands.

"Wrists were bound?"

"Zip tied. This one, too."

I uncovered the second corpse.

"Guys, meet Adolpho Delhijos."

I heard both Sarah and Luke's sharp intake of breath. Even after a week underwater, the mosaic of tattoos on the man's torso, arms and legs, was still vivid.

"There's more," I said, handing Sarah a couple photos from the file. "The man had the word "Chuchis" prison-tattooed in a band around his penis and around his anus."

Sarah made a sound of disgust. "You've got to be kidding."

Luke was examining the tattoos on the man's chest. "Any sign of a struggle?"

"Both were unmarked."

Sarah was peering at the photographs. "But Chuchis. Who or what are Chuchis?"

"Who, I think. Put an apostrophe after the 'i.'"

Luke looked grimly amused. "Hmm. Didn't see it around his mouth, though."

"Probably holding that over his head to keep him in line," I answered.

"Oh, you mean," Sarah said.

I nodded. "Think: Property of."

She made a disgusted sound. "Some bad man's girlfriend."

Luke eyed the prominent tattoo across the dead man's chest. "MS-13."

"I was wondering about that. Some sort of code?" I asked.

Luke nodded. "Mara Salvatrucha, gang from El Salvador. Number 13 is supposed to be a southern California designation. Everything I hear says they're a bad bunch—the worst. Whoever burned this guy better be watching his back. His friends *will* come after him."

"State patrol found his car in Water Pocket Canyon, checked the registration with Phoenix, who confirmed the gang affiliation and prison record," said Sarah.

"So what the hell was he doing up in this neck of the woods?" I asked.

"Maybe he and Rooney were lovers," said Luke.

"Near as we can figure, he was just delivering merchandise to Rooney when a third party intervened," said Sarah. "Highway patrol reported traces of coke in his car."

"So Rooney was telling us the truth after we busted him," said Luke. "The stuff was coming up from Phoenix."

"Except he lied about who the connection was at this end," I pointed out.

Sarah gave me a disparaging look, which I felt was unwarranted.

"Blood gas says both had been sampling the product," I said.

"Product a third party hijacked," said Sarah.

"That makes sense," said Luke. "What doesn't make sense is how they were killed."

"What do you mean?" I asked.

"Well, why go to all the trouble of hauling these two way up the lake and burying them up to their necks to drown? Why not just kill them at the car?"

I covered the bodies.

"Maybe the killer didn't want the bodies found," said Sarah. "Like with Eddie."

We both looked at her.

"So you're saying we may have the same guy here?" Luke asked.

She shrugged. "We only found these two through a fluke. I doubt our perpetrator counted on us finding them anytime soon.

"The MO here points to the same guy in all three murders: he goes out of his way to move the victim from the scene of the original crime. I mean—why move Eddie and his cruiser and dump them in the lake? We know where he was killed, but what is it about that place that's important? It's in the middle of nowhere."

"Someone didn't want him found there," Luke agreed. "But why?"

"And let's say 'killers', shall we?" she added.

"How do you figure?"

"Well, for one thing, it's more believable that two or more guys got the drop on Rooney and Delhijos. Also, you'd need more than one driver to get the murderers' car and Rooney's out of there."

"Was Rooney's car there?"

"State police matched tire tracks at the scene with samples taken from Rooney's place. Of course now it's probably at the bottom of the lake," she said.

"Okay, 'murderers' then. It still doesn't explain why they killed them so far from where they were kidnapped," I said. "Any tire tracks found in the side canyon where Rooney and Delhijos died?"

"No. It would've been impossible to drive out there. They had to have come in by boat," said Luke.

"And none of this explains why the murders were so elaborate. So…ritualistic," I said. "None of this sounds like a typical drug deal gone bad."

"It's almost as if the *murders* were the point, and *not* the theft," said Sarah.

"And here's another thing," Luke said. "Page police told me they talked to Rooney's friends and acquaintances, and no one reported any apparent threats on his life."

"So?' asked Sarah.

"So isn't it odd that no one tried to scare him off first, before killing him? Rooney was strictly small-time. Why kill him? Why not just run him off?"

Nobody had an answer for that.

"Let's look at it another way," I said. "Both events are drug-related. We're pretty sure Eddie wasn't smoking it, but was he dealing it? Was he killed for the drugs in his cruiser?"

"No way in hell," said Luke. "Eddie was a straight arrow."

Sarah agreed.

"Okay, so Eddie wasn't killed for drugs. But we do know he was killed by someone who knew how to kick awfully hard, hard enough to shatter his jaw. Who would he have met out there in the boonies who could've done that?"

"Probably not Kenneth Klain," said Sarah. "And since he's still in custody we know he didn't do Rooney and Delhijos."

Luke nodded.

"So if he didn't kill these two, and we think we have the same guy for all three murders, then Kenneth probably didn't kill Eddie either," I reasoned.

None of us spoke for a minute, all of us lost in thought.

Sarah looked at me with a mixture of shame and anger in her eyes. "You've led us right to it, Jordan. This has to be Tic."

Something inside me went very still. "Sarah," I said.

"Oh, Jordan! I screwed up. I screwed up! We had Rooney in custody. If we'd held on to him, he'd still be alive."

"Sarah, don't beat yourself up over it," I said. "Rooney made a choice. He could've stayed in custody."

"I tried to tell her the same thing," said Luke.

Now she gave us both the same look. "How can you be so complacent?" she asked hotly. "We can't push all the blame onto Rooney."

She was looking at me.

"Go ahead and say it, Sarah," I said. "If I hadn't posted Tic's bond, he couldn't have funded whoever it was that sprung Rooney. Is that what you wanted to say?"

She hung her head. "I'm saying none of us is clean here."

"Look, I feel bad about Rooney too, but I don't feel I'm complicit in his murder."

She shook her head in disbelief. "So you still think Tic is innocent?"

"Let's put it this way. I still think that any evidence we have so far is strictly circumstantial. First, we had testimony from Rooney—a drug user and a dealer who Eddie thought was shipping the goods in from Phoenix, but who tried to frame Tic for it. Now he's been killed, and you're blaming Tic based on what could be Rooney's false witness.

"I mean, if Tic wanted Rooney dead, why didn't he just kill him? Why go through all this rigmarole of having him busted and jailed, then released, just to end up murdering him?"

"Because the murders are the message?"

*****

Whatever the message, the regional media were now all over it. What had been a trickle from the papers in Page and Flagstaff over Eddie's death was now a river with the gruesome discovery of Rooney and Delhijos. The media loves labels, and these were quickly dubbed the Bluebeard Murders. From Phoenix and Salt Lake, even Denver, TV and radio crews, reporters, freelancers—all descended like a plague on our little town. You couldn't swing a dead cat without hitting at least a camera man.

Someone told me the trophy wife who'd found the two dead men had sold her story to one of the tabloids for a quarter of a million dollars—like she needed the money.

Fortunately, all of us "sources" quickly closed ranks. My receptionist, Mabel, was blocking calls at the office, but I was being followed in public. Maybe harassed is a better word. Reporters waited for me at work and at the hospital. A couple even stopped by the house, but word soon got around that there was a very disagreeable old man living there who had offered to punch out the next idiot who rang his door bell. It got so bad that a reporter interrupted my breakfast one morning at Anne's Place, and Anne showed him the door. We may have been under siege, but we were looking out for one another.

Sarah said things down at the lake were just as bad, although Ted Wooster at least had the sense to send a public relations person down from HQ. Probably worried that Luke would toss a journalist into the lake. The PR person had issued a press release and was fielding phone calls, but Sarah said reporters were following her and Luke around, complicating the run-up to Memorial Day, the unofficial opening of the summer season.

On the bright side, she said it was almost comical to see reporters in suits or dresses throwing money at the boat rental vendors, then piling their crews into speed boats, pontoons—anything that would float—to run out to the scene of the crime. One of the savvier reporters had driven down to a stretch of shore near State Line Beach and told the viewers the bodies had been found there, figuring that no one would be able to tell the difference between State Line and the beach in which Rooney and Delhijos had been planted, which was miles up the lake. He was probably right.

On the phone, Frank said the bureau also had issued a release but that he and Luanda were being badgered every time they left the office.

All of us were counting on the short attention span of the American public. Provided nothing developed further, we were hoping the deaths would occupy only a forty-eight-to-seventy-two-hour news cycle, or maybe less if something more interesting came along. Though it sounds cynical, we all prayed for a triple homicide or a plane crash somewhere to draw these pests away. Although we had no reason to believe the murderer would stop at three, we were all hoping that nothing further developed in the short term and we'd be left alone to resume our lives.

*****

The Friday before Memorial Day weekend I got home and Grady had all his camping gear piled out in the driveway. I helped him load it into his pickup. "You're going camping this weekend? Sarah said it's going to be a madhouse."

He shook his head. "Sorry I forgot to tell you, but we're staging a demonstration starting tomorrow at the gate leading to Wahweap."

"What's going on?"

"Strictly local people. No big deal, but since the lake's at a record low, we want to take the opportunity to ask that it be drained. Figured we'd take advantage of this media invasion."

He tucked his battered Coleman stove and a can of fuel into a box of cooking utensils and lifted the box into the bed of the truck.

"Drain the lake?" I asked, trying to keep the incredulity out of my voice.

"Yes, Jordan, drain it," he said, taking a seat on the tailgate. "You may not know it, but lots of people feel Glen Canyon dam should never have been built, not after Hoover dam went up in the '30s."

"Why not?"

"Felt it was superfluous. Lake Mead behind Hoover has never been used to capacity, so why build even more storage? Powell right now is less than fifty percent full. Besides, do you have any idea how much water is lost to evaporation from these two lakes?"

"Well, you're a little late now, aren't you? The dam's been here for forty years."

"No, as a matter of fact, we're a step ahead."

"How's that?"

"One thing the low water has revealed is that the lake is silting up faster than anyone anticipated. Pretty soon it'll just be one big bath tub full of mud."

"But there's no way you can get rid of the dam," I told him.

He gave me a sideways look. "You think *I* don't know that?"

"Sorry."

"The point is—we don't have to take out the dam. We just enlarge the bypass tunnels on either side of it, open them up and leave them open. The lake will drain faster than you think. Of course, it'll take more than our lifetimes for all the silt to wash away and for Glen Canyon to reappear, but that's what this landscape does best," he said, waving his arm toward the lake, "Erode."

"Wash away the city of Page while you're at it," I said.

That made him stop. He looked at me for a moment before he spoke. "Jordan, I understand that Page is your home. It's my home too. And I understand that most of it wouldn't be here if it weren't for the lake. But eventually in your life you have to hitch yourself to something that transcends your personal life, something more—I don't know—universal maybe—less finite, more eternal."

I try to respect my father's involvement in these things, but the protest seemed a little far-fetched. "Okay, let me get this straight," I said. "You're going to protest to the very people who have just driven for hours from Phoenix, Albuquerque—wherever—to enjoy the lake, and tell them it should be drained."

He shrugged. "Remember what Willie Sutton said back in the '30s when somebody asked him why he robbed banks?"

"What's that?"

"'Because that's where the money is.'"

*****

At the diner the next morning, Anne was pouring my first cup of coffee. It was the start of Memorial Day weekend and the place was busy.

"Breakfast'll be up in a sec," she said. Then: "Couple of guys came in yesterday after you left, looking for Tic."

After the media blitz we'd suffered, my first thought was reporters. "They say what they wanted?"

"Nope. Just Tic."

"You tell them where he lives?"

"No. I didn't know them, and they didn't know Tic."

"Oh?"

"All they had was a picture of him, asked if I recognized him, so I just played dumb."

"Why?"

She shrugged. "Something about them creeped me out."

She went and got my breakfast. "They must really want him, though."

"What makes you think so?" I asked, digging into the huevos.

"Last night I was working at the Windy Mesa, and they came in there showing the picture around."

"Anybody bite?"

"I was too busy to notice. Sorry."

"No, that's okay. They leave any way to get in touch with them?"

"Said they were staying at the Page Boy."

I guess I should have just called Tic and let him know these two were looking for him, but with three homicides still unsolved, and after listening to Anne, I thought I might check them out first.

Turns out that Hector, the day clerk, was a patient, and it didn't take the two of us long to sift through the guest list and find our two out-of-towners. He took me out in the parking lot and identified their ride—a brand-spanking-new-tricked-out-gangbanger-style El Dorado with Arizona plates—which I memorized. I had expected something a little more generic.

I had Hector call them down to the lobby. I watched them cross the parking lot. Even disguised as tourists, the two of them stood out here like a pair of crocodiles at State Line Beach. The way they moved, for example, very deliberate with no wasted motion. And they watched everything around them. They never stopped watching. Their blousy Hawaiian shirts hid the weapons tucked into the waists of their cargo pocket shorts, except for when the breeze pushed the shirt against their stomachs. And the fact that they knew they stood out— knew it and didn't care—told you they knew all the ways of doing their job without getting caught, which they felt gave them an immunity of sorts.

I stepped outside as they walked up. "You the guys looking for somebody?"

"Who are you?" the older one asked, not too friendly.

"Might be able to help you out."

"You a cop?"

"No. Just a concerned citizen. Understand you have a picture. Mind if I take a look?" I asked.

He glanced at the younger one, who fished the picture out of his shirt pocket and handed it to me.

Although of poor quality, like a photo taken with a cell phone and in dim light, the picture showed Tic looking off camera, standing in front of a display case containing pottery of some kind. "You know him?" the older one asked.

"The picture's not too clear," I said. "Mind if I ask what you want him for?"

"Guy's name Tic, right?" the younger one said.

"Like I said, it's not a great picture."

"So where's he live?"

"Well, if it is Tic, he's doesn't live here in town."

"Whyn't you show us?"

"Why would I want to do that?"

"Or else maybe we'll come looking for you, next," said the older one, touching the lump under his shirt.

I turned and faced him directly. Out of the corner of my eye, I could see Hector reaching for the phone on the desk. I discreetly waved him off.

"Are you threatening me?" I asked.

He lowered his chin, then looked up at me from under dark eyebrows.

"You're the one said that."

"Maybe we should take this up with the Page police. They're pretty good at finding people. Probably be glad to help you find your man."

"Maybe we should take you on right here, whoever the hell you are. Only your boy in the office there is just itching to call the cops."

"I think you're getting the picture, only it isn't this one," I said, holding up their photograph. I slipped it into my shirt pocket.

The younger started to make a move for me, and I was ready, but the elder stopped him.

"We got copies," he said. He stepped in closer to me. "Look, we're gonna be around town, so if you change your mind, call us on the cell." He scribbled a number on a piece of paper. "Did I mention there's cash in it for you?"

They turned and began walking away, but the older one looked back over his shoulder and said, "Only don't wait too long. This is a small town. Sooner or later we can find you, too."

Jordan sounded worried enough over the phone that even as busy as we were I drove up and met him at his office. Other than at Rooney and Delhijos's autopsies, I hadn't seen much of him anyway since I'd told him up at Telluride about Eddie and me. We needed to talk, but I knew now was not the time.

He ushered me into his office and closed the door.

"Something's going on, something to do with Tic," he began, and proceeded to describe his encounter with two heavies at the Page Boy.

"They had this," he said, handing me the picture he'd taken from them.

"It's Tic, all right," I said. "Looks like it was taken from an angle overhead. Security camera, maybe?"

He nodded.

"They say where it came from?"

"No."

"What did they want Tic for?"

"These two were looking for answers," he said, "not giving them out. Pretty rough and ready. They would've taken me on if Hector hadn't been in the office watching it all…and their vehicle was not what I was expecting. People like that usually drive something a lot less conspicuous."

He handed me a slip of paper and asked, "Can you check these plate numbers?"

"No problem. So these two didn't seem to give a damn about anyone guessing why they were here."

"No, they didn't."

"So why do you think they're here?"

He paused long enough that I thought he might be ignoring my question. Then he said softly, "It's hard not to figure it has something to do with Delhijos and Rooney being killed."

"My sentiments exactly."

"I guess that's why I called you," he said, looking me in the eyes.

It took all I had to smother my first instinct, which was to take him in my arms. Instead I said, "Let me run these plates and I'll get back to you ASAP."

He looked away. "Okay, and in the meantime I'll try to track Tic down, see what he says."

"You find him, tell him to come see us, okay? We've got some questions, too."

TIC

Pete: "Guys bought us a beer."
Paul: "Asking about you."
Pete: "Had a picture—"
Paul: "Of you."
        "What kind of picture?" I asked.
Pete: "Kinda hard to tell—"
Paul: "If it was really you, he means."
Pete: "It was sorta . . ."
Paul: "Fuzzy."
        "You mean a low-pixel photo? Like from a cell phone?"
        They looked at each other, then me. Nodded.
        "So whud' they want?" I asked, casual.
Pete: "Where you lived."
Paul: "Where you worked."
        I laughed. "You tell them I'm retired?"
Pete: "It's not that funny."
Paul: "These guys were . . ."
Pete: "Intent."

"Whud' they look like?" I asked, keeping an eye on the door for Jordan.

They took turns telling me as much as they remembered, until Jordan showed up.

"Okay, you two, beat it," I said, before Jordan spotted us. "I'll buy you a beer later."

"You're on," said Paul.

"Later," Pete added.

Jordan sat down, called for a beer.

"So what's up?" I asked.

"Had a close encounter this morning at the Page Boy with a couple of guys looking for you," he said.

"They say what they wanted?"

"Your address. Offered me money if I'd tell them, threats if I didn't."

"Doesn't sound good. Why didn't you just call me?"

"All the stuff's been going on around here—I thought I'd check 'em out first. They had a picture of you."

"You got it with you?"

"I gave it to Sarah."

I paused, then snapped my fingers. "That's what she was doing!" I said, trying not to lay it on too thick.

"*Who* was doing?"

"These guys both have dark hair—one younger, one older?" I asked.

He nodded.

I laughed. "Friend of mine and I were up in Salt Lake last week. You know—barhopping. Checking out the local flora and fauna. Anyway, I found Flora and he found Fauna. Y'know."

He nodded again, smiled.

"Things were going our way until a couple of the locals objected, so we invited them outside, had ourselves a little dustup in the parking lot. But just before we get down to it, Flora whips out her phone and snaps a picture of me. Beats me, but that must be where these two got the picture from. And now they've showed up here. Looking for more of the same, I guess."

"So this was at night, outside?" he asked.

I nodded. "In the parking lot."

He considered that for a minute. "Well, now they're armed. You better watch your back, Tic. They mean business."

"Maybe we should call the police."

"You definitely should call Luke and Sarah," he said. "They want to ask you about Rooney and Delhijos."

I nodded. "That figures—after Rooney getting busted and trying to drag me into it and now that he's dead."

"There's also the timing of these two guys showing up looking for you."

"I'm telling you, buddy, Sarah's a sharpie, isn't she? She figures I killed Rooney and Delhijos and now these guys are the payback squad."

He didn't say anything, but I could see the question in his eyes.

"I have to agree, it all fits together—except for one big piece. Even if I did the murders, how would these two guys even know I exist? And where would they've gotten my picture?"

Jordan still looked doubtful. "Tic, these guys had Arizona plates, not Utah."

I sat back and laughed. "Hey, I don't have all the answers. I'm just telling you it makes more sense that it's the two guys we tangled with up in Salt Lake. I'll just lay low for a few days, maybe go up the lake fishing."

"Well, don't wait too long. You do, Sarah and Luke might get a warrant."

"I hear ya," I said. "You okay?"

He looked at me for a second. I could see he wasn't sure what to think.

"Me? Yeah, I know how to take care of myself."

"I was talking about the murders."

He paused again, thinking. "I guess we'll have to wait and see about that."

I laughed, said, "Yes, we will. C'mon, drink up. I'll buy you one. Don't worry about me. I'll be fine, just fine."

Next morning, I awoke as usual to the smell of coffee. Grady's always up ahead of me and he makes the first pot . . . Only after a couple moments I remembered that Grady had spent the last couple of nights with the protesters down at the lake.

Quietly, I rolled out of bed and checked his room. His bed was unruffled. Out the window, I could see his truck was still gone—so who made the coffee?

I made my way slowly downstairs to the kitchen. Sure enough, there it was—a fresh pot of coffee. I checked the back door, which was closed, but unlocked as usual. I mean, this is a small town. We never lock our doors.

I quickly surveyed the rest of the downstairs, which seemed to be in order. Now why would somebody come in and not steal anything?

Not until I returned to my bedroom did I realize what was missing—my wallet, gone from the dresser where I always leave it. I went through the pants I'd worn the night before at the bar, but I already knew it was gone.

So somebody had not only entered the house, they'd come all the way into my bedroom without waking me up. Had I slept that heavily? I thought back to last night with Tic. I'd only had two beers.

Which meant that whoever had taken my wallet was one stealthy individual.

Then I remembered the two gangsters I'd encountered yesterday at the Page Boy, and their threat to come after me if I didn't hand Tic over to them. Like I said, this is a small town. Finding my house would not have been that hard.

But those two seemed a little clumsy for this kind of thing. Breaking people's legs seemed more their specialty. And what good would my wallet do them? I never carry much cash, and only one credit card. Why not steal the stereo instead? After all, it's practically an antique— still plays LPs. Surely some collector would value it.

On the other hand—maybe—as Sarah had suggested about the murders—breaking in was intended to send a message.

I jumped into some clothes. If this was a message, I decided, those two could give it to me in person. On my way out the back door, I poured the coffee down the sink.

Things were still pretty quiet at the Page Boy. Hector was at the desk. "Morning, Dr. Hunt. Need to see those bad boys again?"

"They still sleeping?"

"Nope. As a matter of fact, you just missed them. Gentleman showed up here about thirty minutes ago looking for them. Went up to their room. Next thing he's leaving and they're following in their car."

"You know the guy?"

Hector shook his head. "Don't believe so."

"It wasn't the man in the picture, was it?"

"No, sir. This guy was older. Seriously in need of a shave."

"You happen to notice if either of the guests in question went anywhere during the night?"

"No way of knowing that, Dr. Hunt. I got me a little room in the back, bed down there after I lock up at 10 o'clock. Sorry."

I told him it was okay.

"They get back, you want me to call you?"

"Would you mind, Hector?"

"Not at all, Doc. You have a nice day."

I headed home to make a phone call—and to try to figure out who made that pot of coffee.

*****

I called Sarah from the house.

"You caught me on my way out the door," she said. "Luke just called. Something's brewing down at the lake."

"Let me guess—demonstration of some sort."

"How'd you know?"

"Grady headed down there Friday. What'd Luke say?"

"Some time during the night they set up camp on that island that's appeared off of Wahweap."

"Any sign of Grady?"

"None of our people have been out there yet. Luke wants me to go out with him. What did you need, Jordan?"

"Somebody broke into the house last night," I said.

"Are you okay?"

I appreciated the concern in her voice. "I'm fine. They only took my wallet."

"That's odd. Any clue as to who it was?"

"I think it was the two guys looking for Tic. They told me they'd come looking for me if I didn't offer him up."

"But if they got into your house, why didn't they go after you?"

"Don't know."

"Did you find Tic yet?"

"Talked to him last night at the Windy Mesa. He told me these were probably two guys that he and a friend of his got into a fight with last week up in Salt Lake."

There was a pause at her end. "What do you think?"

"I'm not sure."

"Did you ask him about the picture?"

"He said a girl took it outside at night in a parking lot."

"Which doesn't match the picture you took from the two guys."

"That's true."

"Is he covering up?"

"Maybe. Maybe not. He did describe these two guys to me, so I'd have to guess he's seen them before. And we've no way of knowing they're not the same guys as the two in Salt Lake."

"Oh, but we do," she said. "I checked those Arizona plates for you."

"And?"

"Vehicle's registered to a guy named Luis Mondragon. Criminal record—in this country anyway—starts when he was 15. Gangbanger from the get-go."

"MS-13?" I asked, picturing the tattoo on Delhijos's chest.

"Doesn't say specifically."

"So these two aren't the two from Salt Lake. But there could be some other reason they're looking for Tic."

"Such as?"

"I don't know, but he asked me if these guys are looking for him because of Delhijos, how would they know about him in the first place?"

"I don't understand."

"Well, why would they connect him to the murders? And how would they have a picture of him?"

She paused. "These are exactly the type of questions I'd like to ask him personally. Did you tell him to come see us?"

"Yeah, but he said he's going to leave town for a few days until these guys are gone."

"We may have to issue a warrant."

"I'm sure he'll cooperate."

"I'm glad you think so. Listen, Jordan, I have to go. Luke's waiting on me."

She sounded irritated.

"You okay?"

"Let's talk about that later."

LUKE

We'd been using the binoculars since daylight to watch the protesters from shore. During the night, they had staked the banners all around the small island that had appeared about five hundred yards off Wahweap marina as the water level had dropped during the winter. Some we could read without the binoculars. "Pull the Plug!" "Free Glen Canyon!" "Drain Lake Foul!"

Occasionally, the breeze would shift and we'd hear them chanting, "Pull the plug! Drain the lake! Scrap the dam! Shake, shake, shake!" So far, boaters had been giving them a wide berth, but we all knew that eventually some yahoo with a six-pack under his belt would pull in close and start going at it with someone on the island. Or one of the protesters would interfere in some way with someone who was *legally* enjoying the lake.

Which was the point—once the demonstrators entered the park boundaries, their protest became illegal. We should have headed them off, but I'll be the first to admit we'd been caught with our pants down. When most of the protesters at the entrance gate had left last night at dark, we'd assumed it was all over. But all they had done was drive over to the gate at State Line Beach and entered legally. I had to give them credit. It was evidently well planned and well executed. There were plenty of boats out at the island, and, judging from the number of tents erected, the new residents were planning a long stay.

Sarah and I motored out to see what we were up against. From a couple hundred yards off, I counted first and came up with ninety-six heads. Sarah counted ninety-three, so we had a ballpark, which was all we needed. Eighteen boats ranging widely in size and condition ringed the island. The crowd varied widely as well, from a sprinkling of seniors down to what looked to be a toddler.

"Well, it sure isn't a midget," said Sarah, handing me the binoculars.

"Damn!" I said. "Isn't that Jordan's father? Standing beside the bright orange tent?"

"That's Grady all right. Right in the thick of it."

I continued scanning the crowd. "Shit!"

"Now what?"

I handed her the binoculars. "The tall guy with no shirt and no hair. Is he armed?"

She took a look. "The one with the binoculars looking at us looking at him? Yes, he's packing a sidearm. Oh, and it gets better. Guy just walked up to him with what looks like a semiautomatic strapped across his back."

The longer we looked, the worse it got. We spotted at least a dozen men armed with pistols and or rifles. God only knew how many were carrying concealed weapons.

I kept looking while Sarah circled the island and relayed all this to shore.

"You're not going to believe this," I said.

"There's more?"

"I'm looking at a big old baldy with what seems to be a swastika tattooed on his forehead."

"Skinheads?"

I nodded.

"You mean white supremacists? Here?"

"Neo Nazis. Aryan Brotherhood. Whatever you want to call them. Right here in River City."

"What is up with that?"

"I don't know, but we need to alert them to what they already know."

I cleared my throat, thumbed the bullhorn on. "Attention everyone. You are engaged in an illegal demonstration while trespassing on federal property. Please return to your boats and disperse. Do this now and no arrests will be made, but you must leave now."

A few of them started a ragged chant, one I hadn't heard since Vietnam. "Hell no! We won't go!" They were quickly joined by the others.

"Let's get out of here," I said.

Sarah brought us up to speed as we rounded the island. Half a dozen armed men stood in the water at one end, each holding a beer, each giving us the one-finger salute.

We get back to the marina, everyone's donning riot gear: bullet-proof vests, helmets, side arms with rubber bullets, batons, offering impromptu strategy options:

"There's not much wind. I say we use tear gas, then move in to make arrests."

"Militia's sure to have gas masks. And they're the ones who're the most dangerous."

"We got any stun grenades?"

"Whoa, guys," I said. "We need to rethink this. We've got at least a dozen armed men out there. We start shooting—rubber bullets, tear gas, anything—they're going to return fire . . . besides, there's another problem. Sarah and I counted at least half a dozen children out there."

This was greeted with exclamations of disbelief.

"Kids?"

"These people are shameless."

"Kids, for Christ's sake. Why would anyone bring their children into this?"

"Read your manuals, people," said Sarah. "It's standard strategy in these situations."

One of the guys—a new kid—turned to me. "So what's next?" he asked.

"I'm going back out there, see if we can talk."

"I'll go with," Sarah said.

*****

From a hundred yards off, we used the bullhorn to announce our intention to land. All eyes were on us, but no one made a move to interfere, so I beached the boat.

I got out first, asked to speak to whoever was in charge. A slightly built twenty-something male with dreadlocks, wearing a faded t-shirt and jeans, moved to the front of the crowd—hippie with a trust fund if I ever saw one. He was followed by a strikingly handsome older Indian woman.

"I'm Ranger Luke Russell with the National Park Service," I said. Sarah jumped down off the boat. "And this is Ranger Sarah Tanner."

"Call me Ishmael," Dreadlocks said in a voice a couple octaves too low for his age or his size.

"And I am Morgana," said the Indian woman.

I'm guessing Eastern tribe, maybe Iroquois. Couple of aliases, I knew, but my primary purpose was not to establish identities but to get this thing defused.

Dreadlocks jumped right in. "This project is being jointly staged in the name of the Earth Liberation Front and EarthFirst! We demand—"

I interrupted him. "Don't forget your silent partners."

He continued. "We demand first that you remove yourself. You have no jurisdiction on this island."

"How do you figure?" I asked.

"We claim this island as sovereign territory, last seen before the Glen Canyon National Recreation area—and your authority—was established."

I wasn't going to argue sovereignty, either. "Now look. You didn't let us land just to send us away, so tell me what this is all about."

"You've read the banners," said the woman. "Figure it out."

"Your message has been received and relayed up the line, but I can pretty well guarantee that the lake won't be drained any time soon. Not today, anyway."

"We've all agreed that we're staying here until we receive written assurance that the dam is to be decommissioned and the lake drained through the diversion tunnels," said Dreadlocks.

"Well, I just told you that's not going to happen. So what's next?"

"I guess we just settle in and hope the lake doesn't rise," he said.

I shook my head. "That's not going to happen, either. You people are staging an illegal assembly within park boundaries. Furthermore, you constitute an obstruction to boating traffic. You must disperse, or we will be forced to remove you."

"That's unfortunate, Ranger Rick, because any attempt at removal by force will be met with armed resistance," said Dreadlocks.

"And that's where the heavies come in," I said.

"We are willing to shed our blood for this cause," said the woman.

"And that of others," I said to her. I turned and addressed the crowd. "Is that how all the rest of you feel? Are you ready to bleed and die to drain this lake?"

"Give it up, Ranger Rick," said Dreadlocks. "We're all on the same page here."

"Read the badge, junior. I told you the name is Russell," I said quietly. "You need to watch your manners." I turned to the crowd again. "Is it true? Are you willing to follow these people into an armed confrontation?"

Nobody answered, but I was beginning to hear murmuring.

"How many of you thought this was just a demonstration, not a last-ditch fight to the end?" I asked. "Did you realize when this started that there would be armed men involved here today?"

Nobody said anything, but Dreadlocks could hear the undertone.

"Calm down everybody," he said. "He's just bluffing. They're not going to fire on unarmed women and children."

I addressed the crowd. "He's right. We're not, but that's because we're trained, well-disciplined officers of the law. We're well organized. We follow orders. But look around you," I continued. "Can you say the same about the armed men standing in your midst? How do you know one of them won't decide to pull the trigger—that one of them isn't itching right now to blow my head off and start a firefight, devil take the hindmost?"

I could see people in the group looking around at the militiamen, who were beginning to look decidedly uncomfortable.

"That's right, there are militiamen among you. Also, we suspect, white supremacists. Were all of you aware of this when you isolated yourselves out here?"

"We're all here with a common cause," said the Indian woman. "The armed men you see are simply a deterrent to any aggression on the part of the park service."

"Okay, so you've got militiamen as armed guards," I said to the crowd. "But who invited the skinheads? Why are they here? Have any of you asked them? What's their agenda?"

"We are all engaged in civil disobedience in the interest of restoring Glen Canyon to its natural state," said Dreadlocks.

"Sounds like empty rhetoric to me," I said.

I pointed out one of the skinheads—tattoos, piercings, and all. "Do you really think this guy cares about Glen Canyon? Or is he just here, like the militiamen, to challenge the authority of the US government, people like me and Ranger Tanner here?"

"The ranger is talking you in circles," said Dreadlocks. "Remember we're all here to disobey the government's authority."

"And don't forget *this* item on the neo-Nazi agenda—defending and preserving the supremacy of the white race. And another thing: Can't they speak for themselves?"

Now Big Baldy was coming to the front, looking none too happy. He turned to face the group. "And who do we have trying to give us orders right now? Two figures of white authority. So who's upholding white supremacy?"

"Nice try," I said. "But if you've spent any time here at Lake Powell, you know we have rangers of all races. In fact, that's one of the reasons the white supremacists hate the government—its enforcement of equal opportunity laws."

I looked around the crowd. "I see more than just white faces here. Any of you had a talk with this guy—ask him about his full agenda?"

I turned to the Indian woman. "As a Native American, have you?"

I asked the crowd, "Do you understand these men are just using you and your children as human shields to advance their own cause?"

I spotted Grady and looked right at him. "Well, what about it? Doesn't anybody else here besides these two have something to say?"

As I hoped he would, Grady headed my way. He was trailing Pete and Paul. *What the hell are they doing here?*

Grady faced the crowd. "Nobody said anything to me about firearms. First I saw of those was this morning."

A woman with two children by her side moved to the front. "I would never have come and brought my children had I known there were going to be guns involved."

I saw a good number of people nodding their heads at this.

"I was led to believe last night that this was to be a peaceful act of civil disobedience," said Grady. "Illegal, but peaceful."

A couple of "That's right"s and "He's right"s sounded toward the back of the crowd.

Pete stepped up beside Grady. "We weren't looking for trouble."

"We were just here for the beer," said Paul.

I turned to Dreadlocks. "Sounds to me like you're losing your support base." I addressed Big Baldy in a quieter voice. "These people sound like they're ready to leave. So unless you're ready to keep them here at gunpoint, I suggest you pack it up as well."

He looked at Dreadlocks, who said nothing.

"And just to make sure you understand," I said, "without your human shields, you're in a losing battle with a larger, better armed force. Furthermore, you're out on an island in open water, within easy rifle range of shore. We clear the area, get ourselves a couple of sharpshooters, and pick you off one by one. Just ask one of your militia comrades how easy it is."

Dreadlocks motioned to Big Baldy and the woman. "Let's talk."

They stepped a few yards away, but it wasn't hard to figure out what they were saying.

Grady headed for his tent. "I don't know about the rest of you, but I'm bunching it." A chorus of agreement followed.

"Hold on, everybody," I said. "Even though you've participated in an illegal demonstration, those who leave now and go peaceably will not be arrested—even those among you who are armed. However, we are required to identify each of you before you can be released."

I could see the militiamen bristle at this. "See? There it is," one of them called out, "Big brother in action."

Grady turned his back to me and told the crowd, "I don't know about the rest of you, but I'm proud to have my name associated with the demand to drain this lake. It's an obscene offense to the natural world and should be drained."

Another chorus of assent. Then tents started coming down.

"Furthermore," I said, looking right at one of the armed man, "we'll be checking firearm registrations. You can't prove it's yours, we're impounding it."

That really frosted them.

In a few minutes, Dreadlocks and the woman returned. "Hate to say it, but it looks like this round goes to you," he said.

"You hear what I said about ID?" I asked. "You don't have it, you'll be detained until someone can get it for you."

"You guys are all the same, aren't you?" he asked.

"I guess it's convenient to think so," I said.

Sarah and I climbed back into the boat, where, to my surprise, my legs started shaking so hard they wouldn't stop.

Sarah saw what was happening. "You better sit down before you fall down."

JORDAN

I watched Grady motor from the island into his slip. "Hey Willie! Willie Sutton! Over here!"

As soon as he heard me, I saw his shoulders slump. He tied up the boat. "Jordan. What are you doing here? And get that smirk off your face."

"Sarah called me this morning as soon as she saw you out on the island. What the hell's going on?"

Grady looked chagrined. "I guess I got taken for a ride."

"You said this was legal, outside the gate and all that. You didn't say anything about an island."

He shook his head. "A few hours into the protest yesterday afternoon, somebody showed up and asked who wanted to go out to the island. Some elected to stay at the gate, but most of us jumped at the chance to do something more..."

"Dramatic?" I suggested.

"Effective, whatever. So we rendezvoused at State Line Beach and I went to get my boat."

"You mean you helped take them out to the island?"

"Well, some of them. But that's not the point. Listen—"

Luke spotted us and came over. "Say, Grady, thanks for stepping forward out there. I'm afraid I'da been cooked without you."

"Glad to help, Luke. They really did pull a fast one on us."

"I believe you. We got out there, I noticed a lot of worried faces. And it wasn't me and Sarah they were worried about."

"Listen, Luke, is there someplace we can talk?" asked Grady.

Luke looked around. "We could go sit in my cruiser, I guess. What's up?"

We grabbed Sarah on the way.

Grady and I were in the backseat and he was jabbering away. "We get out there last night, everything's fine. People setting up, cooking dinner. I noticed a couple of these guys, they kinda stood off by themselves, but no guns. We get up this morning, that kid and the Indian woman call a strategy session, then's when the guns come out.

"The kid and the woman can see that most of us are not too happy about it, so they explain about how these guys are gonna defend us against you guys—'agents of the fascist state' they called you—keep us from getting arrested.

"I asked the question, 'Isn't that one of the reasons we're out here, to tie up park resources getting ourselves arrested on the busiest weekend of the summer?'"

"Nobody answered me. They just went on about draining the lake, and the kid read some excerpts from Ed Abbey and John Wesley Powell about how beautiful Glen Canyon was before the dam, at the mention of which, one of the militia speaks up, says it should be dynamited—"

"That didn't hurt your feelings?" I asked.

"No, but I did want to explain the impossibility of that. But then one of the skinheads says, 'This whole lake is just a goddamn government-built cesspool. They threw out the Indians to build it, then who shows up? I was up in Page yesterday, saw all kinds of colored people. Just a while ago I saw a whole family of niggers float by on a houseboat. Looked like—'

"Then the kid cut him off, started in on a rant about the degradation of the natural world, asking, 'For what? To make a few farmers downstream rich?'

"But that's when it dawned on me."

"What's that?" I asked.

"The murders! Eddie, and Rooney, and that gangbanger from Phoenix! It was the skinheads!" he practically shouted.

"Grady, get a grip," I said.

"No, Jordan, you should have heard this guy going on about social degeneration, and black people on boats, and why don't we, since the Indians are collected on the reservation, just finish the job of exterminating them? He was a lunatic!"

I gave him a cold stare. "Looks like it was contagious."

"Jordan, wait a minute," said Sarah. "I think I see what he's driving at."

Grady turned to her. "Think about it," he said, counting off on his fingers. "Eddie—Navajo. Rooney—black. Gangbanger—Hispanic. Scum, this guy called them. Eliminate them all!"

"So the skinheads did the murders?" Luke asked. "But as far as we know, Eddie was killed last fall."

"But these guys are local," said Grady. "After the council, I did a little investigating of my own, talked to a couple of them. Turns out there's an 'affiliation' of these people living out on the Arizona strip, way out past Poverty Mountain."

"But—" I said.

"Wait, there's more. These guys have gotten together with a group of survivalists who live out on the strip and formed what this guy called an 'alliance.'"

We all just stared at him.

"Don't you get it? They all hate the government! And that includes the environmentalists, especially these radical groups like EarthFirst! and Earth Liberation Front. They'd all like nothing better than to see the dam destroyed and the lake drained, just because it was all built by the government."

"But *murder*?" I asked.

"Why not?" he asked. "Not only was Eddie Navajo, he was a cop to boot. Rooney and the gangbanger were drug dealers, the dregs of society. Why not clean them all out?"

We all were quiet while the idea sank in.

"Well, Kenneth Klain might have killed Eddie," said Luke, "but he was in custody when Rooney and Delhijos were killed."

"I still say all three murders were done by the same person or persons," I told him. "And I still say all three were drug-related."

"And these militiamen, it's possible that at least one of them is trained in martial arts, could have hurt Eddie the way he did," said Sarah.

"It's not a lot to go on," said Luke, "but I've got a couple friends of the family ranching out on the strip who might have heard something. I'll make some phone calls." He turned to the backseat. "Thanks again, Grady. I feel like we dodged the bullet out there today."

"Thank God it wasn't literally," said Grady.

Psychology.

I tell them: Lust. Greed. Revenge. Passion of any kind makes people stupid, and you two are no different. You were so hot to get your hands on me that luring you out here was easy. All Carey here had to do was tell you I was hiding out, promise to lead you to me. Half the money in advance, half on delivery. And now look at the fix you're in.

Geology.

Trust me, guys, you wouldn't believe how much water can flow through here and how fast it goes until you see something like that, I say, pointing up. The two of them, sitting nude, zip-tied hand and foot on the gravel floor of the slot canyon, look up. There, twenty feet over our heads, the trunk of an old cedar tree is wedged solidly between the narrow walls. Dangling from it are the two ropes I had thrown over it earlier in preparation for their arrival.

You see, these slot canyons start out as cracks in the sandstone. You probably didn't notice, but there isn't much soil around here, so every time it rains, the water funnels down into these cracks, running fast enough to erode the rock and eventually form a canyon. Of course, it takes thousands of years, but then what's the rush? Mother Nature's in no hurry and neither are we.

Science.

Which is why we're going to take the time to perform a couple of little science experiments today, I tell them. That's why we had you shuck off your clothes before we tied you up, see.

Carey and I pick up the hangman's nooses I had fashioned earlier at one end of each rope, fit them over their heads, and slide the knots up snug. Tugging on the other end of the ropes, we pull them to their feet.

First experiment. Anatomy and physiology.

I've heard that when a guy is hanged this way—slowly—something startling happens. He develops an erection, a hard-on that gets stiffer and stiffer the longer he strangles and twists on the rope, then goes limp when he's either A: cut down, or B: finally strangles to death. So Carey and I are going to haul on these ropes 'til just your toes are touching ground, then tie them off and make our observations.

Now remember that repeatability is an important part of any experiment, so of course we'll have to try this several times to make sure we've got valid results.

Second experiment. Devotion versus stamina.

Sonny, you look like you're in good shape. You work out? Anyway, we're going to lift Pops here onto your shoulders with the noose around his neck, then see how long you can hold him up before you run out of gas and he hangs.

Of course, it's important to record your observations, so we'll be using your camera phones to get the pictures we need, which leads to our final step: publication and peer review. In other words, we e-mail the photos to your gangbanger buddies down in Phoenix.

Well, shall we begin?

*****

Narration.

First day back in town, I bump into Jordan at the diner. "Seen any more of those two?"

He shakes his head. "Guess they gave it up, but not before they broke into my house."

"They take anything?"

"Just my wallet. Made me a pot of coffee before they left."

"Mighty considerate of them, but I doubt they'll be bothering you anymore."

"Let's hope not. Listen, now you're back you better get in to see Sarah. She's talking arrest warrant."

"That's not good. I'll check in with her."

"So where'd you go?"

"Just up the lake for a couple of days."

"Fishin'?" he asks.

I shrug. "Nah, just hangin'."

Considering the number of extra chairs and tables that had to be dragged in from the main dining room, I'm guessing that every last member of the chamber was here, and each had brought at least one family member and a friend. I looked around for a copy of the agenda, and realized there was only one item on the table tonight, and everyone already knew what it was.

The room quieted as chamber president Jared Smith walked to the podium. We were meeting in the banquet room of his restaurant.

"All right, everyone," he said. "Let's come to order."

People sitting with their backs to him at the round tables turned around.

"There're snacks at the table back there, so if you haven't helped yourself already, you can do it while we talk. I'd just like to thank everyone for coming. It looks like we're all concerned about the current situation, so I'll open the floor up for questions and comments, but first I'd like to say a few words.

"Even though the media's main focus is on the people investigating the murders, I know we've all been swamped by reporters looking for—" here he made quotation marks with his fingers "—'background' and 'local color,' and I know that's been a pain."

A hand went up at the back of the room.

"Yes, Neum."

"I don't know about anyone else, but I'm charging these people double my summer rate for rooms to make up for people cancelling their reservations because of the murders."

I heard people laugh, saw heads nod. Someone clapped.

"Well, I figure nobody out in the rest of the world would even know what's going on here without all these media types running around stirring things up," Neum added. "And they're happy to pay it."

"Beats camping out down at the lake," someone said.

"I know most of us are seeing a spike in visitors, even if they're only here to snoop around," said Jared. "Our meal count is up for this time of year."

I looked around. Several people were nodding assent.

"Problem is, we all know all of this is temporary," he continued. "Soon as somethin' worse happens somewhere else, these people will be off chasing that."

"And we'll be left with a lot less visitors," said Neum.

"Somewheres down the road, we may have people showing up to visit the scene of the crime," someone added hopefully.

"But only after the murderer is caught," said Jared.

There was general agreement with this.

"So, Jordan, any hope you guys will wrap this up soon?"

Every head in the room turned toward me.

I stood up so everyone could hear. I didn't want to go through this twice. "You all know we found Eddie Watchman dead in his cruiser in the lake last fall," I began. "This spring, we learned he had been killed some distance away from the lake, loaded into his cruiser, which was then driven into the lake. We think the murderer wanted to hide the place where Eddie was killed. Why, we don't know.

"You also probably know last spring we arrested a suspect, Kenneth Klain, who was the last person to see Eddie alive, but he was in custody when Julius Rooney and Adolpho Delhijos were killed last month. He has since been released."

I didn't even bother to mention our pot-hunting friend Harris.

"So you think the same person killed Watchman, and now the two at the lake?" Jared asked.

"We do."

"No chance that we have two killers on our hands?"

"Given the fact that there are certain links, similarities among the killings, we think it's one person."

"What similarities?"

"I can't say without compromising the investigation."

This brought a collective groan from the group.

"Typical bullshit police response," I heard somebody mutter nearby.

"I'm sorry, people, but that's how these things work."

"Putting two and two together, I heard there were drugs in Eddie's cruiser, drugs in Delhijos's vehicle, and it was fairly common knowledge that Rooney was a dealer, albeit small time," said Laman Spell. He owned the McDonald's on the road down to the dam.

I waited. Someone has loose lips, I thought.

"So is that one of the links?" he pressed.

"I said I can't go into that. Look, if they find out how much we know, that will help them stay one step ahead of us."

"Them? You think there's more than one?"

"It looks like the murderer is not working alone."

"You mean, like a gang?" Jared asked.

"More like an accomplice."

"Do you have any suspects?"

I thought about Tic and Carey. "We do."

"Who are they?"

"You know I can't answer that."

Another disgruntled murmur.

"Listen," I said. "Don't you want these guys caught?"

"So how close are we to catching them?"

"One thing we're sure of is they're local, which means they could be walking around among us."

Everyone looked at someone sitting near them.

"So we can keep our eyes and ears open, is that it?" Jared asked.

"Exactly. Most of you deal with the public every day. Scrutinize your customers; listen to what they're telling you. Even if they're not the suspects, they might have heard or seen someone who is without even knowing it."

"Makes sense," somebody said.

"And in the meantime, we're working on this full time, I guarantee you. Those of you who are patients of mine know I've been shifting you over to other doctors here in town who have been nice enough to help out. The FBI and the Park Service are on this, believe me."

"Um, Jordan, while you're standing, there's another matter we'd like to raise with you," Jared ventured.

"What's that?"

"Well, it's the demonstration down at the lake this past weekend."

"What about it?" I asked, although I knew what was coming.

"We understand that in addition to the environmentalists, there were skinheads and militia men down there as well." He paused. "Armed."

A buzz went around the room.

"Where'd they come from?" someone asked.

"I heard there's a nest of them out in the strip somewhere," somebody answered.

"Out by Fredonia?"

"No, further west."

"There's nothing out there but rattlesnakes and scorpions."

"Exactly."

Jared cleared his throat. "What we wanted to discuss with you is the fact that your dad was in the middle of the demonstration."

"So?"

"Well, everyone around here knows about his role in building the dam, of course, and we all admire him for his stand on environmental issues. In fact, I've told him so to his face."

"Get to point, Jared," I said.

"But we can't let that stuff interfere with business. I mean, add armed militia to the murders, well, it's not helping matters any."

"So what are you suggesting?"

He looked around the room, but no one seemed willing to help. "Well, is there some way to corral your dad, at least until the murders are solved and things are back to normal?" he asked in a rush.

"You know, you people have a lot of gall. First of all, my father's not a rabid dog that I can just put on a leash. Second, this town wouldn't even be here if it weren't for the dam, and the dam wouldn't be here without people like my father. Third, my father was there, yes, but he knew nothing beforehand about anyone showing up with weapons, and for your information, according to Luke Russell and Sarah Tanner, he actually helped defuse the situation out on the island when it looked like there was going to be an armed showdown between the militia and the park police."

An uncomfortable silence filled the room.

"So I'd appreciate it if, number one, you let us continue our investigation unimpeded, and number two, you leave my father out of it."

And, with that, I sat down.

Jared, who also had sat down, popped up behind the podium. "Okay. Thank you for the update, Jordan, and you're right, we're not going to solve the crimes ourselves, so let's leave that to law enforcement."

He turned to the group. "And that was an excellent suggestion, by the way, about everyone staying on the alert. But in addition to that, I think we can help ourselves by instituting some damage control."

Everyone was listening.

"Let's begin by all getting on the same page. For example, when people call in or stop by and start asking about the murders, here's what we tell them. One—it's safe at the lake. Eddie, Rooney, and Delhijos were killed in remote parts of the recreation area, places few people ever visit.

"Two—nothing has happened here in town. And Watchman was a cop. I don't want to sound callous, but sometimes police die in the line of duty. And Rooney and Delhijos, these two were just a couple of bad apples, probably involved in a drug deal gone bad. Every community has a criminal element, even Page, although you could point out that one of the dead men was not even a local. Delhijos was from Phoenix."

"Oh, that's good, Jared," Neum said. "Tell out-of-towners that one of the victims was from out of town."

People laughed.

"Good point. All I'm saying is that there were links between the murderers and their victims, and that anyone just vacationing here is probably not in harm's way.

"Finally, the FBI and the Park Service are on it, with help—" here he nodded at me "—from local authorities. Tell people to take reasonable precautions, and odds are, they'll be fine."

"Just let's be careful not to make it sound too scripted in case people talk to more than one of us," Neum suggested. "We don't want them to think we planned this."

"Exactly," said Jared. "Let's think of these as talking points, which is why I didn't make handouts. I don't think we want people reading something to callers over the phone."

People were nodding their heads.

"Then once people get here, it'll be business as usual. When they see we're not curtailing our range of services, that'll make them feel everything is normal. If visitors want to talk about the murders, we've just decided the line we're going to take. In other words, don't run away from the topic, but wait for them to bring it up."

"What about Eddie Watchman?" asked Laman. "These two murders are bringing up his death all over again."

"Again, don't even bring it up if they don't ask. If they do, tell them the rangers have a suspect."

"Not in custody," I said.

Jared looked at me. "But casual inquirers don't have to know that."

JORDAN

All right now, just like the Rangers taught you, I told myself.

Cardinal rule: Always have at least one crab claw attached at all times while climbing.

Then three steps. One, clip the loose claw onto the girder in front of you. Two, unclip the claw behind you. Three, climb past the forward claw. Repeat. In this way I worked myself out onto the bridge trestle. Within a hundred feet I had the rhythm of it.

I silently thanked God for the climbing harness that one of the sheriff's deputies had loaned me. The crab claws—nylon runners with carabiners attached—would be my lifelines. Even so, at every step my testicles were madly attempting to suck themselves back up into the body cavity from which they'd descended oh-so-many years ago. I was so high above the river that I knew I'd have a lot of time to think about what was coming before I hit the water.

I'd been pulling into the parking lot at the office, thinking about last night's chamber meeting, part of me ticked off that people were so impatient, another part understanding their frustration, when Sarah rang and described what she called "another spectacle."

"Same MO as whoever killed Rooney and Delhijos," she said. "From the top of the dam we can see that there's somebody wrapped in the cargo netting."

"And they've hung him—or her – from beneath the bridge?" I asked.

"Dead center. Jordan, you've got to do something."

"These people will go to any length for a piece of theater."

"'These people?'"

"Sounds to me like our unholy alliance of skinheads and enviros, don't you think?"

"I think we need to rescue whoever's hanging in that net."

"On my way."

And then, there I was, placing one foot in front of the other on a steel girder, hearing the faint hum of the turbine generators at the base of the dam far below. Luke, who hates heights, had been game to climb, but I told him I thought I remembered enough from my Ranger days to not kill myself. Now, I wasn't so sure.

I paused to take a deep breath. Sarah was at the other end of my headpiece.

"Thank God there's at least no wind," I said.

"Just enough breeze to keep the heat away," she said. "You all right?"

"As long as I don't look down."

I was almost there. Over my head, cliff swallows had attached a small cluster of their mud nests to the underside of the road bed.

"What I wouldn't give for wings," I told Sarah, as the acrobatic little fliers darted in and out among the steel beams.

"Whoever that poor soul is wrapped in the cargo netting probably feels the same way," she said.

A few more steps and I was there, close enough to lean out and touch the rope. I steadied myself and looked down at the human bundle swinging slowly below me. It appeared to be an old man, speaking into a headset like the one I was wearing. I could hear his voice, but he was too far from me to catch what he was saying.

I called down to him.

He looked up at me, not with relief, but with terror.

Frantically, he poked one arm through the netting and motioned me away.

"Back off!" he screamed. "Back off or he'll kill me!"

I looked around me. He and I were the only ones up there.

"Go back! Get away or he'll blow the rope!" he shouted hoarsely.

Blow the rope? I wondered, then looked up. Damn! Not ten feet over my head a small lump of C4 had been molded around the rope, a detonator poking out of it.

"What's happening?" Sarah asked tersely.

"This rope is rigged to detonate. He's telling me to go away."

"So do what he says."

I had just unclipped my forward crab claw and was turning to reattach it behind me when the charge exploded, scaring the crap out of the cliff swallows.

It didn't do me any good either. I lost my footing and for a precarious second, 700 feet of empty space yawned below me. Somewhere in the background I heard someone scream as I grabbed the strap of my attached claw. My stomach lurched as I spun slowly in thin air.

By the time I had recovered, it was over. I hauled myself up the nylon strap, back to the girder on which I'd been standing. My ears were ringing, the hard bang of the explosion was still echoing in my head. I reattached the loose claw. Only then did I dare look down at the river, where the Park Service boat slowly approached the bundle of cargo netting lying in the water.

Disconsolate, I made my way back to Sarah waiting on the canyon rim below the east end of the bridge.

"Sadistic bastards," I said as I climbed out of the harness. "Whoever blew that rope must have been positioned to see everything. I got close enough to help, and bang."

"You can bet they didn't hang him out there just to leave him," she said. "Your approach was just a convenient trigger."

It felt so good to be standing on solid ground again that I sat down, right on the slick rock. Sarah knelt beside me. I shook my head. "Poor old man," I said. "Sounded like he was praying when I got out there."

She took my hand. "I can't blame him."

"Yeah, but it was funny."

"Funny how?"

"It was in some foreign language, one I'd heard before but couldn't quite put my finger on."

"Could have been a tourist," she said. "They come here from all over the world, you know."

"Something tells me this was no tourist."

Her radio bleeped to tell her the boat had recovered the body. They were bringing it up through the tunnel in the east wall of the canyon below the dam.

"Well, now at least we can start on an ID," she said.

Sitting there, I flashed on my dad's conjecture about the skinheads and environmentalists. Somehow this didn't feel like their work. Too much focus on the murder itself, not enough on the dam or the bridge.

Then I pictured the two goons who had come looking for Tic. I was sure they'd broken into my house and stolen my wallet. Had this been their handiwork too? But why would they kill some random tourist? And Tic had been so sure we'd seen the last of them.

I wondered.

TIC

"Provenance. I like the sound of it," I say. "Sounds French, don't you think?"

"It derives from the French," says the old man, speaking through the headset I'd taped to his head.

The fear trembling in his voice accelerates the rush of blood through my chest. "As I recall, you're the one explained it to me, remember?"

"The day you brought me the Russells. Oh yes, I remember."

I look at the picture of me, the one I'd brought to him a few days earlier.

"I was a little confused at first as to the *provenance* of this picture," I say. "I thoroughly questioned the two morons who showed up looking for me after Delhijos's lesson in lake tides, but neither of them knew where it came from."

Carey and I are holed up among some rocks and trees at the sheer edge of the river canyon, about half a mile downstream from the steel arch bridge, the one that spans the canyon just downstream from the dam. Through the binoculars, we have a clear view of the bridge, as well as the bundle wrapped in cargo netting dangling from beneath it. At this distance, it looks like a little white cocoon hanging by the slenderest of threads 700 feet above the river.

"God knows Carey and I questioned those two—in earnest—before and during our little science experiment. But they just would *not* confirm the source of that picture. Later, we concluded that they really hadn't known who took it.

"Then Carey—God bless his pointed head—recognized that pot in the background. You know, the red and black Kayenta water jug from Keet Seel—the one in your study."

"That one went for a pretty penny," he says. Even over the headset he sounds mournful.

"I'm sure it did. And don't think I don't appreciate it."

"Please—" he begins.

"But how did you know it was me offed Rooney and Delhijos?"

"I read in the paper about the murders. It sounded like your style."

"I like that. My style."

"And I knew the gang would come looking for whoever did it."

He must have looked down at that point. I hear him gasp.

"Dear God—"

I can hear the blood in my ears now. My face feels hot.

"You just made sure they knew it was me," I say.

"I wanted you off my back, so I e-mailed your picture to some friends of mine in Phoenix who knew who to contact."

"I guess in your line of work, you must make all kinds of friends."

Last night, Carey and I had walked him under the bridge at the canyon's edge, wrapped him in the netting, and tied the rope to it. Me being the climber, I had scaled the trestle out to its midpoint, where I attached my end of the umbilicus to one of the girders.

Of course, the fat old bastard had screamed when we rolled him over the edge and he swung out into all that empty space. But that was all part of the fun.

Now it's mid morning and things have really started heating up. I mean, the bridge is crawling with cops, but none of them seem to have figured out yet what the fuck is going on.

"Well, listen to me, going on and on, doing all the talking," I say. "You must have some things on your mind."

"Only that I beg you to spare my life. I'll give you anything."

"Well, you see, that's the problem. You've already done that. Sold off all your pots and rugs, emptied out your accounts just like I asked."

"I've still got a few assets. My house. My car."

"Now what am I going to do with those?"

"You could sell them—anything—I don't know. Only please don't kill me."

This is getting so good I can barely sit still. A million tiny lizards are charging through my veins. "But you're of no more use to me."

"Look. Let's make a deal. You still need money, I'm still in business. Any sale I make, you get half."

I laugh.

"Okay, 60-40, 70-30. I don't care. You can have it all."

"No can do, hombre. You tried to kill me. Our partnership's at an end."

"I'm begging."

"No. You'da been alright you'da just minded your own business. But you had to try and pull something fancy, and now here you are. Look down. See the tiny little police boat down on the river? It's going to look much larger pretty quick.

"Yes, my man. I'm about to teach you the same lesson I taught those two bad boys up in the canyon a couple of weeks ago, a lesson in gravity."

Only silence at his end.

"Think about the word itself for a minute. What do we say when something is important? It's a matter of gravity. When someone's dying? His condition is grave. Look at you. You're in a grave situation—why? Gravity!

"But we don't consider gravity often, do we, given that we can't escape it. Oh, we can float in the bathtub or jump in the pool, but that's only partial relief, only temporary.

"Now you take those two boys died in the canyon. By the time they were done they fully understood just how unforgiving, how inescapable gravity can be. Just as you're about to. It's a tragedy of our human condition, that we can't shed our weight, that our own bodies can be used to kill us."

I giggled. "You could even say they killed themselves. But don't let it get you down," I say, which makes me giggle again. "Sorry. Just cracking myself up. What I wanted to say was we're all on the same journey. Ultimately our weight, our heaviness, pulls us all down, down into—you guessed it—the grave. There's no escaping it. The only difference for you is your trip is about to accelerate. Now, I'll bet you one thing."

"What?" he asks weakly.

"I'll bet you never in your life felt heavier than you feel right now, have you? I'll bet you can just feel that river pulling at you, can't you? You see, that's why angels can't die. It's not time that kills us, it's gravity."

There is no answer, just a soft mumbling in the mouthpiece.

"Is that Hebrew? Don't tell me you're praying! You? Well, if that don't beat all. Who would have thought you believed in God? Pray, then, motherfucker. God knows you'll be seeing him face to face momentarily."

Carey, who is watching through the binoculars, nudges me. I take a look. "Uh, oh. Wait a minute. What's this? Is that the heroic Jordan Hunt I see climbing out to you? Now we can't have any of that. No, I want you to tell old Jordan to back off. Tell him, or I'll drop you right now."

Through the headphones, so loud I wince, I hear the old man scream, "He says to tell you to back off, or he'll kill me! Back off!"

I watch Jordan stop, then put it in reverse.

"That's it, that's it. Out of harm's way, Jordan, old boy. Today is his turn. Yours is coming.

"Well, old man! I'd offer you a last smoke, but, uh, you understand. And a blindfold—shit! Carey, you let me forget the blindfold, damn you!

"So, any last requests?"

The only reply is the low hum of Hebrew through the headphones.

"Okay, then."

Carey hands me the remote. I feel the blood pulsing in the thumb that presses the button. Through the binoculars, I glimpse the sudden puff of white smoke as the charge on the rope detonates, listen to the old man screaming as he begins to fall.

I jump to my feet. I am invincible.

I watch him miss the police boat, but not by more than a few feet.

Turning to Carey, I grin. "Fat fucker. Didn't I tell him once before that his weight was going to be the death of him someday?"

LUANDA

Jordan rolled the body back into the cooler wall in the morgue. "If the fall hadn't killed him, the heart attack would have."

"May have been a mercy," I said.

"Hm. Sheer terror versus high impact," said Sarah. "I don't know."

"Well, it's all academic now, isn't it?" Jordan asked. "Why don't we head back to my office?"

"Fine by me," I said. "These places always give me the creeps."

"So you drove all the way up here by yourself?" Sarah asked. "Where's Frank?"

"Looking into this new-found brotherly love between the militia and the skinheads out on the strip."

"So what else do you know about our guest back there, Luanda?" Jordan asked from behind his desk.

I took a file out of my briefcase. "Name was Vernon Steps, age 72. Lived up in Bluff."

"Bluff? That's not exactly in the neighborhood," Sarah said. "How did you identify him?"

"Checked missing persons. His housekeeper had filed a report. She drove down yesterday and identified him."

"Does she know anything?" Sarah asked.

I shook my head. "Lives in a small house on the grounds. Said he disappeared one night earlier this week."

"And what did Mr. Steps do up there in Bluff?"

That's a good question. Wait 'til you see the house. His heirs are still going to make out okay."

"Still?" Sarah asked.

"Yeah. Couple of things. First, the housekeeper says the place was chock full of Indian rugs, old pots and baskets, arrowheads, that kind of stuff. Then back in January it started disappearing piece by piece. She figures Steps was selling it all off."

"Cashing out, maybe," said Jordan. "He make any big purchases recently?"

"None that we know of, but in checking his financial records, we ran across something else."

"Let me guess," said Sarah. "He'd emptied out and closed everything he'd had in the way of savings."

"You know, you're one smart lady," I said. "I can understand why the doc here would be interested."

I saw Jordan give her a puzzled look.

"Luanda and I have talked," Sarah explained. "It's okay." She turned back to me. "So we're talking blackmail."

"Probably."

"Mr. Steps have any criminal background?" she asked.

"A couple of speeding tickets over the years, but only one arrest. Way back in 1963. Violation of the Antiquities Act of 1906."

"He was a pot hunter?" Jordan asked.

I nodded. "Convicted and fined for illegal excavation of Anasazi artifacts."

"Hmm. I wonder if this relates to Harris," Sarah mused.

"Who?" I asked.

"Guy we arrested last fall in possession of an Anasazi pot he found out in the boonies. Told us some guy drew him a map, but refused to tell us who it was."

"You think it was Steps?"

She shook her head. "Unlikely. It was somebody he met at the Windy Mesa."

"From what you've told us about Steps' house and its furnishings, he doesn't sound like a guy who does his drinking at the Mesa," said Jordan.

"Sounds like he moved up the food chain years ago," Sarah agreed. "Quit digging and started dealing."

"And not just artifacts," I said.

They both looked puzzled.

"Where's Luke, by the way? I've got some good news for him."

"He's checking out another angle on this thing," Sarah said. "Why?"

"We found his great grandfather's paintings in Steps' safe."

"The Russells? But how did Steps get hold of those?"

"Somebody must have figured he could use his connections in the art world to fence them."

"Oh, Luanda! Luke will be thrilled to have them back," Sarah said.

"Guess there's some good come out of this whole nasty business."

"So you're thinking that whoever was blackmailing Steps has now murdered him?" Jordan asked me.

"Wouldn't be the first time."

"But why kill the golden goose? Even if he'd sold off his inventory and cleaned out his accounts, he was still in business."

"He hadn't sold off the Russells yet," Sarah added.

"The murderer might not have known that," I said. "And thought that Steps had run out of golden eggs."

Jordan looked at me.

"You say Frank's checking out the skinhead-environmentalist alliance?" he asked. "Anything happening there?"

"Preliminary. Nothing solid."

"I wonder if they're our boys on this one," he said. "I'm sure they need money, and a flamboyant murder is their style. These could be the same guys who put the crack in Glen Canyon Dam."

"Crack?" I asked.

"Yeah, back in 1981, EarthFirst! unfurled a big banner down the face of the dam to simulate a crack. It was actually quite impressive. Garnered a lot of publicity. I was overseas at the time. My dad sent me pictures."

"You think they'd resort to murder?" I asked.

He shrugged. "I have to admit this didn't feel like their work. On the other hand, Steps was from Bluff. Why bring him all the way down here to kill him, unless you wanted to bring a lot of bad publicity to the dam and the lake?

"After Steps bought it, I also wondered about the two heavies I almost squared off with a couple weeks ago."

"Sarah told me about them. The guys from Phoenix looking for Tic Douloureux. But why would they kill Steps?"

She looked irritated. "They didn't. This is not their style."

"I agree, they're long shots," Jordan said.

"So who does that leave us with?" I asked.

"We're still looking for Douloureux," Sarah said.

Jordan turned to her. "Tic? Why would Tic kill Steps?"

"That's what I'd like to ask him. Jordan, can you find him? Get him to come in?"

"I know he's back in town."

"Then talk to him. Tell him he's got 24 hours to come in on his own or we issue a warrant for his arrest."

Jordan sighed, started to say something, which Sarah interrupted.

"I don't want to be a hardass, but let me remind you that Tic is out on a bond that you paid, Jordan. Furthermore, he was released into your custody."

"Meaning I'm the one ultimately on the hook here," he said.

"Well, you're certainly wiggling like you're on a hook."

"What does that mean?"

"For one, all your gyrations over Tic and his lame explanation of who those two heavies were and how they got his picture."

"The picture wasn't very clear."

"Clear enough that even a nincompoop could see it was not taken outside in a dark parking lot like he said it was."

Jordan said nothing, but his face was getting red. I could see that Sarah knew she had hurt his feelings.

She said, "Oh, sweetie, I understand your loyalty to Tic, and I love you for it, but you know I'm right. Rooney, Adolpho, and now Steps. Tic is in this up to his eyeballs."

He looked at her for a minute. "The picture does raise some questions."

Sarah looked like she was going to shout "Hallelujah!" Instead, she said, "At least that's progress."

LUKE

"C'mon, it's as plain as the nose on your face," I said from my desk. "You paid Rooney's bond just to get him out of jail so you could kill him. Adolpho was just along for the ride, but you couldn't leave him behind as a witness."

Seated across from me, Tic was using a toothpick to clean under a finger nail, his face as bland as an empty dinner plate. Sarah leaned against the wall by the window.

I wanted to nail this guy so bad I could taste it, but I knew I had to be careful. He was not going to simply blunder into incriminating himself. I wanted to lead him through what we already knew—and only what he knew we knew—to see if he'd bite on something, without divulging anything that might give him a leg up on us.

"Then the heavies show up as payback, and they magically disappear," I continued.

"Probably just back from whence they came, in a manner of speaking," Tic said. "And why would I kill Rooney?"

"Eliminate a competing dealer."

"But that's assuming I'm a dealer, an assumption for which you have no proof. You also have no proof I killed Rooney and his friend, or you'd have me under arrest."

"We do have you under bond," Sarah pointed out.

"But that's for another charge—possession—a charge, by the way, whose chief witness is now dead."

"The charge still stands."

He looked up from his manicure. "Would I have come in voluntarily if I thought you had anything on me?"

"Let's talk about Steps," I said. "You sucked him dry, and when he had no more to give, you killed him. Plain and simple."

He looked up at me. "This guy, Mr. Steps, is that what you called him? Now what gives you the idea that he and I were ever acquainted?"

"The paintings, Douloureux. That's the link. I know it was you broke into my place and stole the paintings."

"What makes you so sure?" he asked casually.

"That night in the Windy Mesa with Jordan and Sarah, back before Christmas. Sarah told you Charles Russell was my grandfather."

"Sounds like a lot of people knew that."

"But you're the only one with a bad conduct discharge."

No reaction.

"So you're the one clued Jordan into that, are you?" he asked.

"You know I did. Which brings me back to my point. You have no visible means of support, Douloureux. No job. No pension. Those paintings would have fetched a good price."

"I'll have to take your word on that."

"But you'll be happy to know that Mr. Steps never got around to selling them. FBI recovered them at his place in Bluff."

"Good for them."

I sat back in my chair. "So we've figured out that much. But why Steps, way over there in Bluff?"

Douloureux continued cleaning his nails.

"You just didn't want somebody fencing the paintings in your own backyard?" I asked. "I have a feeling there's more to it than that. I mean, how did you come across this guy in the first place?"

"The Yellow Pages?" he asked.

Sarah could see I was about to go over the desk after him.

"Mr. Douloureux, Officer Russell has been checking your background," she said. "You might be interested to know he's uncovered a few discrepancies."

"Do tell."

"For example, you told Jordan you were dishonorably discharged for freezing under fire, resulting in the deaths of two of your men," she said. "But in fact, you were discharged for attacking your CO after the mission failed. Isn't that so?"

"And your point is?"

"Why did you lie?"

Tic sat forward in his chair. "Let me ask you something, pretty lady. You ever lie to hide something you were ashamed of? I count Jordan as a friend. We go back a long way together. I just didn't want him to know about it.

"See, I moved back to Page to try and put my life back together, a process your partner here seems determined to abort. Even after I agreed to come down here and submit myself to your questioning."

"And you're a guy doesn't like questions, right?" I said.

He shrugged, said, "Just enjoying my constitutional right to privacy." He looked up from his manicure. "You know, I'm starting to get the feeling you don't like me."

"Let me be the first to confirm that, Douloureux. I don't like you."

"And why's that?"

"Because I think your return to Page and the occurrence of these murders is not a coincidence."

"Really."

"For example, Jordan also told me you were a lead climber in the SEALs."

He nodded. "That boy is just a fount of information, isn't he?"

"Well, whoever climbed out under that bridge to suspend Steps in that cargo netting knew what he was doing."

"What's the big deal?" he asked. "Jordan climbed out there."

"How'd you know that?" I shot back.

He paused only for a split second before answering, but long enough for me to know I'd caught him out.

"It was all over town," he said breezily.

"So where'd you learn to climb?"

"Just a gift, I guess."

"Like the swimming?" I asked. "All that bull back in the bar at Christmas about Aqualung? Maybe in addition to the swimming, you did a lot of climbing as a kid."

"Maybe."

"You said you and Jordan went way back. I asked him about that. He said you and your dad used to disappear occasionally for a few days, even a week at a time. Even during school."

"What about it?"

"Well, where did you go?"

"Oh, you know, camping. Fishing."

"Out in the canyons?"

He shrugged. "Pretty much all over."

"Your dad a big outdoorsman, was he? That doesn't square with what I heard. I understood from asking around that he was the town ne'er-do-well, turned his hand to anything that might make him a fast buck."

Tic laughed. "That sounds like dear old dad, all right."

"Furthermore, I did the math. This must have been before the dam started backing up the lake in '63, and probably for a few years after that."

He stopped smiling. "So what's your point?"

"Mr. Steps was a dealer in antiquities."

"Antiquities?"

"Anasazi pots and artifacts."

"So?"

"So Mr. Steps, given his age and his obesity, obviously was no climber. And yet many of the ruins I've seen in this area are almost inaccessible."

Tic smiled again. "So you're saying my old man hunted pots and sold them to Steps."

"You used to climb for your old man, Douloureux?"

He stood up and stretched.

"Officer Russell, you're doing some pretty risky climbing yourself, going way out on a limb," he said.

"Think so?"

"You like to climb, Officer Russell?"

"Scared to death of heights."

"That's wise. They can kill you. Correct me if I'm wrong, but I think you're accusing me of murder."

We locked eyes.

"It's more than murder, Douloureux. I'm accusing you personally of being a sick fuck—pardon my language, Sarah—a whack job who gets off on these murders. Except for maybe the first one, Eddie Watchman. Maybe that wasn't planned—it was just Eddie in the wrong place at the wrong time. But that's what tipped the scale, pushed you off the bubble, wasn't it? The little bubble of sanity you had managed to wrap yourself in after the discharge. Rooney, Adolpho, Steps. You couldn't just murder them, you had to bury them up to their necks or wrap them in a cargo net, take away all their power."

I got up, came around the desk, put my mouth close to his ear. "I'm right, aren't I, Douloureux. It's all about control. You're just a pathetic freak who gets his rocks off hearing the other guy beg, watching him squirm, seeing the terror in his eyes.

"It's better than sex, isn't it? I'd be willing to bet you can't do it with a woman, can you, Douloureux? I'll bet this is only way you can get your jollies, you sick son of a bitch."

He turned and stared me in the face. "You should really see about getting that psychosis looked at, Officer Russell. They have medication for that nowadays."

Sarah jumped away from the wall and grabbed my arm.

"You'd like to, wouldn't you?" he asked.

"Luke, sit back down."

"Better listen to the lady."

"Get out of my sight."

"Now that's downright unfriendly," he said, pushing his chair up to my desk. "I think we're done here, unless you're going to arrest me—again."

He reached the door, turned back to me.

"Glad you got your paintings back," he said over his shoulder.

TIC

Somebody in Russell's office must have leaked the fact that he was questioning me about the murders, because I was mobbed the moment I stepped outside park headquarters. I mean these people were plain rude, shoving microphones and recorders in my face, pointing cameras, shouting questions at me.

There was only one thing to do. They left me no choice. I raised my hands above my head. They immediately fell silent. Nice. I can't imagine Jesus calmed the waves any more quickly.

"All right, now. One at a time," I said.

Instantly, a dozen of them barked questions at me. Guess that wasn't going to work.

Again I raised my hands. "Okay, okay. Let's do it this way," I said. "I'll pick people one by one for questions." I looked over the crowd. At the front was an older woman who, although short and round, had managed to work her way closest to me.

I pointed. "You."

"Your name is Dick Douloureux?" she asked.

I laughed. "That's Tic," I said, spelling it for her.

We then confirmed I lived in Page, retired military. All that.

"Were you being questioned as a witness to Steps' death or as a suspect?"

"I'm a suspect, although I'd like to point out that I did come in voluntarily."

"You've got nothing to hide, is that it?"

"Now I didn't say that, little lady. All I'm telling you is I came in as a law-abiding citizen who wants to help the authorities get this whole thing cleared up . . .Also, as a Page native, I sympathize with the local business people, my friends and neighbors, who are losing money because of these unsolved murders."

I pointed at a gorgeous blonde a few feet away. "Yes darlin'."

"What was your relationship to the victim?"

"We weren't related."

Big eye rolls all around, but she smiled. "I mean, did you know Steps?"

"The authorities seem to think I did."

"Well, did you?"

I pointed at a short guy who looked like he'd slept in his suit.

"Next question."

"Why do the police suspect you?"

I shrugged. "Judging from their questions, it has something to do with my childhood here in Page."

"Can you be more specific?"

"No."

I could feel their frustration mounting. Like I gave a shit.

"You said you were retired military. Can you tell us more?"

"I was a Navy SEAL."

A murmur went through the crowd. Oooh, special ops. I knew they ate that shit up.

A tall guy in the back raised his hand.

"You—with the hand. Manners count."

"What was your team specialty?"

"Next question."

"Explosives? Climbing?"

These guys were quick.

"I said next question," pointing at a woman who was practically jumping up and down, quivering.

"Were you present at Steps' death?"

"I was not nearby."

"Where were you?"

"Next question."

"Do you have an alibi?"

"I think alibis are for people who have done something wrong."

"So you're saying you've done nothing wrong?"

"Sister, we're all guilty of something."

"Do you know Dr. Hunt, the man who climbed out to try to save Steps?"

"I heard about that. Very courageous of him."

"We know he also grew up in Page. So do you know him?"

"Anyone asked him if *he* knows *me*?" I asked. "I mean *really* knows me?"

Silence. I watched them look at each other.

"Why don't you ask him?"

"C'mon, Mr. Douloureux. It's a simple yes or no question." This was from a big guy, ex-jock probably.

I put the stink eye on him. "Listen, you pack of hyena assholes. You're the ones falling all over each other to ask me questions. You're the ones cornered me. So I'll answer what I want. You want to talk to *me*, you go by *my* rules."

Big guy again. "But you're not answering our questions."

"Are you whining?"

I looked down at the short lady.

"Was that a whine I heard?"

This was great. I could say anything to them and they wouldn't leave.

"Maybe you and me could discuss your heartburn once we're through here," I said.

He wasn't sure what to say to that, so he wisely shut his pie hole.

I pointed at a good-looking brunette with a foxy face.

"Are you a suspect in the two murders back in May?"

"I've not been charged as such."

"Did you know either of those victims?"

"No one's been able to prove that."

"You're loving this, aren't you, Mr. Douloureux?"

I smiled. "You want to go home with me, honey, I'll show you what I love," I said. "Give you a great big exclusive."

She just smiled and shook her head.

"So, did you kill him?"

"Steps? I suspect Mr. Steps was a man who was hoist with his own petard."

You should have seen the looks on their faces. They didn't know what to say.

"You might be interested to know that a tourist captured Steps' fall on video."

"Oh? I haven't seen that yet."

TIC

"Sold it to CNN for 50 grand."

"Is this a great country or what?"

*****

"You ever notice it's hotter in a city on a hot day?"

Carey turned in the seat of the van, looked at me like I was asking him a trick question as we drove into Salt Lake.

"Must be all this concrete and asphalt," I ventured.

He kept his eyes on me.

"What's your idea?" I asked.

He evidently didn't have one.

"Maybe the drought," I suggested.

He just turned his gaze back to the highway.

Dumb as a box of rocks.

Fletcher's shop was in a row of pawn shops down on East 200. We pulled round back.

"Your stuff's right over here," Fletch said.

I had called ahead with what we needed. He had it all in boxes in a corner of the big back room.

"Let's go through it," I said.

He started pulling items out as I checked them against my list.

"Generator first, a Coleman 6875 with the Honda engine, inverter technology, still sealed in its original box," he said.

"Run 11 hours on a tank, right?" I asked.

"At 50 percent load."

"This one of them fell off the truck?" Carey asked with a grin.

"In a manner of speaking, yes," said Fletch. "That's why the price is right, you understand. Damaged merchandise."

There wasn't a scratch on the box.

Everything else was the same: the weatherproof speakers, the watertight CD players, even the 100-watt amp and the control board.

"That there was one hard-to-find item, my friend," said Fletch. "I had to go through several different contacts for that. Finally found one up in Twin Falls, of all places."

A couple spools of wire with assorted clips and plugs finished it out.

"Oh, and this," Fletch said, pulling an iPod mini from his pocket. "My boy put a playlist together for you. Let's take a listen."

We followed him through a curtained doorway into the shop. He dropped the iPod into its dock, cranked the volume. The place filled with the mostly ungodly noise you can imagine.

"I must be getting old," I shouted. "They call that music? Guy sounds like he's being strangled and ass-fucked at the same time."

Fletch laughed, switched it off.

"He only downloaded the most deadly of the death metal," he said. "Per your instructions."

Carey still had his hands over his ears.

"Hope it doesn't scare the guests away," he said.

"What are you having, a lawn party?" Fletch asked

"Yeah, a little get together."

"Gonna be pretty wild, huh?"

I looked at him.

"The music, I mean," he said.

"You're done asking questions, let's settle up," I said.

He gave me the number in his head. "That's with the quantity discount," he added.

"Still a hell of a lot of money," I said.

"Hey, you ain't gonna find these prices at Best Buy."

"I know, I know," I said. "Listen, I appreciate what you've done. And on short notice."

"Always a pleasure doing business with you, Mr. Douloureux."

It tickled Carey to order the businessman's special. We had waited thirty minutes for Pruitt. Now I wasn't sure he was going to show, so I told Carey to go ahead and order. I had them bring me another drink.

"Damn, Carey, can't you take that hat off?"

He was wearing his usual tattered straw with the sweat stained band. He removed it and placed it on the seat beside him.

"You seem a little jumpy," he said.

"I don't like to wait. Makes me wonder if something's gone wrong."

He looked over my shoulder, pointed with his fork.

"This him?" he asked.

Then Pruitt and I were hugging, clapping each other on the back. He was dressed in jeans, with a tailored sports coat, boots, and a hand tooled leather belt.

"Apologize for the wait," he said.

"So, you keeping busy?"

"Busy as the law allows," he said with a wink. "And then some."

"Same old Pruitt. What're you drinking?"

We got him set up, I introduced him to Carey, explained that Pruitt and I had served together as basic instructors at Camp Kerry in the Cuyamacas.

"'Til you shipped out to Afghanistan," he said.

"And you got caught shipping that load of—what was it—parachutes?"

"Among other things."

"To Pakistan, was it?"

"You gonna tell everything you know?"

I laughed.

"Pruitt's like me," I explained to Carey. "Parted company with the US Navy on less than friendly terms."

Pruitt raised his glass.

"Here's to the motherfuckers!" he exclaimed.

"Salud."

We sat back after lunch.

"You got my list?"

"Yessirree," he said, patting a pocket of his sports coat.

"We all set?"

"I made a substitution, but I think you'll like it."

"So long as we still got the same killing power," said Carey.

I slapped him up behind the head, looked at him to ask 'Did you forget where you are?'

Pruitt was looking at him like he'd grown a second head.

"Let's get out of here," I said.

Out in the parking lot, the sun felt hot enough to melt the asphalt beneath our feet.

"Let's all go in the van," I said.

We got in, Pruitt made a call. "We're on our way. Everything look okay?" He listened for a moment before he nodded. "All right, unlock the door, but leave it closed, understand?"

He hung up and directed me to a nearby self-storage complex and the unit where one of his guys was waiting.

Inside, he had it set up with steel shelves and racks, bins, crates on the floor.

"Let's check the rifles first," I said.

"This is what I was talking about," he said, lifting the top off a wooden crate. "Tic, meet the Heckler & Koch HK416."

I held it in my hands, put it to my shoulder.

"Good balance. Feels a little heavier than the M4. What round does it fire?"

"It's about a pound heavier, but it fires the same 5.56x45mm NATO as the M4."

"But that was always a problem with the M4 in close quarters."

Pruitt nodded. "Not enough fragmentation. But remember that was only over 100 meters."

"You're right, we'll be working closer than that."

"But if you're worried about it, I think I might have the solution for you."

He reached into a bin, pulled out a box of cartridges. "The Mk 262. It's a 77-grain bullet, 25 percent heavier, and better fragmentation than the M855 ball. Another thing, you're down at the lake, remember the 416 has over-the-beach capability. You get water in it, it's still going to fire."

"Let's look at the M4 anyway," I said.

"A comparison shopper," he said with a grin.

He stepped over to another crate, drew one out and handed it to me. It settled into my arms like a lover. "Now this is what I like."

"This is what you know, is all," Pruitt said. "Believe me, the 416 is a better rifle. Remember all the trouble we had with the M4 heating up and jamming?"

"I can't argue with you on that."

He fished a piece of paper out of the crate. "Read this," he said. "It's a dust competition they ran last year between the 416 and the M4. Six thousand rounds apiece."

I scanned the page. "Eight hundred eighty two stoppages for the M4."

"Compared to only 233 for the 416."

"That's a big difference."

"Four sixteen's a new design, man," he said. "Uses a short-stroke piston forces the bolt carrier to retract. Keeps propellant gases from entering the weapon."

"So it stays cleaner and there's less fouling."

"Reduces cleaning time, parts last longer. I could go on and on."

"So who's using them?"

"Our guys are trying them out."

"Didn't somebody have these in Afghanistan? The Norwegians?"

"And the Poles."

"You fired it yet?"

"We went out last weekend," he said. "I really think you'll like it. And keep in mind, this is the full-on military version, not the semi-automatic.

"What about accessories?"

"It's got the rails you can fit anything on it that you can the M4."

"Grenade launcher?"

He went to a box across the room, came back with one.

"The M203?" I asked.

"The very same."

"I don't want shrapnel grenades."

"You want stun grenades?"

"No, concussion."

"Got 'em."

"You need anything in the way of explosives?" Pruitt asked. "C4? Semtex?"

"I'm okay."

"How'd that C4 work on your last job? You only bought a handful of it."

"All I needed. Worked like a dream."

He pulled a couple of M14 antipersonnel mines from a box.

I shook my head. "I'll be rolling my own."

"You all set up? You don't have a source, I know someone who knows someone."

I held up my hand. "That's our last stop. Got a guy's got me all set up. Let's look at pistols."

We squared accounts. I asked him, "You know anybody knows how to work with all this?"

"What's up?"

"I got something coming up I'm going to need a little help."

"I know some guys down in your neck of the woods always interested in picking up some spare coin."

"They organized?"

Pruitt nodded. "Militia, along with a handful of skinheads."

I laughed. "Now that sounds like a marriage made in heaven."

He shrugged. "They're experienced."

"I don't know," I said. "Lotta those guys they're playing fantasy league ball."

He stepped closer so Carey and his guy couldn't hear. "I'm given to understand they pulled off the Wells Fargo job earlier this year," he said softly. "Here in Salt Lake."

"No shit. Where they all had police uniforms on?"

He nodded.

"Cops never caught up with them?"

"Not yet. So how many guys you need?"

"Not more than half a dozen."

"How much are we talking?"

I gave him a number.

He said, "I'm sure they'd be interested. What kind of work?"

"You just tell them I'm looking, okay?"

"Can do."

"This gonna be today?"

Pruitt pulled out his phone, opened the door and walked outside. He returned after a minute. "I left a message."

"All right, call me."

"Sure thing," he said, turned to his man. "Keep an eye outside."

He turned to me. "Let's load you up."

We had followed our instructions to the letter. Now we'd been sitting out at the intersection of two dirt roads in the dark somewhere east of Capitol Reef for at least an hour.

"I know he's out there where he saw us drive up," I said. "Making sure we're alone."

"Kinda paranoid, isn't he?" Carey asked.

"Slade? Stuff he sells, he needs to be."

I checked the GPS again. Right on the money.

"So when's he supposed to be here?" Carey asked.

"Don't worry."

"I know. You called ahead."

I punched his shoulder. "You're learning."

Sure enough, not a minute later headlights bumped down the dirt road toward us. Old Ford one-ton with a camper shell.

I'd never realized it before, but seeing Slade and Carey together made me question if they hadn't been raised by the same wolf. I introduced them to each other, wondering if they saw the likeness too.

Slade set his beer can on the hood, walked around to the back, opened the camper shell window.

I shone the flashlight inside on bags marked "Ammonium Nitrate." Beside them were a couple of jerry cans. "That the diesel?"

He nodded. "Drained it from my front end loader a couple days ago, nobody noticed."

"Looks like you got everything."

He reached inside the bed, pulled out a box. "This the Tovex you wanted."

"And the blasting caps?"

"Got 'em up here in the cab."

"Class Bs?" I asked.

"Just like you ordered," he said, handing them to me. "Just out of curiosity, you ever work with this stuff before?"

"Oh, yeah."

"You're down at the lake—don't get it wet."

"We used to cook this stuff up along with a dozen other things in the kitchen sink during qualification training."

"It's damned hard to get anymore since that boy blew up the federal building down in OK City. You need a license to buy it."

"How are things at the mine?"

"Same old, same old. Too much work and not enough pay."

"Well, this should help," I said, handing him a thick envelope.

He touched it to the brim of his ball cap, nodded his head. "'Preciate it," he said. "I 'spect I'll be reading about you in the papers, too."

"You probably already have, old timer."

SARAH

"Say what you want about the wages of sin," Jordan said, "this guy had a nice house."

We were standing by the fountain in the expensively xeriscaped courtyard admiring the handsomely carved front door, and the way the vigas supporting the roof extended over the patterned concrete drive to form a porte-cochere trellised with morning glories.

In the two hours it had taken to drive up to Bluff, the day had warmed up nicely. The heat of the day was just beginning, and I was content to stand in it for a few minutes before we went inside.

"Cool and quiet in here," said Jordan.

"Because it's adobe," I said, noting the expensive woodwork framing the deep-set windows and doors. Artfully placed skylights brought out the earth tones in the tile floor. Overhead, the viga and latilla ceiling had been worked in a beautiful herringbone pattern.

"Look at this kitchen," said Jordan. "Steps must have been a gourmet cook."

"Loved having a gourmet kitchen, anyway. That's a $10,000 48-inch Wolf range and a built-in 42-inch Sub-Zero side-by-side." I ran my hand over the counter top. "Marble."

Jordan was amused. "You seem to know a lot about this stuff."

"Catalog shopping."

We toured the master bath with its Jacuzzi and bidet off the lavishly furnished master bedroom. Everywhere we saw built-in electronics—big, flat screen, wall-mounted TVs, surround-sound speakers, intercoms, discreet lighting. The furniture in the living room and the study was a tasteful mix of western antiques and lavish roll-and-tuck leather sofas and easy chairs.

But all the showcases and the built-in shelves were empty, the floor and wall rugs gone, the plastered walls bare, the paintings that once hung under the display lamps sold off, along with the bronzes and sculptures, only their pedestals still standing in corners all around the house.

I shivered. With Steps dead, this place had the same feel the trading post had when my dad died.

A bay window seat looked out on the pool, which had a rock cascade at one end, all surrounded by a high wall. I stood and listened for a moment to the water falling.

"Reminds me of *The Secret Garden*," I said, "only with a pool."

I wrapped myself in an afghan I found hanging on the back of a chair, and sat down in the window seat. "Come sit beside me. We need to talk." I took his hand. "Did you finally find Tic? He came in yesterday for questioning."

He shook his head. "He must have come in on his own. How did it go?"

"Luke tried, but he couldn't lay a glove on him. We couldn't hold him."

"I'm not surprised."

"What does that mean?"

He looked startled. "Oh, I didn't mean about the whole guilty or innocent thing. I only meant that Tic can be the artful dodger."

"You're not kidding."

"I know Luke thinks Tic stole the paintings the FBI found here."

"Did you also know that Tic attacked his CO when he was in Afghanistan and that was the reason for his dishonorable discharge?" I asked.

"That's not what he told me."

"Jordan, you know Luke. You know he double checked, said Tic nearly killed the man."

"Well, I can understand his not wanting that known."

"But why wouldn't he tell *you*, his best friend?"

"Sarah, it's been a lot of years since we were best friends."

"Luke thinks he's hiding a lot more than that."

"Such as?"

"That he not only killed Steps, but Rooney and Adolpho as well."

Jordan was quiet for a minute, looking out at the cascade on the far side of the pool. "I think it's a big jump from assaulting your CO to murdering three people," he said. "What makes him think Tic is responsible for killing those other two?"

I shrugged. "For one thing, those two goons you ran into showing up looking for Tic so soon after Rooney and Adolpho were found."

"Could have been a coincidence."

"C'mon, Jordan. Even you said that was fishy."

"What I said was I thought the photo of him raised some questions."

"Tic knew you were there at the bridge, and that you tried to save Steps."

"Again, it doesn't definitely prove he was there. And Tic being guilty of those murders still doesn't explain Eddie's death."

"You're the one that said you thought he and Rooney and Adolpho were all drug-related killings," I reminded him.

"But why would Tic kill them?" he asked.

"Same reason he killed Steps—money. Luke thinks he's moving in, taking over the drug trade at the lake."

"You and Luke and the rest of the team run into a lot of drugs down there at the lake?"

"All the time."

"I know it's a problem in town, and out on the res. I see a lot of it at the office. But let's face it, the goons are apparently gone, and Tic is still around." He looked out the window, then back at me. "I guess I should have seen this coming after Luke asked me all those questions about growing up with Tic."

"Anything else happen back then when you were kids?"

Again, he gazed out the window, his face troubled. Finally, he began. "The summer after eighth grade, we were out fishing on the lake one day, and our boat sank."

"What happened?"

He laughed quietly. "Well, it was pretty stupid, actually. Tic had a gun he'd taken from home, and he shot out the bottom of the boat. We tried to row to shore, but we had to swim for it."

I watched Jordan's eyes fill with pain.

"I know what happened to Stevie, Jordan," I said. "Luke told me."

"Did he tell you that Stevie drowned because Tic saved me instead?"

I squeezed his hand with both of mine. "Oh, Jordan. I'm so sorry."

Tears filled his eyes. "Stevie and I were both going down for the last time. We were so close to shore. I think Tic thought he could save us both. He was such a strong swimmer, even then."

The tears came and he couldn't talk for a few minutes.

"That was the dividing line, you see? Stevie's death. Things began changing after that. We'd been like brothers, but from that point on, it was like we were walking on opposite rims of a canyon, moving further and further apart as time went by, with no way to get back.

"Ever since then, I've owed a debt to Tic I can never repay. And I think Tic has spent his life second-guessing himself over why he saved me instead of Stevie." He wiped his eyes. "The worst part is that letting Stevie drown broke something in Tic—I think—the same thing that'd made us friends. He'd saved me, but then discovered I couldn't compensate him for Stevie's death, which drove a wedge between us."

We sat in silence for a few minutes, watching the water burbling over the rocks of the cascade and into the pool.

"Well, you need to prepare yourself, Jordan, because Luke is building a pretty strong case. He's not there yet, but you know Luke. He'll get there."

Jordan turned from the window, looked into my eyes. "I need to know where you are on all this."

I held his gaze for a few seconds.

"I think Tic is our man."

As we were leaving, Jordan spotted the elaborate security system panel by the front door. On the ceiling above, a security camera, like those throughout the house, looked down on us.

"Luanda said all the tapes are missing," he said.

"No surprise there."

"Ironic, isn't it, that Steps spent thousands of dollars to prevent someone from breaking in and stealing his collection, only to be the inside person himself who sold it all away. Hmm. Look at this," he said, reaching out to rub a small half cylinder of metal attached to the door jamb. It was inscribed with foreign writing of some kind.

"What is it?"

"A mezuzah. In Deuteronomy, God commanded the people of Israel to love Him, and to post that command on the gates and doorways of their homes."

"So Steps was Jewish?"

"Must've been," he said, then stopped. "That's it!"

"That's what?"

"That's the language Steps was speaking before he fell—Hebrew!"

"Are you sure?"

He was nodding enthusiastically.

"When I was stationed in the Middle East, I heard it all the time. Steps was praying in Hebrew before he died!"

"He was killed because he was a Jew?"

"Exactly! The skinheads, the white supremacists, the neo-Nazis that Grady saw at the protest. They hate Jews!"

"So Steps' murder was a hate crime?"

"It makes sense, doesn't it?"

"You mean they couldn't find any Jews closer to Page than Bluff?"

"Hey, not only was he Jewish, but a pot hunter as well, which would make him a target for the environmentalists, too."

"They being so PC and all," I said sarcastically, "with Steps disturbing the ancestral gravesites of today's minority Native Americans."

"Sarah, it *is* possible."

I just shook my head and smiled. "You remind me of something my mother used to tell me."

"What's that?"

"There is none so blind as him who will not see."

CONNECTION

The rusted-out 4-wheel-drive Suburban diesels to a stop in front of the storage room, where Pruitt's man stands by the unlocked but unopened door. Two men, one of them a bald mountain with a swastika inked into his forehead, climb out as Pruitt pulls up behind them in a sporty new BMW Z4 Roadster.

The smaller man approaches the expensive car, a two-seater convertible, runs his hand admiringly along the fender. "They make a nice car, those Germans," he says in heavily accented English.

"You're the man should know, Conrad," says Pruitt. "You ever drive one of these you lived back in the Fatherland?"

Conrad shakes his head.

"Maybe I'll let you take her out for a spin one of these days."

Conrad looks Pruitt up and down appreciatively. "Yah, Pruitt, you drive a German car—you look German, you know?"

"How's that, pard?"

"Your clothing, your—how do you say—grooming, yah, looks very German, did you know?"

"I didn't, but thanks anyway."

"You remind me of when I was in Germany," he says. "At the ranch over here, the water we have is bad. Bad smell."

The big bald man walks over.

Conrad glances at him. "No one is clean," he says, and adds regretfully, "Not even me."

"You two done fondling each other, maybe we can get what we came for," the big man says gruffly.

Pruitt puts out his hand, smiles big. "Big Bill Baldwin. How you doing?"

"The same. Just came up for some ammo."

"Well, let's step inside then, shall we?"

Inside, Pruitt says, "I called you guys yesterday. You get my message?"

Baldy shakes his head. "We don't get service out there."

"Bill worries anyway about the government monitoring our cell phones."

"Just another advantage of living in the middle of nothing," says Pruitt.

"You got a problem with that?" Baldy asks.

"Personally, yes. I'm like Conrad here. I've developed an appreciation of the finer things."

"Provided by a poisoned system that's already falling down around you," says the big man contemptuously.

"Speaking of falling down, how are things out at the ranch?"

"Like I said, we need ammo."

"Right this way," says Pruitt, leading them to a bin on a rack. He hands the boxes to Baldy. "That it?"

"What's the matter?" asks Baldy defensively. "That ain't enough?"

Pruitt shrugs.

"So what was the message?" Conrad asks.

"Oh, yeah. Had a customer in yesterday bought a shitload of stuff."
He walks over to a crate on the floor, pulls a rifle from it. "Bought several of these," he says, handing it to Conrad "Said he was planning something, needed some help."

Pruitt watches Conrad examine the rifle, put it to his shoulder, and sight down the barrel. "How would you like to handle one of those?" he asks the German.

"This is a fine weapon," he says. "Heckler and Koch. I know them, made in Oberndorf in Baden-Wurttemberg."

"Well, anyway, no offense," says Pruitt, "but I know from our previous transactions that you guys are chronically short of cash, and this guy had plenty, so I told him you might be interested. In fact, this guy is from down your way. Lake Powell. Asked me if I knew anybody knew how to use one of these."

"You didn't give him our names, did you?" Baldy asks abruptly

"No, no, don't get your shorts in a twist. I just told him you guys were in the neighborhood. So should I call him?"

"What is he planning?" Conrad asks.

"Didn't say. Told me he'd discuss that with you if you were interested. So are you?"

"Give us a minute," says Baldy.

He and Conrad step away to talk. It doesn't take long.

"Call him, tell him we'll listen," says Baldy.

"Okay now, you understand I want a cut here for bringing you all together."

"A—what is the term—finder's fee?" asks Conrad.

"Your English is improving by the minute, my friend."

"You talk to your fellow," says Conrad. "Any fee will come out of his pocket, not ours."

"Let me step outside here, see if we can't arrange a meeting."

"Good," says Conrad.

SARAH

Luke held one of the paintings up to the light from the picture window. "I'm so happy to have these back. Thank you, both."

"Luanda actually found them in Steps' safe at his house in Bluff," I said.

"C'mon, let's put 'em back up."

He handed one to Jordan as I stepped back to judge the results.

"I wonder why Steps never sold these," said Luke.

"Luanda thinks he liked them so much he'd decided to keep them for himself," said Jordan.

"Can't say as I blame him."

I looked around. "I'd say you've put the place back to rights."

"It's taken some serious time and cash," he said, walking to a wall shelf, from which he took down one of the kerosene lanterns. "I found chimneys for the two lanterns. Not the same as the originals and not antique, but they fit."

He replaced the lantern, walked into the dining room. "Not everything in the corner cupboard was broken. And a lot of it I just glued back together. It's too bad. Some of that stuff belonged to my great-grandparents, Charlie and Nancy. I got the clock repaired up in Salt Lake, but I haven't gotten it to keep good time yet. Of course, it didn't keep good time before Douloureux pushed it over."

Jordan said, "You still think it was him."

"I'm sorry, Jordan, but I do." He adjusted an antique mirror on the wall. "Repairing the wood wasn't too bad. I found somebody in Phoenix could handle that, but the broken mirror. You just can't get that kind of glass anymore, not unless you come across the exact size you need."

Jordan gazed around the room. "Looking at what happened here, I'd say I was lucky to have lost only my wallet."

"And whoever it was took it right off the nightstand while you were laying there asleep."

Jordan nodded. "Guys were smooth, I'll give them that."

"What I don't know is how Douloureux got by the dogs," said Luke. "Lewis, I know, is a pushover, but Clark can be ornery, especially with someone he doesn't know. And he knew exactly what day to show up, which suggests surveillance."

Jordan waved his hand around the room. "All this must have been pure spite," he said. "If all he wanted was the paintings, why break the place up—"

"He was sending me a message. This was revenge for me checking his background."

"I was surprised *my* place wasn't torn up," said Jordan. "Those two guys looking for Tic seemed like the type who'd enjoy that."

"Jordan, I think if it was those two, they'd have just beaten you up instead," I said. "And what good would your wallet have done them?"

"Remember they did threaten to come find me if I didn't turn Tic over to them."

"But what about the pot of coffee? That sounds more like somebody who just wanted to show you they could enter your house and walk out again without you even knowing it."

"I have to agree with Sarah," said Luke. "There was an in-your-face-you-can't-catch-me quality to both break-ins."

"Just like we've talked about the murders," I said. "Just the fact of them is enough. Who the victims are or in this case what's stolen is secondary."

"I agree it could have been Tic who came in, and it could even have been Tic who did this," Jordan said. "And there is that same quality to the murders, but *none* of that means he's the murderer."

"Now that Sarah and I have questioned him, I'm convinced he's just toying with us," said Luke.

"But I think we can make an equally convincing case for the skinhead militia," Jordan said.

I just shook my head.

"Speaking of the skinheads, have you talked to any family friends out on the strip?" Jordan asked Luke.

"We know the neo-Nazis have staged several rallies in Arizona over the past six months targeting illegal aliens, particularly those crossing the Mexican border," said Luke. "My friends tell me they've seen a couple of the same guys from the TV news reports around town in Fredonia and Colorado City."

"So they're out there and they're active," said Jordan.

Luke shrugged. "I'm not sure it means much, but we can't afford to let it go."

"We're going out there tomorrow to check it out," I said.

"Mind if I ride along, since it's my theory?" Jordan asked.

"Sorry, but we know these guys are heavily armed," said Luke. "It could be dangerous."

"I'd still like to go."

"We're just going to ask them some questions. We'll fill you in when we get back."

We stood in the dooryard a few minutes before leaving.

"Weather forecast says more hot and dry," I said.

"I've never seen the range in such bad shape," said Luke. "I've sold off most of my stock. Can't afford to feed them."

"I saw alfalfa's going for seven dollars a 3-wire bale at the feed store," said Jordan.

"And it's going to get worse. I've got a couple of my guys up in Montana right now buying a load. They said it's going to be the last one 'til the next cutting."

"Well, give me a call when you get back tomorrow," Jordan said.

"Sure thing," said Luke.

LUANDA

I knew from the map that Poverty Mountain was not the geographical center of the Arizona Strip. It only felt that way.

I looked around, shook my head. "This country must be drawn to a different scale."

First had come Jacob Lake, then Fredonia, then Kaibab. Now we'd left the pavement and were barreling down a single-lane dirt road, Frank at the wheel, trailing a plume of dust that could be seen for miles.

"They'll know we're coming," I said.

"Probably better that way," he said. "Get the drop on these guys, Luanda, they don't like it."

"When you think was the last time it rained out here?"

"Judging by the condition of this road, I'd say not this year."

"Map says it's 'improved.' So what do you suppose 'improved' means?"

"I don't know. They grade it once a year?" he guessed. "All I know is the washboard isn't as bad if you go fast."

Sarah spoke up from the back seat. "Just watch the turns or we'll be in the ditch."

I turned and handed a file folder to her and one to Luke. "Let's take care of some business before we get there. These are the only two we've been able to identify. Sarah, you're looking at Conrad Shrump. He's an import—a genuine neo-Nazi, direct from Hamburg, Germany. Made it through immigration before things tightened up after 9/11, gained his citizenship soon after by marrying an American woman. Minor criminal record. Trespass, concealing identity.

"Luke, that's William Baldwin, alias Bill Baldy, or just Baldy. Home grown, a true son of the deep South. Criminal record also minor."

Luke peered at the photo. "Isn't this one of the guys out on the island for the Memorial Day protest?" he asked, showing Sarah the picture.

"Oh my God!" she exclaimed, peering at the swastika boldly tattooed onto the man's forehead. "It *is* him!"

"You sure?" I asked.

"I'd know that swastika anywhere," she said with a shudder. "That—and those eyes. How did you come by these?"

"Photos were taken at an anti-immigration rally down in Phoenix last month," said Frank. "I have to admit I was dubious at first about any link between these guys and the murders at the lake, but then Luke contacted us."

Luke picked up the thread. "I've been talking to family friends out here on the strip. We circulated among them all the photos we have of these guys and these two came up positive. My contacts place them at what used to be the Bar C Ranch, the old Calder place, now abandoned."

"Nice piece of citizen police work," Sarah said.

"Most of the families I know have lived out here for years," said Luke. "None of them want this bunch in their back yard."

We spotted the Calder Ranch a couple miles off, a cluster of low buildings squatting under the heat and the faded blue sky. As we got closer, we could see half a dozen battered trailers dragged up around the old ranch house.

I turned to Sarah and Luke in the back seat.

"Check your firearms."

I glanced down at the Glock 9-millimeter Luke had belted around his waist. "You got a permit for that, mister?" I asked teasingly.

He nodded, gave me a deadpan look. "I even know how to use it," he said solemnly.

"I'm praying you won't need to."

The humor helped dilute the tension, which was growing by the minute.

We slowed as we approached the front gate. Sure enough, two armed men—one of them Baldy—waited for us on either side of the cattle guard. They motioned us to stop.

"Okay, folks, it's show time," said Frank. "Let's remember to stay cool."

Big as a boulder under a sweat stained ball cap, Baldy circled the Suburban, noted the plates, warily approached the driver's side. Frank rolled the window down.

"Feds," Baldy stated. "FBI?"

Frank nodded.

"What do you want?"

"Got some questions for you and one of your comrades."

"This about the demonstration up at the lake?"

"That and other things."

"Fuck off," he said. "Back up. Get the hell out."

Frank stared at him for as long as he dared. "Mr. Baldwin, we can do this one of two ways. We can either have a friendly discussion here and now, or we can leave and come back with additional agents. Your choice."

"Then we got another Waco on our hands, that it?" Baldy asked. "We know you feds won't hesitate to burn women and children alive, that's for damn sure."

He peered past Frank into the cool dimness of the Suburban. "How many more you got in there?"

"Three."

He glanced over the hood at his partner, who gave some sort of assent that I couldn't see.

"Park it over there by the fence," Baldy said, "and get out—slowly."

They covered us as Frank followed instructions.

We stepped out of the air-conditioned Suburban, closed the doors, and the heat was so intense, the smell of dust and sagebrush so pervasive that the inside feel of the vehicle immediately evaporated. I began to sweat.

Frank adjusted his sunglasses, looked around. "You two here all by yourselves?"

In response, Baldy raised his right hand, and a dozen men, all heavily armed, stepped out from behind the house and the trailers.

"So where are the kids?" Frank asked.

"What are you, the fucking truant officer?"

I surveyed the armed men. "Shit!" I said. I couldn't help myself.

Baldy smiled at me, revealing a couple of missing teeth. "S'matter, Miss Chitlin," he leered. "You wasn't s'pecting a welcoming committee? She the chauffeur?" he asked Frank. "Where's her little beanie?"

He guffawed, looked unsmilingly down at me. "Nigger, you on our turf now," he said quietly.

Luke must have seen me stiffen, because he immediately stepped up beside me.

"No point standing out here frying our brains," he said. "Why don't we go inside and talk?"

Any charm the old Calder place may once have had had long since worn away. It looked to be a miracle the house was still standing, which was more than could be said for most of the out buildings.

The four of us, with Baldy and one that might have been Shrump, sat in the kitchen around an old table. The rest of the men arranged themselves around the walls.

We introduced ourselves, but Shrump jumped in before we could ask any questions. His heavy German accent was a giveaway. It had to be him.

"First things first," he said. "Let's see your warrant."

"We have no warrant," said Luke. "Just some questions."

"No arrest? No search?" asked Shrump. He seemed genuinely surprised.

"We're just checking out leads on a case up at Lake Powell," I said.

"All them murders?" asked one of the men against the wall.

"What the fuck they got to do with us?" asked another.

Sarah looked at Baldy. "You and some of your people were out on that island during the demonstration over Memorial Day," she said. "Eyewitnesses said you talked about cleaning the place out."

"Lighten up," he said. "We meant the lake."

Sarah shook her head. "You made specific reference to killing blacks, Hispanics, taking on the federal government."

He shrugged. "None of that scum belongs out there in God's country in the first place. None of this belongs to them. We're taking it back from the drug dealers, the gangs, the gays, anyone non-Aryan— kick 'em out and close the borders. That lake, that dam, just the government sticking its nose in where it shouldn't be. Just like you're doing now."

"So you got no warrant?" asked Shrump, still surprised.

"No, Mr. Shrump, but that doesn't mean we couldn't get one," I said.

"Yah, but maybe not. Maybe you already asked the judge and he said no. Yes? Maybe he feels you have no reasonable cause to come here. Yah?"

He motioned around the room. "We're not criminals here."

"Look, we're not here to confront anyone . . . Mr. Shrump, is it?" said Frank.

Shrump just stared at him.

"We have four unsolved homicides on our hands," said Luke. "All of which could be considered hate crimes."

"Yah?" said Shrump.

"First, we've got Eddie Watchman, killed a year ago this spring," said Luke. "Not only Navajo, but a cop as well. Skull caved in, body dumped in Lake Powell.

"Second, Julian Rooney, drowned in the lake in May, along with Adolpho Delhijos. Rooney was black, and gay. We suspect he was dealing drugs. Delhijos, suspected drug courier, member of Mara Salvatrucha, probably here illegally by way of LA.

"Fourth is Vernon Steps, dealer in illegal antiquities and a Jew, dropped from the Glen Canyon bridge into the Colorado River last week.

"I think you'll agree that the peculiar characteristics of these murder victims, combined with your presence at the lake and in this area, make for a pretty compelling case against you, especially given what you stand for," said Luke, looking at Shrump.

"A case that any judge would deem worthy of a warrant, not only for arrest but for search," Frank added. He pointed at one of the armed men standing by the kitchen door. "For example, I've already seen a sawed off shotgun here. Illegal as hell. We're talking background checks all around, and who knows what we might find? In other words, we'd be so far up your butts we'd be seeing daylight out the other end."

Baldy cleared his throat. "Before Peewee here wets his pants, let me burst your little bubble. First of all, we didn't kill anybody. And here's why. Number one, the Navajo cop. We'd have been a lot happier if Custer had won back at the Little Big Horn and the Indians were exterminated, but we know that killing any cop just brings more cops.

"Second, the nigger drug dealer. You're right, he makes a logical target, but we wouldn't have killed him like that. We'd have just popped him. Same with Delhijos. And why would we bring MS down on us, those guys are the fucking wrath of God, for Christ's sake."

"Maybe you didn't know he was MS until you read it in the paper afterwards," said Frank.

Baldy just shrugged and continued. "And the Jew. You're saying we went all the way to Bluff to find a Jew to kill, brought him to Page and dropped him off the bridge? Again, why not just kill him? Why make a fucking show of it?"

I noticed Sarah look at Luke and nod, as if to say "Exactly!"

"So you got nothing ties us to these murders," Baldy concluded.

"That may be so," Frank said. "But we come back with warrants and subpoenas, you'll be making those arguments in federal court in Phoenix."

"At the lake you said you wanted to clean out the scum," said Sarah. "A few well-publicized murders would go a long way toward running people off."

Shrump was nodding his head. "Also, to provoke a confrontation, make a point, and maybe be martyred for the cause," he said. "Yah, I can see your point."

"You guys keep mentioning martyring yourself for the cause," Frank said. "Let me point out that that could be arranged, and furthermore, it means you'd all be dead or in prison. This could include your wives and children. Is that what you want?"

Baldy leaned his face closer to Frank's. "Remember, pig," he said quietly, "one thing could bring that on is us killing all four of you right here and now."

Luke jumped in. "That's exactly what we're trying to avoid by coming to you like this. But we need your cooperation."

I guess he took their silence as consent.

"Let's talk about your newfound alliance with the environmentalists," he began.

Baldy glanced at Shrump. "Shit, they approached us, said we'd be bodyguards, shit like that. They just fucked up by not telling everyone we'd be there."

Luke continued. "No rogue elements among you . . . couple of guys who might be tempted to take unilateral action? Saw opportunities to kill these four and took them?"

Shrump fielded this one. "Any rogue elements would have to answer for themselves."

"But you can't be sure it wasn't one of your guys who killed these people," Luke said.

Shrump just shrugged.

"You guys usually have your ear to the ground," said Sarah. "Have you heard anything that could help us out on these murders?"

"You've gotta be fucking kidding," said Baldy. "Wipe your own ass."

Luke persisted. "You network with other groups. Heard anything there?"

"Wait a minute," said Baldy. "What do we get for answering these questions?"

"You get to not be arrested, not have to leave your little Shangri-La," Frank answered, looking around.

Now it was Shrump's turn. "Understand, we want the lake drained because it would eliminate the presence here of the federal government. We have a constitutional right to bear arms, and we can live where we please."

He spread his arms wide. "Look at where we are. We've isolated ourselves here, just as those poor souls did in the Branch Davidian compound in Waco and that family in Idaho. They only wanted to be left in peace, which is what we want. So why would we kill these people and bring you assholes down on our heads?"

"Then here's another chance to keep us out," I said. "So what have you got for us?"

There was a long moment of silence. Baldy and Shrump glanced at each other.

"We've heard talk there's a guy at the lake moving in on the drug trade," said Baldy.

Again, I noticed Sarah giving Luke a look.

"Okay, that may account for Rooney and Delhijos," said Luke. "But what about Eddie Watchman?"

"This guy supposedly has a new connection," said Baldy. "I mean Watchman was a cop. Maybe he found out about it. Who the hell knows?"

"You heard anything about this new connection?" Frank asked.

Baldy shook his head.

"And that leaves us with Steps," said Luke.

"That one's totally off the map," said Baldy. "The guy a dealer?"

"Yes, but not in drugs as far as we know," said Frank. "So what do you know about this new guy?"

"Somebody said he's ex-military," said Baldy.

"Anything else?"

Baldy gave a grim laugh. "You don't want to fuck with him . . . we heard that."

"We got a name here? Any way to identify this guy?" asked Frank.

"No name, but he may be planning something big," said Baldy.

"Such as?"

"We don't know, but he's buying a lot of hardware, enough to equip a small force."

"How'd you know that?"

"Let's just say we patronize the same suppliers."

"When is this supposed to be going down?"

Baldy shook his head. "Don't know that either."

"Mind if I ask where you found all this out?" said Frank.

Shrump smiled, an ugly distortion of his face. "We don't mind if you ask."

Frank looked around the room. "So any of you had any direct contact with this guy . . . seen him, talked to him, done any business with him?"

Baldy abruptly stood up. "Interview's over. Time to fuck off."

Frank looked around again, reached inside his jacket. A dozen gun barrels were instantly trained on him. "Whoa, boys!" Frank said, his hand still inside his jacket. He slowly withdrew it, held up one of his cards. "Any of you change your mind . . . want to talk . . . give me a call. There's a serious reward for any information leading to arrest and conviction."

He tossed the card onto the table.

Baldy spit a brown stream of tobacco juice on it. "Blood money."

But Shrump raised his head like a dog sniffing the air, the gleam of an idea in his eye. "Money is money," he said in a thoughtful tone. "How serious?"

Baldy and Shrump escorted us back to the Suburban.

Luke turned to Baldy. "You ink in that tattoo yourself?" he asked, eyeing the big man's forehead. "Use a mirror?"

Baldy just glared at him.

"Thought so," Luke said. "You might be interested to know you drew it backwards. That's actually an ancient sign for water, not a swastika."

"Fuck you," he said, but Shrump actually laughed.

"Well, I wonder how productive all of that was," I said as we were driving out the gate.

"For one thing," said Frank. "They now know we know plenty about them —who they are, how many they are, how heavily armed they are, and where they are."

"Plus, we have another finger pointing back at Tic Douloureux," said Sarah.

"Maybe," said Frank. "Or maybe just a finger pointing us away from them."

"How about this, then?" Sarah asked. "I recognized one of Shrump and Baldwin's posse."

I turned to look at her in the back seat. "Oh?"

"Guy named Shep Harris. Luke and I arrested him last fall at the lake for possession of a stolen artifact."

"I knew I'd seen him before!" Luke interjected.

"He recognize you?" I asked.

"Definitely. Got that deer-in-the-headlights look the minute he saw me."

"Fax me his file. We'll add him to our database."

"Well, if nothing else, remember that these guys are very territorial," said Frank, "so we've gained the psychological advantage of making a successful foray onto their turf."

"Define successful," I said.

Frank grinned. "Nobody got shot."

A mile out on the single track we pulled off the road when we encountered an old beater school bus filled with gaunt-faced women and haunted-looking kids. They stared through the dirty glass at us as they ground slowly past. We stared back, two alien worlds eyeing one another across a few yards of dusty sagebrush and a million miles of trust and understanding. Then they passed, and we continued.

"Those are the ones I feel sorry for," I said. "The women and the kids."

"Well, Luanda, maybe we've done our little bit to help," said Frank ironically.

I just looked at him.

JORDAN

"I always forget how quiet it is out here," I said.

The two of us were fishing off my boat in Face Canyon, adrift past Boundary Butte. The lapping of the water on the side of the boat and the occasional cry of a mud lark only accentuated the stillness.

"How many days did we spend like this when we were kids?" Tic asked.

"Too many to count."

"I can't believe how many stick buoys and ball buoys we saw coming out here," he said. "Must be lots of rocks coming close to the surface again."

I nodded. "Lake hasn't been this low since it was first filling up. You want a beer?"

We sat, drinking and fishing for a while.

"Talked with Sarah last week," I said. "She said you weren't discharged for what happened on that cliff in Afghanistan like you told me, but for what happened afterward."

He turned from fishing and looked me in the eye, held my gaze, then turned and stared out over the water. "So now you know."

"Why didn't you tell me you almost killed your CO?"

He shrugged. "Thought I'd come back here, leave all that behind, get a clean start. And when I found out you'd come back, too, I hoped we'd be friends again. But it hasn't turned out like that."

"So how has it turned out?"

He turned and looked me in the eye again. "We're just too far apart, you and me."

"But we're out here right now, like we used to be. That must mean something."

"Only that we're beating a dead horse, buddy," he said with a sad smile. "You see, Jordan, people's lives have a trajectory, an arc. Sometimes those arcs parallel one another and people can be friends, like you and me used to be. But sometimes one of those parallels wobbles off course a little bit, intersects the other, or not, and keeps on going out into space. The more time passes the further it travels away from the one it used to parallel.

"Don't you get it? There's some things we can never change, like you and me and Stevie. That's where my arc wobbled and intersected yours. I mean, why did I go back for you? Why did I let go of Stevie to grab you?"

He looked out over the water again. "Because I loved you, Jordan," he said, his voice husky. "Don't you remember how things were back then? We were brothers, you and me. In fact, you were better than my brother. Stevie was just a little pest. My father never taught me anything about family, about taking care of each other. Hell, he never even took care of us. It was every man for himself at our house. You know that.

"But you, you, Jordan, you and your family, were something better than that, finer. On Sundays, you all used to go to church together, remember?"

I nodded.

"Well, that's what I mean. You were one step closer to God than I was. You were stronger than I was . . . purer somehow."

"Not stronger," I said. "Just more strongly disciplined. And it's funny," I added, "but I never felt superior, what with no mother and a drunk for a dad."

We both sat silently for a while, sipping our beer.

"What I'm saying is, you were my only chance to be something better, Jordan. I don't think I knew it at the time, but by saving you I was saving that chance . . . But it didn't work. You were still you and I was still me. In fact, it just made things worse. My father used Stevie's death to drive me into the ground, try to make himself feel better. He was still the same miserable son-of-a-bitch he'd always been." He paused, gave a bitter laugh. "And Stevie is still dead."

"Yes, Stevie's gone," I said, "but we're still here. Why can't we go from there?"

He looked at me and shook his head. "You just don't get it, do you? Look at you. A doctor, successful practice, upstanding member of the community, looking after your dad. Hell, buddy, you even got a girlfriend. Pretty one at that.

"But me, booted out of the service, no money, not even a lousy government pension. No job, my friends are all losers, which must mean I'm one, too."

"But think about your SEAL training, Tic. You could teach survival skills, rock climbing, be a guide. You know this country inside and out."

He shook his head no. "There's more to this than just the differences on the outside, the ones people can see, Jordan. The biggest difference between you and me is on the inside, like it's always been."

"Oh, c'mon—"

"No. Listen. Don't you remember when we were kids? You lived in a nice house, your dad was educated, always had a good job, drove a new pickup. Your mom was a school teacher, educated, too.

"Me, living in that junkyard we called a home. Luke was right . . . my dad was a bum, never made an honest living, wouldn't have taken it if it was offered to him. My mom trying to hold it all together . . . waiting tables, clipping coupons."

"Aren't those just visible differences, too?"

"No!"

I jumped. He'd practically shouted it.

"No, those are differences between people," he said more softly. "People with different families, different upbringings, different education. People with different ideas of what's right and wrong, different expectations of life and of each other.

"Let me give you an example. Something I've always wondered. You have a little brother, Niles. What would you have done if you were me, if it had come down to Niles or me in the water that day? Which one would you have saved, which one left behind? Now be honest."

I looked over the water at the massive walls of the canyon, streaked with desert varnish down to where they vanished beneath the reflecting water.

"I was never the swimmer you were," I said. "So I probably would have lost both of you."

"Oh c'mon now buddy, you're being too modest, just like you've always been. You could have saved one of us. Who?"

I was trying desperately to take myself back to that time, to remember who I was back then. "Okay, my first guess would be Niles."

"Thought so."

"Just because my dad would have killed me if I had lost Niles. I would have been in a lot of trouble."

"Now see, that's what I mean. When Stevie drowned I wasn't thinking about my old man. I just knew I had to get you to shore, so I parked Stevie and towed you in. Only problem was, the little fucker didn't stay parked."

I laid my hand on his shoulder, said, "I'll always owe you that, Tic."

I paused. I knew that what I was about to do was wrong, that I was crossing the line, but I told myself that maybe it was one small wrong for a greater right.

"Tic, I need to tell you something," I said.

He looked over at me, but just then there was a sharp tug on his line, and he turned to reel in his catch, which turned out to be a good-sized walleye.

"Well, I'll be damned," he said softly. "Another fucking walleye, like the one Stevie caught that day."

"Just don't shoot it, okay?"

We both laughed. He unhooked it carefully, avoiding the needle-sharp teeth, and threw it back.

I reached back to the cooler and pulled out a couple more beers.

I raised mine. "Here's to Mr. Walleye."

"Long may he swim."

After we had fished quietly for a while, Tic asked, "Any breaks in the death of that old guy . . . Steps was it? One that fell off the bridge?"

"He didn't fall, he was dropped."

"Okay, dropped. Heard you tried to rescue him."

"For all the good it did. I think I just triggered whoever blew the rope."

"You don't know that."

"Sarah and I drove up to his house in Bluff the other day. Place was cleaned out. Just like his bank accounts."

"Any suspects?"

I paused. "Luke and Sarah think you did it. As well as Eddie, Adolpho, and Rooney."

"I know. They told me. But why would I want to kill them?"

"They think you're cleaning out the competition for the local drug traffic."

"No way! I might not be the upright citizen you are, but I'm no murderer."

"They think you're planning some sort of attack."

"And where did they get that idea?"

Again, I knew I shouldn't tell him, but maybe I could scare him off his plan, if indeed that was his plan. "Sarah and Luke and a couple of FBI agents drove out to the Arizona Strip a couple days ago to meet with a group of militia and skinheads."

"Sounds like quite an outfit. What'd the feds want with them?"

"My dad and I suggested that it was those guys who committed the murders as hate crimes."

He nodded, a small smile on his face. "So what'd the skinhead militia have to say to that?"

"They denied it, of course, told them about a guy, ex-military, who was moving in on the drug trade at the lake, and buying enough gear to equip a small army."

"They name any names?"

"No, but Luke and Sarah think it's you."

"And what do you think?"

I swallowed the last of my beer and shrugged. "I still think they could have done the murders, and that they're trying to point suspicion away from themselves."

"You think? I always felt like those guys were a lot of wannabes. All talk and no action. Not reliable."

"I don't know. Sarah seemed to think they were the real deal."

"You trust her judgment?"

"In most things."

"And what about me? You trust my judgment? Because I think the militia's a red herring, too. I think you've got a real killer on your hands."

What the hell's going on here? I asked myself. "What makes you say that?" I asked as calmly as I could.

"Oh, I get around. Scuttlebutt has it that somebody *is* moving in, and that he *is* planning something big."

"How big?"

"Haven't heard."

"Well, what's it going to be? Robbery? Murder? Who's the target?"

He shrugged.

"So is this the same guy responsible for the murders?"

"Quien sabe, hombre? Who knows?"

He turned in the boat, leaned forward and looked me directly in the face. "All I know is that you and yours better watch out for yourselves," he said softly.

A chill ran up my spine. "What does that mean? Am I a target?"

"There's things I could tell you," he said, then he laughed, a burnt, brittle sound. He reached down, lifted the top tray out of his tackle box, pulled a gun from the bottom compartment, pointed it at me. "But then I really would have to kill you."

I did my best to stay calm, although inside I was jumping. "I remember the last time you and me were in a boat with a gun. Didn't turn out so good."

"I carry it wherever I go, and I suggest you start carrying one," he said.

"Even out fishing with a friend?"

He shrugged, and our eyes met. "Do you ever really know who your friends are?"

SARAH

Jordan's brother Merced drove Jordan's boat the same way he drove the spanking new Lexus he'd showed up in the previous afternoon—left arm, cigar in hand, draped over the side, right hand casually steering as we raced up the lake. Grady and Niles trailed in Grady's boat, Merced barely keeping them in view. I had noticed before that being in the lead seemed important to him.

The wind felt wonderful combing through my hair. I nestled further into Jordan's side in the back seat. Holding his hand in both of mine, I lay my head on his bare chest, feeling his sun-warmed skin against my cheek.

"So how far up the chain of command did you have to go to get an entire summer weekend off?" he asked.

"I just told them I was combining work with pleasure, that you and I would be reviewing the case."

He groaned. "Maybe we should quit stirring the pot for a little while, see what settles out."

"Fine by me."

Late morning, just past the Escalante River arm of the lake, we found an isolated cove that Jordan knew, with a long stretch of sand sloping gently down to the water. We pitched our tents among some big rocks at the top of the slope, including our shade canopy, under which we sat for lunch.

After we ate, Merced dragged his chair out into the sun and settled back with a beer in one hand and his omnipresent cigar in the other. Unlike Jordan, who worked to keep himself in shape, and Niles, who just seemed naturally slender, Merced clearly had let himself go. The only thing that kept him from looking like a beached beluga whale was his twice weekly visits to the tanning salon.

"We were here a year ago . . . tied the boats off to these rocks, remember?" he asked. "Shows you how far the lake's dropped since then."

Grady shifted in his seat in the shade. "It can just keep on dropping, far as I'm concerned."

Merced eyed him. "You still on that kick, Pop?"

"It's no 'kick', Merced. The dam should never have been built."

"Sounds funny coming from the guy who was chief engineer."

"Everyone's entitled to change his mind. This lake replaced an entire, living ecosystem with a sterile man-made blanket of water, all so that millions of people could live comfortably in the Sonoran desert, an ecosystem that can't support them, which is being buried under a blanket of black top."

"That sounds good, Pop," Merced replied with a grin. "'Buried under a blanket of black top.'"

"You can laugh, Merced, but the fact is that the population keeps going up while the water supply stays the same, or . . ." he said, pointing at the lake, "drops."

Merced nodded. "I know you're right. Without water from the Central Arizona Project, Phoenix and Tucson would evaporate like water on a hot skillet. But you can't turn back the clock. Those people are there and they're going to stay there. And they need water."

"And as long as there's water, more will come," said Grady, "so why not limit the water supply to a level that supports today's population and call a halt to the madness? People would just stay back in the Midwest and the Northeast where they belong, places with enough water to support them without piping it in from some man-made bathtub in another state. They won't be as eager to live here if they can't have their swimming pools and acres of bluegrass lawn."

He paused for a moment, looking out over the water. "Let the Colorado run to the Sea of Cortez again, like it's supposed to."

"Very romantic, Grady, but, like it or not, the water issue is primarily an economic equation, not an environmental one," Niles chimed in. "Even today, people in Phoenix pay less for their water than people do in Cleveland, which sits on Lake Erie."

"But that's like saying coal costs less than solar to generate the same kilowatt of electricity," Grady protested. "People aren't factoring in the environmental and health costs. We're ruining the environment to subsidize the cost of water. Do you realize how many species of fish and birds, not to mention varieties of plants, are going the way of the dodo bird because of dams like Glen Canyon?"

"But now, you're back to the environmental equation," said Merced.

"Okay, fine, so let's stick with economics," Grady replied. "Only let's factor in the environment and pay what the water is truly worth, which would drive up the price and give people an economic incentive to limit consumption."

"Which would free up more water for more people to move into more subdivisions down in the Valley," said Merced, who seemed to enjoy needling his father. "The whole system was set in motion years ago, Pop. You can't change that."

"No, but we've got to stop sacrificing our environment to support the way we live, which means changing where we live and how we live there. A desert is hot and dry. It isn't meant to support the same population density as Minneapolis or Chicago. I mean, how many more Glen Canyons are we going to obliterate before we run out of wild places to ruin?"

Merced waved his cigar at the lake and the sandstone walls of the cove. "This looks pretty wild to me."

"Only because you never saw Glen Canyon before the dam went in. There's no comparison."

"So you're saying we should drain the lake and restore the canyon," said Niles. "Do you realize how much silt and trash has accumulated down there since the river stopped flowing? It wouldn't be the same place."

"Not at first it wouldn't," Grady agreed. "Trust me, I've kept abreast of how quickly the lake is silting up, and I know it would take years, probably longer than our lifetimes, for all that debris to wash out of the main canyon as well as the side canyons and down the river. But someday, maybe in our grandchildren's or our great grandchildren's day, Glen Canyon could be what it used to be. Nature has a way of healing herself."

"But how in hell would you ever remove that chunk of concrete you guys poured fifty years ago?" Merced asked.

Grady got a sly look on his face. "There's ways around that dam, son, without necessarily moving it."

This made Merced sit up in his chair and look hard at his father. "What the hell are you talking about?"

"I'm saying that this lake could be drained quicker and easier than you think. But I'm not going there today."

Merced shrugged. "Well, in any event, you could kiss Page goodbye," he said casually. "A few hundred rafters floating down the Colorado every summer wouldn't be enough to keep it going."

Jordan nodded. "You're right about that, Merced. With the drought and now these murders, the Chamber of Commerce people are saying business has fallen off considerably. We're even seeing it at the hospital."

"Hell, that old man being dropped off the bridge . . . that was bizarre," said Merced. "Any leads there?"

Jordan shook his head.

Merced turned to me. "Dad told me you guys questioned Tic Douloureux about it."

I nodded. "We're pretty sure that when Tic was a kid, he and his father hunted pots and sold them to old man Steps."

"Sure, I remember Tic and his dad going—" and here he made quotation marks with his fingers—"camping." He turned to his two brothers. "Don't you guys?"

Niles shrugged. "I didn't really hang out much with Tic. Jordan did, though."

We all looked at Jordan, who said, "C'mon, you guys, who knows what Tic and his old man were doing out there."

"But there was that whole thing about Tic being a Lead Climber in the SEALS," I said. "He *could* have been fetching pots for his father."

"Well, his father sure wasn't doing much climbing," said Merced. "He spent most of his life walking around behind a big old beer gut, didn't he? Along with chain-smoking unfiltered Pall Malls."

Grady and the boys laughed.

"How did you remember about the Pall Malls?" Jordan asked.

"One time, me and Tic filched a pack from his dad and came down to the lake and smoked them."

"All at once?" I asked.

Merced nodded. "Made ourselves sick as dogs. Probably what started me on my cigar habit."

We all laughed.

"The point is," said Jordan, "that we all were climbing rocks in those days. It's just that Tic had a special talent for it."

"I'll say," said Niles. "He had absolutely no fear of heights."

"Nor of anything or anyone else, as I recall," said Merced. "But I have to concede that doesn't make him a murderer. So, you got anybody else?"

"When Eddie Watchman, the Navajo policeman, disappeared a year ago this spring we questioned a man named Kenneth Klain, who we think was the last man to see him alive," I said. "But we didn't have enough to hold him.

"We also questioned another local . . . guy named Harris, who we arrested for digging pots right after Eddie was found. Thought Eddie might have caught him in the act on a different dig six months earlier, but a couple friends vouched for the guy, said he was with them."

"He was a long shot, anyway," Jordan added.

"When we found Eddie, we questioned Klain again, but no dice," I said.

"Then Klain's son found Eddie's gun this spring when he was out herding sheep," said Jordan. "Turned out to be the spot where Eddie was murdered, just a couple miles from Klain's place, so we arrested him and held him until the double homicide this spring."

Merced asked Jordan, "That was the local dealer? What was his name?"

"Julian Rooney," said Jordan. "And his connection, gangster named Adolpho Delhijos from Phoenix."

"Those were the two found buried up to their necks on the beach, right?" asked Niles.

"I'll say one thing," Merced stated. "Whoever the murderer is, he—or she—has a flair for the theatrical."

"Not to mention the grisly," I added with a shudder.

"I mean dangling that old guy—what was his name?"

"Steps. Vernon Steps," I said.

"Besides his dad, what makes you think Tic was in on that one?" Merced asked.

"After Steps was murdered, we found two paintings in his house that we believe Tic stole from my partner, Luke Russell. We think he wanted Steps to fence them."

"But you don't know for sure that Tic stole them, or how they ended up at Steps," said Merced. "So basically you got zero."

"Not exactly," said Jordan a little too quickly.

Merced's ears pricked up. "Oh?"

I shot a warning glance at Jordan, but he seemed determined to say what he said next.

"At a protest back in May, Grady . . . well, why don't I let him tell it?"

"Okay," said Grady. "Most of us demonstrators camped out on an island off Wahweap marina. There were a dozen guys out there with us, all heavily armed, who stood out like sore thumbs among the rest of the protesters. Turns out they were skinheads—neo-Nazis who had agreed to serve as muscle if the rangers tried forcing the protestors off the island."

"An alliance of skinheads and environmentalists?" asked Niles doubtfully.

Grady nodded. "Wait. It gets better. Turns out they've joined ranks with a group of militiamen out on the Arizona Strip."

"And you're thinking these guys committed all four murders?" Merced asked skeptically.

Jordan nodded vigorously. "The first three victims were minorities, one of whom was also a cop," he said. "The fourth, Steps, had been blackmailed, and on top of that, he was Jewish."

"So you're saying these guys were killed because of their race, their authority status, their religion and/or their money," said Merced.

"Exactly."

"I don't know, Jordan," answered Merced. "That seems like kind of a stretch. If I had to bet, I'd put my money on Tic. He was always sort of a wild man, anyway."

"Yes, he was. But, like you said, Merced, that doesn't necessarily make him a murderer."

Grady and the boys spent the rest of the afternoon pulling each other and me around the lake on skis. I quickly saw that I was the novice, having just graduated last summer from two skis to slalom. Niles and Jordan were powerful skiers, cutting huge arcs behind the boat; they even made a couple of runs tandem, ducking beneath one another's tow lines, jumping each other's wakes. Even Grady made a couple of short runs, but Merced was the funniest. Standing on the beach at one point, he lit a cigar, waded into the water with his ski, and had Grady pull him up. He then proceeded to ski for fifteen or twenty minutes, grinning behind his sunglasses with the cigar clamped between his teeth, until Grady swung him around to the beach, Merced released the tow line and glided serenely up onto the sand, cigar still lit. We all applauded as he bowed.

Turned out Grady was every bit as good a camp cook as he was the kitchen variety.

"Hey, some of those early dam sites I worked were pretty primitive," he told us. "We had to look after ourselves."

Late that afternoon he built a fire on the sand and let it burn down to coals in which he buried corn, zucchini and potatoes seasoned with salt, pepper and butter and wrapped in foil. After awhile he set a grate above the coals and threw on half a dozen huge porterhouse steaks rubbed in kosher salt and pepper; beside them he set a Dutch oven cherry cobbler cooking for dessert while we ate dinner.

Something about spending the day outdoors always picks up my appetite, and Grady and the boys ate like they were all teenagers again.

"That was delicious, Grady," said Niles, as he scraped the last of the cobbler out of the Dutch oven.

"I'm glad you told me," his father said. "Otherwise I was beginning to think no one was hungry."

The boys and I cleaned up while Grady tended to the fire.

We finished and I said, "I'll say this about you guys. For a group of men, you all take pretty good care of each other."

Grady shrugged. "Years of practice, I guess. The boys' mother's been gone for a long time."

"What was her name?"

"Grace."

"That's pretty."

He nodded. "Her name was fitting. She was graceful in everything she did."

I looked around at the boys, all of them silent, staring into the fire. Each seemed lost in his own particular thoughts of his mother. There was a melancholy in the air that I did not want.

"Niles," I said, "I saw you packing a guitar, didn't I? Why don't you fetch it?"

Night was falling as we circled our chairs around the fire. Merced lit another cigar.

Jordan took a deep whiff of the smoke. "Merced, whenever you're around, I'm glad I pay extra for the more expensive cigars at Christmas and on your birthday."

"That makes two of us brother," he said, waving the cigar in the air.

Tired as we were, it didn't take long for us to sing ourselves out. Soon we were all slumped in our chairs, staring into the fire, which was dying along with the conversation. Jordan went to our tent and got our sleeping bags. We headed down the beach a ways to a flat spot in the sand, where we spread the bags and lay on our backs, looking up at the night sky. With no ambient light, the Milky Way seemed to hover just overhead, its millions of stars glimmering in luminescent clouds.

Jordan took my hand in his. "You haven't had much to say about the trip out to Poverty Mountain," he murmured.

"Not much to say except what I already told you. We pitched every reason you gave us they were guilty, and they were able to bat each one right back at us. Plus they all but named Tic when they coughed up the fact that somebody was moving into the drug trade in this area, somebody who seems to be planning some kind of attack."

"Did you discuss the nature of the killings?"

I nodded. "They asked why they would want to draw attention to themselves, and I had to agree with them."

He seemed to consider this for a minute, then turned his head to me. "So what does your gut tell you?"

"That these guys are a bunch of angry, alienated, heavily-armed misfits living in hovels in the middle of nowhere, that they don't like women and I wouldn't want to be married to one, but none of that makes them guilty of murder."

"And Baldy and Shrump?"

The mere mention of their names made me shiver. I snuggled deeper into Jordan's side. "Baldy's a true believer. He'd go down with the ship. Shrump . . . I don't know."

"What do you mean?"

"They both scare me, Jordan. Do we have to keep talking about them?" I asked, looking up into his face.

He kissed me on the forehead. "Not if you don't want to."

"I don't," I said, drawing his face down to mine. I kissed him softly, probing his lips with the tip of my tongue. He responded in kind as he took me in his arms and pulled me closer.

"Oh, Jordan," I whispered in his ear. "I was so frightened out there. I couldn't stop thinking about you."

He rubbed my back and nuzzled his lips at my neck. "Let's not think about that anymore, okay?"

I nodded and kissed him again, a slow-moving, lingering kiss that brought my breathing deeper. Our hands were everywhere.

He raised his head and looked down the beach. Everyone had gone to their tents, the fire a dull glow in their midst.

Rolling me over on my back, he moved himself up and settled his weight on me. Again our mouths met, hungry for each other. I tilted my hips into his, and could feel his response beneath the thin fabric of his swim trunks.

He sat back, pulled me to a sitting position, and drew my t-shirt off over my head. I squirmed out of my bikini bottoms as he stood and shucked off his swim suit. A sudden chill drove me into my sleeping bag, where he joined me, dragging his bag over the two of us, now warm flesh to flesh. Again he was above me, his bulk a comfort, and as I welcomed him, I opened my eyes to the night sky just as a shooting star slid across the heavens.

I awoke in our tent early the next morning to the sound of one of the boats starting. I looked at Jordan beside me, but he didn't stir, so I pulled on a pair of shorts and a t-shirt and climbed outside. At the water's edge, Niles was just lowering the prop of Grady's boat into the water. The sun wasn't up yet and I shivered in the onshore breeze. Niles looked up and saw me; motioned me down to him.

"I'm just going out to take a look around," he said. "I won't be gone long, but don't wait breakfast for me."

I asked him which way he was headed.

"Probably head up the San Juan arm a little ways. Don't have enough gas to get too far."

I told him to be careful. He nodded, then slowly swung the boat around and headed out into the main canyon.

"What time do you think he left?" Jordan asked.

"The sun wasn't up yet."

We had eaten breakfast, gotten in a couple hours of sunbathing, eaten lunch and broken camp. It was mid-afternoon and still no Niles.

"Why don't you and I go out for a look around," Jordan suggested to me. "He may have broken down or run out of gas."

"I can't believe that knucklehead doesn't carry a cell phone," said Merced irritably.

Jordan retrieved his from his pack and flipped it open. "No signal out here, anyway. But I'll bring mine with us in case we find him in a spot that we can call from."

We were halfway down to the San Juan arm, when I asked, "Is this unusual for Niles?"

Jordan smiled and rolled his eyes. "Unfortunately, not. We really should keep an eye on him at all times."

"So this has happened before?"

"Oh, yes. We were snowshoeing up in the Weminuche when we were teenagers and he disappeared for 24 hours. In the dead of winter! We had the mountain patrol out, we searched all night. Next morning he came waltzing into camp talking about watching the ice form on a stream he'd found and how amazing it was."

"You're kidding."

"Nope. He told us it had gotten too dark to hike back safely so he had spent the night in a snow cave he dug out of a hillside, which is probably why he didn't hear us calling for him."

I laughed.

"Merced and I were ready to kill him except we were so relieved to see him alive."

"So you think he's onto some kind of—" I hesitated, "—science project out here somewhere?"

"Who knows? Let's just say Niles' attention is very easily engaged, and once engaged, almost impossible to divert.

"Which I think is a large part of what makes him an inventor," he added as an afterthought.

We boated as far up the San Juan as our fuel would allow, but no sign of Niles.

On our way back I finally voiced my fear that he might have fallen victim to foul play.

"What do you mean?" Jordan asked.

"I was thinking about Tic, and I remembered you told me he threatened Niles at Anne's Place the day after Christmas."

"I remember Niles was pretty upset."

"Isn't it possible Niles might have come across Tic, or vice versa?"

Jordan looked out on the vast expanse of water we were crossing.

"I don't know, Sarah. This is a pretty damn big lake." He paused, then looked at me. "And besides, even if we assume Tic is guilty of these murders, why would he target somebody like Niles?"

I looked him right in the eye. "That's a good question. Unfortunately, at the moment I don't have a *good* answer, just a *bad* feeling."

The four of us and all of our gear made it back in Jordan's boat to Wahweap, where I put out the word on Niles and told the Hunts that if he hadn't shown up in 24 hours, we'd mount a search for him.

SETUP

Niles motored slowly through the water filled canyon, the rumble of the outboard echoing off the steep walls forming the narrow passage. If he remembered correctly, he was getting closer. He rounded another bend, and sure enough, fifty yards ahead, the water ended abruptly in a sheer rock wall, but the canyon continued, its floor now a dozen feet above the water level.

Niles knew what he was looking at: a rare drop canyon. These were tributary canyons entering main canyons which water and weather had eroded much more rapidly. As a result, the mouth of the drop canyon was left hanging—sometimes several hundred feet—above the floor of the main canyon. This meant they were normally inaccessible to any creatures save those with wings, but many of them, including this one, had been breached by the rising waters of the lake years before and been explored by boat. The last time he had been here, he and his brothers had boated several hundred yards beyond this point.

But this one had now been entered by foot. A boat was tied up to a short steel rod protruding from the canyon wall. Above it, an aluminum ladder hung from two more rods driven into the rock, leading to the now-drained floor of the drop canyon itself.

The rods interested him. Are those engine valves? he wondered as he eased Grady's boat closer to the steel rods hammered into the rock. Sure enough, someone had sharpened them to a point and pounded them into the sandstone as makeshift pitons.

The boat was loaded with half a dozen heavy wooden crates, serial and model numbers as well as various acronyms stenciled on them. A couple of jerry cans had been left on the canyon floor at the head of the ladder.

Someone apparently was unloading the boat. Curiosity got the better of him, and Niles maneuvered closer to the wall. He tied up to one of pitons at the base of the ladder, which he climbed to the canyon floor.

Quietly, he began making his way up canyon. He knew he was in a remote enough part of the lake that he might have stumbled on some kind of illegal activity, and that surprising somebody in the act was a bad idea. He thought of yesterday's discussion about Tic and the murders, but considered it unlikely that this was his doing. On the other hand, he hadn't any alternative explanation, so he proceeded—carefully.

Which was good, because a hundred yards later he heard voices approaching. Quickly, he ducked into a small alcove and plastered himself to its wall, not daring to breathe.

Two men walked by, apparently headed for the boat. A chill went through him. One of them was Tic.

He realized that once they saw his boat, they'd know someone was there. His only hope was to wait for them to disappear down the canyon, giving him a chance to run up canyon and search for a way out.

The two men were almost out of sight around a bend when all of Niles' calculations ceased. He watched as Tic put his hand on the other man's arm and they stopped. Slowly, they turned, and Tic was looking right at him.

The smile on his face was the same one Niles remembered from Anne's Place at Christmas.

"What the hell are you doing here, Niles?" he asked, walking up to him.

"I guess I could ask you the same thing," Niles replied, trying to sound a lot more confident than he felt.

"Except you know I could kick your skinny little ass all the way down to the water. So, again, what are you doing here?"

"Just out looking around, and I remembered this was a drop canyon. The water's gone down so much, I wanted to see if it had been exposed."

"You a regular geologist, that it?"

Niles said nothing, determined not to let Tic bait him into a confrontation.

"Does anybody know where you are?"

Niles knew he was in trouble, and despite his best intentions not to let Tic manipulate him, he lied.

"I radioed in my position before I left the boat."

"Oh yeah? Who'd you call?"

"The ranger station at Wahweap."

Tic just nodded his head, considering his next move.

"Well, I don't mind telling you you've showed up at the wrong place at the wrong time. Just like back in school, remember? Why don't you pull your head out of your ass?"

"Look, this doesn't mean I have to stay. You guys obviously are busy with something here."

Tic turned to the other man. "Don't believe you two have met," he said. "Niles, this is Conrad Shrump. Shrump, this is Niles Hunt, Jordan's brother."

Shrump didn't bother to shake hands. "Tic has told me many things about your brother," was all he said.

"Shrump and some of his men have hired on to help me with a job I'm planning," said Tic. "Temps. You know what I mean?"

"So what are you guys up to way out here?"

"None of your fucking business, you little prick," said Tic.

"Well, like I said, you guys are evidently busy here, so I won't hold you up."

Niles started around them, but Tic took his arm.

"Uh, uh. You're gonna stay with us for a while, until we can figure out what to do with you."

"You and me, we'll talk," Shrump said to Tic. They stepped away from Niles.

"You are sure we should keep him if they know his position?" Shrump asked quietly.

"What, you think we should just let him go?"

Shrump could see that wasn't going to work.

"Look, it's going to take at least a few hours for anyone to realize he's not on his way back," said Tic. "By then, we can have everything loaded back on the boat."

"You mean, abandon this canyon?" Shrump asked. "But you said it's perfect."

"Just a temporary setback. There's plenty of other canyons we can use."

"And what do we do with Niles?"

"Simple. We kill him and dump the body in a side canyon 50 miles from here."

"Can you be sure he didn't already report seeing your boat and all the gear?"

"Shrump, you worry too much."

Tic walked back to Niles. "You're going to head back up the canyon with Shrump. I have to go back to the boat for a minute."

He looked at Shrump. "No funny business. And you'll be all right."

Shrump couldn't tell if Tic was talking to him or Niles.

Back at the water, Tic climbed into Niles' boat, flipped the radio on.

"Wahweap. Wahweap," he said into the mic. "Can you read me?"

Static.

He tried again. Still only static.

A smile spread over his face.

"Just what I thought," he said, looking around at the high canyon walls.

The rest of the afternoon was spent repacking crates and humping them back to the boats. Tic and Shrump made Niles help, along with the two militia men.

The sun was low in the sky as they moved the last of it.

"You go on," said Shrump. "I must, what is the expression, take a dump?"

"*Nobody wants to stick around for that,*" said Tic. "*We'll see you at the boats.*"

Shrump walked further up the canyon, to a point where it widened and the walls opened up.

"*This should be far enough,*" he said to himself, heading off behind a stand of juniper. Behind the trees, he pulled a hand-held radio from his pocket. "*I must speak with Officer Tanner.*"

"*She's off duty,*" said the dispatcher. "*But let me try her on the radio.*"

"*Yah.*"

After a minute the dispatcher returned. "*I have her, let me patch you through,*" she said. "*Okay, go ahead.*"

"*Officer Tanner? I am with Douloureux. He has just captured Dr. Hunt's brother, Niles.*"

"*I'm back at my place,*" she said. "*We just spent the whole afternoon looking for him.*"

"*I don't have time. Douloureux said he's going to kill him. Soon, I think.*"

"*Oh, my God.*"

Shrump looked at the GPS screen on his radio.

"*Write down these coordinates. Quickly, you must come.*"

SARAH

Dear God, I thought as I came to, *my head hurts.*

I was lying on my back on sun-warmed slick rock. I touched the lump on the back of my skull as tenderly as I could, feeling the stickiness of drying blood in my hair. I winced, then made the mistake of opening my eyes.

Before I could slam them shut, the glare of a cloudless mid-day sky shot twin bolts of pure pain into my head.

Then it all went away.

The next time I came around, my head still throbbed—a reminder to keep my eyes shut and my ears open.

A hot breeze sighed its way through the needles of a nearby tree and sprinkled my face with grains of sand. Breathing deeply through my nose, I gathered the baked odor of sun on sand and rock, the resin smell of juniper and pinon mixed with the dried spice of sage.

In the background, I heard the rhythmic ping of steel on sandstone, and suddenly I was a little girl again, standing on the edge of a shallow rock pit, looking down at two Navajo men who were using cold chisels, sledgehammers, and a pickax to quarry sandstone blocks. My father stood beside me.

"Why do we have to use sandstone for the new storehouse, Dad?" I asked.

"That way the walls will be fireproof. And rodent proof, I hope."

I don't know how long we stood there watching the men work and listening to the clink of their tools against the rock, but gradually I realized I really was hearing somebody chopping rock. Slowly, I turned my head toward the sound, shielded my eyes with my hand, and cracked them open a bit.

Through blurred vision I could see I was lying in full sun on the slick rock floor of a narrow canyon. About fifty yards away, I saw a man striking a pickax against an outcropping of rock while two others watched. The image was fuzzy and I tried squinting to sharpen it, but that only brought another wave of pain, which pulled me under again.

How long it took me to regain consciousness I don't know, but it was considerably cooler when I did, and the light was dimmer.

Niles was my first thought. Had that been he quarrying the rock? I carefully raised my head and opened my eyes. The man was now carrying pieces of rock to an open stretch of slick rock closer to me, but my vision was still too blurred to see if it was Niles.

I lay my head back on the gritty rock and closed my eyes, trying to retrace my steps to this point. *I got a tip from . . . whom? I can't remember.*

I probably have a concussion. All I knew for sure was that my head still hurt like hell, but I also knew I had to try to remember.

I was pretty sure I had boated out here. I remembered how hot the sun was, and I had a picture in my head of the GPS screen on the boat.

Focus! I told myself, but there were holes in my memory like those in a folded piece of paper from which a child has cut a paper doll.

I beached the boat on the sand at the mouth of a canyon . . . this canyon? . . . beside other boats. I walked only a short distance up the canyon when—bam! A light bulb exploded in my head, then left me in pitch darkness.

Back to Niles. Have I seen him here?

The tip! Niles . . . in danger . . . reminding Jordan that Niles had been threatened? By whom?

I drew another blank, but I knew I had to do something.

Slowly, carefully, I raised myself up on one elbow, and from there pushed myself into a sitting position. This caught the eye of one of the two men watching the third guy work. He headed my way. Despite my blurred vision, I saw it was Tic Douloureux.

"Guess I musta hit you harder than I thought," he said, an ugly smirk on his face. "Careless of me. Ready to join the party?"

Squatting down, he grabbed me by the armpits and hoisted me roughly to my feet, but the pain in my head was too much and darkness fell again.

It was dark by the time I came to. Someone had propped me up against a boulder, overlooking a scene which was like something from the nightmare paintings of Hieronymus Bosch.

The wind was still up, dancing the uneven light of a small campfire upon the rock outcropping, where the man I had seen working earlier was cracking off yet another big slab of sandstone, about the size usually used to pave a patio or a walk.

But now, there were others present in addition to Douloureux and the third man. Despite the darkness and my blurred vision, I could see two men, both wearing holstered pistols and camouflage.

Beyond the fire, slumped against the opposite wall of the canyon, another man sat with his arms folded on his drawn-up knees, his head face down on his arms. He looked up at me. My breath caught. Niles!

Suddenly, my brain lit up, but my stomach sank. The radio. Shrump's message. I'd jumped to help Niles and landed smack in Tic's ambush.

Niles weakly raised his hand to me, and I nodded in return. Thank God he was still alive.

At a word from Douloureux, the laborer dropped his tool, stooped down to pick up a slab, and carried it back to the open area right by me.

I gasped. I knew him! It was Harris, the pothunter Luke and I had arrested last fall for stealing a pot from an Anasazi ruin in a canyon off the lake. His face was fresh in my memory; I had seen him last week at the militia headquarters out on the Strip.

Right behind him came Conrad Shrump.

I was badly confused, yet something nagged at the back of my mind. I knew Shrump was supposed to be here; I just couldn't remember why. Why he was standing by, watching one of his own men quarrying rock slabs from the canyon wall, I had no idea. My head ached, but I focused as best I could.

Tic was speaking to the two men. "One thing they taught in special ops, always be prepared to use the tools and resources at hand. And here we have them." He held up Harris' pickax, then pointed back with it at the stone outcropping. "What's more, we have the labor necessary to get the job done."

When Harris bent over to place the big chunk of sandstone on a pile of other pieces, Tic kicked him hard from behind, and he fell face first on the slick rock. Tic and his accomplice obviously had worked him to exhaustion.

"Get over on your back, you piece of shit."

Harris did as he was told. Tic squatted beside him.

"Now your comrades and I are going to work—on you," he said, with a mirthless chuckle. "I'm even going to tell you a story as we go along. Wouldn't want your attention to wander, would we?"

He stood, turned to the two men in cammies, said, "Miller. Evans. Let's start with the biggest first."

But the two didn't move, looking to Shrump for confirmation. Tic went and stood before them. "Listen, you two," he said. "I hired you, I'm paying you, and when I give an order, you follow it, understand?"

Shrump lifted his chin toward the rocks, and the two turned and followed Tic over to a piece of sandstone several inches thick and five or six feet in diameter. Stooping opposite each other, they grasped the edges and, grunting, lifted it and sidestepped over to Harris.

"Easy now, boys," Tic was saying. "We don't want to start snapping his ribs too quickly," he added, as the men gently laid their burden on Harris' chest.

He groaned, and tried feebly to push the rock off himself, but he was too weak.

Evans turned to Shrump. "This is bullshit, man—" he began.

Quickly Tic drew his gun and pointed it into the man's face. "You'll do this because I'll kill you if you don't. I don't care. Give me your gun."

Involuntarily, the man looked over at Shrump, who stared at him stone-faced. Slowly, he drew his gun from the holster and handed it to Tic, who said, "You hesitate again, I'll kill you."

He squatted once again by Harris, then glanced over at me. "You'll be interested to know, asshole, that you're going to die for a very good reason," he said, as the militiamen selected another slab of sandstone, this one nearly as big as the first. "By killing you, your brothers in arms are proving to my satisfaction their loyalty to me, and only me. Comprendo?

"Some people think I'm crazy, but I only kill for a good reason. For example, first there was that Navajo cop, Eddie something or other—"

"Watchman," I said, although it hurt like hell to talk.

Tic turned to me. "Good golly, Miss Molly. I wondered when you were going to jump in."

He looked down at Harris. "Hey, shit for brains. Meet Sarah Tanner, Ranger, U.S. Park Service. Every execution needs a witness, and she's yours. I think she'll understand if you don't get up.

"Now, where were we? Oh yes. Watchman. Sneaking up with his gun drawn. And me in the middle of a business deal. Does that seem right?" he asked, as the two men laid the second rock on the first.

Harris let out a high-pitched squeal like a rat being stepped on.

"Then came Rooney and Adolpho. Again, strictly business, although there were a couple of loose ends needed cleaning up after I drowned Adolpho," he said. "Two of his gang banger buddies. But we gave them a big Lake Powell welcome, so not to worry."

Good God, I thought. *Has he killed them, too?*

"Finally, there was Vernon Steps, illicit artifacts dealer and munificent sponsor of Tic Douloureux Enterprises, who ran out of money and had an unfortunate encounter with gravity."

Miller and Evans set another sandstone piece in place. Harris gave out a long, slow moan.

"And the hits just keep on coming, although you'll be pleased to know, Harris, that you won't be the last," said Tic, looking up from Harris to me. "Oh no, I'm just working my way up the food chain to the bigger fish," he said grimly. "That's right, missy. Jordan and I had a little talk while we were fishing. He tell you he told me about your meeting with the skinhead militia out on the Strip? Said you were questioning them about what's turned out to be my handiwork," he said, as the men retrieved another slab from the rock pile and balanced it atop Harris, whose eyes were beginning to bulge from his head.

Tic looked down to his victim, said softly, "So you're special, see? The others I found on my own, but no less a person than the respectable Dr. Hunt led me to you."

Harris cried out in pain, caused my head to swim. I was terribly confused. *Why would Jordan have told Tic about the militia?*

As if he were reading my mind, Tic came over and kneeled in the sand before me, his face only inches from mine. He shook his head, said softly, "That man of yours, I swear. Got some crazy idea he owes me something, thought he'd pay me back with that little bit of information. Now he thinks he's done paying, but he still owes more.

"A LOT MORE!" he suddenly shouted. "HE OWES ME HIS FUCKING LIFE, ALL OF IT—HIS PRACTICE, HIS SAINTLY REPUTATION, HIS FAMILY—EVERYTHING!"

He leaned in so close we were practically touching noses. "Even you," he said quietly. "And I intend to collect."

My mouth was dry as dust or I'd have spit in his eye.

"Go to hell," I said as firmly as I could.

He got to his feet and laughed. I looked up at him from where I sat. He stood between me and the fire, his face in shadow.

"You have no idea," he said, "how long I've already been there . . . Or how soon our friend Harris will be there," he added, signaling to the two militiamen, who laid another rock on Harris, who gasped several times, then screamed.

"Aha! Sounds like he's just arrived," exulted Tic.

My head throbbed every time Harris screamed. Pinpoints of light floated before my eyes as I watched Tic get down, put his head close to Harris'. "Nothing personal, you understand. I just need you to confirm something I already suspect."

I saw Miller and Evans share a puzzled look.

"Give me what I need, and all the rocks will go away."

Harris said nothing; Tic motioned the two men to set another piece of sandstone on the pile. I heard a sharp pop from inside Harris' chest, and I realized with horror that one of his ribs had snapped. He screamed again, and things began to go black. The last thing I saw before my head slumped forward was Tic leaning down to listen to Harris' guttural whisper.

I couldn't have been out for too long because when I came to, the two militiamen were moving another stone onto Harris, whose head was slowly turning from side to side. Tic was still talking to him.

"So I lied about the rocks," he was saying. But Harris looked like he was beyond caring.

"And isn't that just like life?" Tic continued. "It's all a lie. The years go by, and you keep hoping that things will get better, but they only get worse. It's like these rocks. The weight of all the shitty things that happen to you begins to accumulate after awhile, doesn't it? Not at first, no. You're still young, you're strong, there hasn't been enough time for too much to fall apart. In fact, you feel good, overcome some adversity, laugh in the face of trial and tribulation. Actually makes you stronger.

"But time, my friend, time persists. It never quits, never subsides, it just keeps piling on until it finally kills you."

Harris coughed, spraying blood over his own face.

"But that's the funny thing," Tic said. "It's not the individual piece that kills you, and yet it is. It's the accumulated weight of things, all the disappointments, the failures, the fighting and losing. And yet it's not. You keep pushing ahead under the weight of all those things until one fine day, life piles on one rock too many, doesn't even have to be a big rock, and snap!"

He snapped his fingers. "A couple of ribs break, throwing all that weight onto the remaining ribs, which can't support it, so, one at a time, faster and faster—snap, crackle, pop—they begin collapsing, snapping, and as they do, they puncture your lungs, maybe your heart, and suddenly blood is filling your mouth and you realize you're dying. But until that happens, you just don't know which particular rock is going to be the one that finishes you off. So you just keep going until suddenly you can't go anymore."

At that moment Tic broke into song—"That's life, that's what the people say, Ridin' high in April, shot down in May!" he sang in a bad imitation of Sinatra. "Oh, Harris, by the way, part of this is payback for another business deal gone bad. You remember the map I sold you last fall, the map to the ruin where you found that Anasazi pot? The one you were supposed to sell to me? Except you tried to cut me out, didn't you, tried selling the pot to those folks in the trailer park, and Sarah here caught wind of it, didn't she?

"I'm trying to start a business here, can't you see that? Picking up where my daddy left off, only I'm going to do him one better. It won't be me out there scrabbling in the dirt under a hot sun. Oh no, I'll be sitting in my air conditioned office or out fishing, and the pots will come to me.

"Only you won't be bringing me any. You had your chance," he snarled.

And with the strength of madness in him, he picked up a rock that, from the size of it, must have weighed half what he did, and slammed it down on the pile beneath which Harris was now nearly buried. From his chest came the ghastly sound of fracturing bone as the rocks above him settled for the last time. He gave a blood-curdling scream, then lay silent, but for the ragged gurgle of his last breath. In response, my head pulsed so hard I was sure it had split wide open, and I went under.

FRANK

"Damnit! What was she thinking?" I asked.

I saw Luke and Jordan exchange glances.

"Frank, we played back the tape of Shrump's call—" Luke began, but I cut him off, put up my hand.

"Sidebar here. Excuse me, but Jordan, you now understand we've put the skinhead militia to work for us."

He looked around at the group, his face coloring. "Not sure why I couldn't have been told, but we don't have time for that, now."

"Sarah had good reason to believe that Niles here was in immediate danger," said Luke. "So she jumped. And we'll get her back. According to what Niles told us, things could still work out."

"Oh, and how's that?" I couldn't keep the sarcasm out of my voice.

Niles, looking a little worse for wear but otherwise alright, said, "Tic had Shrump and two of his militia men help murder Harris."

"They killed one of their own?" Luanda asked.

"Tic said they needed to prove their loyalty to him," said Niles.

"Guess we're lucky it was him and not you," she said.

"I was just the messenger boy."

"And we're glad to have you back, Niles," I said. "But, Luke, if their allegiance now is to Tic and not us, I don't see how that's going to work out."

"We think that Shrump and his guys were just solidifying their cover," said Luke.

"By killing one of their own men?"

"Maybe they felt Harris had become a liability," said Luke. "Sarah and I arrested him last fall for pot hunting."

"Big deal! Half the guys out at Poverty Mountain have arrest records."

"But not with us," said Luke. "They knew we knew him. Maybe they thought we'd turned him and he was spying for us."

I was only partially convinced, and I told him so.

"Remember too that there's a lot of money involved here," he continued. "Not just the reward that we've put up for Tic's apprehension, but the money that Tic's paying them. Shrump struck me as one cold son-of-a-bitch. I wouldn't put it past him to murder one of his own men to prove his fealty to Tic and get his hands on it."

We all stood quietly for a moment, thinking, until Jordan chimed in. "Let's pose some 'what ifs'," he said. "What if the militia's cover is blown, and Tic now knows they're informing for us? We still don't know what he's planning, and if he knows we're listening, he's going to be very careful about telling the militia anything usable. Still, they might pick up something. And if he gets too paranoid, he might decide to drop his plans altogether."

I nodded. "But he's come this far," I said. "What if he decides to just carry on with his plans anyway, and keeps the militia because he knows he can't get the job done without them?"

"Then they'll tell us whatever they can," said Luke.

"But will he carry on knowing that one of them could shoot him in the back at any time?" asked Luanda.

"In which case, I might add, our problem is solved," said Jordan.

"And if he takes out a few militiamen when he goes, that's fewer headaches for us," I added.

Jordan shrugged. "On the other hand, Tic is a resourceful guy. He's good at keeping himself alive."

"My concern isn't so much Tic as the militia," said Luanda. "Will they stick with him now they know their cover is blown?"

"That's another 'what if'," said Jordan. "What if they *don't* know. It makes sense that if Tic needs them, he just won't tell them."

"But won't Shrump tell them?" she asked. "He called Sarah and told her Tic had Niles, so when she showed up, Shrump knew that Tic would realize he was reporting to us."

Niles shook his head. "I don't think Shrump blew their cover. When he and Tic caught me, I got scared. I lied and told them I had already called in the location, so Shrump might have felt safe giving Sarah the same coordinates."

"And when Sarah showed up, Tic just figured it was because Niles really had called in," I concluded.

Luke said, "Either way, I think Shrump's just in it for the cash. Niles's already seen him sacrifice Harris to stay in the game. Why would he tell the rest of them their cover's blown and chance that they'll walk away from the reward money and the money Tic's paying them?"

"On top of that, there's a lot more of them than there are of Tic," I said. "Maybe Shrump figures they can still pull off whatever Tic is planning."

"So if Tic's not going to tell them, why should we?" asked Luanda, voicing what everyone else was thinking.

This produced an uncomfortable silence, during which everyone stared at the floor.

"Let me be frank," I said. Jordan chuckled softly. Luke grinned and shook his head. "The skinhead militia is no friend of ours. As soon as this operation is over, they'll take the reward money and use it to plan more grief for us and for any other government lawman. And Tic, as far as we're concerned, is a criminal. So why should we hurt the militia's chances of taking him down, or rob Tic of his advantage over them? I say we go after Tic tomorrow as planned. If the militia joins us, fine. If not, we go after him alone."

"And there's an outside chance that they might already have taken him out if Shrump has told them Tic knows they're in league with us," said Luke.

"Maybe," I said doubtfully.

"I know this is playing dirty pool with the militia," said Jordan, "but now that Tic has Sarah, I say all's fair."

I saw Luke nodding approvingly.

To tell the truth, I feel sorry for Hunt. Here he is, duped by a guy used to be his best friend, right out in front of the rest of us. I don't blame him for wanting the guy brought down by any means possible.

SARAH

In the nightmare, there's fire and smoke and rocks in the fire and a claustrophobia that swells until someone cries out. Me? The cry is followed by the muffled sound of two gun shots. I am lying on my back gazing at fire-blackened rock for several minutes before I realize I'm no longer dreaming. Had the gun shots awakened me, or had I just dreamed them?

My face is wet with tears. The dim light is easy on my eyes. It dawns on me that I'm looking at the ceiling of a cave a few feet above my head, which still throbs unmercifully. But all of this seems to be happening to someone else, as though I'm standing at a distance looking at myself.

Suddenly a face leans into my view of the ceiling. Tic. Reality, all of it, suddenly pops back into place.

"I'm guessing you've suffered a mild concussion, Officer Tanner," he says.

"Thanks to you."

He reaches down and helps me to sit up. Surprisingly gentle. He holds a canteen to my lips. The water tastes really good, as though I haven't drunk in days.

But I can't hold up my head. I pull up my knees, fold my arms on them, and lay my head face down on my arms.

After a few minutes I'm able to speak. "You realize you've totally screwed up."

"How's that?"

"Jordan and Luke will come after me."

"Why do you think I let Niles go?" He chuckled. "Fear not. I've something devious in mind."

"Because you're a deviant, like Luke said."

He once again held the canteen to my mouth.

"You think they won't know it's a trap?" I asked.

"Hey, I'd be surprised if Jordan's finally figured out I'm the bad guy."

"I think kidnapping me will clinch it for him."

"But the rest of you, especially Officer Russell, must have had it nailed some time ago. Why was Jordan so slow on the uptake?"

"It's something you wouldn't understand."

"You're talking about his loyalty to me, feeling like he owed me because I saved his life. That's what you mean?"

"The fact that you know about it doesn't mean you understand it."

He sighed. "I have to admit it puzzles me."

It hurt to talk, so I laid my head back down on my arms. I'm not sure how much time passed until a question entered my mind. "So you don't feel funny planning to take a life you once saved? Wouldn't that nullify the choice you made way back when?"

"Everything moves in a circle, Officer Tanner. I've just about completed mine and I'm going to correct that wrong choice."

"You mean choosing Jordan over Stevie? And letting Stevie drown?"

He made no reply.

I raised my head and looked at him. His eyes held not a speck of human warmth. "I don't see how taking Jordan's life is going to give you Stevie back."

He shrugged. "Maybe all it will do is stop the dreams."

"That's what this is all about? Someone in your dreams telling you to kill? You're like Son of Sam, you've got a dog telling you to kill?"

He chuckled and an oily light came on in his eyes. "I took care of the dog a long time ago."

I had no idea what he was talking about, but there was something I had to know. "Why did you kill Eddie Watchman?"

The light in his eyes burned a little brighter. "I understand you and Officer Watchman were friends. Close friends."

"He was the only one of your victims I really knew."

It was uncanny, but he knew there was more to it than that. I could see it in his eyes. He said, "So you and Watchman, you once were lovers, were you not?"

Don't ask me how he knew that. I ignored his question. I said, "We know where Eddie was killed, and how he was killed, and how you tried to hide the body by dumping it into the lake."

"Damn drought caught me out, didn't it?"

"But we don't know *why* you killed him. You told me in the canyon last night—" *Was it just last night?* "—why you killed Rooney and Adolpho and Steps. How does Eddie fall into that pattern?"

"Maybe he was just in the wrong place at the wrong time."

"Whatever that means."

"Ultimately, it means Jordan and I have finally broken up. Split the blanket. Gone our separate ways. You're the one loves him now."

"Oh?"

"You came running when you thought his brother was in danger."

I felt myself blush. "You deliberately told Shrump you were going to kill Niles, didn't you, just to see whether he'd radio me."

"Like I said last night, once Jordan told me all of you were talking to Shrump and Baldy and their boys, I started to smell a rat."

"You realize that Jordan was just trying to warn you off."

"Whatever. I'm through with him. I'm passing him on to you. Save him if you can. Only you're going to have to be a little smarter than you've been 'til now. Lead with your head, Officer Tanner, not your heart."

Now I laughed, even though it hurt. "You're instructing me on matters of the heart?"

He leaned in close to me. "That's how this whole thing went off the tracks. A long time ago, I followed my heart." He sat back. "You're going to protect Jordan, don't let somebody use you like I did."

Again I felt chagrined. "That sounds like a challenge to me."

I saw the gleam in his eye.

"You take it any way you want to, Sarah."

I hadn't realized I'd fallen asleep until I woke up. The light was dimmer, but my head pulsed wickedly when I raised it to look around.

Tic lay on his side close to the far wall, apparently asleep. He had built a small fire in the middle of the cave.

As quietly as possible, I got to my hands and knees and crawled toward the entrance. When I looked back, Tic hadn't moved.

Once I got to the opening, it quickly became apparent that I wasn't going anywhere either. My breath caught as I looked down an almost sheer rock face to a canyon floor 200 feet below. A sudden attack of vertigo made my head spin and forced me to pull back. I lay on the floor and tried to decide what next.

I turned over on my back and looked up the cliff. No way out there, either. After a couple of minutes, however, it dawned on me that something was missing.

Painfully, slowly, I crawled back to the fire. The cave was not filling with smoke, yet there was none rising from the cave entrance. I watched it rise to the ceiling—then toward the back of the cave.

Tic still seemed not to have moved, so I carefully made my way toward what looked like a small boulder, behind which the smoke was disappearing. Not until I reached it did I realize it was a thick slab of sandstone, much like the ones Tic and his accomplices had piled on top of Harris. I shuddered.

Rising to my knees, I took hold of the slab edges and pulled it back toward me, then quietly rested it on the sandy floor of the cave. Before me was a tunnel, at the end of which I could see light. I crawled through and found myself on the flat top of a butte.

The sun was low in the western sky. Carefully I walked the several-hundred-yard perimeter, but could see no apparent way down. Far below and away from me I could see the lake, a miniscule boat cutting a V through its placid face. As I watched it move, I became aware of the sound of a plane engine. Looking up, I saw a single-engine plane far above, heading toward what I guessed was Page.

For some stupid reason, I waved, but it sobered me to realize what a tiny, insignificant speck of life I was in this vast expanse of rock and water. Like a tiny bit of seaweed on a great stretch of beach.

Standing at the edge of the butte, I looked down into the canyon and realized I was just above the mouth of the cave. I stepped back as another wave of vertigo hit me. I would have fallen if Tic had not suddenly appeared at my side and steadied me.

"How did you get me up here?" I asked him. "You must have carried me and there's no way you could have carried me up that," I said, pointing down the steep rock face.

"I'm tempted to lie and tell you I did, but you're not a woman impressed with bragging. No, there's another way up."

"Still, it couldn't have been easy to carry me up here."

He just looked at me, his eyes bland.

"And why am I worth all the effort? What is to be my fate? The same as Eddie's or Harris' or any of your other victims?"

"Only time will tell us that."

The sun was setting, defining the canyons and declivities around us, the curves of the original river channel now exposed by the falling water. Off to my left, at the base of the slopes leading up to Navajo Mountain, I spotted a long narrow crack in the slick rock.

"Is that a slot canyon?" I asked, pointing.

He nodded.

"I never realized there was one there."

"Uncovered by the dropping water."

I shivered. "It's creepy, all of this stuff being uncovered by the water. It's like the dead coming back to life. Like something rising from the bottom that should have stayed down there."

JORDAN

Shrump must not have told the militia their cover was blown, because the next day he and Baldy and a dozen of their guys came with us to get Tic. Careful to keep them in the dark, we used the GPS coordinates Niles had marked down after Tic had set him free. We were halfway there when I pulled my wallet from my pocket, held it up to Luke. "Niles brought it back to me. Said Tic gave it to him."

"So it was Tic who broke into your house."

I nodded. "I can't believe I was so blind for so long. That's why I couldn't be told you guys had hooked up with the militia, isn't it?"

Luke just nodded.

"Hell, I didn't even know they were working for Tic in the first place," I said.

"They must already have been working for Tic when you two went fishing," said Luke. "He didn't say anything?"

I knew Luke wasn't just trying to rub it in. Still, I felt like a total loser. A thought occurred to me, and I gave a bitter laugh. "He didn't trust me not to tell you the militia was working for him, and you didn't trust me not to tell him the militia was selling him out."

"And I can't believe we didn't get any rain last night," said Luke, changing the subject. He stood at the wheel. "Those thunderheads sure looked promising, but here we are again."

The sky was a deep blue, the sun newly risen in a million tiny mirrors on the water. The day promised to be hot, one reason we were out early. Luke, Luanda, and I, along with Shrump and half the militiamen in one boat. Frank and Baldy and the rest of the militia in another.

I put my hand on Luke's shoulder, thanked him for letting me come along.

"I know how you feel about Sarah," was all he said. He turned to Shrump. "You sure all your guys are out?"

He nodded.

"Wouldn't want them shooting each other, would we?"

But he just gave Luke a blank stare.

"Remind them Tic has Sarah hostage?" I asked.

Then he stared at me.

On our maps there was only water at the coordinates Niles had given us, but the lake had been dropping so quickly that we knew it was entirely possible some long drowned canyon could have emerged above water.

I hated the fact that we were going after Tic on his terms and not ours. He knew that Shrump or Niles would be able to lead us back here, and that we would be sure to come once we knew he had Sarah.

I also didn't like having Shrump and the militia along. Frank and Luanda and Luke may have been comfortable with them, but I wasn't. We had talked this morning about the likelihood of Tic ambushing us, and I had half convinced myself that at some crucial point Shrump and his guys would jump to his side. On the other hand, everyone seemed edgy, and they didn't seem to be acting.

What really bothered me was that everyone was on their toes all because Tic was calling the shots, not us, and that irritated me, particularly since he had been calling the tune with me for months. *Well, no more, old friend. Today we turn the tables.*

We followed Niles' coordinates deep into Music Hall Canyon, out behind Navajo Mountain. Niles had clearly described this drop canyon, its floor left stranded a good fifteen feet above the water that was dropping steadily day by day.

"Before the dam went in," Luke told me, "a hundred twenty-five feet separated the floor of Music Hall from the bottom of Glen Canyon."

He told me it was likely no human had walked it until boaters had ridden the rising water into its previously unreachable recesses.

The ladder still hung from the engine-valve pitons driven into the rock. We cut the engines and tied up to the bottom rungs. No need to caution quiet. We could all hear the overhanging rock walls magnifying every sound. We maintained a hush that no one felt comfortable breaking. Silently we climbed the ladder, the only sounds the huffing of breath and the occasional clink of metal on metal.

Once in the canyon, Luke pulled the slide back on his .45 and levered a round into the chamber. This served as a signal to everyone else, and the air was suddenly filled with the ratcheting sound of bolts and slides being cocked. Luke moved to the head of the group and motioned for the rest of us to follow him up the canyon single file.

Judging from the light increasing as we moved forward, I guessed the canyon widened out ahead. A minute later our eyes were dazzled by the sun bathing the vertical wall to our right. It lit up an extensive area of flat sand studded with rocks and boulders fallen from the walls above. The sun's warmth felt good after the coolness of the narrow passage behind us.

The area looked deserted. "Spread out," said Luke quietly. "Stay close to cover."

We fanned out, aware that we were surrounded by plenty of places capable of hiding a gunman. The hair on the back of my neck prickled as I crouched my way around the perimeter and came up behind Luke.

"This must be the open area Niles mentioned," I whispered. "Said it was stacked with gear."

There was nothing left now but footprints and a couple of busted pallets.

"Let's keep moving up canyon," Luke said. He motioned the others in that direction. Ahead, a huge slab of sandstone filled the canyon, with only a narrow passage on either side between it and the canyon walls. Luke, at one wall, pointed at Frank at the other, then pointed him through. We all knew that if someone lay waiting ahead, this would be the perfect place to pick us off, but nothing happened.

On the far side of the slab lay another flat, also riddled with boulders. Singly and in pairs we worked our way around them. Something off to my left caught my eye. One of Shrump's men hurried back toward us, his hand over his mouth. I watched him drop to one knee and vomit onto the sand. I realized that I had been smelling the odor of ripening flesh for the past few minutes. It was getting stronger.

Luke pointed me in the direction from which the man had come. I knew I wasn't going to like what I found there.

My brain at first couldn't make sense of what my eyes were seeing. A low stack of sandstone slabs seemed to have been piled on top of what initially looked like only another slab. Only after I looked more closely did I see the arms, legs and head. The body had been crushed so flat we couldn't be sure at first what it was.

I pulled a bandanna from my back pocket and folded it over my mouth and nose. Kneeling by the man's head, I waved away the flies that had collected thickly on the fluids still seeping from his mouth, which gaped as though he had died mid-scream. Beside me, Luke craned his head, both of us careful not to touch anything.

"That's Harris," he stated matter-of-factly.

A couple of Shrump's men came up behind us. Their whispering confirmed Harris' identity.

"No mystery how he died," I said, walking slowly around the dead man.

The discovery of Harris paradoxically seemed to put everyone at ease. Maybe they felt they had found the worst and there was nothing worse to fear. They gathered around the grisly cairn as though at a funeral.

Baldy was outraged. "What kind of sick fuck—" he began.

"There's nothing we can do for him now," said Luke. "But we can keep the living alive. Don't bunch up."

The group dispersed. In a minute we heard Baldy say "Jesus H. Christ" in a stricken voice.

Beside the canyon wall, face down, lay the bodies of two more militiamen.

"It's Miller and Evans," Baldy said in a hoarse whisper.

I looked at Shrump. He didn't say anything. If he knew what had happened to these two, I knew this wasn't the time and place to ask him. I felt a guilty twinge for keeping my mouth shut.

"Don't touch anything," said Luke. "Judging from the head shots, I'm guessing they were executed."

The group of militiamen began once more to coalesce. Luke looked around, shook his head, and began walking slowly up canyon again.

Because Niles had told me Sarah had been there, I circled back to Harris' body, looking for any sign of her. About ten yards away I saw something glint in the sun. I pulled a hanky from my pocket and carefully plucked a National Park Service badge from the sand. The number on it was Sarah's.

Relief washed over me—she really had been here. I checked the pin on the back of the badge. It was closed, but there was no patch of torn Park Service green cloth stuck on it. Did this mean she had removed it and left it here as a sign? I felt like it was a message to me, but I couldn't be sure.

I turned back to Harris' remains. Niles said Sarah had witnessed his murder. *What kind of shape is she in? Is she even still alive?* Now I looked around me with a newfound terror. *Will hers be the next corpse we find?*

My thoughts were interrupted by the sound of raised voices. Shrump and Baldy were going at it.

"We didn't bargain for this!" Baldy shouted, pointing at the bodies of the dead militiamen. "I'm pulling everybody out."

"Bill, Bill, calm down, won't you?" Shrump said in his clipped German English. "Did you think it was going to be a picnic? This man Tic, he's . . . he's—"

"He's murdered three of our men," Baldy shot back. "And I'm pretty damned sure I know why."

"Well?" asked Shrump, staring at him with cold eyes.

Baldy wasn't intimidated. "Because he found out we're working for those assholes," he said, looking over at Frank and Luanda, then Luke and me. "And here's a question—all his gear is gone. How did he know we were coming?"

"Now Bill, let's not jump to hasty conclusions," Shrump said. "We cannot know for a certainty what happened here."

"What I know for a certainty is we're leaving, and we're taking our dead with us. You can do what you want."

He stomped up to Luke and Frank, mad as hell. "I don't know how you found out, but you guys knew our cover was blown, didn't you?" he asked through gritted teeth. "You just figured you'd keep us in place and fuck the consequences." He spit in the dirt at our feet. "Well, fuck you."

He called to two of his men who were standing near Harris' body. "You guys get those rocks offa him."

Before Luke could say anything, they stepped up and got a grip on the top slab.

"No! Stop!" he shouted, but too late. In a huge explosion, the pile of rocks erupted into a fiery ball of lethal sandstone projectiles. One severed the arm and half the head of one man, killing him instantly. The other was not as lucky. He lurched to his feet in the dust, blood and viscera streaming from a gaping hole in his abdomen. Looking down, he clutched himself and began screaming, but that was quickly cut short by a gush of blood from the front of his head, followed immediately by the report of a high-powered rifle.

He dropped like the rock he'd been holding only a moment before.

"Take cover!" I shouted as I hit the deck.

More shots rang out. Everyone scrambled for the nearest rock or tree. Some were firing randomly up canyon but nobody had pinpointed the source of the rifle fire raining down on us.

A round kicked up dirt in front of me and I scrabbled for a big rock about ten yards away. Shrump was already there.

"You are a doctor, yah?" He pointed out in front of us. A militiaman lay on the ground. I could hear him moaning.

"Help me move him behind that juniper," I said.

The slug had smashed the man's shoulder, but didn't look as though it had hit anything vital.

"He'll be okay." I took the field surgical kit Sarah had given me for Christmas out of my pocket, and used my knife to cut off his shirt, which I tore into strips and began binding the wound.

Shrump watched impassively. "You are practiced."

I looked up a moment later as I dressed the wound. Shrump was gone. The gunfire continued. I kept my head down.

When I looked up again, Tic was there. Startled the hell out of me.

"Come with me," he said, sticking a gun in my face.

"No can do. Got a man down here."

"That's easily solved."

Before I could move, he shot the guy point blank in the face, splattering all three of us with his blood.

"Jesus Christ, Tic! What in the name of God—"

"You want to see Sarah alive?" He pulled me up by my arm. "Come on!"

In shock, I stumbled ahead of him along the canyon wall, his gun jammed into my spine. Behind me I heard Luke trying to organize fire toward a place up on the rim. That fight was over for me. I had only one thought. Sarah was still alive.

*****

Sarah!

I had never been so happy to see someone in my life, yet so saddened by how bad she looked. Blood from a scalp wound along with dust and ground debris had dried and matted in her hair. Her uniform, usually so clean and crisp, now was pleated with dirt as she lay crumpled on the floor of the cave.

I took off my shirt, folded it and, as tenderly as I could, placed it under her head as a pillow. I smoothed her hair back from her face.

Her eyes fluttered open; it took a few seconds for her to focus. I gently clasped the hand she raised to me.

I fished her badge from my pocket. "I think you lost this," I said, as I pinned it back on her blouse.

She squeezed my hand. "Oh Jordan," she whispered, "I'm such an idiot. Tic laid a trap and I walked right into it."

"Niles told us what happened. There was no way you could have known."

I saw tears well up in her eyes.

"My only concern right now is you," I said. "Tell me how you got hurt."

She told me about the blow to her head, her drifting in and out of consciousness, her inability to walk steadily.

"Sounds like a concussion. The best thing you can do is lie here quietly."

I gently touched the back of her head. "You did get a good whack on the noggin. Compliments of our mutual friend?"

She nodded. "I was walking up the canyon. I heard a noise behind me, but before I could turn around the lights went out."

She looked around the cave. "And now he's caught you? What happened?"

"We went after him and he cut me out of the pack, marched me to a neighboring canyon and onto his boat."

"That's exactly the way he planned it. Did you see where we are?"

I shrugged. "He blindfolded me once we were on the boat."

"I've been up on the mesa top, but I wasn't able to orient myself."

"We had to do some pretty difficult free climbing to reach this cave. I don't know how Tic got you up here."

"Now that you're here, I don't care." She reached her arms out to me. "Hold me."

She was trembling. I held her until she quieted. She pushed me away. For a moment, the pain clouding her eyes cleared. "Tic said you told him we were talking to the skinhead militia." There was an edge to her voice.

I looked her right back in the eye. "I told him I thought they had committed the murders. I told him what you told me, that they had heard someone was moving in on the local drug business, an ex-military guy who was planning something big."

"Jordan, you must have known they were talking about Tic."

"I know it sounds stupid now, but I was still hoping the militia was to blame for the killings. On the other hand, I wasn't sure it wasn't Tic, so I tried to scare him off. I hoped that if he knew that other people were on to his plan, he'd ditch it."

"We knew how you felt about Tic," she said. "That's why we didn't tell you about the deal we made with the militia."

I hung my head. "I don't blame you." I realized now, that like Tic, I had blood on my hands. By putting Tic onto the possibility of the militia being involved, I had brought about Harris' death as well as Tic's attack on Sarah.

I cupped her cheek in my hand. "Sarah, I'm so sorry."

She smiled weakly. "Darling, I admire your devotion to Tic, but I think you can see now what it cost."

"I saw the same signs you were seeing. I just turned them around to point at the militia, not this," I said, gesturing to mean not only her injury but all the death and destruction Tic had caused over the past year.

"Of course, if you hadn't persisted, we'd never have gone out to question them, and we'd never have made the deal we did," she said. "Only now I've blown their cover."

"Maybe not," I said. "They came with us when we went after Tic. We don't know which way those guys will fall. The reward money for Tic's capture still stands." I paused. "Although now we may have another problem."

"What's that?"

"Baldy found two of his men while we were looking for Tic. They'd been executed."

"They must have been the two laying the rocks on Harris; I heard Tic telling them they had to prove their loyalty to him. The last I saw them they were alive. But I was passing in and out of consciousness the whole time."

"Well, Baldy told Shrump he was pulling out of the deal."

"So now, thanks to me, we've lost our inside track." She began to cry quietly, tears sliding down her face.

I leaned down and took her in my arms again.

"Oh, Jordan, there was so much blood," she whispered as she clung to me.

After a few minutes, I asked, "Has Tic said anything to you about what he's planning?"

"Only something about going after bigger fish. He told me to protect you. Is there any way out of here?"

"I could probably climb down, although I'm sure Tic or Carey is watching. But you can't be moved, not right now."

"Then stay with me, please."

I took her hand in mine. "We'll sit tight for now. When Tic comes back, we'll see what he has up his sleeve."

LUKE

The lake might have been at record low level, but Fourth of July weekend looked like it was going to be as big as ever, which gave us no time to lick our wounds after yesterday's debacle. The lodge was booked solid for the entire week bracketing the holiday itself. Every houseboat, even the big beasts that went for $15,000 a week, as well as every power boat, ski-doo, and rowboat had been rented.

We'd looked high and low for Jordan once the hostile fire had stopped, but we'd lost his trail on the slick rock above the canyon in which we'd been ambushed. Darkness had seen us leaving the canyon with our tails between our legs. First Sarah gone, now Jordan. On top of that, I was pretty sure we'd seen the last of the skinhead militia. All of it put a bitter taste in my mouth, left me fearing the worst but hoping for the best.

On the bright side, Luanda had volunteered to stay through the weekend to provide backup. We stood outside the rental office on the main dock, looking out over Wahweap Bay, which, although shrunken by the drought, was still huge. Even so, I knew that by the weekend, its surface would be swarming with craft of all shapes and sizes, from kayaks to cabin cruisers. We were going to have our hands full.

Although it was early, I looked behind me at the horizon to the south southeast, hoping to see the monsoon thunder heads forming that would bring us some rain later in the day. The weather guys were expecting the monsoon to boil up any day, but the sky was cloudless.

Stepping inside the office, I took down the clipboard on which were posted all the boats scheduled to sail over the holiday. We figured Tic was planning something, and it would be like him to try it over a holiday, when he'd know we'd be slammed. I was checking every angle, from campground reservations to weather forecasts to police reports, putting out the antennae, trying to pick up something—anything—that might tip us off.

I scanned the names on the list of houseboat rentals and departures. Halfway down I stopped.

"Esquibel, Ernest, Commander. Why does that name sound familiar?"

"Somebody you knew in the military?"

"No, not me," I said, my mind racing back over the past few months. "Not me," I repeated, then it hit me.

"Douloureux! The background check. That's where I saw it!"

"Who is he?"

"Douloureux's CO in Afghanistan. His name rang a bell back in December when I was checking out Tic's story about leaving the SEALs! Commander Esquibel. He owns a houseboat up here, takes it out every Fourth for a big poker run with some of his pals."

"So?"

"Don't you see? That's the link! That's what Tic is planning!"

She still looked puzzled.

"He's going after the commander!"

I watched realization suffuse her face.

"And right in Tic's back yard," she said, nodding.

I was thinking back a couple of Fourths, the commander walking down the ramp to the slip where his boat was tied.

"Now I remember," I said ominously. "The commander was limping, walking with a cane—"

"After Tic attacked him," Luanda finished.

I checked the list again, then rehung the clipboard.

"Come on," I said to her. "I've got an idea."

TIC

Yes, I knew it had been six months since Carey had started tending bar at the Wahweap lounge, but I still had to laugh every time I came in and saw him there in his little red bartender's vest, all clean shaven with a city boy haircut but without that bent-rim straw hat crammed down on it. Thank God his voice still sounded like he gargled with broken glass or I wouldn't have known it was him.

I took a seat at the table he'd marked "Reserved," the only one in the lounge with a clear view of both the reservation desk in the lobby and Carey behind the bar.

"Anything shakin'?" I asked as he set a beer down in front of me.

"Nothin' I know of," he said. "But I've been pretty busy."

I looked around. Nearly every table was filled, only a couple empty seats at the bar.

"Well, back at it, then," I said. "We all set?"

He nodded and hurried off.

Now, it was down to waiting. I turned and looked out the plate glass windows, watching the high summer sun bleach the red from the sandstone bluffs across the bay. I could feel the weight of all the months of planning resting easily on me and thought: *Now it all comes together. Everything is in place. The fucking militia's going to try something smart before it's all said and done, but I'm on top of it, man, on top of it.*

Sitting there with a cold beer in my hand, I was excited, strung tight and yet feeling loose, right where I needed to be for what was coming next.

Turning the other way, I looked out into the crowded lobby, spotted the plain-clothes ranger standing inside the front door. I couldn't see them from where I sat, but I knew there'd be another loitering by the elevator, a third marking time at the foot of the stairs.

For all the good it's going to do them. Still, it's flattering in a way.

"Well, where do you think the fuckin' camel came from?" said a raised voice behind me and to my left, followed by loud laughter. It wasn't even Happy Hour yet and some bozo was already gassed up. I turned, saw the others at his table trying to shush him.

"Okay, okay," he was saying in a softer voice, "have you heard this one?"

I tried to listen in but the place was too noisy. Between frequent glances into the lobby, I watched Carey working behind the bar. *Damn, that old reprobate knows what he's doing back there,* I thought. *Finally earning an honest living—almost.*

I checked my watch. Almost time.

C'mon, you short son-of-a-bitch. Let's get this show on the road. I got something waiting for you—my own little science experiment—and you're the subject. See how you do in my place.

I took a deep breath. *Gently gently now, plenty of time for mayhem later.*

Not long after, the joker behind me set off another one, cracking up not only his table but several around him. I looked around as he swigged his beer, caught his eye. Shithead actually waved at me. I shook my head, then turned to look out into the lobby again.

I felt the shock before my mind registered that it was him. The crew-cut black hair, the short squared off frame. Brought me right back into his office, him sitting up straight when I walked in, standing real sudden as I came around the desk for him. Esquibel!

I watched him walk up to the counter. He was limping and supporting himself with a cane. Happiness flooded me. I knew I had broken his leg that day. Just never realized what a bang up job I'd done. *Serves you right, you little motherfucker. Hiding behind that desk while I was out getting shot at.*

He checked in, headed for the elevator followed by a bell boy with his bag.

I checked the time. Five minutes later, I caught Carey's eye and tipped my beer at him. I watched him turn and say something to the other bartender, who nodded. Removing his little waist apron, he came out from behind the bar and walked to the front desk, where he hailed one of the clerks.

That's right, just like we rehearsed. 'Commander Esquibel just phoned the bar for room service, but I forgot to get his room number.'

I watched the clerk nod and check his screen. No problem.

After a moment, he spoke to Carey, who raised his hand in thanks and headed back to the bar, where he started setting up a tray for the commander. I waited until he headed for the lobby with it, then left using the door to the outside patio and walked to the locked door at the foot of the stairs where we'd agreed to meet.

In less than a minute, he pushed it open and we climbed the stairs to the second floor, where he cracked the door wide enough to see that there was a deputy standing outside the commander's room.

"That figures," I said, then held the tray while Carey straightened his vest and little bow tie.

"You look terrific," I said. "Now get your ass in there."

He grinned and opened the door, which I held open just enough to overhear them.

"Hey, buddy," said Carey. "Want to knock on the door there? Got some liquid refreshment here for the commander, and he don't like to wait."

I watched the deputy knock, his back toward me. I made my move, and I was standing behind him when Esquibel opened the door. His eyes flicked from Carey to the deputy to me, and I saw them widen in shock, then fear, which he quickly managed to convert to surprise.

"Hey, commander," I said, with a wave and a grin, doing my best Gomer Pyle imitation.

The deputy about jumped out of his skin. "Where the hell did *you* come from?"

"Just dropped by to see the good commander here," I said, "so if you'll excuse me."

"Wait a minute—" he said.

The commander stepped forward. "It's okay, officer. He can come in," he said calmly, stepping back to let us pass. The door swung shut behind us.

Esquibel just stared at me without a word as Carey set the tray on a table in the corner. The commander stuffed a tip in his hand and Carey hurried out, but not before giving me a wink and the commander a relaxed salute.

Esquibel filled two glasses with cracked ice, uncorked the bottle of bourbon, and poured us both a drink. "I assume the bartender is a friend," he said.

I nodded. "Today happens to be his last shift, though."

"Somehow I knew that," he said. "So what the hell are you doing here, Douloureux?"

I shrugged. "Heard you were in town. Thought I'd drop by for old times' sake."

"So it wasn't enough that you almost killed me? You have to gloat over it?" His knuckles were white on the glass he was holding.

"My, my, you do get right down to it, don't you, Commander?"

He glared at me.

"I'm not here to gloat, Commander. I actually wanted to bring you a peace offering."

"Bullshit."

"Now sir, let's don't make this any harder than it already is," I said, pulling out a chair and sitting down. "I realize I have a lot of lost ground to regain here, but remember I paid the price for what I did."

"What," he said sardonically. "A couple of years in the brig and a dishonorable discharge? Big fucking deal, Douloureux."

He indicated his leg. "You know how many operations it's taken to get me this far? I'm lucky I still have this leg after you got through with it!"

He was nearly shouting, but I sensed somehow that he wasn't completely sincere.

"Have a seat, Commander," I said, pulling out a second chair. "C'mon. Relax."

But he remained standing, glaring down at me.

"Don't get too comfortable, Douloureux. You're not staying long."

I jumped up, setting my glass on the table. "Have it your way, sir. I understand how you feel." I headed for the door. How did I know he was going to call me back?

My hand was on the knob when he said, "Hold on, Douloureux," grunting it out like it really cost him something. "Come finish your drink."

Once I was seated, he said, "Okay. What are you offering?"

"Well, sir, you probably didn't know I grew up around here—"

"Yes, yes, I know. The rock climbing and all."

"That's right. And you probably know that the lake is real low because of the drought."

"And so?"

"Well, I'm offering to pilot your houseboat while you're out on the lake, sir. I know this country like the back of my hand, and with the water this low I could show you places in these canyons that nobody's seen in forty years . . . and I know some sweet camping spots."

I stood and went to the window, looking out. "You might not realize it, sir. But the discharge has made it hard to find a decent job. It's like being an ex-con. I'm just scraping by."

He gave a snort of disbelief. "You always had a scam of some sort going on, Douloureux. How do I know this isn't another one?"

I turned to face him. "Because this is about more than the money, sir," I said, looking him straight in the eye. "It's a chance to redeem myself."

Now he laughed out loud. "I remember the last time you wanted to redeem yourself, Douloureux. Two good men died."

"I understand that, sir, which is why I want to do this."

"You ever think about the families of those two men, Douloureux?" he asked harshly. "Dylan had a wife and a couple of kids."

I nodded. "Yes sir, I know that. There's not much I can do for them now. But I can do something for you."

He shook his head, set his empty glass on the table. "I will say this, Douloureux, you always had brass ones when it came to talking your way into something."

I grinned. "Is that a yes, sir?"

He wasn't smiling, just staring at me like I was something on the bottom of his shoe that he'd just stepped in. "Call me in the morning. I'll tell you what time to be here."

Why we had to tie up on shore and continue our trip down lake on foot I don't know. The sun was behind the Kaibab Plateau to the west, a cliff wall to our right along a gravel edge.

Tic jabbed his gun into my back.

"What's the rush?" I asked.

"You are *not* going to believe this," he said. Actually excited.

Another hundred yards we came around a bend in the wall and there at the water's edge was Sarah. Sitting in a battered old aluminum boat. She stood when she saw us.

Carey stood off to one side, rifle trained on her.

Now I knew where Tic had taken her when they'd left the cave together. I embraced her. She latched onto me like she was falling. I felt like I was holding life itself.

"Take this," I whispered, palming the small plastic box to her.

"All right, back off," said Tic.

I turned to him. "You've got *me*. You don't need Sarah anymore. Let her go."

"Yeah, yeah, whatever. Don't you recognize it?"

I looked at him.

"The boat, you idiot!"

I looked down. In my mind a distant memory stirred.

Tic was hopping around like he was Jay-Z. "It's the boat!" he said. "The *same* boat."

I stepped over and peered inside. Sure enough, a hole big enough to put your fist through rent the bottom.

"Park Service hired a friend of mine this summer to haul out all the junk exposed by the falling water. Had it piled up in his equipment yard when I saw it."

I ran my hand along the gunwale. "I'll be damned." I looked up at him. "Kind of brings that whole day back, doesn't it?"

"Me, too. Only it made me understand."

"What's that?"

"You have to stand trial."

I glanced at Sarah.

"For Stevie's death."

"I don't get it."

"Of course, you don't. You're Jordan Hunt!"

"And?"

"You're invulnerable! Even unto death!"

"Tic, what the hell are you talking about?"

"Maybe it was a charm. Who knows?"

I don't know who he's talking to. It's not anyone present. I think of how his voice had changed back when he was describing what had happened in Afghanistan.

"But it was always there. Top student. Football star. Army Ranger. Doctor."

"Tic," I said, but he wasn't listening.

"Your life has just been stepping from one stone to the next, never any real fear that you'd fall in, or if you did, you'd just get wet, no danger of drowning . . . all of you Hunts. No. I take it back. Not your old man. He'd understand vulnerability—your mother and the booze. But you three boys, you were insufferable! So aloof. So . . . untouchable."

"It's all in your head, Tic."

"And somehow that makes it less real?" he asked, truly puzzled. "That shield. You just figured we all had one. You couldn't imagine someone coming after you only because of what you were . . . ironic that ultimately that's what's made you vulnerable."

"No, Tic, what made me vulnerable was hoping you had changed and giving you a chance to show it."

"You didn't give a flying fuck about me. It's all come down to shielding her. There's the chink, the one that allowed me to come after you, like they came after me once Stevie died. First it was my old man, then the people in this shitty little town. Even the fucking military. I was among the best of the best. Bullet proof, you understand? But I couldn't keep it up. I couldn't escape Stevie's death."

"But Tic, you saved me."

He looked around like he had suddenly remembered we were there.

"I was going down for the last time," I said.

He gave a bitter laugh. "Exactly! And what did I do the one time you were facing death, the one time you were really exposed? I saved you! I pulled you back behind the shield, where you've lived ever since."

"You saved my life."

"And look how that's turned out. You and the rangers running me to ground."

"You know why."

He nodded. "But you don't."

He reached inside the boat, brought out a length of chain and a pair of padlocks. "Talk. Talk. Talk. We're never going to resolve this ourselves. That day it was me judged who was to live and die. Didn't turn out so good. Now we'll let the water be the judge. You know anything about the New England witch trials back in the 17ᵗʰ century?" he asked me. I shook my head. "You, Officer Tanner?"

"I know many innocent people died, mostly women," she said.

"Did you ever hear of the 'ducking test'?"

Sarah glanced at me. "Isn't that where the accused was thrown into a pond, and if she floated . . ."

"She was guilty," he said. "And if she sank—"

"Innocent," I said.

"Good, Jordan. But did you know the theory behind the test?"

I shook my head.

"They believed that water was pure, and if you floated, the water was casting you out because your spirit was evil."

He looked out over the water. "And if you sank, the water accepted you because you were pure as well."

He chuckled. "Of course, that left you underwater."

He sighed, looked again out over the lake. "All this water, foiled. Trapped when it's supposed to run free. Made its own rivers so it could run. But men made dams. Men like your father. Turned a river into this bath tub, this cesspool filling up with silt and trash . . . this lake, that took Stevie.

"But that's me. I'm willing to let the water judge what you and your father have done, Jordan."

He put the gun on me. Held out the chain. "Run it through the hole. That's it. Now padlock it. That's right."

I had seen the oars in the boat. I knew what he had in mind.

"Kind of tipping the odds in favor of innocent here, aren't we?" I asked.

"I left Stevie to his fate to save you. Now I'm leaving you to yours. Cover me," he said to Carey. He stepped up and patted me down. "Into the boat."

"Give me a minute."

He looked at Sarah. "Make it quick."

She slipped it into my back pocket as I held her. I prayed the hope I saw in her eyes was a reflection of what she saw in mine.

"It's your fault she's here, Jordan. You're the one told me the feds were talking to the militia. You can chalk Harris up, too."

"Why did he have to die?"

"That was an accident, actually. I was only trying to squeeze some information from him."

"So what'd you find out?"

"Nothing I didn't already know after Officer Tanner here showed up to save your brother," he said.

"Then why kill him like that?"

"Guess I was just disappointed in him and his compadres."

"Let Sarah go, Tic."

"Not quite yet, I don't think. She's my witness. And my bargaining chip. Let's tend to the matter at hand, shall we?" He pointed his gun at the chain. "Now the other end. Around your neck. The padlock."

He motioned to Carey, who stepped to the other side of the boat and helped Tic slide it into the water.

"Thanks again for the tip about the feds," he said as I stepped into the boat.

I picked up the oars.

"But see what happens?" he asked. "When somebody tries to help me? People die!"

*****

Tic and Sarah stood in the dusk watching me row for the opposite shore. Carey kept the .30-06 trained on me. Water flowed steadily into the boat. Fifty yards out it was plain I was in a losing battle. The boat was half-submerged. Rowing it was quickly becoming an exercise in futility.

Water slipped over the gunwales and she started for the bottom in earnest. I abandoned the oars and began to swim. I knew right away I would never make land.

I heard Tic laughing. "Twenty years ago you'd have done it no sweat. Price you pay for getting old."

I felt like I was towing a septic tank behind me.

The chain was cutting off my wind. A moment of panic, but I knew that would kill me quicker than anything. I turned on my back. Took several deep breaths before the boat pulled me under.

I went totally limp. No sense in exhausting myself trying to swim. Better to save myself for the job ahead. Better anyway to sink than to give Carey a chance to blow my head off, which I knew he might do just for the target practice.

I started down. Reaching into my back pocket, I pulled out the miniature field surgery kit Sarah had tucked in there a few minutes earlier. Gift from her last Christmas, one I know she was onshore praying I could put to its best use ever.

The padlock up by my neck was too close for me to see what I was doing. I focused my efforts on the other one. Pressure on my ear drums growing. The mirror that is the surface receding.

Don't drop the kit. That blade.

I tried it in the lock.

Too wide. Another. Still too wide.

I plucked a narrower one from the box. Dropped it, watched it flit away like a minnow.

Damn! Panic spiked in my chest. My heart pounded. Lights like tiny candle flames floated before my face. I was deep enough the light was almost gone. The water was getting colder, numbing my fingers.

I fumbled with the kit. Seized a probe, but dropped the lock. Ran my hand down the chain to where it should be, but I'd gone blind. My fingers had turned to wood.

My brain was on fire. Burning up what little air I had left.

And then I felt a hand grasp mine. I swear it. Took my hand and guided it to the lock.

What in the name of God?

I looked down, and there, not a foot away, was a wavering image of a face. Stevie's face, lit by the candle flames, which were snuffing themselves one by one.

Damn! I dropped the lock. Again he moved my hand.

Working by touch, I grasped the lock. Jammed the lance into the keyhole.

My last thought: *There isn't going to be another chance. For me or for Sarah.*

Before my face, I swear I saw Stevie smile like an angel.

LUKE

Although the sun was not yet up, I looked to the southern horizon, purely out of habit, hoping to see some sign of rain heading our way. Billowy cumulonimbus that marked the advance of the moisture-laden monsoon.

And sure enough, their tops just showing on the horizon, was what I had been hoping for. They might take all day to get here, or they might not get here at all, but for now it was enough that they were there.

"You sure you still want to do this?" I asked.

Esquibel turned from stowing groceries in the galley of his houseboat. "Why not?"

"Too many unknowns. For one, Douloureux's no-show this morning."

"And after that fiasco in the canyon, we don't know what's happening with the militia," Frank added.

"I thought you said Baldwin pulled them out," the commander said.

Frank shrugged. "That's what he said."

"Then who does Douloureux have working for him?"

"That's just it," I said. "We don't know. With the militia gone, we've lost our eyes and ears. Our cavalry, so to speak."

"But you never know about them," said Frank. "If they don't stay in place per the original deal, they don't get paid."

"On top of that, Jordan and Sarah are still MIA," I said. "We know Douloureux has Sarah, and I'm guessing he has Jordan, too."

"Russell, this whole idea of an attack on me is just that," Esquibel said. "An idea. I mean . . . have any of the militia told you this is Douloureux's *plan*?"

"He's too smart for that, commander. But I can tell you he's got motive. Now you're proposing we give him opportunity."

"And means?"

"He's been buying hardware by the boat load, enough to outfit a small force, certainly more of a force than you've got here."

Esquibel looked around at his six buddies, all of them busy moving gear on board.

"They're all military, Russell. Either active or recently retired. They know how to handle themselves."

"No disrespect, sir, but you don't know what you're up against."

"Aren't I up against the same loser who froze on a cliff in Afghanistan and got two of his men killed?"

"I might point out that this is the same loser who almost killed you," I said.

He looked at me. "The operative word in that sentence being 'almost.' You might consider that I've got some motivation going, too."

Just then a rusty 4-wheel-drive Suburban pulled up, followed by two crew-cab pickups. Shrump and Baldy exited the lead vehicle. Six of their men joined them.

Shrump looked like the cat who'd eaten the canary. "Good morning, Officer Russell."

"I thought you guys were out of here," I said.

He glanced at Baldy, and said, "It seems we've had a change of heart."

Baldy cleared his throat. "I hate losing any of my men," he said, talking to the ground. "And we lost six good ones up in that canyon. Got two more in the hospital."

He looked up, looked me in the eye. "I want Douloureux dead."

"What are you proposing?"

Shrump surveyed the houseboat. "This is a 72-footer, yes? Sleeps 12 . . . 14?"

Esquibel stepped up.

"And this is the commander, yes?"

Esquibel eyed him. "What's the plan?"

"That we accompany you on your boat, as body guards."

Esquibel looked over the crew assembled before him. "You're well armed, I'll give you that."

Shrump smiled. "And well disciplined."

Bullshit, I thought. *Oh yes, commander, you should have seen how well they handled themselves when we went after Douloureux. Like sheep in a shit storm.*

Esquibel chuckled. "So who's in charge, you or the big guy?"

"We are, what would you say, co-captains, yah?"

Esquibel looked doubtful.

"Much like your famous explorers, Captains Lewis and Clark."

Esquibel shrugged. "I guess."

Shrump turned to Frank. "We also came back for the money."

"Only the original money stands," said Frank. "I'm not authorized to pay out any more."

"Certainly you can find someone who is," Shrump replied smoothly. "If we are to take out Douloureux for you, he will be unable to remit the remainder of our wages."

"And then you'd be short, is that it?"

Shrump merely nodded.

As they hashed out the money, I told myself that this didn't feel right. I could believe Baldy wanted revenge. I trusted revenge. What I didn't trust was Shrump. From the start it had been the money with him. As lowlife as Baldy was, I knew he had bled with his men. Had Shrump?

Frank's conversation with Shrump ended with Frank on the phone talking to someone about more money and Shrump looking smug, which only made me feel worse.

Shrump must have seen the look on my face. "Officer Russell, what choice do you have? It's the weekend of July Fourth. You have no spare officers to accompany the commander, anyway."

Then I was in his face. "I'll tell you what choice I have. By law, I can confiscate this boat and send you *and* your men *and* the commander *and* his buddies *packing!*"

He stared at me blank faced. "And what would that accomplish?" he asked.

My immediate thought was, *It would make me feel a whole hell of a lot better.*

"Give us a minute," Esquibel said. Shrump stepped away, and the commander said, "Listen, Luke. I don't like these guys any better than you do. I understand they could turn on us in a New York minute. But this might be the only chance we have to nail Douloureux. I say we take it."

I thought about it. "OK, on one condition. That Frank, Luanda and I tail you in my boat. If there's any trouble, we can be there."

We explained this to Shrump and Baldy, who had no problem with it.

"Don't worry," Esquibel said. "If Douloureux's not here, how's he going to know where we are on the lake?"

"Besides, if he does show up, he'll be expecting to see us," said Shrump. "He knows we're working for you. But if he sees park rangers, he may abandon the attack."

"In which case he's still at large and you get no reward money," I said.

Shrump ignored me, turned to the commander. "You are armed?"

"None of us are, actually. We were en route when Officer Russell called us about Douloureux."

Shrump pulled a 9-millimeter automatic from his belt. "Then you must have this. Tell your friends to come to the truck."

I watched as Shrump unlocked the tool chest in the bed of the truck to reveal a small arsenal. He told Esquibel's buddies they could take their choice. They looked like kids in a candy store.

"Commander, remember this," I said. "We're thinking logically about Tic. That doesn't mean he's thinking logically about us. He wants his revenge."

He smiled at me. "That makes two of us then, doesn't it?"

JORDAN

"Quit your bitching or you'll be swimming for shore," I told Carey as we sputtered toward Wahweap in his boat.

He sat in the passenger's seat, moaning and holding his head. "You're the one split my forehead open with that rifle," he whined.

"We get back to Wahweap, you'll have plenty of time to heal. Years, if I have anything to do with it."

The early morning sun was staining the cliff tops blood red as we headed down Last Chance Bay.

Last Chance Bay. That Tic has a twisted sense of humor, I thought, recalling the previous evening.

I don't know why Carey didn't hear me gasp as I surfaced. I treaded water and gathered my wits. What the hell had I seen down there?

I could see Carey on shore rummaging through his rucksack in the dimming light, his rifle leaning against a rock. I took a couple of deep breaths, submerged, and headed for shore, down lake and around a bend from where Carey sat.

Once on shore, I took a minute to gather my strength. I couldn't get the watery image of Stevie's face out of my head. Had it simply been hypoxia? Or can the dead return to us in times of great duress? I knew one thing for sure: I would not have made it without his help.

Thank you, Stevie. I owe you my life.

Quietly, I approached the bend in the cliff, peeked around it at Carey. He had found what he was looking for—a bottle, from which I watched him take a long pull.

I was pretty sure I knew what would happen next. The question was: How long would it take? Sarah and Tic were gone, and I needed to find them. I couldn't afford to wait long.

Fortunately, Carey obliged. Twenty minutes later, in the last of the light, I watched him set the bottle down and lean back against the base of the cliff. Not two minutes passed before his head had fallen forward.

With painstaking care I eased around the bend and made my way toward him. I wasn't ten yards away when damned if I didn't topple a river cobble onto its neighbor with my foot.

The noise roused Carey, who grabbed his rifle and pointed it at me. "What the hell? No fucking way!" he sputtered as he scrambled to his feet.

"Way, Carey, way."

"But how the hell—"

"Never mind that now. Where are Sarah and Tic?"

He just stared at me like I was a ghost, something like Scrooge's Marley, I suspect, with the boat chain still locked around my neck.

"Uh. They left," was all he could manage. Voice like a throat full of rusty razor blades.

"Where to?"

He craned his head forward, peering at me as if to confirm I was really there.

"Carey—"

"You've got to be fucking kidding. What the hell am I supposed to do with you?"

He looked around as though there were someone else there to ask. Still pointing the rifle at me, he reseated himself on the rock. "Sit down. I have to think this through."

I sat on the nearest sizable cobble.

He uncorked his bottle and took another big swallow, wiped his mouth on his sleeve and said, "I guess I could just shoot you. You're supposed to be dead, anyway."

"Are you sure that's what Tic would want?"

He looked puzzled.

"I mean, here I am. The water rejected me, so I must be innocent, right?"

"Is that how it went?"

Even in the failing light, I could see the doubt cast in his features.

He shook his head. "That's all bullshit, anyway. Tic's just a crazy bastard."

"But you bring me back alive, he could kill me all over again."

He laughed. "He'd like that."

He set the bottle beside him, fished in his shirt pocket for his smokes with one hand, cradled the rifle in the other.

"You look cold, sittin' there all wet. You want a drink?"

I shook my head.

"Okay." He drank again.

"Carey, listen to me. You let me go, you could make things a whole lot easier on yourself."

"What do you mean?"

"You let me take your boat, I leave you here, it's nobody's business where you go."

I thought I could see the wheels starting to turn.

"You know Tic's going down," I said. "If not tonight, soon."

He snorted. "That your plan up in Music Hall?"

"You tell me Tic's plan, I'll even vouch for you if you ever come to trial."

"Right. And here's another 'if.' Be no trial 'if' Tic got to me first, and he would."

"Tic's going to be dead or in jail for the rest of his life."

"Says you."

"So you stick around," I said. "How does accessory to murder sound?"

"That's only going to happen if Tic talks. And we both know he won't."

"Don't forget we're talking to the militia. Sure they didn't see anything?"

"Nothing Tic didn't want them to."

"You helped kidnap Officer Tanner."

"Says who?"

"Sarah will identify you."

"You sure she'll live that long?"

"Tic's too smart to not keep her as a bargaining chip."

He took a drag on his cigarette. "Doesn't mean she'll come out alive on the other side," he said.

"You just think about what I said."

"Don't have to. Couple hours, we'll head out, meet up with Tic."

Apparently I wasn't going to talk him to sleep, so I shut up and waited for alcohol and darkness to do their work. Carey finished his smoke, took another drink, settled back up against the cliff again.

It probably wasn't an hour, but it was the longest wait I'd ever known. Darkness completely surrounded me, lit only by the millions of distant stars shining faintly above my head, which was crammed with questions. *Where is Sarah now? Tic will keep her alive until he needs her, but when will that be? What is he up to? Have Luke and Frank and the rest gotten any closer to catching him? Is the militia still in the picture? If not, what are our chances of nailing Tic and saving Sarah? And more immediately, how am I going to get past Carey?*

Finally, I began to hear what I thought at first was air moving on the water, or water brushing on the rocks, but I eventually realized it was Carey snoring. I gave it another five minutes, and slowly got to my feet, my legs and back stiff from sitting folded up on the rock. I carefully placed each step and moved slowly toward him. With infinite care I reached down and, by the light of the stars, plucked the rifle from his lap.

He grunted, looked around like he'd forgotten where he was.

"Stand up," I said. Clumsy with sleep and booze, he tottered to his feet.

"Where has Tic taken Sarah?"

He cleared his throat, a sound like marbles in a blender, spit a wad of phlegm at my feet. "How bad you wanna know?"

"I don't have time for this. Where's your boat?"

"Boat?"

He staggered when I whacked him on the forehead with the rifle butt.

"Christ! The fuck you doing?"

"The boat."

Holding his hand to his head, he turned down lake. Two hundred yards on we came to the nautical equivalent of a crate pulled up on shore. I climbed in, stepped on the flattened beer cans and crushed cigarette packs, and tried the radio. Dead.

"Hasn't worked in years," Carey said.

No surprise there.

The key was in the ignition. The outboard turned over but wouldn't start.

"What's the problem?" I asked.

"Aw, she's just old and touchy."

"Get up here and get her started."

"What's in it for me?"

"More of what I just gave you, if you don't."

He climbed in and gave her a try. No luck. He sat down in the passenger's seat, holding his shirt sleeve to his forehead.

"Have you got a flashlight?" I asked.

He went to reach under the dash. I trained the rifle on him and said, "Careful what you pull out."

"Just a fuckin' flashlight."

"Hold it while I track this down," I said, still pointing the rifle at him.

There was plenty of fuel, and it was reaching the engine, although I noticed there was no fuel-water separator in the line. I had Carey fish me a screwdriver out of the five gallon bucket he called a tool box and did a quick spark test. Spark looked strong, so the problem was probably contaminated fuel, which could mean the carburetor jets were clogged, in which case we were dead in the water since I didn't have the time or the tools to tear them down.

There was one other possibility. Leaning the rifle against the motor, I unscrewed the cap on the fuel tank and lifted out the pickup, which looked like it had been sitting on the bottom of the tank. Quickly, I shortened up the line, tore a strip of my shirt off and wrapped it around the pickup as a filter, and reassembled everything.

I picked up the rifle, went to the front of the boat and turned the key. Still nothing. I went back, disconnected the fuel line, emptied it, and reconnected it. Again I turned the key, hoping my ersatz filter would work. Finally, after several tries, the motor coughed to life in a cloud of blue smoke. I gave it a few minutes on idle, aware all the time that every minute might mean the difference of life or death for Sarah.

I gave it some throttle and it revved without dying, so I had Carey weigh anchor and I slipped it into gear. It almost died, but I gave it a little more gas and it held. We began moving slowly forward. I felt like cheering, until I realized we had lost more than an hour just getting underway.

After another couple of minutes I gave it full throttle, and we were at top speed, but it was running rough. The carburetors were both probably fouled, but there was nothing I could do about it. We would just have to limp back as best we could.

Now we faced another problem—all the rocks and boulders, even the bottom in some places, that were sitting right below the surface, ready to rip the bottom out of the boat or at least shear the blades from the prop.

"Keep your eyes peeled for any obstructions," I told Carey.

"Maybe you didn't notice, but it's dark out here."

"You're right. Get up on the bow with that flashlight and tell me if you see anything."

"You're fucking kidding."

I looked at him, and even in the dark he could see he'd better move, so he climbed reluctantly forward.

We continued on like that for another hour, Carey twice shouting at me and pointing at rocks, which worked fine until he missed one.

I felt the thump, followed instantly by a sharp ping as the prop hit a rock submerged just far enough below the surface. The outboard flipped forward and we coasted to a stop.

Only the hub of the prop remained, the blades neatly sheared off.

"You got another one?" I asked Carey.

He climbed back into the cockpit and crawled halfway up under the dash to the forward storage compartment. After a few minutes, he handed me out a battered piece of junk. The tips of all three blades were gone, and one of them was visibly cracked, but it would have to do. Half an hour later, we were on our way again, moving even more slowly than before.

I stood at the wheel, with Carey again on the bow with the flashlight, both of us straining to see what lay ahead in the dark. Although I knew it was pointless, I was urging us ahead with body and soul, with no idea what I was returning to. Was Sarah now dead? Tic had failed to kill me, but had he found another victim? Was Luke still on his trail, or had he somehow been put out of commission?

I hated traveling blind, cut off from the chase, and, crawling through the dark, I swore my revenge on Tic. I had been blinded by our shared past, but the blinders were gone. Stevie had pulled the last shreds of them from my eyes in the black bowels of the water over which I now sailed.

LUKE

I was just bending down to cast off the lead rope of Esquibel's boat when Shrump shouted and pointed out toward the bay.

It was Tic.

He came alongside the houseboat, threw a rope over to be tied off, and followed it carrying a small sports bag.

"Commander," he said, shaking Esquibel's hand. "Apologize for being late, but there's no rest for the weary."

"Or the wicked," Esquibel replied with no apparent humor.

Tic laughed, turned to Shrump and Baldy. "Conrad. Bill." Neither of them moved to shake his hand.

He noticed me standing on the dock, Frank and Luanda behind me, gave us a mock salute.

"What are you doing here, Douloureux?" I asked.

"Didn't the good commander tell you I had agreed to be his pilot and guide?"

"You understand you're under arrest for kidnapping Officer Tanner and Jordan Hunt."

"I'm afraid that's not going to work out right now. I just told you I've got a job."

"Just tell us where they are, Douloureux."

"And?"

I paused. "We find them unharmed, we'll go from there."

"You're going to have to do better than that, Officer Russell. Besides, I'm pretty sure I've already lost one of my bargaining chips. In the lake. Last night."

"Either of them are dead, Douloureux, you've played your last hand."

"Pretty tough talk from someone who hasn't got even a pair." He paused, smiled at me. "Two of the same card, that is."

I was ready to jump on board and get things started, except I had a pretty good idea of what he was carrying in the sports bag.

He looked at Shrump and Baldy. "Unless you've got another ace up your sleeve, like these two fine specimens here."

He took a step toward them. I watched Baldy bristle.

"You thought I wouldn't figure it out, boys? Thought you'd clean up at both ends with me in the middle?"

Baldy was about to go ballistic, and I knew he was armed.

"Douloureux," I said through gritted teeth. "Back off. Unless you want the whole show to go down right here, right now."

He and Baldy stared at each other another few seconds, then Tic stepped back to his bag, opened it, and pulled out a Parker-Hale machine pistol.

"And let all my careful planning go to waste?"

He turned to Esquibel, but spoke to me. "You're right, I've got something more rarified in mind for the commander than a mere bullet in the guts."

He turned back to the militia. "And I've got something special in mind for all of you as well."

"I say we just go for it now," Baldy spat.

Tic drew back the bolt on the Parker-Hale and stuck the gun in the big man's face. "Actually, I can go either way. Let's start with you, big boy."

I jumped from the dock onto the deck of the houseboat. There was an electric crackle in the air. I knew Tic was right, damn him. If he died, we'd never see Sarah or Jordan again.

I stepped up beside Shrump. "This isn't going to end anywhere but in a bloodbath."

Shrump nodded. "The officer is right. We must stay with our plan to accompany Mr. Douloureux." He turned to Tic. "Perhaps you can give Officer Russell some assurance that you will not harm his friends if we sail with you today."

Tic shrugged. "All I'm wanting is a long, relaxed weekend playing cards and drinking beer with my old commander and his buddies."

"So we're trading our lives for the lives of Russell's friends, is that it?" asked Baldy, outraged.

"Looks that way," said Tic.

"Why should I give a flying fuck about them?"

I knew Shrump had the answer to that question. Sure enough, he laid his hand on Baldy's shoulder. "The money, Bill. Remember the money."

Baldy shook his hand off.

"That's right, big man," said Tic. "You're still in the running for the money. And if you come along, there's sure to be another chance to kill me."

Douloureux turned back to me. "Of course, now is not the time. Officer Russell, let's get all these gentlemen off board, and you can remove the tracking devices I'm sure you and your FBI friends have hidden on the boat."

"There aren't any. We had none on hand."

"What was it our old friend Ronnie Reagan told us? Trust but verify?"

He reached down into his gym bag, pulled out a scanner. "You know what will happen if I sweep and find anything, right?"

It pained me mightily to do it, but I knew we had no choice if we ever wanted to see Sarah or Jordan again. With a glance at Frank, I climbed up to the pilot's house and removed the transmitter we'd hidden there, then reached down into the bilge for the second one.

"And the feds. They plant any?"

"That's it."

"You sure? You know how bad they are about getting signals crossed with you locals."

"You're clean," said Frank.

"Then let's do a little weapons check, shall we?"

One by one we took back all the weapons with which the militia had supplied the commander and his men just a short while ago, then did the same with the militia themselves.

Once we had everyone back on board, Tic had one of the militia move his boat to the dock and tie it off. He came and stood in my face. "Remember, I see anything following us—boat, plane, helicopter, it doesn't matter—you'll find what's left of your partner and your friend maybe six months from now, a year, maybe never, who knows?"

I kept my mouth shut, afraid of what I'd say.

He leaned over the side, got his face close to mine. "Me and the commander have a private score to settle," he said softly. "And we don't want any unexpected guests. Comprende?"

I nodded slowly.

He pointed down at my feet.

"You mind untying that line?"

JORDAN

I suppose I should have been grateful that we hadn't run out of gas on top of everything else, but by the time Carey and I limped into Wahweap, I was crawling with anxiety. Things only got worse when we pulled up at the dock and there was no sign of Luke or any other uniforms.

There was no room to tie up, and it dawned on me that it was the Fourth holiday. So I simply pulled in beside a boat that was already docked and tied up to it.

With a short length of rope I'd found in Carey's "tool box," I bound his hands behind him, then looped the rope through the wheel, to keep him from wandering.

Jaime, the marina manager, was overseeing the fueling station. Boats were lined up ten deep to get gas. He looked harassed.

"Have you seen Luke?" I asked.

"He was around earlier, but I've been too busy to keep track."

"Mind if I use your radio?"

He waved toward his small office at the back of the convenience store.

Luke was relieved to hear from me.

"From what Douloureux said, we thought you might be dead."

"I almost was. Where's Tic?"

"Somewhere up ahead of us on the lake."

"Is Sarah with him?"

"She wasn't when he showed up to pilot Esquibel's boat."

He quickly filled me in on all that had transpired since our failed raid on Tic in Music Hall Canyon two days earlier: the arrival of Tic's commander, Luke's surmise that an attack on the commander was what Tic had been planning all along, Luke's secret deal with Esquibel to try foiling Tic's plan, the withdrawal and subsequent reappearance of the militia, and Tic's piloting the commander's houseboat with his buddies and the militia aboard.

"Said he'd kill you and Sarah if we tried tracking him."

"Then what the hell are you doing?"

He explained his tactic of hailing down boats periodically to ask them if they'd seen Esquibel's houseboat pass by, and in which direction.

"Always amazes me to see how quickly the crowds at Wahweap thin out once they're on the lake, it's so damn big, but it's worked so far. We're pretty sure he's not too far ahead."

"For God's sake, please keep out of sight."

"Copy that. Can you get up here?"

"Not in Carey's crate, that's for sure."

"Take Tic's boat. It's tied up at the north end of the dock."

"Will do. Give me your coordinates."

As I fired up his boat, I wondered briefly if Tic had deliberately left the key in the ignition. It might have been an oversight, but I was beginning to wonder if any part of this had been left to chance.

Carey, his hands still tied, sat in the front seat looking pitiful as I slowly backed away from the dock. Only once I was clear did I look at the dashboard.

"Damn!"

The fuel gauge was on empty, so I carefully maneuvered to the head of the fueling queue, ignoring the rude remarks from boaters who had been waiting patiently in the hot sun and comments about the line starting at the end. Fortunately, Jaime saw me coming.

"Hold your places. Let this boat through."

I pulled up at the pump. "What's going on, Dr. Hunt?"

"I've got to get up the lake. Can I pay you later?"

"No problem."

I looked around while he filled the tank, and met the eyes of every person in every other boat around me. Only then did I realize that the chain Tic had locked around my neck was still there. I had draped it down my back last night while working on Carey's boat and forgotten about it.

I looked at Carey sitting there with his hands tied, dried blood streaked down his face and onto his shirt from the gash I'd put in his forehead.

I pointed with my thumb over my shoulder at the lake.

"Anybody heard? They bitin' today?"

Dead silence.

Jaime cleared his throat. "Dr. Hunt, I've got a pair of bolt cutters in the tool shed. Only take a minute to cut that lock."

"Fine, but make it fast. We top her off we're out of here."

I looked around again while we waited for Jaime.

I gestured toward Carey. "Fishin' buddy." Tugging at the chain around my neck, I said, "Didn't want me to go out today." I leaned over, slapped him on the shoulder, and grinned. "Had to talk him into it."

Several guys actually nodded.

TIC

We reached the wide open plain of Padre Bay by mid-afternoon. Even with the drought on it was enormous, still a good two miles across, rimmed by the sheer cliff walls of mesas and buttes. We got to what looked like the middle I had the commander cut the engine. Half a dozen boats dotted the huge basin, but none of them were nearby.

I looked to the south. The thunderheads I had noticed earlier were continuing to build. Was it finally going to rain?

"What's going on?" Esquibel asked.

I picked up the Parker-Hale. "Time we had us a little come to Jesus."

I moved to the back of the boat. "You two, stand aside," I said to Baldy and Shrump, then lined their six men up along the railing. "Now I'm sure you all were just following orders, that Shrump and Baldy here led you into selling me out to the feds, but that's no excuse.

"You should know that even in the military, you're given an order you know is immoral it is your duty to disobey it."

"You're the only one we agreed to work for, Douloureux," one of them said. "We didn't know nothin' about any deal with the feds."

Another said, "We all of us had to leave the room out at the ranch at a certain point."

All of them were looking at Baldy and Shrump, who, I now realized, had kept their men in the dark.

"Now isn't this like the fucking military!" I said.

Baldy was actually reddening with embarrassment. I loved it.

"We knew some of you would object to working for the feds on purely ideological grounds," he stammered.

"To refuse the money was impossible," Shrump added.

I cocked the pistol. "And there you have it. Another sellout. This just gets better and better." I pointed the gun at the militiaman closest to me.

"And now for the payoff."

I heard Baldy say "Fuckin' asshole" under his breath as he charged me. He moved surprisingly quickly for a big man. I waited until the seemingly impossible moment, sidestepped him, and clubbed him hard on the back of his head as he went by. The deck trembled beneath my feet as he slammed into it.

I spun and pointed the pistol at two of the militia who were about to make the same mistake Baldy had. "Let's everybody settle down. Back to your places."

Shrump stepped forward.

"May I say something here?"

"Only if it will make me laugh."

He looked around the bay. "Yah, but consider that there is no wind and that sound travels well over water. Gunfire will be noticed. Furthermore, if you shoot these men their bodies will float, which means evidence."

"So far so good, Conrad."

"So why not let them try swimming for shore? If they drown, they'll sink. What's more, I'm certain that Officer Russell and the FBI are trailing us, despite your warning. If so, stopping to rescue any who survive the swim will further improve our chances of escape."

I grinned at him. "Shrump, I'm good, but you're genius."

I pointed the pistol at the six. "Okay, everybody down to your skivvies."

As they stripped, I gave instructions. "First, I don't care what you've always been told about never swimming without a buddy. I see you pairing up I'll shoot you.

"Second, I'll point you to a shore and you swim to it. Again, any deviation, you're dead. It's about a mile in any direction, not much of a stretch if you're in shape. You assholes think you're survivalists, here's your chance to prove it. Over the rail."

Reluctantly, they climbed over and dropped into the water, except for one, a little guy, white faced and sweating.

"I can't swim," he choked out.

"Not my problem. Over the side."

"You might as well shoot me now."

"And miss out on the fun? No fucking chance."

With that, I grabbed him with one hand and tossed him over the rail. Sure enough, he thrashed around, trying to get back to the boat. One of his buddies tried swimming to the rescue. Too late, he realized his mistake, as the little guy latched onto him like he was the Rock of Gibraltar. The would-be hero tried in vain to disentangle himself, but the drowning man kept pushing him under in a futile attempt to climb up him and back to the surface. In less than a minute, both had disappeared beneath the surface.

Looking over the side, I shook my head. "Pitiful."

I looked out at the other four, who were treading water, staring in horror at the spot where their two comrades had just drowned.

I raised the pistol over my head, fired a shot in the air. Let somebody hear it; I didn't care. "Starting gun, shitheads. I want to see assholes and elbows."

One by one, the four remainders turned and began swimming gamely for their designated shores.

I checked my watch. "Okay, commander. Fire it up. We've got a schedule to keep."

Baldy still lay on the deck, out cold.

"Somebody throw some water on that."

JORDAN

With daylight and maximum speed in Tic's boat, I reached Luke, Frank, and Luanda by mid-afternoon, waiting for me out of sight of Padre Bay behind the long arm of Gunsight Butte.

The July sun blazed on my back, but it was about to be overcome by the first of a formation of clouds sailing out in advance of the towering thunderheads standing like palisades on the southern horizon. I wasn't getting my hopes up, except that with the clouds had come a stillness harboring an expectancy in the air that I hadn't felt for a long time. Would it rain, or would the black-bellied clouds sail away from us again, trailing moisture like ropes dangling from a dirigible?

"We estimate that from the time they left Wahweap, given the speed they can make, that they're somewhere in Padre Bay," said Luke.

"There's a saddle on the north side of the butte that overlooks the whole bay," I said. "Let's get up there and see what we can see."

We found a small opening along the rocky shore at which to tie off the boats. I cut Carey's hands free and all of us began scrambling up the rocky slope to the saddle.

"You sure he won't give us away?" asked Luke as we climbed.

Carey seemed dazed by the lack of sleep, the alcohol he'd consumed last night, and the purple knot on his forehead.

"I don't think he'll be any trouble."

Lying on the hot slick rock, we swept the vast bowl of water with our binoculars. The huge houseboat, although dwarfed by the expanse on which it sat, was not hard to spot.

I focused just in time to see five men in their underwear, followed shortly by a sixth, go over the side.

"What the hell's going on?"

Everyone on board the houseboat seemed intent on something happening in the water alongside. We were too far away to be sure, but it looked like somebody was having trouble. In a minute, whatever it was, was over.

We watched as someone on board raised an arm over his head, and heard the distant report of a gunshot. The men in the water began swimming away from the boat.

"If I had to guess I'd say those are militia," said Frank.

"Or Esquibel's men," said Luanda.

"I don't think so. I think this is what Douloureux was planning when he told the militia he had something in mind for them."

"Maybe you're right. There were six of them, and six went over the side."

Luanda peered through her binoculars. "But there are only four swimming away."

We all watched the swimmers quietly as we digested what that meant.

"Maybe we should have told them their cover was blown," Frank said soberly. "Given them a fighting chance."

It didn't help matters any that we could only watch the men in the water, unable to go to their rescue without Tic spotting us.

"The houseboat's moving again," said Luke.

I for one couldn't watch anymore.

"I'm heading back to the boats."

Luke lay prone, still watching. He nodded. "You all wait at the boats. I'll radio when it's clear and climb down to meet you on the bay side."

We reached the boats, started them, and motored down to the southern tip of Gunsight Butte, where we waited.

I kept visualizing the four black dots inching away from the houseboat in all that water. It was like watching a car accident or some other disaster unfold at a far remove and with the sound off.

If they don't panic, they'll probably be all right, I told myself.

On the other hand, a mile is a hell of swim, I thought. *I'm not sure I could make it, and I keep myself in shape.*

"Any of those guys drown, you're on the hook, you know," I said to Carey.

He gazed at me vacantly.

"You sure you don't want to tell me what Tic has in the works?"

He slowly shook his head.

"Maybe we could swap you for Sarah."

He snickered. "Don't bet on it."

I knew that by the time we rounded the tip of the butte and headed into the bay, Tic would be gone. I wondered how many of the militiamen would be gone as well.

*****

We got to the bay side of Gunsight Butte, Luke had climbed only part way down from the saddle. We spotted him up on the slope, using his binoculars to keep track of the four men in the water. He climbed down to us and pointed them out to me.

"Jordan, I want you to stay behind and pick them up. I'll take Carey with me. Maybe he'll change his mind and give us Tic's location."

"Don't count on it."

"I'm going with Luke," Frank told Luanda. "You stay here and help Jordan."

"We'll catch up as soon as we find them and put them ashore."

Luanda scanned the water while I watched Luke and Frank, Carey sitting behind them, cut a beeline across the bay. She spotted one of the swimmers almost immediately.

She saw another while I was hauling the first aboard. We pulled him out, but there was no sign of the other two.

I had a bad feeling until, as I surveyed the flat expanse, I thought I saw a familiar boat. "Hold on," I said as we headed toward it. Sure enough, Pete and Paul were standing by the transom as I pulled up.

"Dr. Hunt," said Pete.

"What the hell—" said Paul.

"Is going on?" finished Pete.

"We heard a gunshot."

"Is anybody hurt?"

"Have you seen two guys in the water?" I asked.

Paul stepped down into the small cabin and returned with two militiamen wrapped in damp towels.

"You mean these two?" he asked.

"Well, I'll be damned."

"We fished them out—" said Paul.

"Not long ago," added Pete.

"Asked them why they were swimming—"

"So far from shore."

"They looked kind of—"

"Sheepish."

"Said Tic Douloureux—"

"Tried to kill them!"

I nodded.

The two militia men began climbing from Pete and Paul's boat into mine.

"Hold on a minute, boys," I said. "Pete, can you take these guys back to Wahweap?"

He turned and looked at Paul, who said, "Well—"

"Are they good guys?"

"Or bad guys?"

"Somewhere in between," I said.

Pete turned to the four men.

"You guys—"

"Like to fish?"

They all nodded as one.

"All right," I said, "we have to catch up to Luke. These guys will fill you in. You'll be all right."

They nodded their heads in unison.

"We've got extra tackle."

"And plenty of cold beer."

Everybody looked happy at that news.

TIC

The only light I had piloting Esquibel's houseboat into the narrow side canyon was whatever was still reflecting down from the tops of the tall rock walls on our left. We maneuvered around a bend and there in front of us was a broad sand beach filling the canyon from wall to wall. I had just enough water to turn the boat around. I cut the engine and we dropped anchor.

I checked my watch. "We're going to be here for a while. Why don't you have your buddies fix some grub?"

"Nobody's hungry after what happened this afternoon," the commander said.

I shrugged. "Suit yourself, but you won't mind if I get myself a little something."

He followed me down to the galley, watched while I fixed a sandwich. I pointed at the round table in the main salon. "Isn't this usually your big poker weekend?"

"Not after watching two men drown."

"C'mon, commander. These guys are military. They've seen men die before."

"In combat, yes. Not cold blood."

I took a bite of sandwich. "What's the difference? Dead's dead."

"That the plan for me and my men?"

"Commander, Commander. I told you. I'm just here as your guide."

"That's bullshit, Douloureux."

"Hey, I'm just trying to get myself back on the straight and narrow."

"How can you say that after watching those men drown?"

"I didn't kill them, did I? I could have, and I should have, but I let them swim for it."

"Knowing that one couldn't swim."

"It was ennobling to see one man give his life for another."

"You are one sick son-of-a-bitch."

I just grinned.

"Luke Russell and Luanda Wilmington and I had a little talk before I got to the lake," he said.

"I'd have been disappointed in Luke if you hadn't."

"Told me about a series of murders up here."

"Is that so?"

"Is that the plan for me?"

"Oh, I've got something extra special in line for you, Commander."

"So you said back at Wahweap. Well, let's get on with it, shall we?"

"All in good time, Commander. All in good time."

Down below, Shrump quietly closes the door on the head. Inside, he pulls a hand held radio from his pocket and switches it on. He waits a few seconds, and then begins quietly reciting the boat's coordinates over the radio.

LUKE

We came out from behind the point at the head of Anasazi Canyon and the houseboat had disappeared in the dimming light.

"Now what?" I asked.

We hadn't seen another boat for a while, and there were none in sight now. They'd either headed back to Dangling Rope marina or had found a side canyon in which to spend the night. With no one to ask, we were traveling blind and in danger of running up on Douloureux and the commander.

I turned to Carey. "Here's your chance to be a hero."

"Fuck off."

I radioed our position to Jordan and Luanda, but got no response. The canyon walls were high here.

"Let's just sit it out and wait for them here," said Frank.

It wasn't long before we heard the sound of a boat approaching, and soon they were pulling up alongside us.

"We don't know where the houseboat is," I said.

"No word from Shrump?" Jordan asked.

"Steep as these walls are, he probably can't get through."

"Then I guess we wait."

TIC

The untouched bowls of chips and dip, the full beer bottles growing warm on the table, ash trays out but empty. I love it all, but especially I love the looks on the faces of the commander's men, as though they'd all eaten of the same thing that had given them the bellyache, with diarrhea impending.

And absolutely most of all, I love knowing that I am the cause of all this.

I've chosen a seat backed up to the cabinet I understand to be the correct one, facing the double doors onto the deck, where Baldy is now conscious but still down.

Shrump has taken a seat by the doors.

"You going to join us, Conrad?" I ask.

He shakes his head.

I turn to Esquibel. "Commander, I don't believe I've been introduced to your friends."

Stiffly, in a quiet voice, he goes around the table.

"Nice to meet you all," I say. "Now I want everybody to enjoy themselves, understand? Just act like I'm not here."

Which, I know, is unlikely.

"In fact, just to break the ice, I'm going to borrow some money to get in the game. Sound familiar?"

Silence.

"Commander. I'm tapped out. You'll have to stake me."

"No problem."

"Okay, then, gentlemen, let's play some cards."

We play a few hands, the commander at my side, the Parker-Hale on the table before me, the bolt already slid back just in case. I pick it up when I go outside to relieve myself over the side, stick it in my belt when I'm done. In the last light of day, I look up the canyon and see Navajo Mountain looming in the distance. Lightning is dancing around its crown, but I figure it's just another false start to the monsoon.

I return from the deck and, taking my seat, I notice that the cabinet door is slightly ajar.

Not like the commander, I think. He must be pretty sure he's got me in his sights.

Esquibel points a thumb at the bar behind him.

"No beer, Douloureux?"

I know alcohol will unstring me. "Maybe later."

He raises an eyebrow. Keeps his mouth shut. "The game now is Omaha. Hanratty, you're the button."

Hanratty deals the hole cards. Guy to the left of the big blind bets twenty bucks. Hole cards must be looking good. I'm holding an ace, a ten, an eight and a seven, but I know it's going to get better. Tonight is my night.

Nobody folds.

I look at Shrump. "So I guess your dueñas haven't worked out so well, have they, Commander?"

Esquibel chuckles. "Our chaperones? We'll see."

"Take my advice. Keep an eye on them. They can be turned on a dime."

Hanratty deals the flop, an ace, a seven and an eight in the middle of the table. Next guy to lead the betting pushes up a twenty-dollar chip. Small blind folds, along with the two guys to my right.

The same thing that told me Sarah would answer my false alarm tells me this hand is coming down to the commander and me.

Hanratty flips the turn card. A seven.

He peeks at his hold cards and folds. It's down to three of us.

The guy to my right pushes twenty dollars forward. The commander and I see him.

Hanratty deals. I just know what the river is going to be, and it is. An eight.

The bet is to me. I ask the commander to front me a hundred dollars. He glances at me but slides the chips my way. I push them all out on the table.

The third guy folds. I look at the commander.

I know he has me. He's not a bluffer. I also know what comes next.

He folds.

I lay out my cards.

Full house. Aces full of eights.

"Dead man's hand," says Hanratty.

The commander can't restrain a grimace. "Just like you, Douloureux. A bluff. I should have called you."

He shows his cards. Four sevens.

I grin. "Right you are. But see, Commander, that's the point. That's why the militia was useless. In the end, it's what you are that counts, not what's standing between you and what you fear."

Esquibel sighs heavily. "All right, tell me, Douloureux. What do I fear?"

"You know."

"You think I'm afraid of a punk like you?"

I glance at Shrump. "Looks to me like you're still hiring others to do your fighting for you."

"I'm not going to need any help to take care of you, Douloureux."

I'm sure now that he's retrieved the 9-millimeter Shrump gave him back at Wahweap, the one he stashed in the cabinet and has now pulled from his belt.

"You know what I have trained on your balls under the table, don't you?"

"Let me guess. A little item that Shrump passed to you back at Wahweap that you hid in this cabinet?"

I see the doubt flicker in his eyes.

"Big as they are, they shouldn't be hard to hit at this range, even for you, Commander."

"Russell asked me if I thought I could bring you in. I told him I'd be happy to pay back what I owed you for this," he says, lifting the cane in his other hand.

"So you and Luke, a couple of regular guys, throwing in together to gang up on poor old Tic."

"Surely you suspected something when you got past the guards to see me at the hotel."

"Hmm. That *was* suspiciously easy, now that I think of it."

"And especially when I agreed to let you, of all people, pilot this boat."

"I guess I made the mistake of taking you as a man of your word."

"We set you up, Douloureux," he said. "It's over."

He gestured with the pistol at Shrump.

"Get on the radio and give them our location."

But the German just sits there.

"I think he's already tried that, haven't you, Shrump?"

Shrump reddens but says nothing.

"Don't worry, Conrad, you did exactly what I wanted you to do."

Esquibel points the automatic at me. "I don't know what's going on here, but we'll do it this way. Take the gun out of your belt, slowly, and lay it on the deck."

I shrug. "You da man."

I stand and pull the machine pistol from my belt, start bending toward the floor.

But then I drop to one knee and point it up at the commander.

Who reflexively flinches and pulls his trigger.

Nothing.

His face looks as though all the blood has suddenly drained from it.

"But—how—?" he stammers.

Slowly, I rise to my feet. I can't suppress a giggle as I set the Parker-Hale back on the table. "That nine misfire on you, commander?"

He pulls the trigger again. Nothing.

He turns to Shrump. "You son-of-a-bitch."

"Hand it to him," I say.

The commander obeys. Shrump opens the chamber. Shows Esquibel it's empty. "You mean you never jacked a round into the chamber, Commander?" he asks.

He pulls back the slide and cocks the hammer. "How extraordinarily careless of you."

I step up next to the commander. "Now in case any of you boys want to be heroes, remember I haven't made the same mistake."

In a blur of motion, I spin myself around and deliver a powerful roundhouse kick to the side of the commander's head. The man hits the deck like an 80-pound sack of Quikrete.

"Consider that a down payment on what *I* owe *you*, asshole."

Then several things happen in rapid succession.

First, Baldy, who must have been watching this unfold from out on the deck, bursts through the door. Did I mention that he moves surprisingly quickly for a big man? No sooner have I downed the commander than he's grabbed the machine pistol off the table and jammed it into my temple.

"This is gonna be for Harris and the men you wasted in Music Hall Canyon."

"I did Harris. The two idiots who triggered the booby trap, and one more. But if you're counting Miller and Evans you can chalk them up to Mr. Shrump here."

"What the fuck are you talking about?" he asks.

"Allow me," says Shrump. "Simply put, the day Officer Tanner answered Mr. Douloureux's bogus attack on Niles Hunt, Mr. Douloureux and I arranged a business agreement. He posited that he would never be caught. From what I had seen of him and his operation, I agreed."

"So there would never be any reward money paid," says Baldy.

"Very good, Bill. Mr. Douloureux understood that I had to compensate for that loss of income, and he generously agreed to take me into his employ as a means to do so."

"A fucking double agent," says Baldy. "So it *was* all about the money."

Shrump nods. "That and living in such primitive conditions at Poverty Mountain. I had had enough of that. Mr. Douloureux guessed early on that the militia was spying on him, so he went shopping for some, what's a good word . . . insurance . . . to protect his investment in equipment and personnel. Clever dog, he tricked me into calling Officer Tanner after leading me to believe he was about to kill young Niles.

"Mr. Douloureux and I are both men of the world. We know there is no honor among thieves. That's how you say it, yah? So I asked him to illustrate the sincerity of his intent. Which is where Harris came in. But he feared Miller and Evans would object. I told him not to worry. I would take care of them. I took them aside and told them Mr. Douloureux was willing to pay the three of us good money to work only for him. They, how do you say, hemmed and hawed, but eventually agreed. I returned to Mr. Douloureux and told him so."

Shrump laughed. "They even helped us set the stones on poor Harris, albeit reluctantly."

I smiled and nodded. "All that about the loyalty test was just for the benefit of Sarah and Niles, to keep them thinking that I thought the militia were working only for me. Helped me use Conrad here to keep up on what Luke and the feds were up to and to lead them off the track."

"You'll pay for this," Baldy hissed, the pistol still at my head. "I'll kill him and you."

Shrump just grinned. "Of course, once Harris was dead, Mr. Douloureux wanted proof of my own sincerity. So I shot Miller and Evans. Also to make sure our little secret stayed between Mr. Douloureux and myself."

"Just like that," Baldy says.

"Just like this," Shrump says, and swinging his pistol into Baldy's face, he pulls the trigger. Blood and tissue from the exit wound splatters several of the commander's men, on whom Shrump turns his gun. "Now, Mr. Douloureux, you will, as agreed, pay me Bill's portion as well."

"As agreed, partner."

"And the rest of you, you will follow our orders. Or you can join Bill here. Understood?"

You can hear the lake tapping against the hull.

"Good. All of you. Out on the deck."

"Wait." I look down on the mound of flesh that had been Baldy. "Get this pile of shit off the boat."

Two of Esquibel's men drag Baldwin's corpse outside. Dump it over the side.

We follow them out.

"Everybody stand over by the side."

I begin to raise the Parker-Hale toward them.

Shrump steps up beside me.

"Perhaps we should simply have them swim to shore. Partner." He looks at me. "As a contingency, should things not proceed as planned."

"Things are going to go as planned, Conrad. Depend on it. This, I don't give a fuck either way, although I will say you're turning out to be a real buzz kill. Partner.

"Okay, all of you. Into the water."

No one hesitates.

We were back out on the lake, Shrump at the wheel with me, Esquibel still out cold on the floor of the salon, when I told Shrump to give me the hand held radio.

He pursed his lips and handed it over.

"You think I didn't notice the trips to the head, when a real man would just have hung it over the side?"

He looked embarrassed.

"That's okay, Conrad. Like I told you back there, you served a purpose. And now you can serve one more time."

I handed him back the radio. "Call your friends waiting down the lake and tell them you've gotten the jump on me, that you've got me down but that the commander's been badly hurt. You got that?"

He nodded.

"And Shrump? Make it real, then I want to see you throw the radio overboard."

JORDAN

Shrump's voice, high-pitched and excited, crackling out of the night, startled us. His message got us all excited.

We were about to dash into the side canyon when I asked, "How do we know this isn't another ruse, like the one that snared Sarah?"

Luke nodded. "I guess it all depends on whose side you think Shrump is on."

"So if he's working for us, the message is genuine. If he's working for Tic, it's bogus?" I asked.

"He could be drawing us into a trap," Frank added.

"We're close enough we'd have heard if there was any gunfire," Luanda said.

"Don't be too sure," I said. "Sound travels well over water, but the canyon they're in goes back quite a ways, even in low water."

"And we still don't know what Sarah's status is," added Luanda.

"I will say this, Shrump has been no help in that regard," said Luke.

"But let's not forget what Tic said he'd do to her if he caught us trailing him," I said.

"Nor did Shrump warn us about what we'd face in Music Hall Canyon," Luke continued, "or tell us about the cave where you and Sarah were being held, Jordan."

Frank nodded. "We didn't know anything about Douloureux trying to drown you."

"On the other hand," said Luanda, "the militia did come back to us even though Baldy had pulled them out after the disaster in Music Hall Canyon."

"But only because Shrump wanted the money and talked Baldy into reconsidering," said Luke.

"And Douloureux did make the militia leave the boat and swim for it, probably as punishment for double dealing him with the feds," said Frank.

"Question is, are Shrump and the militia on the same page?" I asked.

"He did tell us about Tic's plan to visit Esquibel at Wahweap," said Luke.

"But if Tic knew Shrump was talking to us, he'd be very selective in what he told him," said Frank.

"And he's told us nothing about what Douloureux plans to do with Esquibel," said Luke.

"If he even knows," said Frank. "He hasn't radioed us Tic's position all day."

"Again," I said. "Tic knows he's working for us, he's going to be watching him very carefully."

"So once again, who the hell's side is he on?" asked Luke.

"For all we know, his own."

"So are we going to debate this all night?" Luanda asked.

"I say we err on the side of doing something more than just sitting here," Luke replied.

"Then I think we have our answer," she said.

We reach the final stretch of the canyon, there's nothing between us and the beach but water.

"I was afraid of this," I said.

"Fire on the beach," said Luke.

The commander's men were waiting for us when we pulled up on the sand. Baldy lay dragged up on the beach, dead.

"What the hell's going on here?" Frank asked.

There was embarrassed silence until one of Esquibel's friends came forward and explained how Tic had ordered them off the houseboat.

Luke nudged Baldy's body with his toe. "How'd this happen?"

The same guy related Shrump's double-dealing the commander and his murder of Baldy.

"That at least explains why we haven't heard from Shrump," said Luanda.

"Give me a minute here," I said. I took Carey by the arm up the beach. "Listen carefully, shithead, because you're about to change your mind and give me Tic's coordinates and the circumstances of Officer Tanner."

He laughed out loud. "Yeah, and Michael fucking Jackson is going to crawl out of my ass and sing Thriller."

"That's unlikely."

I showed him the radio in my hand. "What's more likely is that I'm going to radio Shrump and tell him we're headed his way because you were chicken shit and gave up Tic's location."

Now I had his attention. "Shrump relays that to Tic, you think you and Tic are still close after that?"

He swallowed hard. "I'm fucked either way," he said. "I tell you and he'll kill me."

"Not if we take him down first. Then you're safe. We'll just tell him Shrump turned him."

"Trust me, he'll know the difference. That motherfucker is uncanny."

"Then all the more reason we use the element of surprise to take him out permanently, right?"

He stared at me.

TIC

The further back into the canyon we floated, the worse the smell got. It even brought Esquibel to. Shrump tied him to a deck chair.

"Christ! What is that?" he said.

"Just a couple of guys thought they were tough coming after me last spring," I said. "We've been marinating them in the lake since then. Brought them up just for you."

I knew what was coming and even I had to admit the smell was bad.

A flash of lightning lit the canyon, followed closely by a crack of thunder.

"Damn, that storm's closing in," I said.

"So what's the plan, Douloureux?"

"Getting a little anxious are we, Commander?"

"You're not dragging me all the way out here just to kill me. You could have done that at any point."

"You're right about that, but remember, Commander, God doesn't ever put us where we shouldn't be. All those years I spent training recruits, I didn't know that. Always wondered why He'd sidetracked me into a dead end."

"He instructed the Navy to do that because He knew you were a dangerous lunatic."

"Year after year, batch after batch of overachieving, fucking eager beavers. Mold each one, then send them off to operations all over the world, while I stayed behind."

"Always the bridesmaid, never the bride? That it, Douloureux? You're lucky you weren't out on your ass years ago."

"Every time I ship off a bunch, I turn around, here comes another, the Navy forever keeping my nose in it.

"But something always told me to hang on. Remember you told me there was something else going on with me?"

He nodded. "As in, you weren't all there."

"What you never understood, Commander, there *was* something going on. Like I could read other men's minds, knew what they were going to do before they did it. Like playing cards back there. I knew that eight was coming my way. I knew you had me beat, but I also knew you'd fold . . . And that's how I knew, all those years, something would come, something like the world had never seen before.

"9/11 . . . Thank God for 9/11. I saw those planes going into those towers I knew it was my ticket out of that goddamned training camp . . . God bless Al-Qaeda. They sprung me right into the middle of the action."

He snorted. "We were scraping the bottom of the barrel when we found you."

"That climb was a bad call, Commander. We should have never been out there."

He shook his head. "You're the one choked, Douloureux. You know it and I know it."

"But see, I already had what I needed from the Navy. I already knew what I had to know. How to simulate combat conditions right down to the ground. In the finest tradition of the SEALs, I've made full use of the opportunities available.

"That's why it was okay to beat the shit out of you, Commander. I already knew they weren't going to send me back to training camp after what happened on that cliff."

"You made sure of that, Douloureux."

"Damn straight I did. But I didn't need the Navy anymore."

"So *you* cut *us* loose, right? You're a fucking head case."

We came around the final bend in the canyon. Ahead was the beach. Esquibel began to choke on the stench.

"We'll see who gets inside of whose head. You like to climb, Commander? How do you feel about heights? Any problems with vertigo?"

"I've seen enough, Douloureux, to know you're out of your mind."

"We're just getting started, Commander."

Carefully, I aimed the boat directly at the beach a hundred yards ahead, held the wheel, reached over and opened the throttle full bore. The mammoth houseboat heaved itself forward and began gaining speed.

"I always wanted to do this!" I shouted over the roar of the engines. "EEEHAAA!"

JORDAN

Back out on the lake, we took only Carey with us, headed for the coordinates he gave me, which I found on the map. We took the lead. I radioed Luke on his boat.

"Crooked Canyon. Narrow and twisted. Like a sidewinder moved across the map and stopped. On the San Juan River arm."

Several miles away, on the flanks of Navajo Mountain, lightning flared and thunder rolled.

"Looks like we might finally get some rain," Luanda said.

"We do, we better be careful in these canyons," I replied.

"The lake going to rise that fast?"

I shook my head. "Flash floods. You're standing on dry ground in one of these narrow canyons, you look up and here comes a wall of water ten, twenty feet high. Where you gonna go? You sure as hell aren't going to outrun it."

"You couldn't just ride the tide?"

"Water's moving too fast. Besides, it's really half water, half mud, chock full of debris. Dead trees, logs, sagebrush, drowned animals and livestock, rocks and boulders rolling along underneath. Whatever was in the canyon is washed downstream. Including you."

It wasn't long before we reached the mouth of the canyon.

Just as we did, a red flare arced over the slickrock between us and the mountain.

I said to Carey in the back of the boat, "I guess you were telling the truth. This must be the place."

I called a stop. Pulled our boat right up beside Luke's.

"Jordan, you and Luanda hop on over here," he said. "Let's let Carey go in ahead by his lonesome."

Carey gave him a sharp look.

"That's what I thought," said Luke. "You go on ahead now, hear?"

No sooner had we entered the canyon than Carey stopped ahead of us.

"What's the problem, pard?" Luke called out.

"You know what the problem is, you ratshit bastard."

"Now let's watch the language. There's a lady present."

We maneuvered up beside him. Luke pointed his .45 at him.

"You'll go forward or I'll kill you where you stand."

Carey gave him the look from hell, but throttled ahead slowly.

As soon as Carey started forward, Luke let out a deep sigh of relief and re-holstered his gun.

Now we were hearing explosions and gunfire ahead. Occasionally, one of the bigger explosions lit up the sky overhead. Sounded like a battle royal, only I couldn't figure out who Tic was shooting it out with. The thunderstorm was moving closer.

We also began to get whiffs of something, something gone bad. Really bad. I wondered if maybe a cow or a horse had fallen into the water, which had receded and left its carcass exposed. Whatever it was, the smell was getting stronger the further in we went.

I had just turned to comment on it to Luke when a tremendous explosion filled every nook and cranny of the canyon with deafening sound. I ducked and looked ahead in time to see pieces of Carey's boat peeling themselves off a huge fountain of spray shooting up out of the water.

Stunned, we stopped and stared.

No sign of Carey.

Slowly we moved ahead. All of us with our ears ringing. "There he is!"

Carey had surfaced off to the port side. We fished him in. He seemed dazed but miraculously unhurt.

"Now you're on your own, motherfucker," he mumbled.

I asked him if there are anymore underwater surprises up ahead, but he had been deafened by the explosion.

I shouted the question. "Better tell us before we hit one. You might not be so lucky the second time around."

He knew I was right.

"It's clear from here to the end."

"And what the hell's that smell?"

But he just smiled a small smile.

"Well, so much for sneaking up on them," said Frank.

"Everything going on up ahead, and with the storm moving in, I doubt they even heard it," I said.

I knew this canyon, but the lake had dropped so much I wasn't sure where the water ran out. Fortunately, we could gauge that from the explosions as we drew closer to them.

Luke slowed to a crawl. "We're getting close."

Sure enough, we nosed around the next bend and there before us was a scene like every disaster movie ever made rolled into one.

Silhouetted against the brilliant explosions on land was the wrecked houseboat lying at a crazy angle half on the beach, its pontoons smashed. Several small fires were burning in the dry grass and sage. By the canyon wall, an explosion had caught a dead piñon on fire and it was flaring like a huge torch. The sound of small arms and semi-automatic rifle fire filled the air.

As we watched, a mine exploded in the shallow water on the beach, followed in rapid succession by several more on land. Suddenly a heavy machine gun opened up somewhere. All of it shrouded in a dense pall of smoke and the stench of decomposition.

"Better follow the path of the houseboat in case of more mines," Frank shouted.

We all drew our side arms and crouched in the boat as we slowly motored in.

"Remember, as far as we know Sarah's still alive," I said. "It's likely that Tic will have her close by, so hit what you're aiming at."

But no one was there.

Luke drew us up behind the houseboat and tied off on her.

We'd made it through the underwater mines, but God only knew what lay ahead of us on land.

Where is everybody? I wondered.

Then Luanda pointed.

"There! On the wall."

How she had spotted them through the dust and smoke I don't know, but two hundred yards up the canyon were two figures, one above the other, crawling up the sheer sandstone wall.

TIC

I know there's a rock shelf a couple of feet underwater just off the beach. We hit, it shreds the Fiberglas pontoons. Shrump and I are holding on, but Esquibel tumbles down the deck in his chair like a bowling ball and crashes into the railing. I cut him loose and drag him to his feet.

Where the hell is Carey?

The houseboat has come to rest half off and half on the shelf.

I turn to Shrump. "Remember, I'm worth more to you alive than dead, so make sure you're firing high or low. You hit either one of us on that wall and we're both dead."

He nods and disappears up the canyon. A moment later a flare splits the night. Everything is bathed in its deep red light. We look like devils.

We hit the sand, an underwater mine blows a fountain of water into the air. It drenches us. A split second later, a land mine explodes down the beach, showering us with sand and rock.

The commander looks like his head is about to spin off.

Way to go, Shrump.

Smoke is filling the air. Esquibel's head ducks as the sound of small arms fire erupts from behind a boulder 50 yards away. A round shatters a window on the houseboat.

"We better get off the beach," I shout.

"My cane!" the commander bellows.

"Fuck that, it's just pain management!"

I know the way. We head up the canyon. I have the commander by the arm.

Another mine blows nearby. We're knocked down by the blast and deafened by the tremendous noise of a string of explosions. Overlaying everything is the gagging odor of the putrescent corpses pulled up on the beach, and roar of the death metal coming from the speakers.

We stagger to our feet. I see Shrump rise from behind a boulder ahead of us, an RPG launcher on his shoulder.

"Get down!" I scream as the grenade zips over our heads and explodes somewhere behind us. The shock seems to rock the whole canyon.

Shrump must have been paying better attention than I thought when Carey and I were orchestrating all this.

Again we're sprinting up the canyon. A couple of rounds wicker their way past our heads. The commander flinches. I let go of him and start jumping up and down. Strictly not in the plan, I know, but I can't help myself. I turn in a circle and shout, "Happy fucking New Year! Merry goddamn Christmas! Happy Fourth of July!"

Another flare arcs into the sky and pops. Shrump sends a couple more rounds over my head. A reminder.

I grab the commander. We're almost to the canyon wall when the rapid chugging of a machine gun stitches a line of .50-caliber slugs diagonally up the rock face. Sandstone splinters rain down on our heads.

Everything is where I laid it. The odor of cordite is heavy in the air.

I climb into my harness. The commander can only stand and stare at me, dazed.

Once I'm in, I step him into his, cinch it at his waist. He moves as though he's in a trance.

No sooner does one flare die than another goes aloft.

I've tied a loop into both ends of a short stretch of climbing rope. Hook one into the carabiner on the commander's harness. Tighten it down.

He finds his voice. "You're out of your fucking mind, Douloureux."

I slip the other loop through my carabiner.

"You understand what's happening here, Commander?"

Just then Shrump detonates a mine further down the wall. We're both deafened.

I'm shouting but I can't hear my own voice. "This is what it was like that night, Commander. The noise. The confusion—while you were sitting all comfy cozy at your desk, cup of hot coffee. Jerking off in the men's room."

Suddenly there's a huge flash above us. Almost simultaneously a peal of thunder splits the air.

I look up. A single fat drop of rain strikes me dead center in the forehead. I scream a welcome to the weather.

"We're going up. I'll lead. You follow."

I look up the wall, probably fifty yards high.

"Funny, isn't it, Commander, that an even playing field turns out to be a vertical wall."

"You're insane! One of us falls, we both die!"

I nod. "Difference between you and me, Commander. I don't give a shit."

The good commander knows his only salvation is to follow my every move, which he does—for a couple minutes anyway.

"Stop," he shouts. "I need to catch my breath."

"We've only made half a dozen moves, you pussy."

An explosion drowns out his reply.

"You made this climb before?" he asks.

"Commander, your sang-froid is slipping."

"Fuck you, Douloureux."

"But that's what most people don't understand about climbing, Commander. On a new climb—"

Shrump pops a couple of rounds into the rock above. The commander flinches.

"On a new climb, it's all about improvising. Sure, you can stand on the ground and try to plan your route, but things always look different once you're up here. The important thing is to keep moving up. Closer to heaven, further from hell."

Reaching up, I jam my fingers into a narrow vertical crack not more than two inches deep. Check the slack between me and Esquibel and move up.

White faced, he follows.

I can't see any holds ahead. The explosions and the flares provide only an uneven light. I pass my hand over the smooth rock face. Right at my finger tips is a ledge. I stretch and I've got it.

"Okay, we're going to have to work together on this one. You move when I move. Ready?"

Below me, the commander's mouth is moving, but with all the noise in the canyon, I can't hear a word of it.

I repeat my instructions. He nods.

"Okay. Reach."

We move in unison up the wall, the rope taut between us. I can see a small jut of rock above me just big enough for a hand hold. Again we move together.

Two more moves and we're standing side by side on a narrow ledge, leaning into a slight depression in the cliff face.

"Ultimately," I tell him, "you have to believe in yourself, that you can grasp what you're reaching for."

He looks down. I can see his legs trembling.

"You believing in yourself right now, Commander?"

He raises his head but says nothing.

"Mouth too dry to speak?

"That wall in Afghanistan. You think we had time to plan our climb? In the dark? That was a bad call, Commander. You pushed us too far, asked for too much. We paid the price. Dylan and Rocker paid with their lives. But for me, it was worse."

I grabbed him by the collar.

Far below on the canyon floor, a mine shatters the air. Shrapnel ricochets past us.

"Absolute focus," I shout into his face. "That's how you climb. You think about falling, you narrow your focus on the next stretch of rock. Close out everything else.

"Falling is a tiny closed door in my mind, Commander."

I showed him with my fingers. They were bloody and bruised.

"Up here, there's always a huge temptation to open it. Just crack it a little bit. Just a peek."

Another flare coats us in red light.

"But now I know if I even crack it, it's going to bust wide open. I've seen what comes through. I don't want to see it again.

"You opened that door, Commander, and I've paid hell closing it."

"You want to kill yourself, Douloureux, go off somewhere and blow your brains out. Leave me out of it."

"But this way I can kill two birds with one stone."

I survey the rock above, find what I hope will be our next handhold.

I start up, but the commander won't move.

I come back down.

"Found what you think is a safe place, Commander?"

I jerk on the rope.

"There are no safe places," I shout. "You move or by God I'll yank you off this wall and we'll both die.

"There's no going back. It's up or we're dead. Understand?"

Shrump rips another string of .50-caliber slugs into the wall below us and jump starts the commander.

I don't know if Shrump plans it this way. With all the smoke he probably can't see the cliff too well. We just reach a stretch of rock near the top with a slight overhang, he cuts loose another RPG.

The impact blows me right off the wall.

I see the look on Esquibel's face as I fall past him.

"Hold on," I scream.

I know we're going down, and I feel a moment of silent peace.

But the rope jerks me short and I'm scrabbling at the rock for a hold.

I look up. Esquibel is looking down at me, his face full of horror.

I catch back up to him.

"I wouldn't try *that* move if I were you, Commander."

I feel rain falling in earnest now. Fortunately sandstone doesn't become slick like limestone or granite. Maintains its grit and makes it easier to climb.

Every time I look up now the raindrops fill my eyes. I shake them out and refocus.

I'm just about to make my next move, when I suddenly realize something has changed.

I can *hear* the rain falling.

JORDAN

"Everybody stay put," Luke shouts.

He retrieves a small metal case from under the dash. "Let's hope this damn thing works," he says as he opens it. "Here we go."

He flips the switch.

For a split second I feel my heart flutter in my chest, as though the electromagnetic pulse has knocked it out of rhythm. I draw in a sharp, short breath.

The electrical signals to the heart, I realize. I'm suddenly grateful for what complex creations we are—that we somehow survive.

I glance at the others. They look awed.

The human ear responds to the sudden halt of deafening sound by creating its own noise, or maybe what we hear when Luke flips the switch is simply the dying echoes of the tumult in which we'd been submerged so completely.

Either way, it takes a few seconds to adjust to the new silence.

"God bless Niles," I say. The pulse had worked exactly as he'd predicted it would. All of Tic's electronics are fried.

Frank is plucking something from his ear. "Damn thing killed my hearing aid." He sounds mildly amused.

I look at my watch. Ditto.

Staying low, we climb out of the boat, make our way on shore.

Now, we're halfway up the beach when the newfound quiet is suddenly shattered by two rifle shots in quick succession up canyon.

Luke spots the muzzle flash. He points the way, but I raise my hand. "Everybody wait. Let's put Carey to work again."

"Good idea," Luke agrees, and shoves Carey out in front of us.

Once off the beach, we begin spotting bits of brightly colored surveyor's ribbon tied to sage bushes and trees.

"He's marked out a trail," I say.

The noise had been overwhelming, and it's soon clear why. Behind several bushes and rocks are big speakers from which had poured the sound of shells exploding, rifles firing, and the screams I remember hearing from men badly wounded in combat. Not to mention the shrieking death metal.

We come across smoke generators and craters blasted out of the sand by mines.

The smoke is dissipating in the rain as we silently approach a screen of boulders and the big juniper from behind which the shots had come.

Luke trains his gun on the tree. "Come out in the open!"

Looking closely, I can see Shrump standing at what looks like one of those boards you see at concerts for controlling sound and lights and other stage effects.

"All right. Hands where I can see them," Luke says.

'Dying for the cause' is not a phrase in Shrump's vocabulary. He's more one of those 'live to fight another day' guys. Only that doesn't work out for him so well this time.

"Gun on the ground!" shouts Luke. "Step out in the clearing where we can see you!"

Shrump is following instructions perfectly when he takes one step too many. Off the trail.

Watching it happen reminds me of a turkey wishbone. No need of an autopsy to determine cause of death. The mine blows off his legs in two entirely different directions. He's dead before his trunk hits the ground.

The dust is settling, the noise echoing down the canyon.

Frank turns to me. "Couldn't have happened to a nicer guy."

Tic and the commander are just reaching the top of the cliff when we get there. We can hear the commander's exhausted grunting.

Tic looks down, says to me, "You passed the water test!"

"So, what is this, Tic? The gravity test?"

Far overhead I hear him laugh.

"Well put, my friend. But you need to lay down your guns. The commander and I are tied to one another. If I fall, he falls."

"He's telling the truth," the commander says.

"Commander, you okay?" Luke shouts.

"So far."

The rain is coming down harder all the time.

"So Tic, what's next?" I ask.

"I'm just making it up as I go along, buddy."

"Shrump is dead. We've got Carey."

"But I've got the commander. He's trump."

"Where's Sarah?"

"Omigosh, I nearly forgot!"

He disappears for a moment. When he returns, he's holding Sarah in front of him, hands bound, mouth gagged.

"Sarah! Are you all right?"

She nods.

"I'm coming up!"

"No need," says Tic.

Helpless, I watch him hook his foot in front of hers. I know what's coming.

I scream as he shoves her from behind. She screams through her gag as she plunges toward the canyon floor.

TIC

I call down to Jordan, his face tilted up at me in the driving rain. "The cost of a coil of rope? $39.95. A climbing harness? $79.95. An aluminum carabiner? $12.00. The look on your face? Priceless."

I see the body of Officer Tanner dangling limp halfway down the rock face. The rope tied to the base of the piñon beside me had held. At the very least, the fall must have broken her back.

Far below, I see Russell raise his .45. But, Doyle grabs his arm. "Wait," he says. "You might hit the commander." The canyon walls bring his voice up to me.

"That's right, Agent Doyle," I call down. "And now the commander and I have some unfinished business to attend to, so you must excuse us."

Only after we start out over the slick rock do I realize that the RPG has done more than knock me off the wall. A clicking in my left knee tells me a piece of shrapnel or a sliver of sandstone has blasted its way in.

We stop for a second while I try fishing it out. No luck. It's bleeding freely but it's not going to matter, anyway.

"In all the commotion I never did thank you for saving my life back on the wall," I say.

The commander's face is filled with disdain. "Why would I give a shit about you, Douloureux? I just held on to save myself."

I nod. "The benefits of mutual self-interest."

He just shakes his head.

"And that's why God put us all on this same little planet, Commander. Back there you were just trying to save your own skin, a task which just coincidentally happened to involve saving mine. There's beauty in that."

I stand up, take him by the arm and frog march him along. "If we weren't meant to help each other, don't you think that God, in all his majesty and power, would have created for each of us his own little planet on which to live out his life?"

"There's no doubt *you're* living in your own world, Douloureux."

"Take your cheap shots, Commander. The point is, we're all here together, helping each other."

"And hurting each other. What you did to Tanner was cruel. She's probably dead."

"Just a necessary part of the plan. But I will grant you that I wonder sometimes if God has the same plan. In other words, are we on the same page? Or at some point is He going to step in and throw a big left turn into what I have in mind?"

We walk on. The lightning's glare shows me we're headed the right way.

"Or maybe he's already done that," I continue. "Take Jordan for instance. God gave me what I needed to arrange things for Jordan, and I put those things into play. According to my plan, he should never have been here tonight. But according to God's plan, he is. And I'm willing to accept that.

"Which tells me I'm in the post-planning stage of this whole operation. Granted, I have an idea in mind, but whether or not God will arrange circumstances such that I can put that idea into play, I don't know.

"Where the hell are we going, Douloureux?"

"To your own particular circumstance, Commander. See, that's what it's all about. Circumstances. God builds you with circumstances, then sets you down spinning like a top into circumstances, and away you go. Whether or not He knows what's going to happen after that, I don't know, but I have an idea.

"We're made in God's image, and we're curious, so God has got to be curious too, don't you think? We're told that He knows everything that ever *has* happened and everything that ever *will*, but that doesn't leave any room for curiosity. So I vote in favor of Him not knowing. Just sitting up there looking down and waiting to see what happens. We're doing the same, we who are made in His image."

We continue across the slick rock. It's like walking across the sand dunes from which this rock came millions of years ago. Up onto the crests, down into the valleys. Only with firmer footing. Even with my knee, we're making good time. The commander is limping without his cane, but he seems to have recovered from the climb.

"I don't know if God is going to give me what I need to finish out my idea. I do know he's moved me to a higher plane. I started out killing for gain, then moved on to revenge, both of them impure motives. But now I'm merely an agent, arranging circumstances in order to let God decide who dies and who lives. That's what I did with Jordan, and God has given me an answer."

The flashes of lightning are coming one atop the next. Finally ahead of us I can see what I've been looking for: the dark narrow crevasse in the rock.

"My job now is just to recognize opportunities, arrange the circumstances, and let God sort things out. Isn't that what you trained us to do as SEALs, Commander? Recognize opportunities and use them to our advantage?"

"You just better hope that nobody back in that canyon is the climber you are."

"And if someone is, and he catches up to us, I say so be it."

The rain is now coming down in buckets. We are on top of a deep narrow slot canyon.

The Colorado is a deep carving river, I tell the commander, and the water in her tributaries has to carve just as quickly to reach down to her. This canyon has been carved over millennia by scouring flash floods. It's only a few feet across at the top, but it widens out as it deepens. Man, in all his God-given ingenuity, could not build a more efficient water accelerator. This slot drains hundreds of square miles of solid slick rock, it gathers all that moving water and funnels it into a narrow crevice and sends it crashing down to the river.

We walk along the edge. I'm looking for a place to wait for what I think is coming, for what I think God is going to send me. Just as we reach the perfect spot, a flash of lightning illuminates it for me to see. A good sign.

"Down here, Commander."

"What for?" He looks around. "There's nobody to hide from."

"We're not hiding. Now climb down or I'll just shove you in and the fall will kill you."

Together, we climb a half dozen yards to the ledge I've spotted in the canyon wall. Peering down into the darkness, I wait for a flash of lightning to show me the canyon floor far below. When one comes, I see no water flowing.

"Okay, Commander, now we wait."

JORDAN

"Sarah! Sarah, can you hear me?"

Nothing. She hangs unmoving far above us.

"I have to get up there."

"You mean *climb*?" Luke is incredulous. "Jordan, there must be some other way. Otherwise, how would Douloureux have gotten Sarah up there?"

"There's no time. Besides, there're probably still mines up canyon, and the pulse has killed the boat engines, so we can't search by water for a way up."

"You know I'd go up, but heights—"

"It's okay. I can't climb like Tic, but I'm the most qualified here. Besides, I can do the most for her medically."

We pack a first aid kit, water, a flashlight, and other necessities into a backpack. I shoulder it and walk to the wall, Luke behind me.

He unholsters his .45 and hands it to me. "Stick this in your belt. Good luck, Doc."

I scan the wall, searching for any evidence of where Tic and Esquibel had gone up. There, to my left, is the faint scuff of a boot sole.

I start up, searching after every move for another scuff mark, any sign of which way to go.

Steeling myself against looking down, I keep my focus instead on Sarah dangling above me. She struck the wall so hard, she may well be dead. The closer I get to her, the more frequently I peer up at her, desperately hoping for some sign of life. Nothing.

Only a couple of moves away from her I reach a narrow ledge and have to stop. And my legs are trembling with fatigue; I'm panting. I lay my cheek against the cold stone and offer a short prayer that Sarah is still alive.

Finally I'm beside her. Her pulse is faint, but there. Thank God.

There's little I can do until I get her off this rock face. By climbing above her and grabbing the rope, I make short work of the distance to the top.

From the bottom, Frank shouts up, "Can you lower her down to us?"

"Not enough rope." Using everything I have, I haul her up to me.

Carefully, I stretch her limp body out on the ground, aware that I could easily worsen any possible spinal cord injury. I check her pulse again—a little stronger.

I untie the rope from her feet and remove her gag, try shielding her face from the rain.

"Sarah," I say, gently stroking her face. "Sarah."

Her eyes flutter, and then she's looking up at me.

"Jordan! You're okay?"

I nod.

"But that boat. The chain. How did you escape?"

"I don't have time to explain, but your surgery kit helped. Now, you've had a bad fall. We need to check for concussion and paralysis."

She reaches up and touches my face. "You're the doctor."

As I check her over, Sarah tells me about Tic bringing her up here after watching me go down with the old rowboat; his attaching her to the tree; that Shrump is definitely still working for Tic.

"Not anymore. He's down there, dead."

Shuddering, she says he's a horrible little man.

I continue checking her.

"Am I okay?"

"You're still concussed. But I don't think the fall made it any worse."

"My back feels like it's broken."

"Severe muscle strain as far as I can tell. We'll need x-rays to see more. Can you move?"

I want her out of the rain. With her feeble assistance, I move her under the piñon, where I make her as comfortable as possible.

I call down to Luke that she's okay for now, pull Luke's gun from my belt and give it to her.

"In case Tic circles back."

"I don't think he will. I think I know where he's gone."

She describes the slot canyon she had spotted from the top of the mesa in which Tic had held us captive. "I can't be sure, but I think it's in that direction," she says, pointing.

When I stand, she says, "Let me come with you."

"I've got to move fast, and you're too badly hurt. I'll come back for you."

"Jordan, please be careful. Losing you twice might be more than I can bear."

I walk out along the line where Sarah had pointed, then travel an arc left and an arc right. After a few minutes I break what I think is their trail: a footprint-shaped smudge in a patch of sand.

Unless he knew exactly where he was going, Tic would travel more or less a straight line until he hit the slot canyon, so I try to maintain a straight line of travel myself. Using the direction Sarah had given me as an axis, I zigzag back and forth, hoping to pick up more sign.

Why is Tic heading for a slot canyon? If his goal is to kill Esquibel, why not just shove him off the top of the canyon wall, like Sarah only without a rope?

There'll be no footprints on the slick rock and precious few sand patches like the one I already found. Any blood marks will be washed away by the rain.

I see something glinting in the flashlight beam. I bend down and pick up a button, thread still attached. Obviously torn from a shirt.

I hurry on, then stop to listen. Off to my left, in the general direction of Navajo Mountain, I hear above the splash of the rain a faint roar, like the cheering of a distant crowd. The wind shifts and it's gone.

There's no time to stay still. Up and down the rolling surface of the sandstone I hurry. Questions continue to bubble up. *What will I find at the canyon? Is the commander already dead? How can I overcome Tic without a gun?*

Further along I stop at a small piñon growing from a sand-filled crevice in the rock. The broken tip of a branch dangles in the rain. Getting close?

Again off to my left I hear the distant clamor on the wind, only louder this time. Closer. Or is it just the wind itself, echoing through the huge ramparts and palisades of the sacred mountain?

Aligning my path with my clues I move straight ahead. It doesn't seem possible it can rain any harder. I splash through puddles forming in the depressions, trying to stay low in case Tic's checking his back trail.

The roar is so close now, I can pinpoint its source. Straight ahead. Now I know what it is. *Hurry.*

And suddenly, in the flashlight beam the irregular black slit in the rock. The slot canyon.

I crouch at its edge and shine my flashlight down. Far away, the holy mountain is shaking its shoulders, sending torrents of water racing down to the river. Fifty feet below, water speeds along the canyon floor, crashing into the sculpted alcoves in the walls, sending spray up toward me, issuing a roar like a thousand voices telling me there isn't much time left.

Carefully, I make my way along the canyon's rim, keeping an eye out for Tic and the commander, when a movement below the edge catches the corner of my eye. It's Tic, pointing a machine pistol up at me. The commander's crouching beside him.

"Jordan! You continue to impress!" Tic shouts over the roar of the water in the canyon below him. "That's far enough."

"So what's the plan, Tic?"

"Get the flashlight out of my eyes."

I shine it down into the canyon at the rising water. "You better get out of there, Tic. You see what's coming?"

"Exactly. I thought I'd give the commander here a swimming lesson."

"What's the point?"

"This is the guy who screwed up my last chance."

"Last chance for what?"

He pauses. "To make it all right . . . to make it all up and undo . . ."

His voice trailed off as he looked down at the steadily rising water.

"Killing Esquibel is only going to make it worse," I shout.

The water is rising—quickly.

He shakes the gun at me. "In your world, maybe. Not in mine. This will put me back on top. This . . . and your death, Jordan."

"Killing me isn't going to solve anything either."

"I beg to differ. It will eliminate a living, breathing reminder of a bad choice I made a long time ago."

"But it won't undo the choice."

"Then I guess I'll just to have to settle for what I can get." He glances down at the muddy torrent now swirling only a few feet below him. "I'm thinking I climb back out, leave the commander on this ledge, let him decide. He tries climbing out, I shoot him, or he takes his chances with the water."

"It's murder either way," I yell down to him.

He either hasn't heard me or is ignoring me.

"You get the same choice," he shouts. "Into the water or a bullet in the face."

"Tic. Wait. I—"

They say you don't hear the shot that kills you, which may be. Still, I hear a shot. But there's no muzzle flash from Tic's gun, which suddenly spins out of his hand and into the rushing water.

I whirl around. Sarah. Behind me. Feet planted firmly. Arms straight out in front of her. Luke's .45 grasped tightly in her hands.

"Jordan! The commander!" she shouts above the roar of the wind and the water.

I turn back to the canyon. Esquibel has broken free from Tic and is trying to scramble up to me.

I climb down, grab his outstretched hand, and pull him up.

Tic, standing on the ledge holding his bloody shoulder, looks up at us. The water is at his knees. I can see he's having trouble keeping his footing, and I start down for him.

I'm halfway to the ledge when Sarah screams.

I look up and the commander is sliding back down toward me. Sarah drops the gun and lunges as best she can to catch him. Too late. He's coming down.

I catch the full brunt of his weight. Fortunately, my feet are on solid rock, and as he scratches and claws at the rock wall, I'm able to shove him back up toward Sarah. She grabs his wrist. I see her look past me, pointing, her expression terrified.

I turn. The ledge is empty.

Tic is gone.

I spot him downstream. In an instant he's ten yards away. Lightning flashes, and in the electric glare he raises an arm as if to wave. His expression is serene. The torrent slams him against the rock wall, and pulls him under.

For what seems like a long time, I cling to the canyon wall, staring downstream, as if waiting for Tic to bob to the surface.

When I feel water washing over my feet, I climb up to Sarah, and hold her tightly to me in the pouring rain.

"What happened?"

"Oh Jordan, he was holding on. I think he was waiting for you to climb back down and help. But then, upstream, I saw—"

"What was it?"

"For a second I thought it was a tree limb, but then the lightning flashed and I swear it moved. Like an arm. The arm of a child reaching up from under the water."

I hold her from me and stare at her.

"It . . . seemed to . . . hook Tic. It pulled him off the rock. Into the water."

"Are you sure?"

Looking down at the muddy torrent racing below us, she just shakes her head.

EPILOGUE

That thunderstorm opened the floodgates. The prevailing wind shifted to the south-southeast, and we had the heaviest monsoon that anyone in these parts can remember. The lake's coming back, slowly re-covering all the secrets it had exposed.

One it never surrendered was Tic's body. Whether he was washed into the lake or buried under the tons of sand and debris scoured out of that slot canyon we'll never know. Of course, there's a third possibility. Unlikely, but you know what it is.

Carey, for one, must have believed Tic was gone, because he sang like a canary in exchange for a more lenient prison sentence. He confirmed that Tic was indeed taking over the local trade in drugs and artifacts in order to fund his attack on the commander. As Rooney had told us, the pot came from Mexico through Phoenix, but, probably fearing retribution, Carey was deliberately vague on how it arrived at the lake, or how traces of it had wound up in Eddie's cruiser.

Carey willingly identified the two badly decomposed bodies in the canyon as the gang bangers who had come looking for Tic after he drowned Rooney and Adolpho, and he confirmed the relationship between Vernon Steps and Tic's father.

But all of those people were dead. He resolutely refused to finger anyone still alive: the pawn shop owner, the illicit arms dealer, or the mine worker from whom Tic had purchased his explosives—on the premise that he'd be a sitting duck in prison if any of them decided to get even.

Luanda Wilmington leaves in the fall to begin classes at the academy's Forensic Science Research and Training Center in Quantico. Frank is still holding things down at the shop in Flagstaff.

Tommy Two Clouds and Ella Watchman got married last week. He's going to adopt Adella, Marcus, and Junior. I told them at the wedding I thought they'd make a great family. Ella said she was going to try talking Tommy into leaving the Navajo police, but I don't think she can.

Commander Esquibel, roughed up, but otherwise okay, said he'd be back again next year for his Fourth of July poker run, that his buddies are all game. His houseboat is totaled, but he said he was planning on buying a new one, anyway.

Luke said the monsoon is greening up his pastures and the huge chunk of Forest Service land he leases for grazing, and he's purchasing stock to put out on it. He told us he's looking forward to things getting back to normal for a while, once Sarah returns from medical leave, which should be soon.

Grady's still on the wagon, still drinking his heavily sugared tea, and traveling to protests, but he has agreed to sell the house. I asked him what changed his mind, but he hasn't really said. I wonder if it has something to do with Niles being abducted or my own near-death experience, but all he'll tell me is that life is for the living.

He felt bad about steering us wrong on the militia, until I pointed out that that was as much my fault as his, and that using the militia was how we had gotten to Tic. By the way, they're still dug in out at Poverty Mountain. Although with Shrump and Baldy dead, they've kept a low profile since Tic sent them off with their tails between their legs.

Niles and Merced will be joining us for Christmas dinner. Niles, with Merced's help, is trying to patent his miniature electromagnetic pulse generator that we used to quell all of Tic's electronics in Crooked Canyon.

With Grady looking at new houses, I toyed with the idea of finding one big enough for him and me and Sarah to share, until I realized no house was big enough for that. In fact, I'm still not sure Sarah and I should live together. She thinks it's because I resent her not telling me the feds were working with the militia to double cross Tic. I told her she was wrong, but then she asks me why she had to learn from Tic and not me that I had told him the feds and militia were talking at all. Why hadn't I told her myself? My question for her is, Why wasn't I allowed to visit the militia with the rest of the team in the first place?

"Didn't you trust me?" I asked her.

"Frankly, no."

"Or were you just jealous of my devotion to Tic? Instead of to you?"

"You think I'm that immature? That I lack that much confidence? You're the one who can't commit to me. You condescend about your dad living in the past. How long is your mother's death going to keep its grip on *you*?"

Which is usually where the argument ends, with her pushing the whole thing onto the fact that I feel abandoned by my mother after she died in the car crash, which is why I won't commit.

Brady, who has overheard a couple of these discussions, is advocating for us moving in together, since, he says, we already fight like a married couple, anyway.

Once Sarah was better and the dirt roads were passable again after the rain, we all drove out to where Eddie had died. I rode along with Luke and Sarah. Tommy, Frank, and Luanda were in Tommy's cruiser.

On the way out, we stopped by the Klain compound. Tommy wanted to check on the grandfather. We also wanted to apologize to Kenneth, who came out of his family's trailer carrying a camping lantern.

"My son found this somewhere out where you're headed," he said. "Let him show you."

Once on scene, the boy led us to a small niche in a rock mound only a few hundred yards from where Eddie had been killed. The opening was thinly covered with pieces of sage brush. Inside was a cache of several dozen camping lanterns. How we had missed them in our search of the area last spring, I don't know.

Luanda recognized them as the same type found crushed by the roadside back in the spring. "Guess we've all been so caught up in the murders that we've missed pieces of the puzzle lying right in front of us," she said.

"And here's another piece," said Tommy. "Anyone notice the small plane going over just now back at the Klains?"

We all shook our heads.

"Grandpa commented on it."

Frank's face lit up. "Just like he did when we interviewed him after we found Eddie."

"Want to bet that that's what Kenneth saw when he told us there was a light in the sky?" Tommy asked.

Frank nodded. "He was just too drunk to identify it."

"And that explains why Eddie went west instead of returning east when he left the Klains that night," said Luanda.

I went out and stood in the middle of the dirt road. It was plenty flat enough and straight to serve as a landing strip for a small plane using the lanterns as landing lights.

"The camping lantern hadn't fallen from a passing vehicle, it was probably overlooked in the dark when the rest were picked up after the plane took off," said Luanda.

"So Eddie surprised Tic while he was waiting for the plane to land, and somehow Tic disarmed him and killed him," said Sarah.

"Tic was trained in the SEALs to kill people using only his hands or feet," I said. "He could have crushed Eddie's jaw."

"Then they put him in the passenger side of the cruiser, loaded the marijuana in the back, and drove down this road, which leads to the lake," said Sarah.

"Where Carey was probably waiting with a boat," said Frank.

I nodded. "After unloading the pot, they shoved the cruiser into the lake, figuring it would never be found."

"Which explains why they didn't bother to move Eddie into the driver's seat or move the seat back to its original position," said Frank.

The July sun burned down on all of us, but nobody made a move for their vehicle. We just stood silently for a minute, on the chance that Eddie somehow lingered there with us.

Luke was the first to say something. "So it took all of us coming all the way out here to figure out something this simple," he said, shaking his head. "We're damn lucky they pay us anything at all to do this job."

Like Luke, I'll be happy to settle back into the routine medical stuff I see at the office and in the hospital. I think a lot about Tic, and I wonder what went wrong with him. Losing Stevie. Watching his friends die in Afghanistan. Getting the Big Chicken Dinner. Maybe what he told Luke that night in the Windy Mesa was right: maybe every man does reach a point in his life at which he's trying to avoid being crushed by the weight of his personal history. Did he just get there sooner than the rest of us?

As for those of us here in Page and at the lake who haven't yet reached that point or may never reach it, maybe the best we can hope for is no more droughts. Let the lake keep its secrets.

CPSIA information can be obtained
at www.ICGtesting.com
Printed in the USA
FSOW01n1108200416
19471FS